Reluctant Adept

by

KATHERINE BAYLESS

Scry
media

Printed in the USA

First Printing, December 2015

ISBN 978-0-9971055-0-6

www.katherinebayless.com

For Natalie, my sister, my forever friend—I'm a better person because of you.

(Navigating the social minefield of adolescence was hard enough. I can't imagine what growing up would have been like without you.)

I love you, lil' sis.

NOVELS IN

A CLAIRVOYANT'S COMPLICATED LIFE

Deadly Remains

Deceiver's Bond

Reluctant Adept

Song of the Lost

NOVELS IN

THE COVENTRY YEARS

A Jot of Blood

OTHER NOVELS BY KATHERINE BAYLESS

The 7th Tear

CONTENTS

ACKNOWLEDGMENTS

My books are better because of my test readers and their feedback. If not for them, I wouldn't have the confidence to release my stories into the wild. Michelle, Trish, Sarina, Natalie, Scot, Dave—from the depths of my qwerty little heart, thank you.

Dave, as always, thank you for finding the time in your schedule to copy edit my book. If not for you, Lire's voice would probably be *horse* and *sleep-groveled*. Oy.

To my awesome husband: Without your encouragement, patience, and invaluable expertise, my creative writing would have remained a private hobby. I love you.

To all my readers who took the time to drop me a note over the past year to ask about Lire's next adventure—my thanks! I won't lie, the main reason I write is purely selfish, I love doing it. I write for myself, first and foremost. But knowing there are people reading and enjoying my stories gives me an incredible sense of satisfaction that's hard to beat. It motivates me to keep writing, even when I'm busy making lemonade out of life's little lemons.

A QUICK NOTE ABOUT THIS BOOK

Reluctant Adept is the third book in the *A Clairvoyant's Complicated Life* series. Thanks so much for giving it a go!

To get the most out of *Reluctant Adept* with the least confusion, start with my first book, *Deadly Remains*. Although each of my novels is a self-contained story with no cliffhangers, there are overarching plot threads and character progression that span all three books.

It's always a tricky proposition to get readers up to speed while steering clear of info dump territory. I'd rather err on the side of too little info than too much (although I hope to get it just right). However, if I missed the mark and a time comes when you need to refresh your memory about someone, I've included a list of characters with their relevant descriptions at the back of this book. The descriptions are written from Lire's point of view at the start of *Reluctant Adept*, so there are no spoilers. (See: Lire and the People She Knows.)

I hope you enjoy Lire's latest adventures!

Double, double toil and trouble,
Fire burn and cauldron bubble.
Cool it with a baboon's blood,
Then the charm is firm and good.

O well done! I commend your pains;
And every one shall share i' the gains;
And now about the cauldron sing,
Live elves and fairies in a ring,
Enchanting all that you put in.

By the pricking of my thumbs,
Something wicked this way comes.
Open, locks,
Whoever knocks.

– *Macbeth*, Act IV, Scene 1

PROLOGUE

My best friend Julie frowned, staring at me as though I'd admitted to having a conjoined twin hidden beneath my blouse.

"How is that even possible? No psychic has more than one gift." She leaned in, her forearms braced on the edge of the small table. Mid-afternoon wasn't the busiest time for her coffee shop, Peabody's Beans, but she lowered her voice anyway. "I mean ... are you sure? Maybe this is a trick the demon— "

I focused on her cup and saucer, levitating them until they hovered in mid-air, just below the level of her chin.

She jerked back, her breath catching as I pulled the heat from the cup's contents, freezing her mocha latte solid. Finally, I directed the white porcelain back to the tabletop, setting it down with nary a *clink*.

Julie covered her mouth, her face unnaturally pale, her wide brown-eyed gaze meeting mine. "Lire ... oh my God. And ... and pyrokinesis too?"

I nodded. I wasn't demonstrating that one. It still scared the hell out of me. Maybe, when things calmed down, I could ask her brother Tom for some pointers.

"Holy crap. This is just ... it's just ..." Blinking rapidly, she shook her head.

"Freaky?" I blew out a breath. "No shit. And the crazy thing is: I haven't even told you the weird part yet."

"You're kidding." She gawped, taking in my serious expression, and blurted, "You get three new psychic powers after helping the police with a murder investigation *and that's not even the weird part*?"

I shook my head and sipped my cappuccino, using two hands to keep my cup steady. I tipped my chin at her mocha. "Okay, that was sacrilege. I'll wait if you want to make yourself another one."

"And miss out on this story, now that I've gotten you down here after an entire month of not seeing you? No way." She called out to her husband, Steven, who was somewhere behind the counter, asking him to bring her a new mocha when he got the chance. She gave me a determined glare, her color restored. "*Now spill.*"

I sagged, smiling for the first time since sitting down. I'd been dragging my feet about telling her this stuff—about telling *anyone*, to be honest. Deep down, though, I'd known Jules wouldn't recoil. We'd been friends for seven years, after all, and having a pyrokinetic sibling made her more accepting than most normals. But when something as strange as a clairvoyant with more than one gift came along, not to mention one who was currently mired in dealings with the sidhe, a race even many in the magic community considered to be pure fantasy ... well, it wasn't exactly an easy story to swallow.

With a deep breath, I told her everything—about the sidhe and their belief in the coming demonic invasion; how Maeve, sidhe princess and bitch extraordinaire, snatched my almost-boyfriend Vince from under my nose and ordered her cousin Kieran to glamour me; about Kieran's transformation from antagonist to boyfriend material; how my childhood friend Daniel died at the hands of the archdemon Azazel; about freeing Tíereachán from his demon enslavement and closing Azazel's gateway to Hell; and, the kicker, how I learned to sidestep to a higher dimension.

"That's what the elves call it? Sidestepping?" By this point, Julie's raised eyebrows had been hidden beneath her smooth brown bangs for so long I wasn't sure I'd ever see them again.

I nodded. "They prefer 'sidhe,' by the way—'elf' is what Tolkien used in his books. But, yes, apparently sidestepping is something their adepts have been known to do."

"Adept? What's that?"

"A sidhe who can create portals to other worlds, which is a super big deal for them. The surface of their planet is majorly hostile, so all of their cities are underground. They depend on magic to make living there possible. Their portals to Earth give them the extra potential they need to survive."

She blinked. "Are you saying ... they're siphoning magic from us? Like some skeevy neighbor tapping into our cable box for free HBO?"

I snorted. "Sort of, I guess. For whatever reason, our universe seethes with magic potential. We have way more than we could ever use, so it's not as though we don't have it to spare."

"And these 'adepts' ... they're the ones who set up the ... the *cables* to steal it?"

"Not sure they'd appreciate the cable guy comparison." I snickered. "Adepts are über rare. And the sidhe are down to just one. They call her the amhaín. She's King Faonaín's estranged sister. He held her and her son Tíereachán hostage for over a thousand years, just to harness her power. It led to a civil war and, now, they have separate kingdoms. The king still doesn't have a portal adept and, by all accounts, I'm the first candidate to come along in something like two thousand years." I widened my eyes sarcastically. "You can imagine how excited I am about *that*."

"Just because you can do this sidestepping thing? They think you're an adept?"

I shrugged. "Pretty much. Kieran says he knew from the first time he touched me."

Her look of surprise compressed to a knowing smirk. "The first time he touched you, huh? Mr. TD&D—tall, dark, and dreamy?" She folded her arms and scowled at me. "I can't believe you haven't at least brought him by for a quick espresso."

"I think you mean a quick inspection."

"Exactly! I must see this *amazing* hair and absolute gorgeousness of which you speak," she said, drawing out the 'amazing' with a few extra vowels. "And he doesn't have my seal of approval yet," she added, flicking her wrist at me as though to swat me under the chin and making a 'pfft' sound. "What were you thinking?"

"Clearly, I wasn't." I mugged at her and then sighed, tipping back the last of my coffee. "Things have been a little crazy lately."

She leaned back, her expression turning serious. "I'm sorry about Daniel, Li-Li. I can't imagine how horrible that must have been for you." She shuddered and then shook her head. "And the whole thing with Vince ... obviously, the detective had some serious baggage to unpack. You do not need that drama, girlfriend, know what I'm saying? Besides, Kieran sounds incredible." She looked at me speculatively. "But ... aren't you worried about taking things a little fast? You guys just met ... and now he's living with you?"

I shifted in my chair. It wasn't as if I hadn't winced over the speed of our relationship too, but somehow, when Kieran and I were together, my worries melted away at the astonishing *rightness* of it, as though I'd known him for years instead of weeks.

With the warmth of Kieran's favor burning inside me, I met her concerned gaze. "I know it's been fast, but we've been through a lot over the past few weeks. Evading certain death has a way of accelerating a relationship."

"I suppose so." After a moment, she brightened, her mouth quirking up at the right corner. "Girl, I think it's time for another party. Don't you?"

Little did she know ... I hadn't even let slip about going to the Otherworld for my 'sabbatical' yet.

Resigning myself to her incoming freak out, I began, "You have no idea how good that sounds. Because, there's something else I have to tell you ...

ONE

Damned if I'd let a demon invasion keep me away from Julie's party.

Kieran obviously didn't approve. But, *darn it*, it's not like the Apocalypse was showing up tomorrow. Or even, next month. This had nothing to do with preparing for battle. He just didn't like me leaving the protection of my building's wards and house djinn.

Red had always been the voice of caution when I wanted to do something stupid or reckless, but now, I was getting it from Kieran too. Red stood on the coffee table, his teddy bear paws folded across his ample tummy. From the couch, Kieran glowered at me under his dark, keenly-tapered brows. The concern of my protectors was both sweet, annoying, and complete overkill.

"Why do you insist on taking such a risk for something so frivolous?" Kieran asked.

I'd managed to keep my cool so far, but that about tore it. "I don't consider having friends *frivolous*," I said, biting out the word with the precision of a linguist. "And if you remind me one more time about being 'the one' and how important I am to the fate of the sidhe and humankind, I might strangle you. Did you know that Jackie's started calling me Neo?"

Reluctant Adept - Chapter One

The Matrix used to be one of my favorite movies. Not anymore. "It's no wonder with the way you and Kim and Brassal go on about your oracle's stupid-ass prophecy," I huffed.

Kieran's expression turned stony. He hated it when I dared to impugn his people's hallowed soothsayer.

Red tsked at me. "I believe Jackie's ribbing has more to do with your penchant for flying around Seattle's skyline and efforts at deflecting bullets."

"The business with the oracle and everyone telling me I'm 'the one' doesn't help," I muttered, but tamped down my indignation. Impersonating a petulant adolescent wouldn't help my cause. "I don't understand what has you two so worked up. It's a night out—three hours outside my building, tops. Now that the Invisius telepaths have stopped trying to turn my brain to mush, my life expectancy has improved tenfold."

Before either of them could issue a protest, I admitted: "I know things aren't perfect. Lorcán's still out there. I get it, but I'm not planning to wander down a dark alley at midnight. I just want to see Julie. Hang out with my friends for one darn night. Take my mind off this demon business for a few hours. I need a break. I want to talk about normal things to normal people who don't know what's coming."

Served me right. I mean, what kind of idiot thinks rallying a magical army to protect the world from the coming demonic scourge would be easy?

I sighed and massaged my forehead. *This kind,* apparently—a red-headed freckle-faced psychic with more power than skill.

Kieran abandoned his perch on the couch to stand before me. He squeezed my arm. "You've accomplished much. Thanks to you, Michael has Invisius Verso's telepaths well in hand. The vampires and the others will come around. If not ..." He shrugged. "Eventually, they will see the truth. When they do, they'll seek you out."

"Later isn't good enough," I said tiredly. "If we wait for them to figure it out on their own, the demons will have time to infiltrate their ranks, just like they did with the telepaths.

Fighting the invasion will be hard enough without possessed strigoi to deal with. We need them on our side, or at least *clued-in*, as soon as possible."

So far, I hadn't been able to get a single meeting with any of the major leaders. My street cred clearly sucked, or, perhaps it had something to do with the fact that I sounded like a doomsday prepper on the last day of the Mayan calendar.

Hi, my name is Lire Devon. As the Earth's first adept, I'm spearheading an alliance of the magically gifted to fight an invasion from Hell. How'd you and your friends like to join in the fun?

Was it any wonder getting a call through to the strigoi domn seemed to be about as easy as booking a private tryst with Bono? The vamp in their PR department had thoroughly stonewalled me, claiming he had no time to concern himself with unsubstantiated warnings, and the conversation went downhill from there. Maybe when the condescending prick saw the photos of the carnage that followed the demons' attack on the Invisius telepaths, he'd pull his fanged head out of his ass. The envelopes went out by FedEx two days ago, one to the domn at his compound in Iceland and the other to the PR twerp. I could have gone through Diedra, my friend from high school who worked for a strigoi clutch, but I didn't want her reputation to be on the line if my relationship with the domn went sideways.

I was still working on the werewolves. The isangrim's secretary promised to pass on my message when their council reconvened after spring hiatus. At least she hadn't threatened to send someone to drain every last drop of blood from my mangled body if I dared to call her again.

Thank God I had Jackie, Claude, and Duran helping me with the witches and warlocks, otherwise I'd be zero for four. Jackie and Claude were in discussions with the local Rowan collective, and Duran was using her juice with the largest Glindarian sect in the Pacific Northwest. Once relations were established, we'd use the Rowans and the Glindarians to approach the Arcane Council.

Reluctant Adept - Chapter One

Not for the first time, I wondered how the heck I was going to persuade all these groups to cooperate. Six weeks ago, I'd been a thirty-year-old human clairvoyant—a psychic with the power to learn the secrets of anything I touched. A few magic curve balls later, I found myself wielding more power than I felt capable of handling, which is why Tíereachán had urged me to visit his mother, the amhaín. She was the last of the sidhe's portal adepts and the only one who could teach me what I needed to know. We were leaving for her domain in less than a week, and I had no clear idea when I would return. I just wanted to relax and enjoy one of my few remaining evenings in Seattle with my friends, and I wanted Kieran with me.

He smoothed a stray lock of my hair behind my right ear. "The Dawn of Convergence is still a few years away. Until the demon hordes can enter this world on their own, without the help of their summoners, we have time. But if you continue to take risks, you won't be here to exploit it."

I relished the concern in his deep, musical voice. And when he looked at me like that, with his striking angular features and intelligent gaze set with such tenderness, it was hard not to melt. I wanted to pinch myself whenever I thought of him as my ... what? 'Boyfriend' seemed a little juvenile. Although he didn't look much older than my thirty, he was a twenty-seven-hundred-year-old sidhe. 'Lover' was a more accurate designation for what we were to each other, but no matter how inadequate 'boyfriend' sounded, there was no way I'd refer to Kieran as my lover in public. Way too much information.

"Lorcán is lying low," I reasoned. "He's not going to chance coming after me. Not when he's trying to avoid the king's notice. And certainly not when I'm at a party with you, surrounded by dozens of people, most of them magic users. Besides, now that Princess Bitch is on trial, why would Lorcán bother? It's not as though Maeve can reward him for claiming me. Kim says the king has Maeve locked up tighter than a leprechaun's— " I stopped before uttering

Kim's memorable epithet and amended, "Uh, somewhere that puts even Alcatraz's anti-mage unit to shame."

Since I'd been responsible for bringing Maeve's treachery to light and ruined her chance to become the sidhe's next ruler, hearing Kim speak so confidently helped put my mind at ease. Pretty sure I'd shot to number one on Maeve's 'Top Ten Humans To Kill Slowly' list.

"It is not simply Lorcán, nor Maeve, who concern me," he said, spearing me with a meaningful look.

Yes, I knew, but I was doing my best to ignore it, which wasn't wise, all things considered. King Faonaín, ruler of the sidhe and Maeve's father, wasn't an adversary I should discount, not if I wanted to enjoy my continued freedom. And I wasn't sure that he thanked me for uncovering his daughter's machinations.

"It's a few measly hours," I said, chastened but no less determined. "Julie worked hard putting this party together, and I want to say goodbye to my friends."

I looked away. I was grateful for the opportunity to train with the amhaín, but I couldn't say I was entirely happy about it. I mumbled, "Who knows? It could be months, maybe years, before I see them again."

Kieran slipped his fingers under my chin and gently coaxed me to meet his gaze. His dark eyes conveyed the regret I might not have picked up in his voice. "You're a quick study. It won't be years."

"You don't know that."

"But it is a reasonable guess based on how easily you sidestepped and closed the demon gateway without training." He arched his brow, giving his features a deliberate, superior slant. "Surely, even my dear cousin would not argue with that, despite his fondness for contradicting me."

I smiled as he knew I would. Although Tíereachán took great pleasure in needling Kieran, there seemed to be an undercurrent of respect between them. They were family, after all.

"I thought we agreed the king won't break the Compact," I said. "He knows I'm going to his sister strictly for training.

Reluctant Adept - Chapter One

I have no intention of becoming one of her subjects. I'm not taking sides in their power struggle. I'm doing this for Earth, so we can fight the demons. Everyone knows that." I frowned at him. "Or is there something you haven't told me?"

The Compact, the ancient accord between King Faonaín, the amhaín, and the telepaths of Invisius Verso, had been in place for centuries, since the end of the sidhe civil war. Without an intact covenant, the king would be free to resume his efforts to exterminate the human race. Of course, such a response would likely reignite hostilities between King Faonaín and his sister, the amhaín, since it was the main reason for their rift.

Kieran's lack of response troubled me. So did his grim expression.

"Hello?"

His jaw tightened. "I've told you the facts I'm aware of, but Kim has been avoiding me. I don't like it."

As King Faonaín's emissary, Kim provided a means of communication with the Otherworld through her bond to her soulmate, Brassal, Kieran's most trusted friend. Neither of them would avoid Kieran without good reason.

"You are an outcast. Why does this surprise you?" Red asked.

I bit back a sigh, wishing Red hadn't spoken so candidly. Kieran's banishment by Maeve was a sore spot. Even more so, now, since the king didn't seem inclined to reverse it.

"She's not forbidden to *talk* to us," I replied. "She just can't share sensitive information about the realm, that's all. Same goes for Brassal."

I tried to recall the last time I'd seen either Kim or her partner, Jackie. It had been a couple days, I decided.

"Kim would find a way to warn us if she knew something," I said. "She'd tell Michael or Jackie if we were in danger, knowing they'd come to us." I frowned at his closed expression. "Don't you think?"

"I'll feel better once you're in the amhaín's territory. At least there you will have more protection."

For the moment, I ignored the fact that he hadn't answered my question. "The king's had three weeks to act. He never sent word that he objects to my decision train with the amhaín. You think he's going to send the Hunt for me? He's that threatened by his sister? She gave her word that my training would be free from debt or obligation. He doesn't believe she'll honor that?"

Kieran's body language grew more taut with every one of my questions. He folded his arms, the sleek material of his button down shirt conforming to the defined muscles of his upper arms. He had the build of a martial artist—toned and lithe without being bulky—a beautiful yet deadly package. His offensive magic and physical prowess were a combination against which few sidhe could stand. But King Faonaín wasn't *any* sidhe. He commanded the *Wuldrífan*, the Wild Hunt, a spectral and by all accounts unstoppable hunting party. Even if I discounted this ghostly force, the king ruled over a magically empowered populace with a preternaturally powerful army at his fingertips.

"I think the king has more to worry about of late than the amhaín," Kieran replied.

I took in his rigid stance and crossed arms, everything still except his index finger, which he tapped in a slow, deliberate rhythm against his left bicep. It was that restless gesture that had me biting out a curse, the four-letter word slipping out before I pressed my lips together.

"You've been keeping things from me." I closed my eyes and breathed past the disappointment that settled on my chest. "I thought we were past that."

"*Bídteine*, if I shared every care I had for your safety, you'd soon think I was a hand-wringer with nothing better to do than worry day and night."

My eyes popped open. Truth. Kieran didn't lie. Like all sidhe, honesty with him was a near-fanatical point of honor, but he was as agile as a politician when it came to evading questions he didn't want to answer. No doubt he hoped I'd swoon at his concern for me and lose my train of thought.

Sadly, it had been known to happen, but I liked to avoid acting like a star-struck idiot whenever life and limb were on the line.

At my raised eyebrows and dubious stare, he blew out a breath. "I have nothing ... concrete," he explained, his voice edging precariously close to being huffy, or as huffy as a proud male sidhe ever managed. "The king has enemies, those who want his power for themselves. If they learn of your existence—that the first adept in almost two thousand years is openly roaming the streets of Seattle—it would be to their advantage to claim you." He narrowed his eyes. "You may not enjoy being lauded as 'the one,' but the value of a proven adept is beyond calculating. There are many who would do anything to leash that power."

He paced away, his body tense and hands clenched. "Brassal has refused to discuss this with me, so I am forced to speculate. But if I were the king, this is a threat I would not dismiss. In fact, it is something I would take steps to *immediately* counter. I would not, for instance, assume that an outcast sidhe could provide enough protection for such an important asset, nor would I want this asset disappearing into my rival's territory where she could not be protected by my own forces."

I decided I hated being described as an 'asset' almost as much as being called 'the one.'

"He'll want me under his thumb, not just because he wants access to my power but so his enemies don't get it."

He nodded, turning to face me. "From his point of view, if he claims you and takes you for his mate, it both assures his continued rule and guarantees your well-being. Kim is deliberately avoiding me. She and Brassal seek to send a message without breaking their oath of loyalty to the king."

Thought of the king taking me against my will and coercing me into becoming his soulmate wound me tight enough to feel sick. The power of sidhe glamours was insidious. I wasn't sure whether I could thwart King Faonaín's sway, even with my partial blood connection to Tíereachán helping me. I wanted to ask, but Kieran disliked discussing my relationship with his cousin, even though it had been platonic from the beginning. (Okay, yes, Tíereachán was breathlessly sexy, but he was also one of the cockiest and most exasperating individuals I'd ever met.) I didn't know whether Kieran's annoyance stemmed more from his cousin's lecherous banter or the knowledge that Tíereachán had forced me into a blood compact when he'd been enslaved by the archdemon Azazel.

I slid Tíereachán from my thoughts and focused on the possibility that Kim was trying to warn us. "How long have you suspected this?"

"Since yesterday. I saw her out in the hall. When I spoke to her, she all but ignored me and the look on her face was ..." He frowned. "She's scared. It's not an expression that suits her."

No, I could see how it wouldn't be. Kim might not be as brash as her partner Jackie, but she wasn't timid either. If Kim was worried and unable to tell us, acting this way would give us warning without technically violating her loyalty to the king. And if she was afraid, I had reason to be concerned.

Unease flashed across Kieran's face.

"What?"

He paused, his normally full lips compressed to a flattened line. "Wade called while you were at Claude's this morning."

Wade was the amhaín's soulmate and, therefore, her most intimate liaison. He didn't telephone to shoot the breeze. I folded my arms, pressing them against my stomach as it churned with the all too familiar feeling that came whenever I was about to hear crappy news.

"Two days ago, Maeve testified during her trial that her dealings with Azazel were, while repugnant, necessary in order to learn the identity and location of the prophesied adept." The taut muscles of his jaw flexed as spoke. "She announced the truth of your existence to the Tribunal. Vince was forced to testify, as was Brassal. Your identity and powers are no longer a secret shared by a trusted few."

Reluctant Adept - Chapter One

My lips tingled numbly as the blood drained from my face, and it was all I could do to keep my trembling knees from dumping me on my ass. I staggered to the nearest chair and sat down hard. With my adept status exposed, worry over King Faonaín and his enemies wasn't unfounded.

Not good. Not good at all.

In less than a week, Kieran and I were scheduled to meet Wade in Vancouver, where he'd then drive us to the closest gateway to *Thìr na Soréidh*, the amhaín's sealed enclave within the Otherworld. Our airline tickets to Canada were booked. Kim knew about it, therefore so did the king.

I straightened in my chair, squared my shoulders, and considered where this left us. "Since Wade knows, it's safe to assume the news has leaked beyond the Tribunal," I said. "And, for the sake of argument, let's also assume that all of the king's enemies know I'm an adept and where I am."

I met his gaze. "How are these enemies going to get here? I thought it wasn't easy for you guys to come to Earth nowadays. There's just the one gateway in Evgrenya's territory. Since the king has a treaty with her and she's on his side, that gateway will be heavily guarded, right?"

I knew next to nothing about Evgrenya, except for the fact that she controlled the only gateway outside of the amhaín's sealed domain, which made it the only access point to Earth within the king's reach.

"The only side Evgrenya is guaranteed to support is her own," Kieran said, lips curled in distaste. "It was Maeve who negotiated the treaty, giving Lorcán passage to Ireland. I don't know the specifics of their arrangement. It may have been for temporary access. Now that Maeve is disgraced, there's no telling where Evgrenya's allegiances lie. It would be foolish to assume she'll deny the king's enemies access to her gateway. And even if she did, it could be because she plans to send her own contingent to claim you."

I threw up my hands. "Of course it would. All I have to do is merely *think* of the worst possible scenario and it's sure to happen." I bit back another choice four-letter word. "All right. Options?"

Before either he or Red could answer, I held up my index finger. "One: Hide in my apartment building under the djinn's protection for the rest our days." I raised my second finger. "Two: Leave as planned and try to make it to the amhaín." With the addition of my ring finger, I felt like a Girl Scout repeating her pledge. "Three: Negotiate with the king for your reinstatement and then give myself up."

I abandoned the finger gestures and flopped back in my chair. "Four: Escape to a remote tropical island and go native. Personally, that's my favorite. At least I'd get to see you in nothing but a loincloth for the rest of my life."

No amused reaction to that last bit. Instead, he closed the distance between us, his jaw set and eyes intent. He loomed over me. "Negotiating with the king is, at best, ill-advised and to do so in the hope that he will overturn Maeve's outcast decree is quixotic. I will not allow you to do such a thing."

Well, hello, Mr. Bossy.

"Quixotic, huh?" I launched upright and feigned a frantic glance about the room. "Quick, Red, where's my pocket dictionary?"

Kieran snorted at my antics and gazed down his nose at me. "El Ingenioso Hidalgo Don Quijote de la Mancha?" At my befuddlement, he said, "Apparently, Don Quixote is no longer taught in your schools. Shame."

I shouldn't have been astonished that Kieran knew more about human literature than I did, but I was. The man never stopped surprising me. Quixotic wasn't a word I'd ever heard in conversation, but I knew a little about the seventeenth-century Spanish novel. Precious little, but it was enough for me to puzzle out the word's meaning. Knowing Kieran, no doubt he'd been personally acquainted with Cervantes.

"Negotiating with the king is the equivalent of attacking windmills, huh?" I asked wryly.

"Exactamente."

"Spanish is such a sexy language, so expressive." I tipped my head, examining him archly. "I should warn you, though.

I came by some of my dialect by reading items that belonged to more than a few eighteenth-century pirates."

"Attempting to negotiate with the king, in any language, will be your downfall. I'll not allow you to attempt it."

So much for levity. I glared at him, exasperated. "We're going to discuss it, along with the rest of our options, pros and cons, and then *together* we'll decide what to do."

"By all means," he said deliberately and raised his index finger, his expression turning grim. "Option one: Keeping to your apartment for the foreseeable future, allowing the djinn to protect you. For a long term strategy, this will not work. The king or his enemies will seek your friends and family. Your loved ones will be tortured or killed until you submit to their demands."

The speed at which my self-righteous anger turned to fear made my head spin, but he plowed ahead with barely a nod, taking my expression for tacit agreement.

He raised his second finger to join the first. "Option two: We leave as planned, meeting Wade and allowing him to escort us through the amhaín's gateway. This is foolhardy, although the idea is viable. We cannot leave as planned. We must leave now, while everyone expects us to attend your friend's festivities, using your sidestepping ability to evade our enemies when necessary."

"After what you just said about my friends and family?" I gaped. "There's no way I'm leaving them unprotected! I'll go to Kim. Brassal is your best friend. You told me he's trustworthy. He and Kim will help me negotiate a deal so the king will ensure my family and friends are protected."

He stiffened. "Even with Brassal and Kim on your side, the king cannot be trusted. Sacrificing your freedom in return for your friends' protection will only result in your enslavement, and once you are within the king's grasp, I'll be helpless to aid you. As soon as we arrive, I'll be sent on a suicide mission or assigned duty in a far off province, leaving you at his mercy."

I jutted out my chin. "I would make your job as my bodyguard one of my stipulations and bonding with the king would be off the table too."

If Kieran and I were soulmated, it would keep anyone else from bonding with me, but I knew better than to suggest it. If Kieran and I bound our souls, Kieran would become a prime target for assassination.

He shook his head and cupped his hand against my cheek. At his touch, my insides immediately warmed, and I stared into the depths of his dark-brown eyes, wanting nothing more than to stay there forever.

"*Bídteine*, no. The king is ruthless and clever. There is no bargain you can make that will prevent him from claiming you as his mate, killing anyone who interferes. He will have his way unless you can counter his leverage against you. The amhaín can teach you the necessary skills to accomplish that. Take my word as someone who knows—this is the surest path toward protecting your friends and family."

Wilting, I hugged myself. "I never wanted any of this." I stared up at him. "I just want a normal life ... a normal life with you. Is that so much to ask?"

His expression softened. "Normal? Or do you mean ordinary?" I opened my mouth to explain, but he beat me to it. "No, my sweet. I understand. I do. I would like nothing more than to find a place where I could be assured of your safety and enjoy my time in your company. But you and I ... we are not ordinary, not in your world nor, even, in mine. You because of your abilities and me because of my bloodline and my prior deeds. No amount of wishing will change that ... nor would I want to. You are the most extraordinary woman I have ever encountered. It is not possible for you—with your magic and intelligence and generous spirit—to live anything but an extraordinary life." He leaned down to rub his nose alongside mine, making me feel warm and cherished. "It is my honor to be allowed to occupy a part of it, even if things are not exactly as we might wish."

I placed my hand over his heart as I always did whenever he said the things that touched me most. I wondered whether he had any idea what his words did to me. And not just his words, but his actions. With every caress, each tender glance, he'd burrowed his way into my life, and though I'd done my best to resist, I realized he'd found his way into my heart. Kieran was the most honorable, sexy, thoroughly captivating man I'd ever known, and we'd spent the past three weeks practically living in each other's pockets. Protecting my heart had been a lost cause from the start. He was smart, wise, and made me feel as if I was as necessary to his survival as water. I'd teetered on the edge of the slippery slope weeks ago, maybe even from the moment he stepped foot in my apartment and offered me his service as protector, even when his views on humans had been discriminatory at best.

I parted my lips to tell him so, but then he ruined it by adding, "Keeping you safe is but a small price to pay."

Any heartfelt words died in my throat, smothered by a hefty dollop of reality. I was the *prized* adept to be protected at all cost.

I tried to thrust the bitter thought aside but couldn't. I didn't doubt that Kieran respected and cared for me. I knew he did, but it wasn't the sole reason he'd chosen to remain at my side.

There was Nuala to consider, the amhaín's adept-in-training who, years ago, he seduced into becoming his soulmate in order to bring her under King Faonaín's dominion. Once she discovered that Kieran had deceived her, she withdrew from him. And even though he'd fallen in love with her, Nuala had never forgiven him, never opened herself up to him, not in the near century they were together, ending when she died in an earthquake. The mistake continued to haunt him, even after nearly two thousand years, and it was why Kieran was known to many as 'the Deceiver.'

I think in some small part, the reason he sought to protect me from King Faonaín's threat was to make up for what he'd done to Nuala all those years ago.

So, instead of babbling something sappy, I looked away and muttered, "Right ... keeping me safe."

I stepped out of his reach, smoothing my hair as I forced myself to consider our current predicament instead of our relationship issues. If I let him make all the decisions, we'd be heading out the door without so much as a goodbye to anyone.

"Lire?"

"I think it's time to pack, don't you?" I said, ignoring his troubled expression, and then spun on my heel to cut a path upstairs to my bedroom.

Inside my walk-in closet, I snagged my paisley duffel from the floor and shook it roughly so my yoga gear spilled onto the carpet at my feet. While I toed aside my rolled-up mat, hand weights, and exercise clothes, Kieran's presence filled the doorway.

"We'll leave tonight," I told him. "But we're going to the party, at least for a couple of hours. If we don't show up, my friends will worry and our enemies—if they're even out there—will know we're up to something. Afterward, we'll slip away. I think we should drive to Whistler. Airline tickets are too easy to track. I have emergency cash in my safe to cover our expenses, and we'll take ... Daniel's car."

I faltered over the name of my childhood friend and had to stop to suck in a shaky breath. Memories of Daniel's recent murder at the hands of Azazel hijacked my thoughts all too often.

If I'd known how to close the portal sooner, I could have saved him.

I buried the frequent recrimination before I could beat myself up with it anymore, adding, "I'm pretty sure Michael hasn't sold it yet and it's safer than taking my Mercedes, even if it does have armor plating."

When my suggestion was met with silence, I glanced away from the clothes I was snatching from their hangers to consider Kieran. He'd donned his customary mask of superior neutrality. It was the look that said he'd lived long and nothing he encountered at this point could surprise him. I knew better, though. Oh, he'd definitely seen it all—after twenty-seven-hundred years, that was a given. But I'd come to learn that he also used the façade to cover his emotions, to prevent anyone from knowing what he might be thinking. In the Otherworld, where lies weren't tolerated, emotions would reveal too much and invite potentially uncomfortable questions.

I had to wonder whether this cool detachment was the main quality that drew me to him as surely as a newly turned strigoi to fresh blood. I longed to strip away the impassive mask, to find the very truth of the man underneath, to know him like no other, and to show him that he was so much more than a fallen sidhe with dubious honor.

It was a challenge I relished.

I turned to him, clothes draped over my arm. "Why so quiet? I figured this is what you wanted."

"It's a reasonable course," he replied. "Will my cousin be an attendee at this soirée?"

"I think so. Michael said they'd be late, so I assume that means they're both planning to come." I narrowed my eyes, examining him. "Why?"

"You'll be tempted to tell him our plans, to include him. We're safe to discuss it here, with your building's wards and guardian djinn, but at the party, no matter how discrete you try to be, it's possible for our enemies to overhear anything you might say. Keep our plans to yourself unless you're under the protection of my shroud. Even then, the fewer who know our intentions the better." Leaning against the door frame, he folded his arms. "Let me take care of informing Tíereachán."

"Informing him?" I swallowed my bark of laughter. "If you tell him to stay put, you know he won't listen, right?" I went back to yanking various items from their hangers and muttered, "You guys are worse than adolescent siblings with the way you peck at each other."

"If I intended for him to ... *stay put*, as you say, I'd know better than to inform him of our plans." He sniffed. "The man is worse than a disobedient mongrel."

I managed to hide my smirk at his disgruntled tone, ducking behind my armload of clothes and turning to rummage in my lingerie drawer. Satisfied that I'd pulled out at least a week's worth of panties and bras, I snagged my duffel with my foot and kicked it toward my bed.

Kieran examined me suspiciously as I passed. In better spirits now that we'd agreed on a plan, I rose up to give him a peck on his cheek. "Grab the black backpack from the middle shelf, you gorgeous, sexy elf. Hurry and pack, or we'll be more than just fashionably late."

He scowled at my favorite taunt, but when he turned to do as I asked, I caught a flash of his smile. It zinged through me, bouncing off every nerve ending like a pixie on a sugar high. *Yum.* It was crazy what the man could do to me with a single spontaneous smile. I'd never done recreational drugs, but they couldn't possibly compete with Kieran.

Gazing at his retreating backside from over my shoulder, I teetered at the threshold before dumping everything on the floor and chasing him back into the closet. I smiled, wicked purpose infusing every step. Guess we were going to be late.

When my fingers slid under his shirt, eliciting a hungry growl and eager response, I couldn't find it in myself to be upset about it.

TWO

Laughter and Lady Gaga's 'Applause' greeted us when I pulled open the glass door of Peabody's Beans. A bright yellow notice flapped in the rain-scented breeze, informing anyone not already deterred by the bright-red neon CLOSED sign that this was a private party.

As I stamped my damp boots on the doormat and shook the ever-present Seattle drizzle from my hair, the smell of espresso, overlaid by the aroma of Julie's signature nachos, stirred my hunger. A growl issued from my stomach almost loud enough to be heard over a boisterous cheer. Behind me, Kieran slipped inside, and I watched him take in our surroundings, fascination crinkling the delicate skin at the outer corners of his eyes.

While I hung up my jacket and gently repositioned my purse at my hip, so as not to disturb Red, I surveyed the large shop for the source of the raucous cheers. A small group of six or seven had gathered near a vintage Ms. Pac-Man arcade game, no doubt watching Julie's brother compete with whoever he'd suckered into going head-to-head with him, a challenge that no doubt involved shots of tequila for the loser. Tom was a lot like his sister, he approached everything he did with an infectious *joie de vivre* that even a toga-wearing frat boy would envy. Although, when the morning-after hit, maybe not so much.

Reluctant Adept - Chapter Two

My mouth watered at the piquant fragrance of pickled jalapeños, onions, and cheese. I'd dig ditches through hard-pan for a plate of Julie's nachos.

Dozens of friendly eyes met mine as I searched the familiar crowd in search of my good friend. Clusters of people peppered the spacious coffee shop, some sitting at tables or in the padded chairs surrounding the in-the-round fireplace, others standing in small groups, chatting over their drinks and plates of food. A mob hung out at the back counter where Julie usually set up the refreshments. Here and there I caught a few new faces.

The loiterers hovering near the counter parted and Julie bounded toward me. I waved at people I knew, responding to variations of 'Hey, Lire!' until my friend of seven years halted practically in my face, hands on her hips, sleek brown ponytail swinging.

"You're never late! I thought you forgot!" she exclaimed. Her attention wandered to Kieran. She blinked long, her eyebrows pursuing her hairline, as her gaze flitted from his face down to his toes and then reversed course. "Never mind. I forgive you."

She shook herself and turned to me, her grin wide and a little sloppy. Someone was tipsy. "Holy crap, Li-Li, you weren't kidding. Get out the Dustbuster. Worth every crumb," she gushed, admiring Kieran and nodding her head gravely. "Monday through Saturday and twice on Sunday. Your eyes do not lie, girlfriend. I'll never doubt you again. Swear." She held up her hand, pinkie waving.

I gazed heavenward. "God save me from drunken best friends," I grumbled, cheeks heating, and then narrowed my eyes at her. "I've got three words for you: The Lucky Caldron. Behave, or a certain someone's going to learn all about the bachelorette party gone wrong."

She rolled her eyes. "Please. That secret's following us to the grave and you know it. Pinkie swears are absolute."

I pursed my lips to hide my grin and leaned closer. "Remind me to stop confiding in you." Straightening, I said, "Kieran, this is Julie, my soon-to-be *ex*-best friend." I shot her a warning glare, knowing it was a lost cause but unable to help myself. "Jules, this is Kieran."

She stuck out her hand and Kieran shook it, his lips quirked by an amused smile. After they exchanged good-to-meet-yous, Kieran looked at her askance. "Dustbuster? I imagine there's a hidden meaning at work here," he observed, glancing at me before his eyes narrowed and turned conspiratorial.

I leveled a finger at Julie. "Don't even think about it," I said, voice pitched low, but she just snickered.

Ignoring me, she took Kieran by the elbow. "Kieran, hon, I'm so glad you asked." Smug grin firmly in place, she guided him toward the refreshments. "It's a private joke Lire and I cooked up after a night of one too many drinks. You ever hear the saying, 'I'd let him eat crackers in my bed any day?'"

He chuckled. "No, I can't say I have."

She stopped to peer up at him, unsteady in her stance as she cocked her hip. Her chain-link belt, which perched low on her hips, clanked softly. "I don't need to explain it, do I?"

"Crumbs in one's sheets are a terrible business," he replied in mock seriousness.

After a moment of looking puzzled, she brightened when his words apparently sank in. "I know, right?" She beamed. "Now, decide how many days of the week you'd put up with it and there you go. I agree with Lire, you're definitely a seven-day-a-week guy, but don't go getting cocky. Personality counts. I haven't accounted for that yet." She shot me a devilish grin and giggled. "Although, Lire has ... along with performance." She waved her hand dismissively and rolled her eyes. "I'll be taking her word for *that*."

"Good grief." I smacked my palm to my forehead. "Kill me now." I stared at her, exasperated. "Remind me: Why did I come here?"

"Nachos. And the BFF Seal of Approval, of course. He's stealing you away for a three-month sabbatical and this is the first I'm meeting him." She shook her head and tsked at me. "Girl—seriously? You didn't *actually* think you could come out of this unscathed, did you?"

She folded her arms and eyed Kieran authoritatively. "Lire is my best friend. She's part of my family. You hurt her and I will hunt you down, and most of the people in this room will join me. Here, or the Otherworld, it doesn't matter. I might be human, but I'm inventive and persistent and very, very devious. Just ask any of my brother's skanky ex-girlfriends." She poked him in the arm with her index finger. "Got me?"

Kieran regarded her thoughtfully and bowed his head. "Of course. You have my word, Lire's well-being is my highest concern."

Looking satisfied, Julie nodded. "Good. Then we have an understanding." She dusted her hands together and grinned at us. "Let's party!" She bounced on the balls of her feet and then strode around the rustic fireplace toward the counter. "Warming up your food now, Li-Li," she announced. "Grab a drink, you two."

Shaking my head, I risked a glance at Kieran. Thankfully, he continued to look amused. "You want a beer?"

"Certainly." He followed me to the large tubs filled with ice and various beverages.

As I straightened from the container, cold Blue Moon in hand, he grasped my waist and whispered over my shoulder, "For you, I would not be deterred by one crumb nor ten thousand, day of the week notwithstanding."

I shivered at the warmth of his breath against my cheek. When I turned, he smirked and tucked a stray lock of my hair behind my ear. *Holy cow.* With Kieran around, who needed a roller coaster for a case of plummeting stomach?

Although I did my best to hide it, a goofy grin spread across my lips. Being cool was a lost cause. Going, going, gone.

Because I could, I tugged on his neck and, when he leaned down, I kissed him soundly on the mouth, earning his immediate reciprocation. Afterward, I sighed and rubbed my lips together, savoring it. "That's something I've not been able to do in a long time," I murmured.

He chuckled, taking the cold bottle I handed him. "I think it's been all of twenty minutes, not that I mind."

I shook my head. "I haven't had a boyfriend I could touch without a barrier for over ten years." I gave him a sly smile. "I've missed the novelty of being able to mark my territory in public."

"Well then ... I'm happy to oblige." His grin turned wolf-ish. "Mark me anytime. Since it works both ways, it's to my advantage."

Julie shoved a plate between us, unrepentantly breaking up our quiet conversation. "I figured you guys could share. With the two of you going at it, Kieran needs to stick to psi-free," she said with a knowing wink.

I took the plate from Julie, responding with an exasper-ated widening of my eyes, and thanked her.

"It twists off," I told Kieran, when I saw him frown at his bottle's cap and then scan the nearby table, probably for a bottle opener. Many of our more modern conveniences were lost on him since, until a month ago, it had been over fifty years since he'd spent any appreciable time on Earth.

Julie pulled off her disposable gloves and tossed them into the trash. Grabbing a beer, she said, "Come on, Kieran. Let's introduce you around."

I liberated a psi-free mineral water from the tub, stuck it under my arm, and then trailed behind with the plate, stuff-ing a loaded tortilla chip into my mouth and trying not to dump it all over my blouse as I walked. *Oh, man. Heaven.* The fingers of my gloves were going to be an oil-stained mess by the time I was done, though. Why could I never seem to re-member to take at least my right one off before stuffing my face? *Bonehead.* Fortunately, I kept several extra pairs in my purse.

A few steps past the fireplace, Julie stopped to whisper intently into Kieran's ear. *Uh oh.* I knew that look. She was up to something, but between my chewing, our distance, and the ambient noise, I couldn't overhear what she'd said.

Kieran faced away from me, so his expression was no help. He gave her a nod and then continued to follow in her wake across the room.

Damn it. With my mouth full of nachos, I couldn't scold her, and when I realized she'd headed straight for her husband and Glen, my ex-boyfriend—the one who dumped me last year because he was sick and tired of dealing with all my 'necessary precautions'—I wanted to yank her back and threaten her with horrible things if she didn't behave. Why had I shoved the entire mile-high chip into my mouth? No doubt I had cilantro stuck in between my front teeth, and to top everything off, I couldn't take a swig of my water because the bottle was still encased in its protective shrink-wrap.

Resigning myself to the coming discomfort, I offloaded my plate on the nearest table and then sidled up to Kieran.

"Hey, sweetie." Julie beamed at her husband, pausing to greet Glen before going on, "Hon, I want you to meet Lire's beau. Kieran, this is my husband Steven and his friend Glen."

They shook hands while I did my best to avoid looking at my ex.

Why was I so uncomfortable? Yes, he'd hurt me, badly in fact, but I'd been over the jerk for months. Maybe my sudden cold sweat was because I had little experience with ex-boyfriends, having had so few of them. Honestly, this was a novelty I could have lived without, in spite of Kieran overshadowing him. Not because Glen wasn't attractive; he was, in a clean-cut Microsoft executive sort of way. It was just that Kieran—in addition to being incredibly sexy and well-built—possessed an enigmatic aura that marked him as being dangerous if provoked. He stood out in the room like a fallen angel among the rabble. Glen was so far removed from Kieran's league, it was laughable.

I busied myself with unwrapping my water bottle, needing to hide behind it.

Maybe most women in my shoes would be feeling smug and victorious right about now, but for some reason I itched for a hole to fall into. Julie was my dearest friend and I loved her to bits, but this whole setup smacked of … of high school.

As I gulped from my bottle, I almost cringed, wondering what Kieran must think of it. The guy was a twenty-seven-hundred-year-old dignified sidhe.

Strange as it seemed, it was only at odd times like these that the age disparity occurred to me. After all, we were both adults. By all appearances, Kieran didn't look any older than my thirty, but Julie's mischief had me considering the bizarreness of it. His teenage years were so long ago, at this point they must be an indistinct fog lurking in the furthest corner of his mind. Besides, the sidhe were far too superior to experience anything as plebeian as angst. Most of them no doubt popped out of their mothers' womb wearing tuxedos and ready for higher education, skipping puberty entirely.

Why had I decided this party was a good idea?

The touch of Kieran's caress on the back of my neck startled me. I jerked my attention upward to find him gazing down at me, his lazy grin and twinkling eyes speaking of mischief. To my shock, he leaned down and pressed his lips to my temple, soothing my anxiety with a gush of warmth. I blinked up at him, mystified and pleased in equal measure, until Glen's shocked voice reminded me we had an audience.

"Hey, don't— " Glen reached out, as if to grab Kieran, but stopped short. His confused gaze ping-ponged between us, eyebrows raised and mouth slackened with shock. I swear I heard Julie snicker, but that could have been my imagination.

"You— " he stopped, dropping his arm and stepping back as he took a breath to regain his cool. "He can touch you. You said … I mean, I thought that was a problem."

Problem for you, *dickwad,* I thought as I slid my drink to the nearby table, freeing my hand to wrap around Kieran's waist.

"Not for the right man," Kieran replied, his fingers still curled possessively at the back of my neck.

Whoa. Okay, maybe I was starting to enjoy this. Glen looked nonplussed. If not for some of the hurtful things he'd said when he dumped me, I might even have felt bad about it.

I leaned into Kieran when his arm snaked to my waist, encouraging me closer. He sure knew a little something about marking territory, and I planned to reward him later. He hadn't needed to go along with Julie, who'd certainly instigated this, but he'd done it anyway, surprising me yet again. There was a playful side to Kieran, and I enjoyed uncovering it.

"You mean the right *elf*," a statuesque brunette threw in, her sultry voice failing to conceal a sneer.

Perhaps an inch taller than Glen's five-foot-ten and looking way too young for his late-thirties, she insinuated herself into the conversation, perching her narrow chin on his shoulder and wrapping her arms around his waist. With her heavily made-up eyes, stylishly tousled hair, and what little I could see of her skintight leather ensemble, she wouldn't have looked out of place at the MTV Video Music Awards. For a party among friends, though, it was a little much.

Her turquoise-blue eyes narrowed as she examined Kieran and me and added, "Although, any elf would do. Like the strigoi, touchies can't read them."

I bristled at the derogatory terms. Interesting, though, that she'd used the formal name for vampires.

She stalked to Glen's side, draping a possessive hand on his left shoulder and fingering the top edge of his black turtleneck with the tips of her glossy-red nails. "But as far as elves go, this one has little to crow about." Predatorily, she scrutinized Kieran and sniffed. "Pity."

What the hell was she smoking? If Kieran walked the runway, he'd be a slam dunk for hottest male model of the year. Whenever we went out in public, he drew appreciative stares from practically every female we passed, in addition to a fair number of men. It would have irritated me if not for the fact that Kieran dismissed it, as if the attention meant less than nothing to him. At first, I thought it was because he continued to harbor a dim view of humans—he'd once told me, in his experience, human women had proved to be 'vain, weak-minded, insipid creatures' who only craved to bed him a their 'earliest convenience.' However, I'd come to realize that Kieran simply didn't view himself as being particularly attractive.

Squeezing my side in warning, Kieran placed his beer on the nearby table, but I was too incensed to spare it any thought. Who did she think she was, anyway?

"Clearly, you don't have eyes," I scoffed. "Not that we give a flying crap." I dismissed her with an eye roll and turned to Julie. "I must have missed the 'Rude Skanks Allowed' sign on your door, Jules."

Julie didn't react. In fact, our exchange seemed to have left both her and Steven lost for words.

Kieran's magic swept over me and blurred movement wrenched my attention back to Glen and Miss Brunette-and-Bitchy.

Joining the two of them was an eye-catching newcomer, another MTV-wannabe by the look of his trendy, monochromatic wardrobe. Slim ebony suit, silver-gray shirt, and meticulously trimmed goatee, the man was a six-foot-three study in how to be tall, black, and handsome without trying. He stood at the brunette's side, restraining her outstretched arm, which he'd plainly grabbed mid-strike.

No way. The idiot woman had dared to take a swing at me?

Kieran's protective shroud surrounded us. Since the brunette remained on her feet, instead of collapsed into a bloody heap on the floor, her companion must have interfered before Kieran could unleash his corrosive shadow on her skinny ass.

"Now, Eva," the man crooned in a deliciously cultured British accent. "What is it Americans say? Sticks and stones? Besides, that was a rather coarse thing to say, even if true."

He was dissing Kieran's looks too? What was this—opposite day?

Reluctant Adept - Chapter Two

Somehow, I'd stepped into that Twilight Zone episode where the model-perfect blonde laments the fact that her 'treatments' hadn't fixed her horrible facial disfigurement, and then the camera pans back to show all the doctors and nurses with pig snouts instead of noses. If these two thought Kieran wasn't much to look at, I couldn't imagine what their idea of a showstopper might be, although, the two of them weren't exactly hard on the eyes. Not a snout in sight. Maybe they had curly tails that I couldn't see. I almost snickered at the thought.

Eyebrows creeping upward, I shook my head. This whole encounter bordered on the bizarre.

The man tucked Eva's arm under his, stroking her still-clenched fist soothingly, easing her fingers apart. His graceful brown hands contrasted prominently with her fair skin, calling attention to his long fingers and smooth caresses. The sensuality of each stroke sent a shiver through me. When I glanced into his dark brown eyes, he stared back with an intensity that shot sparks of alarm clear down through my heels. This man might be a lot of things (intimidating, striking, and sexy to name a few), but I was fairly sure *human* wasn't one of them.

In one swift move, Kieran turned into my one-armed embrace, pulling my shoulder firm to his chest. With a flick of his wrist, his magic sword manifested in his right hand. "She is mine," he said in a tone that was both calm and inexorable at the same time.

It all happened so quickly, I didn't have time to gasp, much less issue protest.

"Of course she is," the man replied, smiling with all the humor of a shark swimming in chum-filled waters. "Lovely party. Allow me to introduce myself, I am Nathan."

My eyes widened at his elongated, sharply pointed canines.

Oh shit. My first contact with the strigoi and Kieran acting like a possessive Neanderthal did not project the message I wanted to convey. I came close to jabbing him in the ribs with my elbow, but the ominous absence of party chatter finally permeated my indignation.

I glanced around me. Julie and Steven hadn't moved. They stood riveted in place, both of them blinking slowly, eyes glassy. Glen, too, seemed to be some kind of trance. A glance about the shop revealed more of the same. Interspersed among the dazed partygoers, I spotted at least six other strangers, all of them eying me with cold malevolence and projecting tightly coiled menace.

Nathan and his cohorts had mesmerized and taken control of everyone in the freaking room!

No, not Jules! And Steven?

Oh shit, oh shit, oh shit ...

I swallowed hard in a hopeless effort to control my skyrocketing alarm. There was a reason an unsolicited strigoi bite was a felony in most states. More powerful than the strongest roofie, strigoi venom acted on the central nervous system. Enhanced by magic, it produced a highly suggestive state that lasted indefinitely, without physiological side effects, other than being at the mercy of the vampire who wanted a meal and whatever else. Worse, its continued effect could only be countered by the strigoi's antidote. Victims could be told to go about their lives, just as my friends had been told to enjoy the party, but unless they received the anti-hypnotic or the strigoi died, they'd be forever compromised, unable to resist the call of whichever vamp had bitten them.

I turned back to the British vamp. At least, he *sounded* British. For all I knew, he was a two-thousand-year-old Celt who'd spent the last few centuries in the UK ... aside from being black. I didn't think that quite fit the image of an ancient Celt, but I'd not read many Celtic artifacts so I could hardly call myself informed.

Shaking off the useless, random thoughts, I clamped down on my distressed need for air. "You guys know those photos I sent weren't meant to be a threat, right? I wanted to get the domn's attention, to prove that I'm not a prank. Your PR guy wasn't particularly ... gracious when I called."

Somehow, I managed to avoid sounding panicked and even diplomatically added, "I guess I can't blame him. A demon invasion does sound pretty farfetched."

Nathan's dark gaze briefly wavered. "You spoke to Frederick? When?"

Frederick was the prick who'd threatened to drain me for wasting his time. *A-ha.* Maybe it had become clear to Nathan that delightful Freddy had stonewalled me.

"I don't remember the exact date," I replied. "About a week and a half ago."

"And after this ... contact, you sent photos?" His eyes narrowed. "Directly to the domn or through Frederick?"

"Both," I said, relaxing with the hope that this was just a misunderstanding. I'd even consider overlooking what he and his associates had done to my friends if he backed off and set things right. "Didn't Frederick send you the photos? I hope he at least forwarded you my cover letter."

"No." Curiosity played on his face, along with darker things.

I donned my 'don't worry, I can be reasonable' smile—although, Kieran's continued protection was seriously cramping my style. Projecting confidence wasn't easy when my boyfriend kept me caged inside his one-armed embrace and brandished a sword as though we were surrounded by a pack of rabid wolves.

"Then I can see why you thought you were dealing with a crank," I said. "Why don't we start over? Release my friends and I'll give you the important details. Then we can go from there on how best to involve your domn."

He stared at me for a long moment, and his frank evaluation left me with the distinct impression that he'd deftly cataloged all of my potential weaknesses in the off chance he had to run me down like a gazelle. Clairvoyants were immune to strigoi venom, as were telepaths, but we could still be drained readily enough.

"What you say intrigues me," he said, "but that's not why I'm here."

"You're— " I stumbled over his admission. "Wait. It's not?"

"Indeed, no." He grinned broadly, displaying a disturbing length of fang.

I glanced around, taking in the scene, not liking that the song playing over the shop's speakers was 'The Monster' by Eminem. I shook my head at him. "I don't understand."

He chuckled. "Allow me to elaborate. *You* interest a friend of mine. And what interests him, interests me." He raked me with his gaze. "Although, I must admit, you aren't what I expected." He raised a pitiless eyebrow. "So ... *human*," he observed, lacing the word with considerable distaste.

"Looks can be deceiving," a harmonious baritone interjected, proving without a doubt that Murphy's Law applied, even at parties.

One night of normal. That's all I wanted. Really, is that so goddamned much to ask?

Disgusted, I trilled, "And now about the cauldron sing— "

Ow!

Kieran's hard squeeze stopped me mid-verse. Whether he'd done it in silent warning or recrimination, I didn't know. Honestly, he was lucky I didn't stomp on his foot. I didn't need to see the voice's source to know a male sidhe lurked to our right.

Or, that because of my decision to come here, we were knee-deep in shit.

Again.

Resonant, bewitching laughter filled the room, vibrating the air itself. I shivered and would have tried to rub away my gooseflesh if not for Kieran's continued embrace, which pinned my right arm against his rigid body.

Tension rolled through him as he deftly drew me several steps backwards, providing better view of our newest threat but still maintaining a defensive position against Nathan.

Snap out of it, dummy. Protect what's yours.

Spurred by the thought, I unfurled my telekinesis to encompass Kieran and myself within my magic's hold before extending my reach into the room. To my dismay, my invisible tendrils skidded off the strigoi as though they were coated in grease, leaving a series of oblong dead zones within my netting. Even worse, the slippery barrier extended several inches beyond each one of them, which prevented me from grasping their human victims.

I looked about me. Each vamp held at least one captive tightly, using either hands or fangs (or, in one surprising case, a switchblade) to threaten immediate harm.

Jesus.

Still, if I overlooked the hostages held by each vamp, there were a little over a dozen partygoers I could grasp freely. Of course, this was only good news if I could *do* something to help them.

Why did Julie and Steven have to be so darn popular?

I'd never attempted to sidestep so many people at one time. The most I'd managed, with Kieran bolstering my focus, had been five. I wasn't sure I could manage seventeen, not that it mattered. Even if I could shift everyone to that higher dimension, it wouldn't counter their catatonic state. They were now intrinsically tied to whichever strigoi had bitten them and easily tracked through their blood, thanks to the strigoi curse. No place would be safe. And where would I keep them? They were essentially human vegetables. Unless ordered to go about their lives as usual, they wouldn't feed themselves, much less attend to their other bodily functions.

My gorge rose at the thought, but I swallowed thickly and shoved the thoughts aside. Later. I'd deal with that problem later.

I turned my attention to the source of the delicious laughter—a remarkably handsome sidhe sitting near the fireplace. He lounged in one of the shop's few upholstered wing chairs, long legs crossed at the ankles, forearms draped on the padded armrests, and his head arched back in mirth, exposing his smooth, muscular neck. At first glance, my breath didn't just catch, it vaporized. How the heck had I not noticed him earlier? This was not a man you missed. He was so hot, climatologists probably had to factor him into their weather predictions. I ogled him, gobsmacked, while understanding crashed down on me in the form of this golden, able-bodied visage.

Eva and Nathan's comments about Kieran made a little more sense now, although not because this new guy was drastically better looking. With his long, honey-blond hair, luminous skin, and warm hazel eyes, he seemed to radiate a captivating, seraphic glow; whereas Kieran, raven-haired and flinty-eyed, appeared brooding and austere. Personally, I'd go for Kieran's dark intensity every time, but everyone's tastes were different. Apparently, the two vamps favored the fair-haired, ethereal type.

The sidhe in question directed an amused, panty-vaporizing smile at me. "Live elves and fairies in a ring, enchanting all that you put in," he recited, continuing the Shakespearian verse where I'd left off, his lyrical voice an intoxicating purr.

He chuckled. "How delightful. The Scottish play. And who is Macbeth in this scenario, I wonder? Would that be you, Kieran? Did the oracle's prophecy raise such high hopes?"

Kieran snorted. "You know well—one such as I do not aspire to such things."

Lord. Not that stupid prophecy again. When I'd blurted the memorable line, it was because of the elves and fairies reference, not because of Macbeth's foretold kingship. Apparently, Golden Boy figured Kieran had wooed me in the hopes of becoming their next ruler—the one who would unify their fractured populace and be soulbound, not to a sidhe, but to a mate who straddled worlds.

I couldn't fathom why anyone would count *me* as a possibility for the prophecy's soulmate role. I wasn't a half-blood like Kim, who was naturally a part of both worlds. I was a born-and-bred Earthling. As Nathan had already pointed out: *Human.* I didn't straddle worlds.

Reluctant Adept - Chapter Two

Yet ... you can sidestep to a higher dimension, my little voice added, *which is pretty dang otherworldly. And an adept can supposedly open gateways to other worlds. That's what a gateway does—it straddles worlds.*

Not that I'd ever opened a gateway. I'd merely closed one, so that didn't precisely qualify.

I shook myself.

This was not the time to let my thoughts ramble on unchecked. None of it mattered. As far as I was concerned, anyone who thought I was the awaited soulmate was a deluded idiot. For all of two seconds, I basked in the superiority of my strenuous belief, until I realized ... it wasn't *my* opinion that mattered.

If King Faonaín and all his enemies were drinking the oracle's Kool-Aid, then in their minds I was a twofer—an adept *and* the future ruler's soulmate.

Christ. I'd be lucky if kidnappers didn't start crawling out from under the goddamned floorboards.

Hello, Earth to Lire ...

If Blondie thought I was the prophesied, world-straddling mate, I had to get my act together.

The sidhe chuckled, directing a perfectly arched eyebrow at Kieran. "Yes, I suppose Maeve did cure you of that ambition, didn't she? Ruined your standing as surely as she plies her virgin lovers. And, yet, you continue to play her fool." He scoffed, "Just the mention of Nuala's human kin and you rushed to dance to her tune once again."

Human kin? Had Kieran's former mate hooked up with a human at some point and conceived a child? That didn't make any sense. Nuala had been dead for almost two thousand years. Any half-human child of hers would be dead by now. Although ... if her child had taken a full blooded sidhe for a soulmate, it would have prolonged his or her life.

Had Maeve sent Kieran here to find Nuala's half-blood child? If so, once he found this person, what had she ordered him to do about it?

"Then you haven't been paying attention," Kieran replied. "I grew tired of that tune, long ago. You, I believe, cannot say the same, yet here we both stand. Outcast and rogue. Which of us is the more foolish?"

Rogue? *Oh crap.* Unless more than one rogue sidhe wandered the Earth, this was Lorcán, Maeve's right hand, the one she'd sent to claim me when Kieran had refused her order to bond with me.

The golden-haired sidhe laughed, rising smoothly to his feet. "Which of us, indeed. I am not the one seeking to redeem my past through my dead mate's bloodline. But, I digress, where are my manners?"

He beamed at me. "My dear Miss Devon, I shall take it upon myself to make the introductions since the Deceiver seems disinclined." He bowed. "I am Lorcán."

I tipped my chin at him, and, although I tried, I don't think I kept the distaste from showing on my face. The fact that he'd referred to Kieran by his rude sobriquet didn't help. "Lorcán. I'd say it's nice to meet you, except we all know you're not here to do anything nice." Even though my knees felt weak, I met his level gaze with one of my own. "Are you?"

"Now, wherever did you get an idea like that? Perhaps you would do well to consider the source of your assumptions. For example, I for one do not seek to deceive you with glamour." He twirled his hand through the air, gesturing at his face. "What you see is what you get," he said, shooting Kieran a challenging glare, "scars and all."

"If you're trying to imply that Kieran has seduced me with a glamour, you're wasting your breath," I told him. "Glamours don't work on me. Or didn't your precious princess mention that?"

He barked out a laugh. "Then why does he wear his mask? It certainly isn't for my benefit. I can see through such magic, as can my associates."

My stomach fluttered at the increased pressure of Kieran's protective embrace, which told me Lorcán had revealed something Kieran didn't want me to know. The realization might have driven me out of his arms, but Kieran wasn't the only one who'd warned me about Lorcán. Kim and Brassal both distrusted and actively disliked him, but more significantly, Lorcán was aligned with the demon-conspiring Princess Maeve.

Even if Lorcán spoke the unvarnished truth and Kieran *was* employing some sort of mask, such a thing couldn't disguise his actions, which spoke louder than any superficial glamour he might be using.

It wasn't hard to decide whose side I wanted to be on.

"You should talk," I said, my voice calm in spite of my gyrating insides. "Kieran isn't the one working with strigoi to illegally enslave my friends."

"Ah," he drew out, eyebrows lifting. "I see." A satisfied smile broke over his lips. "You were unaware of this deception, too. How interesting."

He tilted his head dismissively, gesturing at our surroundings. "As for your friends ... necessity, I'm afraid. For my protection. A rogue does not venture into the open without some assurances, especially when meeting an adversary who has so very much to lose. You must know, Kieran's done you a great disservice."

"Why? Because he protects me from *you*?"

"No. Your protection I cannot begrudge. Your continued survival is paramount. No, my ingénue. It's because he hasn't told you *why*."

"Why? Why *what*? Why he protects me?"

He angled his head, indicating partial agreement. "Why you are what you are."

"What I am, huh? And what, exactly, am I?"

"The second potential adept to be born in over four thousand years." He peered at me. "Do you know the identity of the other?"

I frowned, sure I didn't want to know, but I had a strong suspicion that I did.

"Nuala, of course." He took a step closer. "His former mate. And you, my dear, are born of her familial line."

I blinked, the air going out of me as though I'd been sucker-punched.

Born of—? My mind wheeled. *I* was somehow related to Nuala?

That wasn't possible. When Kieran and I had first met, he told me I had no appreciable sidhe blood and asked how I'd acquired my additional psychic gifts. But the fact that he now remained ominously silent and tense at my side led me to believe that 'appreciable' was the operative word. And since Kieran didn't accuse Lorcán of lying, that meant ...

I was Nuala's human kin—the one Maeve had used as bait to lure Kieran into doing her bidding.

I was so damned stupid. *This* is what drove Kieran's single-minded interest in protecting me. I'd suspected it had something to do with Nuala and atoning for his past mistakes, but I thought it was due to the similarity of our situations. The irony stung. Kieran had come to Earth with Maeve, for no other reason than because I was related to his former mate.

God! This explained Kim's surprised reaction to my green eyes when she and Brassal had first seen me. Apparently, I'd inherited the trait, which, according to Kieran, was a rare attribute among sidhe.

Was this why Kieran had seduced me? Because I reminded him so much of his former love—the one he'd called 'a treasure'? All those times he looked longingly into my eyes, had he seen her staring back at him?

My skin itched to crawl away, and I felt sick.

As far as the camel's back went, this latest straw was a freaking steel I-beam, further taxing my already shaky control. Magic surged from my core and spread throughout my body, galvanizing my nerve endings and straining the limits of my psychic shield.

It clawed for escape.

I dropped my arm from Kieran's waist. When I tried to wobble out of his embrace, his arm tightened at my side.

"Don't," he whispered fiercely into my ear. "This is what he seeks, to drive you away from me."

"If you know what's good for you, you will *let ... me ... go*," I growled, leveling him with a molten glare so there was no mistaking my warning. Of course, the spiking air temperature surrounding me likely clued him in, even before I'd opened my mouth.

Whenever my emotions got the better of me, most notably anger, my pyrokinesis tended to boil over. And, right now, Kieran's betrayal, combined with Lorcán's threat and my friends' subjugation, fueled it. The fiery potential heated me inside and out, the anticipation of its release so intoxicating, it had me seeing red.

Even though I was angry and reeling, I had no desire to hurt Kieran, which was inevitable if he remained as close as he was. In truth, what I longed to do was verbally rip him a new one, but I couldn't do that if I accidentally fried his ass. Instead, I tore out of his grasp, shaking him off, and strode closer to Lorcán, since it was the one direction that didn't put me near someone I cared about. Actually, that wasn't entirely true. I could have moved to the shop's exit, leaving nothing to stand between Lorcán and Kieran, but as stupid as it was, my abiding desire to protect Kieran forbade it.

Lorcán smiled, and the thought of scratching that smug expression from his deceptively angelic face almost pushed me into temptation. Potent memories taunted me—as foreign as they were familiar—the thrill of release, the rush of heat flowing through me, and the exultation of reducing an enemy to a screaming, flaming sack of charred skin and bone. Nothing matched that feeling of absolute power. God help me, I craved it.

I laughed, full throated and brazen and utterly unlike me. If I hadn't experienced the sensation of it coming out of my own throat, I might have thought a maniacal clown had used me for his ventriloquist dummy. It was a venomous cackle, derived from the darkness that I kept locked away—the source of my pyrokinesis—Patty Schaeffer. No matter how hard I tried, I couldn't seem to separate the memories of the woman who'd unknowingly bequeathed me her power and the magic itself. It's why I avoided using it.

I fought the rising power, my hands clenched into fists as the flaming potential pushed through every pore, filling my body and driving the temperature around me to dangerous levels.

It took a shaky moment, but I managed to stop throwing off heat like a radiator with a faulty thermostat. Too bad my anger wasn't as easy to govern.

"Lorc, hon, here's a tip. My control isn't the greatest. In fact, it damn well sucks. Push me too far and it won't matter that you've enslaved my friends—there won't be enough of this building left standing to ensure anyone's survival, much less my own."

He looked at me thoughtfully, his smirk turning into a brittle smile. "Duly noted. You are a genuine wonder, my dear. I have no desire to push you to such extremes. I merely wish to see that you are fully informed."

"If that was all you wanted, you'd have simply petitioned me for a meeting on neutral ground under a flag of peace. Instead, you went for a position of power, using my friends for leverage, which tells me you want something I wouldn't otherwise do freely. I can tell you right now, though, if it has anything to do with becoming your mate, you can forget it. I'll bring the building down around our ears before that happens."

"I believe you would, at that." He chuckled. "Be assured, I have no wish to tempt fate. I'll leave that to Kieran." His gaze veered over my left shoulder and, at his slight nod, Julie gasped.

I didn't need to look. The jolt through my telekinetic web broadcasted Nathan's superhuman attack. In a blink, he snatched Julie. By the time I turned, he'd yanked her head to the side, barring her throat.

"In short, I want Maeve," Lorcán said, drawing my attention back to his serene expression. "You have three days. Bring her to me, alive and undamaged, and I will release your friends unharmed. However, if you fail, at dawn on the fourth day, one of your friends will die, and another, every dawn thereafter, until Maeve stands alive and well at my side." He narrowed his gaze. "Is that clear enough?"

"Are you insane?" I barked out an incredulous laugh. "I've heard all about it. She's in the most secure of your prisons! Nathan's right. Four boons or not, I'm human, not a super-hero. And the king ... I've heard enough to know he puts the bad in badass. And don't get me started on that Wild Hunt thing that supposedly no creature can escape." I widened my eyes and shook my head at him. "There's no way. You can't be serious."

"But I am," he said with a charming smile. "In fact, let me show you how deadly serious I can be." His voice was calm and pleasant. *Come here, dear. I've something wonderful to share with you.*

Kieran growled a thunderous warning, "Lorcán."

The blond sidhe smiled wider. "Nathan, if they interfere, kill the girl."

"As you wish," the strigoi replied, although, I was re-lieved to note that he didn't sound overly enthusiastic.

"Whoa." I raised my hands, palms out. "Okay, look, let's not be has— "

"Eva," Lorcán purred.

Her attack was preternaturally swift. I felt her efficient, brutal movements even before I turned to look, and worse, there wasn't a damned thing I could do about it. The gloppy sound of Glen's throat being savaged coincided with my frantic scream.

No, no, no! This can't be happening!

I took in the ghastly scene, which unfolded in impossible clarity. Blood coated Glen's dress shirt and chinos. Dozens of thin, red rivulets streamed down the length of his limp body, over his splayed legs, soaking into his clothes and dribbling onto the floor. Eva gripped Glen's shoulders, hold-ing him upright as she hunched over his ruined neck, her face and upper chest a blood-coated mess. She lapped en-thusiastically at his gaping wound, her head bobbing up and down with each sloppy, squelching lick, as if he was as de-lectable as an ice cream cone on a hot sunny day.

Oh, God. But it is *happening. And it's my goddamned fault! I could have gone along with him, but no, I had to be a fucking smartass. This … this is all on me! I own this. Glen … stupid, innocent Glen … murdered … because of me … all because of* me*!*

With those useless, soul-destroying thoughts, my control shattered. Magic flared from my center, pulsing over my skin in an instantaneous red-tipped conflagration, surrounding me and blocking my view of Glen's grisly, ravaged neck. With my psychic shield in tatters, there was nothing to hold it back. The inferno exploded outward, zipping along the lines of my telekinetic web as readily as a burning trail of gasoline. It shot through the room, whipping through and around furniture, between bodies, painting the floor in a veneer of molten, shimmering striations that heated the air and threatened to ignite anything nearby.

And above the directionless tumult, the roaring in my ears, and the glory of release, I screamed.

After a time that might have been minutes or long seconds, a shock of cold slithered up from my feet and coiled around my body like a frosty, unearthly boa. It prepared to consume me, wrapping tighter and inching higher, until it pinned my arms to my sides and the succor of darkness flooded my vision and filled my ears. Engulfing me from head to toe, the dark coil pulsed around me, constricting and soothing with its strangely familiar resonance.

Gravity shifted and the sensation of movement, of weightlessness, hit me. Words flowed through my mind, thoughts that weren't my own.

Cúairtine, stop fighting me. Calm down. You'll kill yourself if you don't.

My head snapped forward and then back, my body coming to a abrupt halt. Heat roared through me as the fiery potential building inside of me fought for escape, but the dark coil prevented my magic from manifesting and breaking free.

I'm here with you. Open your eyes. Find yourself and look at me.

Slowly, my fire died and I became more aware of my body. The darkness retreated.

I blinked. Cold, damp wind ruffled my hair and buffeted the exposed skin of my face. Someone held me. I stared into a set of piercing blue eyes, narrowed by concern.

"Tíereachán?" I croaked.

Relief flickered over his expression. His head snapped up and he frowned grimly at something in the distance. I registered shouting, the clank of metal meeting metal, and over it all, a crackling, like crumpling paper, but there wasn't time to dwell on it before another face filled my view. This one was also familiar, but looked extremely pissed off.

Agent John Fisk.

His hand covered my forehead. He growled something foreign and my world spun to black.

But not before I registered the distinctive smell of smoke.

THREE

Subtle motion and the steady rumble of road noise woke me. I blinked several times, my eyes unfocused and gritty with fatigue. My left cheek felt sweaty and hot against the pillow supporting my head. Little wonder, I slowly realized, since it wasn't a pillow at all. Even in the car's dark interior, I could see I'd been sleeping on someone's leather-clad thigh—a decidedly firm, muscular thigh. Since my clairvoyance hadn't kicked in, the leather was either faux and psi-free or not from Earth. I clambered upright, hoping I hadn't left drool marks, and swiped my disheveled hair out of my eyes.

Tíereachán's surprised gaze met mine from across the backseat.

The party came back to me in a rush. Fire. *My* fire.

Jesus.

I remembered smelling smoke.

"Oh, no!" I croaked and clutched at Tíereachán's arm like he was my sole anchor on a crumbling rock face. "What have I done? Julie! Kieran! Where's Kieran?"

My gaze darted around the car's interior. Red sat on top of the front passenger seat's backrest, facing me, his stubby legs hanging over the edge. Fisk drove, his wary eyes meeting my frantic ones in the car's rear view mirror. The front passenger seat was ominously empty. We headed down a four-lane interstate, I-5 by the look of it.

"What happened? Oh my God," I shrieked. "We have to go back!" It was still dark. Maybe we hadn't been driving for long.

Tíereachán peeled my hands from his arm and squeezed them hard, a lifeline. He frowned, his lips compressing to a hard line. "We cannot go back. We barely got away as it is. Kim and Jackie and the king's coterie weren't far behind, but without their immediate help, Fisk and I were outnumbered. Lorcán has aligned himself with a contingent of extremely powerful vampires." His mouth curved down in distaste as he added, "I believe he's been sharing his blood with them. It makes them more deadly and harder to kill than usual."

My brain stuttered as I tried to parse his words. "H-h-how long have I been out of it?" Remembering Fisk's descending hand, right before I blacked out, I gasped and yanked my hands from Tíereachán's grasp. "He put me to sleep. How could you let him do that to me?" I focused my rant at Fisk in the driver's seat. "Asshole! You kidnapped me!"

If they hadn't done that, I could have fought by Kieran's side. I could have helped him and everyone else to escape.

Fisk's narrow-eyed gaze flashed in the mirror as he snarled at me, "We saved your ass, you stupid cu— "

"John!" Tíereachán snapped, the increased volume making me jump. "Watch your mouth. Do I need to remind you who you're talking to? Show some restraint. She's upset enough."

Fisk grumbled under his breath, something about overburn and clueless fucking bitches.

I buried my face in my hands. He wasn't wrong. Without their interference, if the fire hadn't killed me, overburn—the result of pushing too much magic through my body—would have. Bottom line: I was a stupid bitch who'd lost control. The whole clusterfuck was my fault. Kieran and Julie and the rest of my friends might be dead, burned alive or butchered by the strigoi, all because I had less control than a five-year-old at an all-you-can-eat candy store. I turned away, falling against the door while I fought to swallow the sound of my strangled sobs.

The light pitter-pat of Red's paws hit my thighs as he climbed across me to ascend my arm and perch on my tensed, quaking shoulder. His paw stroked my hair and he murmured soothing things into my ear, but even his kindness couldn't ease the mantle of guilt that squeezed my heart.

"Michael or Kim will call one of us with an update soon," Tíereachán assured me, voice soft, his cocksure demeanor starkly absent. "Don't worry. Kieran is a worthy adversary. More than once, my cousin has faced worse and survived." Lowering his voice, he muttered, "He's harder to kill than an ill-tempered *tonngéar*."

If the situation had been different, I might have been amused by his acerbic aside and asked for a description of what was no doubt an ugly and tenacious Otherworld beast. As it was, I nodded stiffly and dried my eyes with the heels of my gloved hands, feeling numb.

Bit by bit, Tíereachán's words percolated through the knot of despair in my mind.

Someone would call. With news. I latched on to that single thought more doggedly than a toddler clutching at her mom's leg in a crowd of strangers. My phone. Where was my purse? Red was here, so my shoulder bag had to be somewhere in the car, right?

I must have mumbled something because Tíereachán shifted in his seat and then offered me my bag. As soon as the faux suede hit my lap, I ransacked it, coming away with my iPhone in nothing flat. Bluish light illuminated the backseat, thanks to my Cookie Monster wallpaper. I squinted at the brightly lit screen and then sagged in my seat. *Damn.* No missed calls or texts. I sniffled and fought another wave of useless tears.

It was 10:15, now. We'd arrived at the party around 8:30. If I factored in another twenty minutes of socializing prior to my meltdown, it hadn't been more than ninety minutes since Tíereachán whisked me away. So, perhaps not long enough yet to panic, I reasoned.

I tapped out an urgent text message to both Kim and Kieran, checked the settings to ensure my cell would both ring and vibrate if a call came through, and then maxed out the volume. When I was sure I couldn't miss a call or text, I clutched it to my stomach and stared at nothing through the passenger window as darkness, tinged by the amber glow of the dashboard's control panel, once again claimed the backseat.

Memories of the party weighed on me so heavily I had difficulty drawing breath. "I ... I remember smelling smoke," I choked out, bowing my head closer to the window, not wanting to know the details but compelled to ask, "Did ... did I ... was anyone—?"

I sucked in a shuddering breath, but Tíereachán answered before I finished voicing the question.

"I saw no burning bodies nor did I smell any," he said. "When I pulled you out, a few tables had ignited. Kieran had charged to engage Lorcán. Between the spot fires, my cousin's deft blade, and the hostages, the vampires had plenty to keep them occupied. It helped make our escape somewhat less complicated. While I got you into the car, the alarm sounded. We were hard pressed at that point, so I had little wherewithal to notice more."

"The sprinkler system triggered along with the alarm," Fisk said, shrugging. "Fucking bloodsuckers kept me too busy to see much beyond the tip of my sword."

"Where are we going?" I asked when it seemed Fisk wasn't going to add anything more.

"Another of my mother's gateways. One the king doesn't know about," Tíereachán replied. "Wade is there waiting for us, along with a sizable detachment."

"You may as well stop." I turned to stare at him across the darkened seat. "Everything is off until I know what's going on with my friends and Kieran."

"John and I cannot stand alone against a contingent of sidhe-suckled vampires. We'll not risk stopping for more than refueling until we reach my mother's forces."

"I'm not crossing until I know my friends are safe," I said, but my little voice wondered, *What if they're dead?*

"I expected nothing less," he replied.

After a moment, he touched my elbow and I jumped at the unexpected contact.

"Lire, tell us what happened," he urged. "What did Lorcán hope to achieve with such a brazen attack? Red told us he'd been listening to music and missed much of what happened."

Dread sliced through me, and I hunched over my knotted stomach.

What was I going to do about Lorcán? If Julie and Steven and the rest were still hostages, did I have a choice but to find a way to give in to his impossible demand?

Covering my face, I turned back toward my window.

Tíereachán squeezed my arm and tried to pull me toward him, but I shrugged him off. I dropped my arms, my hands thumping to rest limply on my thighs. "His strigoi thugs enthralled everyone, held them hostage. He wants me to retrieve Maeve." I went on to explain the details of Lorcán's ultimatum. "There's no way I can bust her out of there. I'm not a djinn with untold powers. When I told him the whole idea was ludicrous, he ordered one of his vamps to murder my ex-boyfriend. She tore open his throat, and I stood there, stuttering like an idiot while she did it."

I turned to stare at him. Even in the dark, it was easy to discern the shock and sympathy in his widened eyes. "Maybe if Lorcán hadn't told me about Kieran and Nuala and ... *who I am*— " I faltered, sucking in a breath at the memory. "I might have been able to keep it together, but— " I shook my head vehemently. "I warned him. I tried. I told him it wouldn't take much to push me over the edge, but the fucker didn't listen. He killed him. Poor Glen ... he ... he didn't have a chance," I said, my voice breaking. "The rest could be dead too, and it's all my *stupid* fault!"

Reluctant Adept - Chapter Three

As I slumped to the seat, he pulled me into his arms. Red scrabbled over my back, jumping to the window's ledge to avoid inflicting his defensive spells on him. I collapsed against the warmth of Tíereachán's chest, grief-stricken and too wrecked to resist the enticing comfort of his embrace.

He tucked my head under his chin and shushed me, whispering tender endearments and holding me close. Boneless and sniffling, I swallowed my tears and tried to think positive. Kieran would call any minute. It took time to save everyone and defeat Lorcán. He'd be okay. Soon enough, he'd tell me, in his alluring, musical baritone, that Julie and Steven and the rest of my friends were okay. The disheartening bombshell about his continued deception ... I didn't have the strength to dwell on it, not when I awaited news of their possible deaths, knowing the fiasco was my fault.

After several minutes, Tíereachán murmured, "I'm sorry I didn't get to you sooner. I didn't receive Wade's warning message about the revelations at Maeve's trial until late, and Michael neglected to inform me of your friend's party until afterward. I felt your anguish and we were still blocks away." His arms stiffened, crushing me against him. At my squeak of protest, he eased his hold. My head rose and fell along with his heavy sigh.

This was the first I'd heard that he could sense my emotions through our blood connection. A spark of unease fluttered through me, but I cataloged the disturbing thought under the heading, 'Things To Freak Out About Tomorrow.' Or next week. Better yet, how about never?

He muttered bitterly, "What was my cousin thinking, allowing you to attend that party in the first place?"

I crumpled the smooth weave of his shirt as shame swelled up to lodge heavy in my throat. I turned my face into his chest, trying to hide from the world, from my mistake, from everything. "My fault— "

"No, Lire," Red scolded from his window perch. "I will not allow you to bear this burden. You have every right to live your life—more cause than most, in my mind. Any fault in this lies entirely with Lorcán. The decision to leave the relative safety of your building was mutually decided. Even had we stayed, you know as well as I, the safety there is an illusion. A fact proved by Lorcán's brutal yet effective tactics."

Red explained the strategy behind our evening plans to Tíereachán and Fisk. If either one thought it naïve or misguided, they kept their opinion to themselves.

As my frantic, guilt-plagued thoughts quieted, I became aware of Tíereachán's gentle stroking along my spine. At first, the unsolicited contact had been a dimly noticed comfort, but now that the heat of his body and his clean, citrusy scent had risen to the fore of my mind, unease hitched along for the ride, troubling me like a pebble under my heel that grew more noticeable the longer I walked on it.

Tíereachán must have sensed my growing disquiet because he pressed the whole of his hand against my back and, in an affected, haughty tone, said, "When you speak to my cousin, be sure to tell him of my virtuous behavior despite your delightful proximity. When you finally acknowledge me as the better sidhe, I want no thought spared to underhanded influence," he tsked. "And you simply must stop pawing at me, woman. It's embarrassing."

As he no doubt intended, I uttered an indignant growl and pushed at his chest, levering myself away from him to sit upright. I raised my arm to deliver a backhanded smack, but his hiss and pained expression halted me, my snarky retort frozen on my tongue.

I eyed him critically. "You're hurt."

He straightened in the seat and crossed his arms, but the grimace that had replaced his cocky smile told me the move wasn't an easy one. "It's nothing. I'm fine."

"Good. Then you won't mind proving it." I scooted closer while I tried to recall where I'd placed my hands when I'd shoved myself away from him. "What happened? Show me."

"Mate, sit down. I don't need your fussing."

I ignored the irritating endearment, which he'd used because he knew it got on my nerves and no doubt hoped it would distract me.

"You're gonna get more than fussing," I said, passing my phone to Red who'd retaken his perch on the back of the front passenger seat. "You'll get a knuckle sandwich."

I ran my fingers over his arms, checking the fabric of his black button-down shirt for tears or the wet, sticky signs of blood. Not finding anything, I attempted to pry his unyielding arms loose for access to the parts of his torso he'd deliberately hidden.

Stymied, the truth dawned on me. I froze and stared at him, horrified. "It was my fire. You're burned. I hurt you."

"You didn't hurt me."

There was no hesitation in his reply, but I didn't buy it. When his dark appendage wrapped around me, I'd been going up like a dead pine in a forest fire. Why hadn't I thought of it sooner?

When I continued to stare at him, distress knitting my brows, Tíereachán tilted his head and peered at me. "After all this, you will not take my word?"

We'd been through a lot together, true. I'd rescued him from Azazel's clutches. And, even when he'd been under the archdemon's thumb, forced into the guise of a demon by a blood pact and unaware of his true sidhe identity, he'd never lied to me.

But I also knew it was possible to skirt the truth without lying. And there's no way he'd missed coming into contact with my fire, not when his magic had wrapped around me so securely.

Given sidhe touchiness when it came to their honor, there was no tactful way to answer his question, so I didn't even try. "I'm not stupid. You guys parse the truth like nobody's business. Technically I didn't hurt you, but my fire did, right?"

One look at his narrowed eyes and inflexible jaw told me I was most definitely *not right*.

Where was an open well when I needed one?

"Unlike Kieran, I have never sought to deceive you, *Lire*. You do all other sidhe a disservice when you cast us in his mold."

For once, he'd used my actual name in lieu of a cocky endearment, but instead of pleasing me, it stung as if I'd been slapped.

Chastened and heart-heavy, I retreated to my side of the car. I glanced up in time to catch Fisk's disapproving eyes in the rear view mirror, but when he spoke, his voice was surprisingly calm. "He took a blade tip to his side when he yanked you out of the shop. It's a minor injury that I've tended to, so stop worrying."

I felt the weight of Tíereachán's scrutiny, a near palpable pressure along my left side. At that moment, with shame and anger burning in my chest and heating my cheeks, nothing shy of physical force would have prompted me to meet his gaze. Hugging myself, I huddled at the window, wishing I was anywhere but inside the car with these two imposing men, even if they had saved my life.

"You said Lorcán told you something before he issued his ultimatum," Tíereachán observed, sounding wary. "It obviously upset you. What was it?"

I gritted my teeth, pressing my arms tighter to my abdomen. *Nope. Not going there.*

"He revealed something," he pressed, ignoring my silent protest. "Something Kieran hadn't told you. Something that concerns Nuala and who you are."

"You don't know?" Fisk's surprised inquiry pierced the night-dimmed interior. "She's descended from Nuala's father. They've tracked both sides of his line for generations, hoping the spark would manifest somewhere along the way, even with the years of diluted blood."

I bit my lip. My relation to Kieran's former mate was less like a daughter and more like a half-sister. Although, genetically speaking, after two thousand years of intervening lineage, one could hardly say we were related. Not that it mattered, of course, since neither consideration made the situation with Kieran feel any less smarmy.

"Kieran knew?" Tíereachán's voice rose. "He kept you ignorant and then seduced you?" He bit out a curse. "I should have suspected as much. When I get done with him, my cousin is going to wish Lorcán had gutted him." He spewed a long series of harshly bitten Silven words that I didn't have to work hard imagining as curses.

When Tíereachán finished his rant, Fisk grunted his agreement and said, "At the soonest," and then, with a severity that almost surpassed Tíereachán's, he snapped, "I'll fucking help." Which, considering Fisk's surliness toward me, came as a shock.

Call me crazy, but their threats eased some of my crushing worry. If they were imagining what they'd like to do to Kieran, both men must harbor little doubt that he'd survived the fight with Lorcán.

It wasn't enough to distract me from the ongoing humiliation of Kieran's betrayal, however. It was one thing to have a preference for women with green eyes, quite another to seek out the distant relation of your former lover. I wondered whether doing so had bothered him. Had it made him feel guilty? Couldn't he see how creepy it was?

I gritted my teeth. This constant emotional tug of war—fear and worry followed by humiliation and betrayal—had left me feeling wrung out and carsick.

"I'm sorry," Tíereachán said, his words clipped by his remaining anger. "If I'd known Kieran had been keeping this from you ... I'd have forced him to tell you."

I nodded, relieved when he didn't pile on by using Kieran's mistake to paint himself as the better man. Both his and Fisk's reactions had already made that point painfully clear.

Gaze firmly averted, I shifted in my seat. "So ... I have to ask ... is there, I don't know, maybe something I should know about Kieran's appearance?" I paused, tucking my hair behind my ear, not sure whether I wanted to know the answer, but nevertheless compelled to learn it. "Two of the strigoi said something bizarre about his looks, as though he was flawed somehow. What they said, it just— " I huffed. "It struck me as odd—crazy, in fact. And then Lorcán said something about Kieran wearing a mask, like it was something Kieran did for my benefit, since he and the strigoi could see through it."

From the front seat, Fisk's muttered curses rose above the road noise, doing nothing to help my frame of mind. If I hadn't already melded myself to it, I might have shrunk further against the car door.

Tíereachán didn't respond, but his silent outrage washed over me, the ominous calm before the mother of all storms. I held my breath, primed for his response, as if any second it would thunder through the car and startle me out of my seat.

I couldn't stand it any longer. I gave up window gazing and peered across the seat.

Tíereachán stared two holes into the car's ceiling, his arms folded across his chest, head pressed into the seat's neck rest. The darkness did nothing to hide the stark relief of his rigid posture and flexing jaw.

"*Again*, I didn't— " Eschewing the ceiling view, he straightened and then cocked his head from side to side, easing the muscles of his neck.

After a moment, he turned to me, his expression neutral. "Kieran was badly burned in a fire after an earthquake." He pressed his lips together, frowning. "Sidhe healers are more skilled than yours, but they can only restore so much, even with willing donors. It's not uncommon to use a glamour to hide our imperfections from humans. When one lives as long as we do, scars are inevitable. We may not physically age as humans do, but life takes its toll. Glamours allow many of us to blend into your society without drawing unwanted attention to our ... otherness."

He studied me, then subtly jerked his chin upward. "As your lover, he should have told you. But for that, I cannot denounce him, much as I might wish to."

My thoughts splintered as I tried to decide whether to be angered or saddened or frightened by this revelation. And since I'm an idiot, I blurted the question that tipped my tongue. "Why? Because you do the same thing?"

"No," he replied, voice going hard. "Because I am not heartless."

A flea could squish me, I felt so tall. I slapped a hand to my face and scrubbed. Honestly. How many faux pas could I cram into the space of five minutes?

I sighed. "Come on. You know I— "

The trill of my phone's ringtone cut off my fumbling apology, all but goosing me onto the floorboards. Hands trembling, I yanked the bright beacon from Red's extended paws and scrabbled at the screen, squinting to read the contact information. I swiped to answer and, before it had even made contact with my ear, burst out, "Kim?"

"Lire, thank God," Kim said in a whoosh. "You got out. Are you with Tíereachán and Fisk? We didn't know for sure— "

"Kieran," I choked out. I closed my eyes, squeezing my cell and fixing it taut to my ear. "Kim, please … Kieran … is he okay?"

Silence, as forbidding as it was deafening, hammered down the open line. For a half a tick, the moment spanned forever and back again. Finally, she said, "He's alive. Out cold, but alive. Duran just got done healing him."

"He needed a healing?" My voice emerged abnormally high. "How serious is it? What happened?"

"He's going to be okay. The injury wasn't crippling, but he took a sword hit to his left shoulder. It was deep enough that we asked Duran if she could help him out, instead of taking him to the hospital."

I could only breathe into the receiver.

"He's okay, hon. Don't worry." She mumbled an aside, probably to Jackie, saying that I sounded fine. "What about you? You okay?"

"No. This is all my fault. If I hadn't lost it— "

"Lorcán wasn't about to leave empty-handed. You did what you had to."

I wondered whether she'd be as understanding if she knew Lorcán hadn't been a threat to me at all, the destruction was because I'd lost control.

"What about Julie and Steven and my friends?" If I clenched my muscles any tighter, I'd be inside out.

She hesitated. "One was already dead when we showed up. Looked like a vamp kill."

"Yeah. That was Glen."

"Ah, okay ... well, I didn't stay long after the fire department and police showed up, so I didn't get word about casualties. I didn't see any other bodies though, besides the one, but that doesn't necessarily mean anything. I was pretty busy at the time. We eliminated two vamps, but Lorcán and the rest escaped. They took the hostages with them. What does your friend look like?"

"Long, straight brown hair. She had it in a ponytail. Petite. About five-five. Her husband Steven is six-one or so, medium build, blond buzz cut."

"I'm not a hundred percent sure, but I think one of the vamps, black dude in a suit ... I think he had them. I know he and several other vamps had hostages. They made it out with Lorcán—along with a top-heavy brunette with a thing for leather and Louboutins."

"She's the one who killed Glen."

"Then I'm doubly sorry I couldn't fry her ass. I think Lorcán found a way to share his shroud at distance. The vamps were resistant to my magic. My lightning affected them, but not as much as it should have."

"Tíereachán thinks Lorcán's been sharing his blood with them."

She sucked in a shocked breath and then spat out a few fervent curses. "That explains how she could run in those ridiculous stilettos," she said acerbically and then sighed. "Lorcán is depraved. If that's true ... shit. If he's sunk that low, the king will hunt him. He's signed his death warrant."

"I thought the king was already hunting him."

"With his agents, yes. If this proves to be true, though, the king'll definitely spare a— " She faltered but continued smoothly, "He'll find a way to send the *Wuldrífan*."

Find a way? What did that mean? Wasn't it easy for him to dispatch the Hunt? Maybe I didn't have as much to worry about as I thought I did. At least, from the king.

There was so much Kieran hadn't bothered to explain to me.

"Kim, what's going on with Kieran? Can I talk to him?" I just wanted to hear his voice.

And then ream the shit out of him.

"His injury wasn't minor," she replied. "You know how healing magic is. Duran supplemented as much as she could, but Kieran's reserves had to sustain the rest. She figures he'll be out for at least ten hours. He's crashed on the couch here with us."

He should be in our bed, not on the neighbor's darn couch!

Fortunately, I smothered the uncharitable thought before voicing it.

Duran's healing was a great gift. Performing the ritual up in my apartment would have been complicated, requiring Duran, who was human and therefore not immune to my clairvoyance, to wear a skin-suit. I couldn't fault them for not wanting to bother with the inconvenience. And now, to get Kieran across the hall, up the stairs, and into our bed, he'd need to be carried. The djinn could handle that, but it was easier for Kim and Jackie to keep an eye on him if he stayed where he was. Based on my own experience, he'd be dead to the world until late tomorrow at the soonest.

I'd received one major healing in my life, back in my Coventry Academy days when I'd run afoul of a desperate teen with a poisonous bite. My history teacher, a Glindarian like Duran, saved my life, neutralizing the poison and healing tissue damage that would have taken my own body weeks to mend. Compressing that much healing into the span of a few minutes takes its toll, both in pain and energy. Besides the steep monetary cost, it was one of the reasons most people didn't seek out magic healing unless absolutely necessary. The more severe the injury, the more energy required and pain endured. If the healer couldn't (or wouldn't) supply all of the necessary power, the patient's body bore the cost and there's a limit to the energy a person has available to give. Even with a full coven, there's no cheating death, at least, not without resorting to black magic, exchanging one death for another.

I shivered at the sickening thought.

"Lire, have Tíereachán bring you home," Kim said, breaking into my scattered thoughts. "My lord King Faonaín has extended you his offer of protection. You're not safe here right now. This attack proves it. Brassal wants me to tell you that he's crossing over, tomorrow, to escort you to the king's fortress. He'll keep you safe."

"You know as well as I do, he can't protect me from the king."

"The king's not going to hurt you, but his enemies aren't so honorable. You'll be safe in his territory. There's no one stronger or more capable. He commands an army of thousands, all of them trained warriors and skilled in magic. Nothing can stand against them. Listen to me, hon. I've been to his fortress. There's no place safer."

Maybe, but my friends and family would remain unprotected on Earth. And safe was a relative term. I had no desire to be King Faonaín's mate, much less his prisoner. Ostensibly, I'd end up being both.

"It doesn't matter. I'm not going anywhere without Kieran. And we have to get my friends back from Lorcán and force the strigoi to administer their anti-hypnotic."

"Let the king deal with Lorcán. I'm sure he'll send the *Wuldrífan*. His hunters will deal with the vamps. Antidotes won't matter when they're all dead. Your friends will snap out of it none the worse for wear. And, as far as Kieran goes, he's heading back to the Otherworld tomorrow. The king reversed Maeve's decree."

My mouth froze half open before I sputtered, "He's … *what*?"

Heading back home? No. There's no way he'd commit to that. Not without at least consulting me first.

I frowned, shaking my head. "No longer outcast? Why would the king suddenly do that?"

Tíereachán shifted in his seat, reminding me that at least one side of this conversation wasn't private. I wondered if he could hear Kim's voice over the ambient noise, too.

She hesitated. "I guess because the trial's over and the truth has all come out."

If that wasn't the vaguest answer ever, I didn't know what was.

I turned toward my window and shifted my phone to my other ear, lowering my voice. "Kieran said he's going back? He's going back, tomorrow. He actually said so?"

Again, the slight pause. "Yes."

Much as I didn't want to believe her, it must be true. Like the sidhe, part-bloods, especially ones bound to a full-blooded mate, wouldn't deign themselves to lie.

Although keeping secrets was another matter.

"I don't understand," I said. I hardly recognized my own voice. It sounded oddly distant. "He didn't even consult me."

The silence went on for so long, I worried the line had dropped.

"Kim? Hello? You still there?"

"Yes."

I breathed again, not realizing I'd stopped, waiting for her response. "This isn't something Kieran would do without at least talking to me about it." Maybe it was pride, but I had to believe that. "Is there something going on that I don't know about?"

Another delayed response. Something was definitely up.

"Jackie's worried about you," she said. "Talk to her. She wants to know if you're okay."

"What? No. Kim, hold up— "

Jackie's voice cut in, "Hey, Lire ... I think Kim needed to talk to Duran. What's going on? You with Tíereachán?"

I sighed. "Yeah."

"That was some dicey shit at Peabody's. You all come through it okay?"

"Yeah. I think so." I shifted in my seat as if it might restore my equilibrium. The world had taken a dire turn, slipping from under my feet like a Teflon-coated flying carpet. "Tíer's hurt, but I guess it's not bad. One of the vamps had a knife or something."

"More than one of them did. Fucking biters," she said, and I pictured her studious brown eyes pinched scathingly. "That's the last thing any of us expected. Christ. If they'd gone down as easy as they do in the movies, life would've been a hell of a lot simpler. Between me, Kim's lightning, and the few part-bloods already in the neighborhood, we barely kept them off us. Never a nice surprise when the only thing in the arsenal goes over like week-old Pepsi. Thank fuck the furniture in that place was wood. A couple splintered chair legs made all the difference, let me tell you."

I cringed imagining how Julie and Steven's shop must look. I'd managed to destroy their business, instigate one of their friend's murder, and get them kidnapped, all by showing up at their place for twenty goddamn minutes.

I clenched my jaw. *Focus, Lire.*

"Jackie, what's going on over there? Kieran told Kim he plans to go back home tomorrow. Any idea why?"

"Some," she replied, her single word managing to convey many unsettling things—reluctance, anger, and something that felt a lot like pity.

I waited. When she didn't elaborate, my patience snapped. "Jesus! Is no one going to tell me what the fuck is going on?" I huffed. "I know you don't want to violate Kim or Brassal's confidence, and I don't expect you to, but can you throw me a goddamn bone? Something? I'm stuck in a car speeding down I-5 to God knows where and I'm getting really tired of being clueless all the time!"

She exhaled sharply and then cursed. "I'm in a difficult spot here. Believe me, I'd fucking love to give you an earful over what complete and utter *shit* this is, but I gave my word to Brassal that I'd keep my damned teeth together. All I can say is, *yes*, the king overturned Kieran's outcast status." She virtually chewed on the last bit and then blew out another exasperated breath.

After a moment, though, in a tired whisper that I strained to hear, she added, "Lire ... just ... use your head. Now that Maeve's out of the picture, think about what that means in terms of Kieran's duties. Okay?"

Duties?

She cleared her throat. "Look, I gotta go."

"Uh, sure." I frowned, trying to puzzle her out. "Thanks, Jackie." *I think.* "As soon as Kieran wakes up, can you please have him call me?"

"I'll tell him," she promised. "And, Lire?"

"Yeah?"

"You should ... call Michael. He's, uh, probably been too busy with *all his travels* to call you. And I bet he's worried."

Travels, huh?

"Gotcha. I owe you."

We disconnected.

"Trouble in paradise?" Tíereachán asked. I didn't have to spare him a glance to know his left eyebrow had twitched upward. No doubt, he had his arms crossed too.

I closed my eyes, not in the mood for his usual banter, and said, half in jest, "You're lucky I'm not holding anything sharp, but give me a minute. I'm sure I can come up with something."

I stabbed at my cell's screen to dial up my friend Michael, not wasting the energy to shoot the infuriatingly handsome sidhe next to me a dirty look. It'd be lost in the dark, anyway, and no matter how often I screwed up my face at him, it never made a bit of difference. Apparently, being an arrogant smartass was part of Tíereachán's genetic makeup.

Michael picked up on the third ring.

"Lire?" he said, "You okay? You with Tíereachán?"

"Not really, and yes. I just got off the phone with Kim and Jackie."

"How's Kieran?" he asked. "Did Duran do her thing yet?"

"Yeah. Kim said he's sleeping it off," I replied, sagging in my seat. "You didn't follow them back to my building?"

"No. Kim took off with Kieran and Jackie after the cops and fire trucks showed up," he replied. "I'm still here at Peabody's, in case I need to head off any issues with the authorities."

As a telepath, Michael's skills were invaluable for keeping the police from sticking their noses where they weren't wanted. A small tweak to someone's memories meant not having to deal with answering some potentially difficult questions.

"Right, of course," I murmured, stifling a sigh. "So ... was there just the one human casualty?"

"Yes. The police ID'ed him on scene. Glen Porter. I'm sorry, Lire. He was an ass, but he didn't deserve that."

"Yeah." I swallowed. "Being my ex is turning out to be a high-risk occupation," I said bitterly.

Two were dead, three out of four, if you counted Daniel, my sweetheart from middle school. Vince, my sole living ex, had been kidnapped by Maeve. (Although, calling Vince my ex was a bit of an overstatement. We'd never even made it out on an official date.) I should warn Kieran before he did something stupid like break up with me.

"No. This isn't your fault. It's all thanks to sidhe bullshit politics and that demon fuck, Azazel. You know that. We'll deal with this. I've got your back."

"I know you do. Thanks. That means a lot." I turned toward the window. "So, Michael ... do you happen to know anything about what's going on with Kieran?"

"You mean, besides his injury?"

"Yeah."

I wasn't sure why I still cared. No matter how distantly related Nuala and I were, he should have told me. The fact that he *didn't* was a big red flag, one that my little voice was having a field day with. But my emotions were dumb. I couldn't switch them off like a robot with a removable empathy chip. Much as I might have wanted to.

"*No.*" Michael gave the word several extra vowels, clearly curious as to why I'd asked. "He's been his normal closed-off self whenever I've seen him."

He and Kieran would never be BFFs, mostly because Michael thought Kieran wasn't good enough for me. It didn't help that Michael's feelings in my direction hadn't always been strictly platonic. He'd secretly read my mind over a period of years, knowing it was a mistake, and fallen for me in the process—all of which I'd learned when I'd touched him a few weeks ago in an overhasty meeting of our minds without our psychic shields. He wasn't spending all of his time mooning over the fact that we'd never be more than friends (me being a clairvoyant and him being a telepath made that impossible), but it made him testy when it came to Kieran. If he knew about what I'd learned tonight, he'd give me an earful.

Michael's voice dipped down, low and suspicious. "Why?"

"Apparently, he's no longer outcast. The king reversed Maeve's decree."

"Oh ... huh. Wonder why the king changed his mind."

"Kim said it's because the trial's over and the truth has come out."

"But you don't believe that," he said without any trace of uncertainty. So much for my efforts at being circumspect.

"Let's just say I don't think that's the only reason. Something's not right, Michael. According to Kim and Jackie, Kieran agreed to return home *tomorrow*, without even talking to me about it first. And thanks to him being passed out from his healing, I can't find out why. Kieran and I ..." I faltered and shook my head even though he couldn't see it. "More than once, he's said that even if he could return home, he wouldn't. This ... it's totally out of left field."

Michael grunted in thought. "Maybe I should have told you as soon as I got back in town ... before I spoke with Kim." He blew out a sharp breath. "Fuck."

I pressed a palm to my nervous stomach. "Told me *what*, Michael?"

"The draíoclochs. There are others, like Daniel suspected. King Faonaín ordered me to find them. For the past week, I've been flying all over the country, visiting all the Invisius chapters. The six we have sitting in our vault now, I found yesterday in Chicago."

That explained it. With one of those single-use talismans, Kim could summon a temporary gateway to the Otherworld in any location she chose.

"So that's how Brassal is getting here," I said. "I was wondering."

"Yup. We're set for five o'clock tomorrow, down in our meeting room. Kim's bringing Jessica, one of the Seattle coterie part-bloods. Not sure if you've met her. She's agreed to be their next emissary. Apparently the king doesn't care which part-blood takes the position, just that they do it tomorrow without fail. Her and some appointed male sidhe are expected to bond inside the gateway and then go their separate ways. Sounds fucked up, but what do I know? I hope the guy isn't a total jerk. Jess is a sweetheart."

A bad feeling snaked its way into my chest.

I huddled further against the door and lowered my voice, not wanting Tíereachán or Wade to hear my wild suspicion, in case I was being paranoid and insecure. "Michael ... when, exactly, did you tell Kim about finding the draíoclochs?"

He thought about it. "I found them late last night but didn't tell her about them until early this morning. Why?"

"What about the thing with Jess? Did it come out of the blue or have they known about it for a while?"

"No. That's the crazy part. Kim called an emergency meeting to work it out, this afternoon, while I was in the air coming home. She claimed there wasn't time to call a regional meeting, even though it would have made things easier. The Seattle coterie has just the three women members—Jess, Trish, and Wendy—and none of them are single." He sighed and then grumbled, "Things are a mess down there. I don't know if you know this, but apparently, becoming an emissary has always been a voluntary thing. A love match makes a stronger connection. It's why the part-bloods spend at least six months in the Otherworld after they turn eighteen and go back every few years. But with so few emissaries, the king issued an order this time. His new retainer needs a mate—ASAP. End of story."

"*New retainer*? She said those exact words?" I could hardly force out the question as I fought to catch my breath. The air inside the car had gone impossibly thin.

I clutched the armrest and pressed the phone hard to my ear, as though they were solely responsible for anchoring me inside the vehicle.

"That's how Jess put it to me when she told me about it." He sounded puzzled. "Whether those exact words came out of Kim's mouth, I can't tell you. Why? What are you thinking?"

Bad, bad things. Heartbreaking things—as if my heart wasn't already in pieces.

"Stop the car." My thready croak scarcely penetrated the rumble of the road.

My lungs had shrunk. I couldn't get enough air. Everything pressed against me, too close.

I turned to grip the seat in front of me. "Fisk ... stop the car."

He glanced into the rear view mirror. "We're on the fucking interstate. I'm not stopping the car. You can wait until— "

"Stop the goddamn car. I need some air," I snarled. "*Now*."

"Lire— " Tíereachán started.

"I've never sidestepped at seventy-five miles per hour," I barked. "Not sure what will happen, but I'll do it if you don't pull over and let me out before I effing explode!"

"Do it," Tíereachán directed Fisk.

The car hadn't even come to a complete halt. I opened the door and levitated out, sucking in the cool evening air as though I'd just run a four minute mile. A semi roared past, shaking the ground and buffeting the air around me. Diesel exhaust coated the inside of my throat, making me cough.

I flew across the darkened, tufted terrain to the right of the interstate, dodging a wire fence, until the roadway retreated to a distant rumble and nothing but damp, lumpy grass and shadowy bushes surrounded me. In the distance, lights of a nearby housing development flickered through a line of trees. Above, a gibbous moon pierced the thin clouds, illuminating the landscape with its silvery cast, highlighting every bump and hollow with the stark contrast between dark and light. I shivered as the steady breeze bit through the thin fabric of my blouse, chilling my car-warmed skin.

After a moment, I registered Michael's tiny voice coming from my phone, still clutched in my hand.

"Michael ..."

"Lire! Jesus. What the hell is going on?"

"I ... had to get out of that car. I could hardly breathe with all of this."

"All of *what*?"

"I don't— " I grunted, smacking my fisted left hand against my thigh hard enough to hurt. "I need to talk to Kieran, to know for sure. Maybe I'm being paranoid. But if I'm not ..."

"For fuck's sake, spit it out!"

"Kieran is the new retainer," I blurted. "The king has ordered him to bond with Jess. That's why he's going back to the Otherworld tomorrow."

Michael was quiet for a beat. "Lire, just because he's going home doesn't mean— " He paused. After a sigh, he continued, his voice soft but resigned, "Have you considered that maybe he's not as, well, committed to you as you think? Up until now, there was no way for him to go home. Now that he can ..."

You're expendable. Maybe this wasn't precisely what Michael had in mind to say, but close enough.

"He cares for me, Michael. There's no mistaking it." Forgoing levitation, I landed on the lumpy ground and paced, pounding out my frustrations with each determined step. "But even if he does want to return home, he wouldn't commit to it without at least talking to me first."

A niggling doubt snaked his way into my thoughts, thanks to Kieran's recent betrayal, but I ruthlessly squashed it. "And both Kim and Jackie are acting strangely," I added. "Whatever's going down, they're not happy about it. Jackie flat out told me she's been sworn to secrecy. But she gave me a couple cryptic hints. She told me to think about Kieran's position, his duties, what it means now that Maeve is out of the picture, and she mentioned your recent travels, told me to call you."

"Okay," he said, his protracted drawl telling me I'd hooked him.

"With Maeve gone, Kieran now reports to the king." I stopped pacing and gazed out at the distant houses, imagining Michael's broad face and keen brown eyes as I explained, "Think about it. If King Faonaín wants me for his mate, to keep me under his thumb for all time, ordering Kieran to bond with a part-blood is a genius move. No matter what Kieran decides, it gets him out of the king's way. If Kieran follows orders and bonds with Jess, he and I are finished and the king figures I'm free for the taking. If Kieran disobeys, he'll be hauled in front of the Tribunal for insubordination. Now that the king has gateway access, disobeying orders isn't something that will go unpunished. If Kieran can't get away—if he doesn't escape with me to the amhaín's territory—I guarantee Kieran will occupy the cell next to Maeve's in less than a day if he disobeys."

"I suppose," he murmured, mulling it over. "And with both Kim and Jackie acting weird— " Michael exhaled into the phone. "The question is: Even if it's true, what can you do about it?"

I barked out a humorless laugh. "Are you kidding me? No way am I going to stand by while Kieran is forced to bond with some other woman. If Tíereachán and Fisk won't take me home, I'll sidestep and fly back on my own."

"Yeah? And then what? Kieran's injured. You said he's sleeping off his healing, right?"

"That's what Kim said."

"What are you going to do? Drag his unconscious body down to the parking garage, stuff him into your Mercedes, and hope he's okay with disobeying the king when he wakes up?"

This plan sounded way better inside my head.

I stifled a growl. "Yes, damn it. Although, I'm hoping I can convince Tíereachán to help. My Mercedes is too conspicuous and I don't know where the hell we're going."

"We aren't going back," Tíereachán announced from behind me.

I jumped and spun on my heel to find him standing firm, arms folded in displeasure, just five feet away. I wondered how long he'd been listening. Long enough, apparently.

"Fine. Stay here," I snapped. "I'll sidestep and fly back on my own. The djinn will help me. Kieran and I'll figure something out."

"Sinking ship, no land in sight, and you insist on tying yourself to an anchor," he scoffed. "He will drag you to your doom."

"Please. Can you be any more melodramatic?" I returned his scowl, keeping my phone at my ear but tilting the microphone away so I didn't blast Michael. "It's not as if Kim's keeping him prisoner. And the king isn't sending Brassal until tomorrow night. So, that means we have, what? Eighteen hours? If we turn around now, it's about ninety minutes to backtrack. How far is it to this other gateway?"

Tíereachán maintained his obstinate stance, his elegant brows dipping downward, disapproval driving them to practically meet over the bridge of his nose. "You are operating under the mistaken belief that Brassal cannot cross over earlier if necessary. Even if you sneak into your building undetected, Kim will notice Kieran's absence. Although the cost is dear, if the king knows you are within his reach, he will release the Hunt. Even your djinn cannot protect you from their spectral grasp."

"I can sidestep."

He snorted. "Once they gain your scent, it won't matter."

Reluctant Adept - Chapter Three

"The Wild Hunt can sidestep too?" Alarm pitched my voice higher. "They can follow me to that other dimension?"

"No, they are restricted to the material plane, but their tracking skills are unrivaled. Once set loose, they are compelled to pursue their quarry until it's trapped or killed. They are unrelenting and eternal. They cannot be killed or banished. They cannot be bargained with and are utterly merciless. They require no sustenance and have no need for sleep. Even if you escape to a higher dimension, as soon as you return to their plane, they will have you. Only a trained adept can escape them by harnessing a conduit to another world. This is why it's imperative that you go to my mother without delay."

Tíereachán stepped closer so that the lines of his face were plain in the moonlight. His expression was calm. "Kieran has a choice. You cannot make it for him, no matter how much you might wish to."

"Bond with some woman he doesn't know or face the Tribunal? Those aren't choices, they're punishments!" I fumed. "All because King Faonaín is a self-absorbed asswipe of the first order. Kieran deserves another choice—to escape with me—and I'm going to give it to him."

"What makes you think he doesn't already have that choice?" he asked. "Kieran isn't without resources. It is well within his abilities to follow in our path."

His response, aggravatingly composed and level-headed, as though we were discussing a camping trip instead of a life-changing escape into the Otherworld, pissed me off.

"He shouldn't have to follow," I exclaimed. "If I hadn't had my own personal Chernobyl, we'd be together right now. This wouldn't be an issue. I won't abandon him!"

"He doesn't deserve your loyalty."

I might have snapped back something hurtful if his tone had been harsh, but he'd sounded almost pitying. I frowned, unsure how to react.

He sighed. "Regardless, there are some things, even you, with your considerable power, cannot control. Kieran must decide what is most important to him. And you must find the strength to let him."

"So, that's what you expect me to do?" I glowered at him. "Sit on my hands and allow the king to shit all over our lives?"

"No, *Cúairtine.* I expect you to calm down, stop reacting emotionally, and *think* about what you're doing."

World Walker. I almost snorted at his not-so-subtle reminder of my supposed importance.

My body flashed hot in spite of the cool late-night breeze. "Well, Mr. Iceman, since I'm obviously incapable of making smart decisions due to my hysterics, tell me, what would you do in my shoes?" I pinned him to the spot with my gaze, narrowing my eyes to mere slits. "If the woman you cared about most in the world was about to bond with some other guy or face prison time, you'd have no problem with this, right? You'd sit back, miles away, in the middle of a moonlit field, and let her face that decision on her own without lifting a finger to help. Easy as pie. Is that what you're telling me?"

A dark expression flashed over his features that I had a difficult time deciphering in the moonlight. "Easy?" he ground out. He laughed brutally. "I have no need to don your shoes, Lire. I know their torment all too well. And even though I'm no longer a world away, their fit seems to grow more intolerable by the day."

Huh?

At Tíereachán's brisk nod, cool fingers slid across the back of my neck and I flinched, realizing too late that Fisk had circled around to sneak up behind me in the dark. His minty breath tickled my right cheek as he muttered something foreign into my ear.

No!

I shifted to the balls of my feet, tensing to launch myself into the air, but my body had other ideas. All at once, my muscles gave way, every fiber suffused by tingling warmth, as though I'd been worked over, head to toe, by the world's best masseuse.

Reluctant Adept - Chapter Three

Unvoiced protest dying in my throat, I crumpled. Before I could worry about the ground rushing to meet me, oblivion rose up instead.

FOUR

Show me one of your favorite places.

The thought floated to me in the darkness of my warm cocoon. Even in my mind, with no sound to vibrate my ears, the voice resonated deeply. A man's voice. Its lyrical cadence was familiar and comforting. It made me feel safe, but at the same time, I had the strongest urge to give its owner the middle finger.

I snuggled into the darkness as though it were a fur coat. I should have been angry about the voice's intrusion, but I was far too relaxed to do anything but drift, senseless and content.

Is it so much to ask that you would refuse? the voice asked.

Unbidden, the image of a blond, vastly-appealing sidhe surfaced, followed by a surge of complicated emotions.

Tíereachán.

It all came back to me. The jerk had ordered Fisk to put me to sleep! And, now, because of our blood connection, Tíereachán had the gall to gatecrash my slumber. Not that this was unusual. Until a few weeks ago, before I'd rescued him from Azazel's millennia of torment, he'd visited me nightly for almost a month. In our joint dreamtime, I'd taken him places he couldn't have hoped to see in person.

With him back in my mind, I realized I missed sharing this unique connection with him.

And then I mentally shook myself. *He put you to sleep to keep you from helping Kieran! What kind of friend does something like that?*

Wake up. Wake up now! I needed to be aware of my physical body in order to sidestep. Besides, even if I could somehow sidestep while dreaming, I wouldn't leave Red behind. I had to be awake.

I tried to sense my body, lying on the back seat, and imagined feeling the rumble of the car as it motored down the interstate. Maybe I could will myself back to reality if I thought about it hard enough.

I've missed this too, Tíereachán thought.

A jolt of pleasure sparked through me at his admission, but before I could even begin to scold myself over that particular brand of idiocy, his final word landed on me.

Did he say ... 'too?'

He thought I'd missed this? How the hell would he know? It's not as if I'd been following him around with puppy-dog eyes. *Cocky bastard.*

Okay, yes. I'll admit we shared a connection and, yes, I found him attractive, but that didn't mean I wanted to act on it. Kieran and I were together. I'd never given Tíereachán *any* indication that I felt more than a platonic friendship toward him—attraction notwithstanding. *Hello!* I thought Hugh Jackman was a superior male specimen too, but I wouldn't throw away Kieran like last week's cold pizza in order to go out with him.

Yeah, but Hugh Jackman hasn't shared dreams with you, my little voice supplied. *Nor is he immune to your clairvoyance.*

And proving that my little voice is a complete bitch, it added, *Besides, Kieran betrayed you—more than once.*

I told my mind to put a goddamned cork in it. This was Tíereachán's default setting, nothing more. The guy had chutzpah to spare. And he was trying to distract me from waking up. Well, it wouldn't work. I'd find a way to wake up and then I'd—

I'm sorry. His silvery voice cut into my thoughts. *If I'd known how you felt, I wouldn't have forced myself to stay away. Without a world to keep us apart, I hadn't wanted to take unfair advantage."*

Was he kidding? Unfair advantage? He knew how I felt? *Of all the arrogant, egotistical ...*

If this was his attempt to get me riled up, he'd thoroughly succeeded.

His chuckle rumbled through my mind.

Cúairtine, what are you afraid of? His question hung in my thoughts, taunting me.

Afraid? As if!

Maybe if I continued to ignore him, he'd eventually go away.

Somehow, he managed to convey a sigh. *Please, indulge me. Likely, I'll not see these places but in your dreams. It's a simple enough pleasure that costs you nothing. Why not enjoy this time while we have it?*

Incensed, I broke my stubborn silence to shout my thoughts at him, *Are you insane? You kidnapped me, and now you want us to enjoy our time together? What the hell is the matter with you?*

In a swirl of blinding light, I shoved us into the most breathtaking landscape I could imagine from memory. *You want a favorite place. I'll give you a favorite, all right.*

Oh, yes. High, high up. Overhanging Rock on Glacier Point—a precarious, natural platform shoehorned over a sheer three-thousand-foot drop to the floor of Yosemite Valley. I made sure to settle him with his heels pushed to the unforgiving rock's edge, the pristine view spreading out behind him, a tree-studded, glacier-carved granite wonder.

Blue eyes wide, blond hair blowing in the warm, pine-scented, afternoon breeze, he peeked down past his right shoulder.

I surrounded him within my telekinetic grasp and pushed ever so gently, not enough to cause misstep but to press my point. His arms flew out as he attempted to keep his balance.

Now that I had a voice, I shouted at him, "This is my life. But apparently, my dreams are now the only place I have any say. How could you do this to me? How could you take away my control? You, of all people! You're no better than Azazel. I should pitch you over the goddamned edge, remind you what it's like having zero control."

The nearby drop-off sent a tremor of unease through me, despite the fact that, here in my dream, it presented no physical danger to either of us. Even so, the thought of him plunging half a mile toward the inevitable *splat* at the bottom made my insides cringe.

"Control is precisely what I'm determined to give you," he replied, his wavering, outstretched arms the sole concession to his precarious position. "I seek to empower you, to give you the skills that will prevent anyone from taking advantage of your weaknesses. Yet, unlike Kieran, or Kim, or, even, Michael, I demand nothing in return. Who else in your life, besides Red, can say as much? That you freed me from Azazel's enslavement is a debt I can never hope to repay. I will not rest until you have the skill and knowledge to chart your own life. If it means you will despise me for my methods, then so be it."

God! I wanted to grip his stubbornly set jaw and give it a hard shove. Instead, I issued a very unladylike shriek of frustration and stomped away. I vaulted over the stone safety wall and kept going until I'd pounded my way several hundred feet along the viewpoint's tourist-worn path, breathing hard.

Damn him! And damn Fisk!

If I could just wake up, I'd grab Red, sidestep us the hell out of the car, and then jet through that weird dimension all the way back home as fast as my body could stand. I'd never traveled long distances in the higher plane, but there was a first time for everything. I was pretty sure the djinn did it all the time. It was how they transported themselves from one place to another in a blink. Of course, unless they willed it, they didn't have flesh and bone bodies. My physical body, however, would limit how fast I could levitate myself. The higher dimension was devoid of physical obstacles, allowing me to travel in a straight line, but I could breathe there. Air meant friction. From my experience flying around the Seattle skyline, I knew my body, specifically my eyes and ears, could handle only so much buffeting.

Still ... I could probably fly back home half as fast as Fisk had been driving. So, a few hours, then?

I'd never levitated myself for longer than twenty minutes at a stretch, mainly because I'd gotten too cold out in the elements to stay out any longer. In the higher plane, though, I wouldn't have to worry about the weather, but energy consumption was another matter. I'd never pushed myself far enough to know my physical limitations. Was it possible for me to run out of steam? Maybe, but if I did, I could afford to stop and rest. There was plenty of time to rescue Kieran and get away before Brassal showed up.

But what if Tíereachán was right? What if Kim alerted Brassal as soon as she noticed Kieran missing? Would the king demand that Kim open a gateway so he could send the Hunt after us? And, if Kieran knew of this risk ... would he resist leaving?

Damn it!

He would. If he thought he was saving me from the king, he'd totally resist. He'd shroud himself to prevent me from using my magic on him. I could threaten to give myself up to Brassal if he didn't accompany me. That might work.

But if I had to blackmail Kieran to convince him to come with me ... what did that say about our relationship? And, now ... did I even want to continue our involvement, knowing part, if not all, of the reason he'd seduced me was because of my relation to his former mate?

I wiped my sweaty palms on my jean-clad thighs. Thinking about what he'd done made me feel ... bad. Not quite dirty, but close enough to make me uncomfortable.

I stalked down a half dozen rough-hewn steps to a section of the rock wall that edged the lookout's rocky precipice. A cluster of low lying scrubby bushes and a lone intrepid pine tree had somehow found purchase on the broad granite plateau, green gems embedded in the dusty silver-gray stone. Half a mile below and stretching a good seven miles away from me, the high pile carpet of lush forest coated the valley floor, the iconic shape of Half Dome rising four thousand feet above the greenery like a stone giant's big toe.

I gripped the sun-warmed iron railing that capped the wall and stared out at the view, thinking.

I didn't want to admit it, but Tíereachán had a point: If Kieran wanted to accompany us to the amhaín's territory, it was within his power to escape. Two weeks ago, I'd given him a cell phone programmed with all of our numbers. Help was just a text or call away. I had no doubt Wade and Fisk had associates who would pick up Kieran if he called to ask.

If I sidestepped and flew back to him, I'd be putting the both of us in danger. What's more, if I fell prey to King Faonaín's hunters, I wouldn't be free to rescue Julie and Steven and the rest of our friends.

I gripped the railing as though it could expunge the burn of helplessness and frustration in my chest.

Loose pebbles crackled under Tíereachán's boots as he sidled up next to me.

We stood in the precious silence, broken only by distant bird song and the mellow swish of the afternoon's warm breeze, taking in the magnificent view.

"Was this another of your father's favorite places?" he finally asked.

My father had passed away a little over three years ago, but the ache of his absence still managed to sneak up on me. "Yes," I replied, subdued. "Yosemite National Park. You know it?"

He nodded, looking thoughtful, and then returned his attention to the natural spectacle below us. "Before my mother and I coordinated our escape, I accompanied the king and his retinue to this valley often. We call it *Búancodail*. It's been many, many years since I've seen it." His head tilted slightly as he mused, "The king favored to visit in winter. Me ... I preferred autumn."

"King Faonaín brought you here?" I stared at him, eyes going wide. "I thought you were his hostage."

He glanced at me. His dark-blond eyebrows tilted downward at my obvious surprise. "Did you imagine me confined to a dungeon? For near a thousand years?"

I had, actually.

Sidhe royal succession wasn't a simple matter of inheritance by the oldest child. Skill with magic factored into the Tribunal's decision too. Since the amhaín possessed such a rare and powerful gift—the ability to create and maintain the Otherworld's portals to Earth—King Faonaín's younger sister might have inherited the crown. To counter this threat, the king abducted Tíereachán prior to the Tribunal's vote. The move forced the amhaín to accept the subservient role as portal adept instead of petitioning the Tribunal for succession.

Knowing this fact, along with all the talk about the king's desire to hunt me down and his own daughter's malevolent behavior, I'd eagerly painted King Faonaín as a cruel master and Tíereachán as his wretched prisoner.

He smiled in amusement. "My uncle held me for political reasons. He raised me as his son."

"A carefully watched son," I guessed.

He cocked his head to the side in subtle assent.

"Did he love you as one?" Curiosity prompted me to ask the question before I considered its personal nature.

His expression hardened and he turned away. "In his own way ..." He shrugged. "Perhaps."

"Is that why Maeve fed you to Azazel? Because she thought you were a threat to her own succession?"

He barked out a laugh. "Fed me, is it?" He shook his head, his flaxen hair gleaming in the afternoon sun, and tutted. "Love, you do have a way with words." He sighed. "Yes. Unlike Kieran, I wasn't easily plied into doing her dirty work, but I fell nevertheless."

My blood boiled at the reminder. Maeve was a scheming, cold hearted bitch, as bad as her father, if not worse. Through manipulation, she'd utterly ruined Kieran and tricked Tíereachán into enslaving himself to Azazel. And last month, she abducted and seduced Vince, my almost-boy-friend, into becoming her soulmate in the hope that it would more closely align her to their oracle's prophecy. Last I heard, Vince had been confined to the Otherworld under King Faonaín's watchful eye, since Maeve refused to break their soulbond. As far as I was concerned, the wench deserved every lonely, depressing, agonizing second in prison. I hope she rotted there for all eternity. I just wished Vince didn't need to suffer along with her because of their shared connection.

If I had to bust her out of jail for that asshat Lorcán, I was going to be so effing pissed.

I considered Tíereachán's profile—impeccably straight nose, strong jaw, proudly set brow—his was a visage truly befitting a prince, but his aristocratic mien was an illusion. It belied the unfortunate truth that, even though I'd rescued him from Azazel's immediate grasp, he remained tied to the archdemon by blood compact. Because of this, he would likely be distrusted by his own people despite his royal lineage.

"Fell?" I shook my head. "I see it more as a stumble." I pushed away from the railing to face him. "Even Azazel's geas couldn't hide what you are from me—a good man struggling to recover from a poor choice. It's why I grew to trust you, why I helped you." I tilted my head to the side and studied him. "How can you suggest I do anything less for Kieran?"

Scowling, he turned away.

"He's made mistakes," I conceded. "And there's no question, this latest one ... it changes things."

When he considered me, his eyes held a piercing combination of surprise and scrutiny. Uncomfortable, I gazed at the view and shrugged. "I'm not sure how I feel about it yet, but the one thing I won't do is abandon him without a word."

"Erring once, I'll grant you, is a mistake. But he's had nearly two thousand years to learn from it. Now, he no longer makes *mistakes*," he said, lips curled in reproof. "They are deliberate acts. He is the Deceiver. He does not deserve your devotion."

"I disagree. There is good in him. I've seen it. He risked his life for me. Before this latest— " *Deception.* I waved my hand, helplessly, unable to say it. "He had every opportunity to pressure me into bonding with him, but he's done nothing of the sort. He wants me to go to your mother, not the king."

"Because he knows you need proper training," he retorted, eyes flashing. "Summoning the spirits of long dead adepts was tried and failed with Nuala. Only a living adept can train you. Kieran is simply ensuring that you reach your true potential while he presses his advantage."

"Advantage? Advantage to do what?" I asked. "To bond with me? If he does, it puts him at odds with the king. That's not an advantage. According to you and Fisk, it's a death sentence. So what are you implying he wants?"

"Redemption. Absolution from his past mistakes. But such a thing can never come from selfish acts. The more he pursues it, the more it will evade his grasp. True redemption must come from within. Until he realizes this, he will continue to deceive both you and himself under the guise of protection. His choices will drag you down until you don't know who to trust."

Tíereachán's emphatic tone goaded me. Whether sidhe or human, why were people so eager to perceive the very worst in someone and then look no further? We weren't black and white. Dismissing Kieran as worthless, based solely on his past mistakes, was no different than the bigoted people who took one look at my gloves and hated me.

It struck me as ironic that Tíereachán held such a one-sided opinion, since most people, sidhe especially, were sure to balk at his tie to Azazel. I had no doubt he'd be written off as evil for dealing with a demon in the first place, even though the reason for his enslavement had been a noble one.

"Can't you see? He's spent the last two thousand years being told he's the Deceiver. A person can live with something like that for only so long until coming to believe it. And he *does*. It's sunk so deeply that he's allowed it to define him. Its shadow permeates his soul." I took a steadying breath to shore up my unsteady voice. "Someone needs to believe in him. If I don't, then who will?"

"You cannot save him. It's a mistake thinking you can."

One could say the same thing about you, I thought.

"Maybe. But it's my mistake to make." I tipped my head upward to stare into his fierce blue eyes and poked his chest. "He's more than a fallen sidhe," I said fiercely. Then, easing away, I turned back to the view and added, "Same. As. You."

After a few moments enduring my silent treatment, he sighed. "We cannot risk going back. Not with Kim in possession of the draíoclochs."

Kim ...

I drew in a sharp breath, remembering Michael's offhand comment. Eyes wide, I snapped my gaze to Tíereachán's face. "But she's not."

He frowned, puzzled.

"Kim doesn't have them," I clarified. "Michael does. He's got them in Invisius' basement vault. He told me."

I barely restrained myself from tugging on his arm like a little kid outside the doors to Toys "R" Us. "Wake yourself up. Tell Fisk to head back to Seattle, to Invisius HQ. I know the combination. We can sneak inside and steal the darn things out of the safe! Without a gateway, the king can't send the Hunt. We'll be safe." Contrite, I amended, "Well ... safer."

His eyes narrowed suspiciously. "And it will prevent Kieran from leaving," he said, voice low and disapproving.

The draíoclochs were also my ticket into King Faonaín's territory, in case I couldn't learn how to world walk before Lorcán's imposed three-day deadline. I wasn't sure where Tíereachán and Fisk might stand in regards to my vow to save my friends at all costs, so I kept that part to myself. I didn't want the two of them on guard in case they intended to stop me.

I ignored his scowl. "A side benefit. It will at least give me a chance to talk to him," I said, reluctantly adding, "but if he wants to leave, I won't stop him. Once we're at your mother's gateway, we'll find a way to give back the draíoclochs, so we don't cause a diplomatic incident." *All of them, except one.* And I knew precisely how to go about stealing it.

I met his gaze. "Okay?"

He considered me, expression hard, but plainly thinking it over. "I'll be right back," he said and disappeared.

I blinked at his abrupt departure, wishing it was as easy for me to wake up. *Freaking Fisk.* It was just my luck that the angry, foul-mouthed, half-blood jerk possessed mind magic in addition to being a skilled swordsman. From now on, I wasn't letting him get anywhere near me, particularly if we disagreed on something. *Bastard.*

I tapped out an anxious rhythm on the iron railing, the metal warm against my fingertips from the late afternoon sun. Below me, most of the valley had sunk into shadow, leaving Half Dome and its neighboring lofty granite rock faces swathed in apricot-tinged light. The view was spectacular but lost on me as I pondered the likelihood of waking up in the car, en route to raid Invisius' safe, or in the Otherworld with no way to help Kieran or get my hands on the draíoclochs.

Would they go for it? It seemed like a strategical advantage to curtail or eliminate King Faonaín's access to Earth, but maybe the amhaín didn't care, since the king's access would be limited to half a dozen trips—one temporary gateway per draíocloch. Would stealing them be enough to breach the Compact, regardless of whether we returned them? I was pretty sure I could swipe one without anyone noticing. All I had to do was substitute it for the depleted draíocloch I happened to have at home and I'd be good to go.

Before my fidgeting devolved into pacing at the railing, Tíereachán popped back into my dream looking like a divine messenger, golden hair flying, shoulders firm, hell bent on dispatching his grim tidings, even if it meant cracking skulls.

"We're heading back," he clipped out.

Hoo-kay. Somebody was miffed.

I wished I'd been awake to know what he and Fisk had discussed, or, rather, argued about, because, clearly, there'd been an argument. I wondered whether Red had spoken up and what he thought about all of this. I fully intended to grill him as soon as we had some privacy.

"Then why are we still here? Wake me up," I said.

He sighed, looking almost rueful. "So eager, are you, to spend more time in the dark, closed space of John's backseat?"

"Yes," I replied stiffly. "Mark my words, if you ever tell Fisk to put me to sleep again, I'll maroon you in The Between for a goddamn week."

He snorted, the right corner of his mouth curving upward in amusement. "If you started listening to my counsel, I wouldn't feel so compelled."

I sucked in a breath, ready to explode, but he dropped the smile and stepped close enough to touch my arm. "You have my word."

His sober expression mollified me. I exhaled loudly and examined him with narrowed eyes. "How is it you can pop in and out and I'm stuck here? What's the trick?"

"No trick. I'm not in a forced sleep. I'm not asleep at all, in fact."

I don't know why I assumed he had to be asleep in order to enter my dreams. Probably because it made our connection seem less intimate and, therefore, less terrifying that way. Self-deception at its best. I wanted to kick myself. Or run away screaming. I wasn't sure which.

You really are a goddamned moron.

"Stop," Tíereachán scolded. "Don't let me hear you speak harshly about yourself again."

I blinked at the non sequitur until I realized ... it wasn't a non sequitur at all. "What the—?" I sputtered. "Son of a bitch! You are. You can read my mind." I waved my hands and then pushed at him, shooing him. "Get out of my head. Get out, right now!"

He had the nerve to chuckle, the creep. "*Cúairtine*, calm yourself. Your mundane thoughts are a mystery. I can *hear* the most focused, that is all."

I recalled his earlier comment. "You can sense my emotions too!" I accused.

He frowned, looking nonplussed. "The strong ones, yes. More when I'm touching you. Why else did you think I wanted to share my blood if not to equalize our bond?" He sounded genuinely puzzled. "If you'd done so, you would have the same ability to know mine. At the very least, it would make you less distrustful," he pronounced, mouth pursed as though he'd discovered I short-sheeted his bed.

"Well, excuse me," I drawled. "You started pestering me about strengthening our bond when I still thought you were a demon." I huffed. "How was I supposed to know you weren't trying to enslave me?"

"Is that so?" He gazed at me archly. "And now that you know me for what I am?"

My heart jolted and sped up.

Jeez. Calm down, idiot. He's not asking you to share his blood. He wants to know whether you trust him.

"You wouldn't do anything to hurt me. I know that."

But people often hurt each other, even without trying to.

Dismissing the thought, I glared at him. "But you're still on my shit list for putting me to sleep."

"Although you understand why I did," he replied without hint of remorse.

Honestly. Sidhe and their damn superiority. It made me want to argue, or maybe accidentally pinch his ear. But he was right. I did understand.

I just didn't have to like it.

"I wasn't going to run off," I muttered. Knowing that wasn't strictly true, I rolled my eyes and added, "At least, not right then." Even to my own ears, I sounded sullen.

He snorted.

Someone was a little too full of themselves for my taste.

"So ..." I said, leaning against the low wall. "Our connection is increased if you're touching me, eh?"

His expression didn't veer from neutral, but something flickered behind his eyes. Unease, possibly.

He nodded.

"Are you touching me right now?"

He responded with silence. He wasn't dumb. He knew a loaded question when he heard one.

I didn't care that he wasn't the type to grope me while incapacitated. He had his hands on me when there was nothing I could do about it.

Not. Cool.

I folded my arms. "Then you know how that makes me feel."

He wiped a hand over his jaw, trying to hide his chagrin, and, for the first time, his gaze veered away.

It was a new look for him, boyish almost, but I refused to soften. "What do you think you should do about it?"

He sighed, flashed me with a crooked smile, and then blinked out of my dream.

"You'll be lucky if I don't kick your ass when I wake up!" I bellowed at the sky.

As my surroundings faded to black and the echo of my voice reverberated in my ears, I wondered whether my threat had been 'focused' enough for him to hear.

I smiled, sure of it.

FIVE

We hit the South Lake Union neighborhood well after midnight. Fisk deftly parallel parked his luxury import between a beat-up Chevy pickup and a blue, late-model Subaru Impreza, two blocks from the red brick building that Michael and more than a dozen Invisius telepaths called home. I shivered as I unfolded myself from the backseat onto the damp, downtown Seattle sidewalk. The cool late-night air bit into the warmest parts of my body, drawing out goosebumps and making late spring feel more like winter.

Not all of my shivers were due to the cold. Less than three weeks ago, I'd stood not far from this exact spot with Kieran, Michael, Daniel, Kim, and Jackie, on the morning of our attack on Invisius. Now, Daniel was dead and I found myself at odds with the very people I still considered allies, if not friends. The reversal didn't sit well.

Hugging myself against the cold, I examined the moonlit street.

At least this time around, I didn't have to worry about the possibility that I might need to kill someone.

I frowned at the thought and turned to Fisk. "These are friends. I want the draíoclochs, but not enough to consider hurting anyone. No physical force. Understand?"

Even standing in the shadow of the nearest maple tree, Fisk's disgust wasn't difficult to read. "No. Really? Any other pearls of wisdom to share?"

"Sure," I replied sweetly. "Don't antagonize the person who's about to sidestep your ass into another dimension. She might be tempted to accidentally leave important bits behind."

To my delight, Fisk's eyes grew wide as I engulfed both him and Tíereachán within my telekinetic grip, but before I could get a feel for Fisk's resonance, his shroud slammed over his body, shutting me out and reflecting my magic with a reverberating slap.

I gasped and staggered backward at the unexpected jolt as I scrambled to reabsorb the backwash that boomeranged into me. Maybe if I'd been prepared for Fisk's indecorous reaction, I'd have successfully redirected the returning magic, but the surprise left me flat footed. With the power I'd spooled to sidestep readied and flowing through me, the profusion had nowhere to go. The surplus power spilled over, following the lines of my magic like the overflow drain in my bathroom sink, and surged into Tíereachán.

Tíereachán stiffened and bit out a Silven curse at the unheralded deluge.

Too late, I banked my power and strengthened my psychic shield to prevent further backwash from inundating him.

Bonehead!

This never would have happened if I'd drawn the power I needed, instead of topping myself off like a greedy child taking yet another cookie, in spite of having one in each hand and another stuffed in her mouth.

Overspoolers are preschoolers. How many times had I heard that annoying rhyme, growing up? Even though overspooling was something only offensive psychics had to worry about, you'd think the lesson would have sunk in, regardless. I'd heard the inane verse chanted around the playground enough times, for God's sake.

Worse, I'd allowed my excess to spew all over Tíereachán! Why didn't I stamp an 'L' on my forehead and have done with it?

"Shit!" I croaked. "Sorry."

Ignoring me, Tíereachán leveled Fisk with a furious scowl. "Are you thick? If she saved a fallen good-for-nothing sidhe like me, she's certainly not going to harm you, even if you *are* an unmitigated ass."

"What did you expect?" Fisk growled back. "She's over-topping and slinging magic faster than a *ùruisg* in heat."

Tíereachán leveled him with a withering glare. "Had she years of experience, I might echo your sentiment. But she's had a mere three phases to learn control—with little instruction. Even if you are so arrogant to believe you could do better under the same circumstances, she doesn't deserve censure."

After a moment of dueling with their belligerent stares, Fisk looked at me, ground out a half sincere apology, adding crisply, "A little warning before you force your magic on me would be appreciated."

"Because, when you put me to sleep, *twice*, you did the same for me, right?"

Tíereachán cut in, "Enough! You two are worse than an unhappily mated couple in their second thousand years."

Eww. I wrinkled my nose at the thought of being mated to Fisk. The guy was grumpier than a gorgon on a bad hair day.

What the hell was Fisk's problem anyway? I couldn't figure out what I'd done to warrant his near constant animosity, other than simply breathing.

Okay ... yes, there was that time when I'd helped break the defensive ward in the Invisius telepaths' basement. We all thought the elders had erected it to keep everyone except their brainwashed telepaths out of the building. How were we supposed to know Wade had placed the ward to restrict a demonic gateway? If they'd bothered to warn us, we'd have left the darn thing intact. That's right, *we*. It had been a group decision to bring the ward down. But for whatever reason, despite Kieran, Michael, Daniel, Kim, and Jackie all being there, Fisk chose to blame the whole thing on me!

Now that I thought about it, Fisk's surly attitude went all the way back to when I'd first met him in FBI Agent Cunningham's office, weeks ago—*before* the whole ordeal at Invisius and prior to my initial meeting with Kieran and Maeve. At the time, I thought Fisk was nothing more than a prickly FBI agent annoyed at needing a clairvoyant's unique skill. I'd chalked up his animosity to the fact that I refused to help him with the case he'd been investigating ... but maybe there was more to it. Perhaps he'd disliked me from the start because of who I was: A clueless human psychic everyone had pegged as the next adept.

I sighed. Whatever. Derision was nothing new to me. Every day, people avoided, even scorned me, because of my gloves and what they meant. The reaction was so familiar, I hardly noticed it anymore. Of course, those reactions typically came from normals, plain humans, not the magically inclined. But lately, with all my blundering, it was little wonder Fisk treated me like an airhead who'd play hopscotch on a pile of explosives.

I turned a jaded eye to Fisk, but I resolved to stop rising to his bait. "I have your back, for however little you think that's worth. Hate me or not, I don't give a crap. We're on the same side. Either you trust that, or you don't." Ignoring his rigid stance and affronted expression, I said, "I plan to sidestep the three of us so we can enter the basement in secret. That's what I was about to do until you shoved your shroud in my face."

Before he could issue what was surely an indignant retort, I added, "It was rude to grab you without warning you first. From now on, I'll try to remember." Somehow, the grudging admission didn't choke me as it left my mouth.

See? I could be professional.

He evaluated me, coolly assessing, until the invisible, oblong bubble that surrounded him disappeared.

"Okay, then," I said tentatively. "Here goes ..."

Taking it slow, I eased my magic around the two men, spooling the power I needed to encase them within my telekinetic grasp and no more. With scarcely a thought,

Tíereachán's resonance nestled into my mind, as familiar and comfortable as a favorite pair of fuzzy slippers. I might have worried about the speed and ease of our connection, but the dreaded anticipation of so intimately touching Fisk smothered what might have otherwise freaked me out.

I turned my attention to Fisk, forcing the invisible fingers of my magic to wreathe around him. As my magic slid over his body, each of his stiffly coiled muscles twitched in response. He was worse than a skittish horse, watching its groomer with wary eyes, poised to deliver a swift kick. Honestly, I wasn't any happier than he was. Fisk was the last person I wanted to know so thoroughly.

The guy was *physically* attractive; I'd give him that. Beauty seemed to be a universal sidhe trait that extended to part-bloods too. Fisk was six-feet-four inches of able-bodied, square-faced good looks with arresting amber eyes that made me think of the deadly allure of a lion. And, while not as heart-flutteringly gorgeous as Tíereachán (or as darkly handsome as Kieran), Fisk's physique made him the most imposing of the three men. He outweighed Tíereachán by a good thirty pounds, all of that surplus bulk in the form of toned musculature and four extra inches in height. Where Tíereachán's physique was cut and defined, like a swimmer's, Fisk's was brawnier, more befitting of a linebacker.

I held their unique resonances in the fore of my mind, like fondly remembered melodies, and then slipped every one of our finely tuned molecules ...

　　... one
　　　... dizzying
　　　　... whisper
　　　　　... sideways.

The darkened street warped and elongated as it both veered away and rushed closer. My stomach lurched and my ears throbbed with the familiar feeling of movement while my feet remained incongruously rooted to the solid yet now distorted ground.

I laughed at our arrival, the joyous sound echoing oddly in the stagnant atmosphere, but stopped myself short before I could spin around, hands raised in the air. When I caught Fisk's eye and took in his sickly grimace, I almost cracked up again, but by sheer willpower, managed to squash the impulse. I didn't need to give him yet another reason to hate me.

Ignoring his obvious discomfort, I considered our dark, deformed surroundings. "Crud. The last time I did this, it was early morning. It's going to be hard to find the building in the dark with everything so ..." I trailed off, looking at the obscured, topsy-turvy world around us, and then settled on, "wonky."

"Ever heard of a veil?" Fisk rasped, along with something that sounded suspiciously like, 'fucking amateur.'

My hackles rose.

"Jesus," I spat. "I got the message already. You hate me. *Get the fuck over it.* I'm doing my best and being an asshole won't make it any better."

Anger had kept my voice at an even, if not indignant, keel, but on my last word my bottom lip trembled alarmingly. I bit it, hard, welcoming the pain as it forced any self-defeating emotions back where they belonged—buried deep.

Fisk would not, *could not*, hurt my goddamned feelings. I didn't have time for this shit.

"Oh, I don't think it's hate, precisely," Tíereachán murmured, his arms folded, gazing down his nose at Fisk in a superior, assessing way, as though he'd discovered something interesting.

"Close enough," I bit out.

If Fisk was in the least bit sorry for his behavior, it didn't register on his broad, chiseled face. Whatever. It no longer mattered. I was done worrying about the jerk. Obviously, he had a problem with me, but it was just that: *His* problem. Not mine. And I'd be damned if I let myself be a party to it any longer.

Strengthened by my resolve, I calmly addressed both men, "Your veils would cover us on the street, that's true, but Jackie warded the building a couple weeks ago. It announces all arrivals, even those keyed to it, like Tíereachán and me. But it won't allow *you* inside at all," I said, flashing my eyes at Fisk. "Unless you want to go in neutered. Magically speaking, of course."

I folded my arms. "Like I said, I was running on autopilot bringing us here. You're right, it makes more sense to walk to the building veiled. At that point, I can sidestep us through the ward."

Tíereachán dismissed this with a sibilant snort. "It is well within your skills to find our destination, dark and ... *wonky* view or not."

I almost laughed. "Yeah? With what? My magic flashlight?"

"One of these days, you will cease underestimating yourself," he admonished. "*Think.* How did you separate me from my master?"

"I pushed you *here*—to the higher plane," I replied, although I didn't see how his rescue from Azazel had anything to do with finding our way through the Stygian, obfuscated view.

"Yet you remained behind, in the material one."

I frowned at the memory. Yes, I'd done it, but the act had terrified me. At the time, I wasn't sure I could send him to the higher realm without going along with him. I'd been afraid of pushing him too far, perhaps even losing him to the void.

"Yeah, " I drew out the word, leaving it hanging. *So?*

"When it came time, what did you do to retrieve me?"

"I pushed my magic into the higher plane and searched for you."

"Exactly," he said, tipping his head back and gazing down at me. "Tell me how."

"I don't know. I, uh ... made my magic act like ... fingers." Talking about how I internalized my gifts always sounded lame. I'd been asked countless times how my clairvoyance worked, usually by normals who had no clue about magic. I hated putting it into words. It always came off so clichéd. Evidently, describing my new abilities was no different.

"Tell me about these ... *fingers*." Predictably, he looked nonplussed. "Where does the power come from?"

"From my center, my core. You know, the usual." I shrugged, pulling my arms tighter to my stomach. "It's nothing special, just my TK."

"TK ... " His head jerked to an inquisitive angle. "*Telekinesis*?"

Tíereachán never blurted things. He was one of the most confident, self-possessed individuals I'd ever met. I shifted my feet, glancing at Fisk who appeared almost as riveted. "Well ... yeah," I replied, frowning at his astonishment. "Couldn't you tell? How else did you think I wrapped us up to come here?"

"I've been grasped by telekinesis, many times," Fisk said. "Your magic feels different. More ... invasive."

What the heck did that mean? Was the difference because of the unnatural way I'd acquired my additional gifts? All three—my telekinesis, cryokinesis, and pyrokinesis— had been unknowingly conferred to me when I made the mistake of reading the remains of three unidentified murder victims. My clairvoyance triggered the remnants of a nasty spell, one that the Circle Murderer had used to rip the psychic ability from each victim. Thanks to that interaction, I'd ended up with each victim's gift.

My TK had come from Jason, a type-three telekinetic whose magic worked on both organic and non-organic objects. As far as I knew, there wasn't anything unusual about Jason or his TK, and I had no reason to think his gift had mutated when I'd inherited it.

No. More likely, Fisk's perceived difference had to do with the methodical way I 'learned' his body in order to memorize his resonance. It had obviously made him uncomfortable. I shouldn't have snarked about leaving important bits behind when we sidestepped. No wonder he'd responded the way he did.

"That's how you found me?" Tíereachán asked, his brows spiking upward. "You sent these telekinetic *fingers* into the higher plane and ... felt around for me?"

I was dangerously close to feeling like a candidate for *Oddities* show regular, but I shrugged, managing to feign nonchalance. "Yeah."

"And you knew it was me?"

I laughed. "Who else would it have been?"

"Ah. So you simply grabbed the first thing you found."

I rolled my eyes. "Of course not. I knew it was you."

"How?"

Jeez. What was this? A job interview? "Your resonance— I know how it feels; what your body, your soul, sounds like; how you vibrate." Heat rushed to my cheeks. "It's hard to explain."

I half expected him to leer at me, but instead, his eyes lit up. "Perhaps your abilities are similar to my mother's after all. She speaks in the same terms about places." He considered me. "Do you know Michael's resonance? He accompanied you when you sidestepped Wade's ward, did he not?"

I hesitated, struggling to keep up with his unexpected segues. "Uh, yeah. He did."

"I had thought to instruct you in the plagency of a place and how to use it as a beacon, but this will serve."

Plagency? Leave it to the sidhe to use words I'd never heard uttered in mainstream conversation. He couldn't have said 'resonance' like everyone else?

He nodded briskly. "Michael is in his building. Seek him out and take us there."

I opened my mouth to set the bossy bastard straight. I knew all about the *resonances* of places. How the heck did he think I sidestepped? My building's djinn had deposited me here in the higher dimension, last month, when I'd needed a private moment with Michael. The feel of this place had sung to me, the tune seeping into my bones like a top ten favorite, one that, once remembered, had stuck fast in my mind. And the Earth with its beautiful, discordant, vibrant symphony ... it had called me home more than once.

I knew about *plagency,* and, besides, I wasn't a damned taxi to be ordered about! I fumed but snapped my mouth shut, just short of issuing an irritated retort. Tíereachán was simply ... being Tíereachán. And he *had* pointed out something that should have been obvious to me from the start. I could sidestep my magic and use it to navigate. *Duh.*

Saying nothing, I closed my eyes and thought about Earth, her complex, tumultuous arrangement of melodies that seemed to both fight and jive, grate and please, thousands of harmonies interlaced to form the brilliance of life that was nothing short of miraculous. It was *home,* familiar and comforting and easy to find, as though the damp street, two blocks from the telepath's building, was a warm hearth that beckoned me. Careful to keep myself firmly rooted in the higher plane, I slid my magic toward that warmth and almost gasped at the physical sensations of the sidewalk, neighboring tree, and Fisk's sedan parked at the nearby curb.

Jeez Louise. It worked!

As I wound my magic's tendrils experimentally through the nearby foliage, Earth's complex symphony rippled in my mind as notes came and went in a subtle yet marked permutation that changed with each minuscule movement.

"Huh," I mumbled. "Would you look at that?"

Each location possessed a unique signature, in the same way each cell in my body contributed to the whole of my being's resonance.

Until now, I hadn't realized when I sidestepped, I zeroed in on the loudest melody of my destination's overarching song and allowed it to guide me. Sort of like standing out on a street lined with an infinite number of houses and choosing to enter the dwelling that blared music the loudest. With all the houses playing music at the same volume, the loudest and most distinguishable music emanated from the closest doorway. This was why, when I sidestepped, I shifted to the target plane without changing my relative location. To sidestep somewhere else, I was willing to bet I needed to seek out the specific melody being played by whatever 'house' I wanted to enter, and then ... go there instead.

I reeled at the possibilities. If I memorized the *plagency* of a place, knew it by heart in the same way I *knew* Tíereachán's resonance, I could jump to that location instead of where I'd been standing seconds prior. I could ... *teleport*?

No. That couldn't be right ...

Could it?

I think I stopped breathing for a second or two as I marveled at the idea.

"Not much to look at. Have you located Michael?" Tíereachán asked, breaking my dumbfounded reverie.

"Mmm?" I opened my eyes, while still keeping metaphysical tabs on the Earth-side street we'd recently vacated. "Oh, no. Just noticing what you meant about the plagency thing," I replied, chagrined. I'd been prickly with him—even if it *had* been confined to my thoughts—and he hadn't deserved it. Evidently, Fisk's ongoing disregard had made me hypersensitive to anyone who called attention to my ignorance. Not a healthy attitude if I wanted (and needed) to learn about my burgeoning abilities.

Sighing at this bit of introspection, I admitted, "I'm not sure how to use it to navigate, though. For now, I think we're safer if I use my TK like a white cane." I tilted my head to the side, considering him. "But if you lend me some of your focus, or whatever it is you sidhe do to share power, I might be able to find Michael in one go, instead of feeling around like a blind woman."

Tíereachán blinked, his shock plain despite the meager lighting.

"*Jesus,*" Fisk bit out. "Why don't you ask the guy to fuck you without a condom, too, while you're at it?"

I recoiled, staggering two steps backward, as much due to Fisk's savage disgust as the vulgar comment itself.

As I stared stupidly at Fisk, speechless and agog, something blurred past my peripheral vision, too quick to be followed. If it hadn't been for Fisk's flinch, I might have attributed it to a shadow, possibly from a car passing on the street in the material plane. However, before I could spare it a second thought, Fisk's shroud slammed into place, instantly cutting me off from his resonance. Once again, I found myself scrambling to absorb the backlash without spewing magic like a toddler, which proved to be considerably easier when I wasn't stuffed to overflowing to begin with.

"What the—?" The rest of my furious response died in my throat when I spied a fine, vertical line of red that welled up through the smooth, fair skin of Fisk's face.

As his expression drew down into a hard, angry grimace, Fisk touched his fingertips to the stark crease at the center of his left cheek, smearing the perfect ruby line and rendering his fingers and cheek bloody. I'd seen this type of injury before—all over the Circle Murderer's body as he died a slow, painful death. This was the result of Tíereachán's offensive magic. He'd flayed a knife-thin strip of skin from Fisk's cheek!

Without any thought spared to the possibility of danger, I flew to stand between the two men, my backside a few inches from Fisk.

"What do you think you're *doing*?" I demanded, glaring at Tíereachán, my voice bordering on shrill.

Tíereachán ignored me, staring daggers over my head at his target. "I have warned you more than once about your disrespect. No doubt this will improve your disposition."

Anger burned away my fear, heating my cheeks and neck. I stalked into Tíereachán's personal space and got right into his face, or as close as I could manage considering our height difference. "Have you lost your mind?" I snapped and then jerked my arm behind me, leveling an accusing finger toward Fisk's face. "*That* is not how friends deal with personality conflicts."

"No," he snarled, never taking his eyes from the part-sidhe behind me. "It's how a *flaith* deals with disobedient half-blood *scolacas*, who allow resentment to poison their thoughts and rule their actions. One who will suffer painfully at my hands if he permits his petty emotions to interfere with his duty." Tíereachán's blue eyes were positively glacial. He narrowed them to slits. "This was but a *small* reminder."

I shivered at the menace in his tone, knowing well how much worse a more demonstrable reminder could be. His gruesome methods still haunted my dreams, even though, when he'd dispatched the Circle Murderer amid a sea of blood and gore, he'd saved me from becoming the killer's fifth victim.

I jumped at the unexpected contact of Fisk nudging my back, belatedly aware that I'd almost run into him. Over my shoulder, I caught his inquisitive gaze as he examined me. Since Fisk tended to border on dismissive whenever I was around, the intensity of his attention made me want to squirm. I might have sidled away if I hadn't been worried about Fisk and Tíereachán coming to further blows.

Tíereachán, however, was no longer paying Fisk any mind. He regarded me with a focus that rivaled Fisk's in its fervor, although instead of puzzlement, his eyes sparkled with defiance. They dared me to argue, which had the predictable effect. Righteous anger flared through me, as satisfying as it was fortifying, drawing me up and squaring my shoulders like a puppeteer had pulled my strings.

If he assumed I'd sit back and let him brutalize Fisk, he obviously didn't know me at all.

"I don't care if you're freaking God Almighty," I ground out. "If you do anything like this again, I ... I'll ..."

Do what? Hurt him? Kill him? He'd know those were empty threats. If I didn't endorse hurting people who criticized or vilified me, I certainly wasn't going to do something horrible to someone I considered a friend. And, as unwise as it seemed at the moment, I cared about Tíereachán. I valued our friendship, which was why his physical assault on Fisk bothered me so much. It was behavior that befitted Paimon the demon, not Tíereachán the sidhe.

In the weeks since freeing him from Azazel's grasp, I hadn't seen him do anything remotely nefarious, much less aggressive. Nothing prompted me to believe he'd been corrupted by his millennia of demon enslavement.

That is ... until now.

He raised his eyebrows, waiting, eyes taunting, and, perhaps, behind that superior veneer of his, looking uneasy. Although, the uneasy part might have been a projection of what I desperately wanted to see.

I frowned at him. "I won't be a party to that," I said, softer than I'd intended. I narrowed my eyes and added some fire. "No—not just that. I won't tolerate it. If this is something you're in the habit of doing, you won't be a part of my life. I'll cut you out. Period. Even if it means not training with your mother."

Even as I said it, I knew it was the truth. Yes, Tíereachán had ample reason to be concerned about Fisk's growing animosity. The part-sidhe's attitude had gone far enough to breed distrust, something unacceptable in an ally who we needed to rely on, but that didn't warrant such an over-the-top reaction. Although, truth be told, Fisk's wound bore more resemblance to a severe cat scratch than a monstrous goring. Was the scratch any worse than Fisk receiving a split lip after a punch to the face? Probably not, but a knuckle sandwich wasn't a great solution either.

I held Tíereachán's gaze, and, even in the dim light, what he saw in my expression must have given him pause because an underlying emotion flickered behind his eyes. Something that might have been satisfaction, but it evaporated so fast, I didn't have time to know for sure. And the threatening expression that slid into its place increased my doubt that I'd seen an intervening emotion at all.

He narrowed his eyes at me. "You would challenge my authority as flaith? As prince and heir?"

"No," Fisk said, and I jumped at the reminder of his presence so close behind me. "My lord, I beg your pardon. She doesn't have a goddamned clue."

Fisk moved in front of me to stare into my eyes. "You— "
He stopped and then snapped his mouth closed. His brows
dove together as his expression went from concern to con-
sternation. "Why did you have to be so fucking *human*?" He
blew out an angry breath and then barked at me, "He was
within his rights and I deserved it. For once, shut your clueless mouth and stay out of it."

Was he kidding? Playing the human card? Who the hell
did he think he was, anyway? He was part human himself,
the hypocritical jerk!

I opened my mouth to tell him off, but closed it when I
took in his pointed, exasperated look. It said, 'Shut the hell
up or you'll cause more problems for the both of us.' It was
an expression I never expected to see on Fisk's face.

"You enjoy getting flayed alive? Fine. Next time, I'll sell
tickets." I dug into my purse, mumbling under my breath to
Red about the stupidity of idiot sidhe males, and then
shoved a moist towelette packet at Fisk. "Here. You're a
mess."

Tíereachán, apparently placated by Fisk's comments,
watched placidly while I folded my arms and gave both of
them the stink-eye. What had I been thinking? As soon as
Tíereachán had dropped my purse into my lap in the car, I
should have nabbed Red, sidestepped the two of us out of
the freaking backseat, and not told Fisk or *his royal highness*
a darn thing. Although, admittedly, in light of all I'd learned
over the last few hours, running back to Kieran, rose-col-
ored glasses in place, wouldn't have done me any favors.

After Fisk had staunched his bleeding and cleaned his
face, Tíereachán jerked his chin at him. "Now that you remember who you serve, perhaps you'll appreciate the more
troubling concern regarding our future queen's earlier, rather ... *libertine* suggestion." He stared down his nose, evaluating Fisk coolly. "After all, you've already speared the
heart of it, pointing out, as delicately as always, what you
find so objectionable about her nature."

I frowned as I worked this over in my mind, trying to decide whether I should be offended, not liking the 'future

queen' bit, wondering whether he agreed with Fisk's assessment of my 'objectionable' nature (whatever that might be), and, at the same time, puzzling over what 'troubling concern' he was worried about. With everything tangled up in my head, it took me a moment to recall what had prompted their altercation to begin with.

I'd proposed that Tíereachán share his power with me.

I flushed at the memory of Fisk's harsh response. He'd compared sharing power to unprotected sex, which struck me as odd since sharing power with Kieran hadn't felt nearly as pleasurable as sex. It was nice, sure. I wouldn't turn it down on a regular basis. Having the extra focus was a potent feeling, a rush, but not what I'd call orgasmic.

Obviously, his rebuke had nothing to do with unwanted pregnancy, so it had to be about something else.

Was it because the sidhe viewed sharing power as a private, intimate act? Or could the connection convey a disease of some kind? A mental STD? If so, Kieran had never once hinted at either scenario. My stomach lurched sickeningly as I wondered whether this was yet another place where Kieran had deceived me and taken advantage of my ignorance.

Fisk's puzzled expression shifted to alarm as he obviously connected the dots, which did nothing for the queasy state of my innards. Sadly, I hadn't found my way out of the dark. *As usual*, I thought. But knowing Tíereachán, I wouldn't be left clueless for long, especially if revealing the truth further illuminated Kieran's deceitful nature.

Fisk cursed and stalked several feet away, hand raking through his thick brown hair.

"Let me guess," I said dryly. "Sharing power isn't something that's condoned."

"Between a soulmated pair, where malfeasance is impossible to hide, it's common enough," Tíereachán replied. "But the fact that you are unattached and aware of this ability raises the troubling question: Is this an act you and Kieran have shared? Or merely a capability he, or someone else, mentioned in passing?"

I felt distinctly as though he'd asked whether or not Kieran had deflowered me. From the corner of my eye, I noticed Fisk turn, his attention focused on me, waiting for my answer. It was a struggle to avoid cringing, and I looked away, avoiding both men's gazes.

I nodded. "Kim mentioned it once." I shot a scathing glare at Fisk. "The first time Kieran shared his power with me, he did it to save me from Azazel's grasp when I touched that cursed necklace *you* tricked me into reading."

Fisk didn't flinch but his eyes widened at the accusation. Weeks ago, when Fisk had been introduced to me as an FBI agent in need of my professional expertise, I'd refused to read a piece of evidence that belonged to a serial killer—the same killer who'd orchestrated the murders of King Faonaín's emissaries. Not wanting to take no for an answer, Fisk found a way to sneak the necklace into the group of items I'd been scheduled to read as a part of a cable television show.

And he had the nerve to be pissy with *me*!

"The first time?" Tíereachán echoed, pulling me out of my memories. "He's shared power with you more than once?"

I nodded. After several seconds of grave silence, I blurted, "For God's sake! You're acting as if the guy did something horrible, like rape or something. He didn't! He shared his power to help me focus my magic, so I could break that necklace's evil spell and then to make it easier to sidestep five … no, *six* people when we stormed the telepath's stronghold. He did it to help not hurt me."

He'd also done it when I levitated the both of us across Puget Sound, so we could get to Kim and Jackie's house on Bainbridge Island, but I kept that one to myself. I was already embarrassed enough, which more than anything else pissed me right off. I had nothing to be embarrassed about, darn it!

Fisk muttered something under his breath that sounded a lot like 'fucking clueless.'

"Yeah?" I challenged. "I wouldn't be so *clueless* if you guys took the time to educate me! Do you have any idea how god-damned condescending you all are? Clueless doesn't mean stupid. And if I'm clueless, it's because nobody tells me jack shit!"

"Lire, answers are coming, I promise you," Tíereachán said. "But, we need to know what happened. When Kieran first shared his power with you— " He hesitated and then sighed. "Forgive me for asking: Did he share his power before or after you succumbed to his advances?"

"Succumbed to ..." I straightened. "You mean ... sex? Are you seriously asking—?" I blinked at him, astonished, and virtually squeaked, "You want to know when Kieran and I first had sex?"

"Yes—whether it was before or after he shared power with you." He didn't even have the decency to bat an eye-lash.

I tightened my arms around myself and considered ordering him to take a long walk off a short pier. My sex life was none of his damned business.

And then I realized *why* the question had me squirming.

I'd slept with Kieran after knowing him less than three days. It had been the first time I'd done something like that, mainly due to there being precious few men brave enough to date a clairvoyant. But even the times it had come up, casual sex hadn't my thing, no matter how touch-starved I'd been.

I straightened my spine. I absolutely refused to feel anything but good about taking Kieran to my bed. It had been close to ten years since I'd last experienced sex without the necessity of a skin-suit. To say I'd missed the pleasure of skin contact was a massive understatement. Kieran was caring, intelligent, drop-dead sexy, and, as a sidhe, immune to my magic—an irresistible combination. I had nothing to feel guilty over, and I sure as hell wasn't going to slut-shame myself!

"I can't believe you're asking me this," I muttered, but I was a grown woman, dammit. I was thirty years old. I could talk about my sex life without blushing. All bets were off at giving him any kind of blow-by-blow description, though.

A near-hysterical giggle almost slipped out of my mouth at my mind's unintentional double-entendre.

Get a grip, Lire.

"Timing-wise, the power sharing came first," I replied, my voice miraculously under control. "Kieran helped me break the necklace's compulsion spell and then—later that night, actually—we, uh, hooked up."

Unbelievable. I'd uttered the words 'hooked up.' That was something Monica would say, I thought disgustedly ... and then froze.

Here I was all worked up about being slut-shamed for sleeping with Kieran, and yet ... ever since she'd been hired as our receptionist at Supernatural Talent & Company, I'd been doing practically the same thing to Monica. Never out loud, of course. I'd never be so heartless. But I'd been plenty judgmental inside my head. My heart sank. No—not just inside my head—I'd gossiped about Monica to Julie, once. I cringed, recalling what I'd said. Why had I done that? Monica had never treated me badly, but based on her provocative, highly styled and flirtatious mien, I'd labeled her a man-trolling bimbo. I'd been Miss Judgy Judgmental. My inner voice and I needed to have a long talk about this, I decided. Apparently, I had some hangups about sex. *Hell*, I could chalk up half of my reaction to green-eyed jealousy and the other half to being self-conscious about my lack of experience. And the combination, it seemed, had turned me into a self-righteous snob.

"At that point, you'd known him how long?"

Tíereachán's question jolted me back into the here and now, as did his frown.

"Look," I said, exasperated. "Do we need to have this conversation *now*? The night's not getting any younger and the draíoclochs are waiting."

"I spoke with Michael while you were asleep in the car. Kim will not come for them tonight. They are safe for many hours yet. We can spare the time to ... educate you."

"I think you're confusing education with titillation."

Tíereachán's eyes narrowed. "If you believe I enjoy hearing of Kieran's exploits, especially with regard to you, you are mistaken."

Okay. That was one comment I did not want to touch.

I pursed my lips and then blew out a disgruntled sigh when I realized he wasn't going to back off. I sounded like a grumpy schoolmarm, but damned if I could help it. "Not quite three days," I bit out, jutting out my chin, daring him to criticize.

"Based on past experience, would you say this is typical behavior for you?" he asked.

"Sex with men? Yep. I'm not into women," I replied breezily. "Although, I did kiss a girl once, in ninth grade. You want to hear about that too?"

The pointed look he gave me said he wasn't fooled by my deflection. Surely, my jutted chin and narrowed eyes had nothing to do with it.

Sighing, he stepped closer, almost near enough to touch me. "Lire, there is no right or wrong in this, no judgment to make or receive. Sidhe hold a different view of what constitutes acceptable social behavior, one that isn't biased toward a particular gender, orientation, race, or, even to some extent, species." He shook his head chidingly. "The proclivity for guilt in pursuit of pleasure between consenting adults is a human inclination, one I've never understood, frankly." He leaned in, saying quietly, "I realize this is a sensitive subject. I wouldn't ask you this question if it weren't important. Is it your habit to share such favors with someone you've known for a matter of a few days?"

Despite his reassuring words, I took a step back. "No. It's not my *habit*. Hard to have a habit when you've got little or no experience with something. Most guys run in the other direction as soon as they see the gloves." I raised my hands and wiggled my fingers. "And the ones who don't … they're just out for the novelty. A night of freaky psychic sex. The bragging rights to tell all their friends about how they lived on the weird side, banging a clairvoyant." Disgusted, I blew out a loud breath. "With Kieran, for once, it wasn't about that. It was about me. He wanted *me* and the gloves didn't matter." On the last, my voice splintered, but I bit my cheek and embraced my anger before any further hint of emotion seeped out against my will.

His expression softened, but the last thing I wanted to see on his face was sympathy.

"Don't," I growled. "I don't need your *pity*. Tell me why my screwed up sex life is so damned important to you."

He eyed me, his expression returning to his more neutral, superior slant, and then stepped back. "Sidhe rarely share their magic with anyone other than their mate, and, if they do, it's reserved for immediate family members, specifically their children. *This* for good reason, because without the intimacy of the soul connection, the recipient is blind and open to any offensive magic that might be used against them by the donor. Curses or enchantments that you might have otherwise detected and countered can ensnare you without your knowledge. The fact that Kieran lent you his power is troubling enough. That he did so without warning you of the risks is both unscrupulous and abhorrent, and it prompts us to question his motives."

He folded his arms. "The timing of your seduction is troubling. The part-blood Vince was, if not your lover, at least a man you cared for. When you thought me a demon, you sought my help to get him back from Maeve, in spite of the danger inherent in such dealings. Yet, after Kieran lent you his power, you cast that relationship with Vince aside, almost without second thought."

"That's not true! I ... he ..." I blinked, aghast. "Vince chose Maeve over me. He bound himself to her. Kim confirmed it. Vince didn't want me. He ..." I shook my head. "Kim said he wouldn't want to leave the Otherworld, even if I'd found a way to get there. Because of his sidhe-blood, Maeve would open up things for him that I never could."

"She used her glamour and abducted him. *Maeve*—a more than three thousand year old sidhe with questionable motives." Tíereachán paused to gaze at me pointedly, the atmosphere rife with the dismal truth. "The choice may have been his to accept her bond, but he didn't stand a chance."

I stared at him, horrified. He was right. I'd abandoned Vince. I'd let my feelings of rejection rule me and left him to his just desserts.

Shame, as pernicious and insidious as a foreign parasite, wormed through me, stoking my guilt until I could barely tolerate myself. Trembling, I pressed my palms to my burning eyes and turned away. "God ... you're right. I deserted him there. He ... he ... probably needed help ... and I turned my back on him." I dropped my arms to my sides and clenched my fists. "What the hell was I thinking!"

"For fuck's sake," Fisk snapped. "Even when he takes the time to educate you, you're still clueless. Weren't you listening? Kieran enthralled you."

I laughed, and the ugly sound grated even my ears as I whirled around to face him. "You got that right, but Kieran didn't need magic to do *that*. Ten years without intimacy was more than enough."

"Doubtful," Fisk scoffed. "Your past history amply demonstrates that you're protective to the point of lunacy."

"My past? You've been keeping tabs on me?"

He shrugged. "What interests King Faonaín interests my lady. Not that it matters. Knowing you, you won't be satisfied without definitive proof of the Deceiver's meddling. Lucky for us, that's easy enough to supply."

I frowned at him, wondering why he'd become Mr. Helpful. What did he have to gain by proving or disproving that Kieran had enchanted me? I already looked the fool, no matter which way things turned out. Either I was a naif who'd fallen for a con artist, or a touch-deprived sex fiend too obsessed with her new bedfellow to spare a thought for a friend in need. Honestly, both scenarios were so repugnant, so altogether painful, I wanted to ignore the whole miserable business. Go home. Become a recluse.

But I knew I couldn't bail out. Not for anything. Julie and Steven and the rest of their party guests were in grave danger. I had to save them, neutralize Lorcán, and ensure Vince had the chance to come home. But to do those things, I needed to pull myself together.

Priority one: *Steal the draíoclochs.*

No problem. Half-way there.

Priority two: *Go to the amhaín and learn how to harness my adept abilities in less than three days.*

Was this remotely possible? No clue, which is why I had to get my hands on one of those *draíoclochs*. My new motto was 'hope for the best, plan for the worst.'

Speaking of worst ...

Priority three: *Break Maeve out of the king's prison before dawn on Wednesday.*

Just the thought of helping that treacherous excuse for a sidhe made my skin crawl, but unless I found another more palatable and foolproof way to deal with Lorcán's threat, there wouldn't be a choice.

But I'd figure that part out later. Right now, I had to be sure I could follow through without interference, not from Kieran, not from anyone.

SIX

I was anxious to get going, but if Kieran had snared me with magic, if something lurked inside of me, just waiting to control my actions … there was no question—I wanted it neutralized immediately. Besides, Tíereachán and Fisk thought the whole reason for stealing the draíoclochs was to prevent King Faonaín from sending the Hunt after us when I rescued Kieran. They had no idea that I wanted one of those *draíoclochs* for myself. Although, I'd be lying if I said that I didn't want to at least speak with Kieran—to confront him. And I couldn't do that if I went weak at the knees at his command.

Straightening, I swallowed hard and glared at Fisk. "Fine. You said the proof of this enthrallment is easy to get. How do we go about it?"

Fisk's eyebrows went up and he glanced at Tíereachán.

His prince scowled back at him. "Easy enough, perhaps. Convenient … no."

"What's that supposed to mean?" I smothered the urge to tap my foot.

"There are those who can sense the aftereffects of even the most subtle of enchantments—an *animtùr*, some healers. But Fisk and I are neither."

"What's an *animtùr*?"

"Aura reader," Fisk supplied dismissively. He turned back to Tíereachán. "Wade."

Tíereachán thought about it, eying me. "Possibly. But not all healers are so nuanced. And even he is several hours away."

Apparently Wade was a healer. Interesting.

"*You* could," Fisk said scathingly. "If she'd— "

"No."

The sharpness of his response left little room for argument, but unsurprisingly, Fisk ignored it. "You know damn well, without proof, she'll insist on continuing this ridiculous charade. She'll want to see him." Fisk scowled in my direction and added, "No doubt to *rescue* him."

"He isn't completely wrong," I admitted, drawing another surprised glance from Fisk. "If Kieran did this ... if he enchanted me, I have to know. Not just because it affects my decision of whether or not to speak with him, but because, if he didn't do it ... it means ..."

That I'm shallow and weak-minded.

It meant I'd been too consumed by my lust for Kieran to be concerned about Vince. Or, worse, that I was I so petty I'd deliberately left Vince in Maeve's despicable hands as punishment for rejecting me.

These were things I could hardly find the courage to consider, much less voice. But I knew that if I didn't learn the truth, the doubt would eat away at me. I'd end up spending half my time questioning my motives, not to mention the motives of anyone who might express an interest in me. Anyway, we had hours yet before the telepaths' alarm clocks went off, and thanks to the weekend, most would be sleeping in.

"For my own sake, I have to know." I narrowed my gaze at Tíereachán. "What did Fisk mean? You could do it if I did ... what?"

"It's irrelevant," he replied, his voice as firmly set as his jaw.

"Obviously it isn't. But why hide it from me?" Suddenly nervous, I asked, "Will it hurt or something?"

As the silence grew, I examined him. He stared at me before shooting Fisk a silent *shut-the-fuck-up* directive that I wanted to smack off his face with the flat of my hand.

"Oh, *hell* no," I blurted. "You're not going to pull that silent crap on me. That's something Kieran would do, the whole lying by omission bullshit, and I'm sick of it." I stalked closer, until I was a foot away, staring at him brazenly. "Tell me. What do I have to do so we can figure this out?"

Maybe it was the Kieran comparison that did it. Tíereachán's eyes flashed defiantly. "Accept my blood. Strengthen our connection."

I blinked.

Okay ... I'll admit, I wasn't expecting that.

His expression turned scornful. "*Exactly*," he said, as though I'd announced to God and everyone that there was no way in hell I'd ever consider doing such a loathsome thing.

Except, I didn't think being tied to him would be loathsome. That wasn't it at all. For some reason, the thought of getting closer to him scared the bejeezus out of me. Precisely *why* the idea made me so uncomfortable, I couldn't say. Heck, I was already bound by a blood covenant to my building's house djinn. So what was the deal with Tíereachán? I knew he'd never hurt me and I knew he was honorable, but thinking about a formal blood connection made something inside me clench so tightly, I found it difficult to breathe. I wanted to explain it, but what was I supposed to say when I didn't understand my own feelings? They didn't make any damned sense.

I considered his flinty narrowed eyes. My reluctance to strengthen the bond between us had told him, *you're not worthy of my trust*. And, in spite of his brash demeanor, that had bothered him. Maybe even hurt him. Here was a man, a sidhe, who had never lied to me, who'd gone out his way to educate me, who'd risked unthinkable horrors to provide me with the clues I needed to fight his master, Azazel. Just hours ago, he had rescued me from a room full of über-vampires. Yet, repeatedly, I'd returned his kindness and courage with distrust.

"You've never lied to me. Not once," I said. "You've risked your life to save mine. Twice."

I frowned. "And ... I can't believe ..." I drew in a shaking breath, almost too stunned to speak. "Oh my God. What the hell is wrong with me? You've done so much, you saved my life ... and I ... I never said thank you." I shook my head, my eyes widening in slowly dawning horror. "I never even fucking said thank you!"

How could I have been so utterly self-absorbed? I don't think I'd ever felt as low as I did at that moment. I'd been wearing blinders, ones that allowed me to see Tíereachán's sex appeal, cocksure mien, and little else. I could hardly believe I'd been so callous. It was as if, for the past three weeks, I'd been walking around as a different person. And she was a self-centered brat who I didn't like one bit.

"I'm sorry," I choked out.

"You have nothing to be sorry about," he said fiercely. "I allowed pride— " He clenched his jaw before he released his breath in an angry huff. "If I hadn't kept my distance, I'd have noticed the signs sooner. I'm the one who should— "

"Don't," I burst out. "Don't even think about being sorry. Because you don't even *know*, okay? All of this could be me, not Kieran at all. Just *me*!"

He clipped out something in Silven, but I had the sense that, although he held my gaze, he wasn't directing the words at me but at himself. Fisk's incomprehensible reply sounded similarly aggravated, even though it was pretty clear Tíereachán hadn't addressed him either. Fisk was just piling on.

After a moment, Tíereachán seemed to remember himself, shaking his head and relaxing the set of his shoulders. "It's not you, Lire. You've been deceived. I'll prove it, if you can find it in you to trust me." In a blink, his magic sword appeared in his right hand and he sliced across the heel of his left. Blood welled in the narrow wound. "Remove your glove."

"You'd strengthen our tie?" I asked, astonished. "Even if it's not what you think? You'll be stuck with a shallow, clueless, fu— "

"Stop," he said. "Give me your hand."

Hesitantly, I removed my glove and extended my left hand, which, despite my trembling, he cut as efficiently as he'd sliced his own. I gasped at the bite of pain, but I could see that the wound was marginally worse than a paper cut. What was it about shallow cuts that made them so painful?

His sword disappeared, and he clasped my hand in his, our wounds together, mingling our blood. "Lire Devon, I offer you the gift of my blood as proof of my solemn and enduring promise. I will now and in the future dedicate myself to the protection of your well-being. I will cause you harm neither by action, nor inaction, nor deceit. I will defend your person with all I possess or I will die in the trying. This I bestow freely, without coercion, demanding nothing in return, save your blood equally shared. Do you endorse this oath, which is gladly given in the spirit of lasting friendship? Speak thrice your consent and it will be so binding for as long as we both shall live."

I swallowed. "Whoa."

"Is that a yes?" He stared down at me with a small, amused smile that, for a scant second, eased his grave expression.

My heart thundered as I considered his promise. Everything in me said to back away. I shivered enough to make my teeth chatter and my stomach seized so acutely, I pressed my free hand against my abdomen for relief. But there was nothing nefarious in anything he'd said. I'd paid close attention. It was an oath of protection and a promise to do no harm. And, curiously, with the way he'd worded it, accepting his blood didn't even obligate me to that same oath, which struck me as unfair. Although, in truth, I didn't need to be compelled by blood oath to protect him. As Fisk had already pointed out, I defended what was mine—

friends, family, whatever—sometimes (okay, most of the time) without thought for my own safety.

Gritting my teeth to keep them from banging together, I glanced at Fisk, who gaped at our bloody, joined hands. I wasn't the only one who'd been surprised by Tíereachán's bold move. Fisk had been the one to suggest the idea, but now that I considered his growing frown, I wondered whether he hadn't expected his prince to go for it. Or, maybe, it was my compliance that troubled him. Maybe Fisk had suggested strengthening our bond because he assumed I'd spurn Tíereachán's offer once again. Was that his game? Was he trying to drive a lasting wedge between his prince and me?

Fisk became aware of my scrutiny and his eyes narrowed. Any second now, he'd say something scathing about being blood-bound to a human. But he remained silent, his expression growing more angry by the second.

And then I realized it wasn't the blood oath that drew his ire, it was my lengthening hesitation. He thought I'd gotten cold feet.

Despite Tíereachán's years of enslavement to Azazel, Fisk was ready to defend his prince. He was loyal, something that surprised me, given his argumentative attitude and perpetual sour mood. Maybe Tíereachán would be accepted by his mother's people after all. The thought filled me with hope.

Even though I disliked him, knowing that Fisk endorsed Tíereachán's offer made me feel better about accepting it. In the face of his malevolent glare, I couldn't help but smile.

When I turned back to Tíereachán, my delight floundered at his grim countenance. I tweaked his hand, which had grown notably slack within my grasp, and shook my head. "So ready to assume the worst?" I chided. "I guess I can't blame you."

I tightened my grip, the answering sting of my wound a physical reminder of our purpose, and ignored the surge of unease that washed through me. "Yes, Tíereachán, that's a yes," I said, replying to his earlier question. "More than a yes, because, along with my blood, I make you the same promise, even though it's something I would have done anyway. From here on out, I promise to protect your well-being and cause you no harm, either by action, inaction, or deceit. I will defend you with all of my skills or die trying because you are my friend and my life wouldn't be nearly as entertaining without you in it. But don't take that to mean I won't kick your ass if you do something stupid." I shot him a disapproving glare.

He snorted. "Very well," he replied. "I acquiesce, now twice spoken. How say you?"

"Twice now, I accept."

"And thrice, do I. How say you?"

"Thrice, I accept."

No sooner had the final word left my lips than a tremor of magic coursed through me, distinct and resonant, reverberating deep in my bones, as though I stood atop a train tunnel at arrival time. When the momentary feeling passed, I stared at him anxiously, waiting for him to do ... *something*. Whatever it was that would prove beyond a doubt that Kieran had or hadn't used magic on me.

After several seconds of feeling nothing untoward, I frowned up at him. "So, uh ... what now?"

His grip loosened but he didn't release my hand. He turned it palm up, raised it to his mouth, and, without preamble, licked a long, languid stripe along the line of my wound. The combination of the crisp, stinging pain, along with his direct stare and the feel of his flexing tongue as it slid over my skin coiled things low in my body, driving a gasp from my throat and a spike of alarm straight through to my toenails.

When he'd placed our palms together to mingle our blood, I figured it would be enough to inaugurate our oath.

Apparently not.

I yanked my hand but he held it firm as he tsked at me. "Calm down. I won't bite ..." He smirked. "Unless asked." He arched a single, supercilious brow and offered me his own bloody hand. "The moment of truth, my dear."

My already queasy stomach lurched and my gaze jumped from his bloody hand to meet his half-lidded eyes.

The oath was one thing, but now, I had to ... lick him? *Taste him?*

Oh, no. No, no, no. Not happening.

And not simply because it was way too intimate and therefore scared the crap out of me, okay? There had to be *ample* reasons to refuse ... if I could come up with any.

Or, even, *one*.

The recent hepatitis C outbreak sprang to mind, but thankfully, rational thought kicked in before I made an ass of myself mentioning it.

Sidhe lived long for a reason. Not only were their bodies impervious to the ravages of advancing age but they were also immune to human disease. And, according to Kieran, there were very few sidhe illnesses. Even the effects of poisons tended to be short lived.

"It's rather ... *earthy* this way, I know," Tíereachán said, dryly, "but I seem to be fresh out of chalices at the moment."

Was he trying to put me at ease? If he'd hoped to lighten the mood, it hadn't worked. It jerked me right back to the issue at hand, which, incidentally, awaited half-a-dozen inches from my chin, bloody and unwavering at the end of his extended arm.

Or was his sarcasm due to my hesitation and anxious expression? Since he'd once again donned his cocky, self-assured persona, it was difficult to tell.

Not that it mattered. I couldn't help the way I felt. Just the thought of drinking someone's blood from a cup was enough to make me squeamish; licking it directly from the source was a whole different kettle of fish—particularly when that kettle looked like Tíereachán. Because, let's be honest, it wasn't the blood that was the problem here.

Jesus. Only you would get worked up over licking a guy's palm during a blood ritual.

It's his hand, not his dick, scaredy pants. Shut up and do it!

My hand trembled as I grasped his outstretched fingers, reluctantly pulling his open hand toward me. Smeared blood coated his taut skin. It had pooled along the length of the shallow wound and settled darkly into the creases that intersected the center of his palm. Now that the lines stood out so starkly, it was clear that the pattern wasn't quite human. Different, yet so similar, I mused, which rekindled my theory that the sidhe occupied a branch somewhere on the human evolutionary tree. For weeks now, I longed to broach the subject, but I knew better. Anything that hinted at likening the sidhe to Neanderthals would never be a welcome discussion. But with such intimate access, I couldn't stop myself from wondering whether our two species weren't as genetically different as the sidhe wanted us to believe. How else could we interbreed?

Okay, maybe not the best time to be thinking about breeding.

Focus, Lire.

I shook myself. After a quavery breath, I lowered my head, touched the tip of my tongue to his wound, and gave it a tiny, tentative swipe.

When the nip of salt and metal invaded my mouth, completing the circuit, magic exploded through me. Potent and electrifying, its addictive power filled my core to overflowing, prompting the sharp taste of electricity to mix with the copper already on my tongue. The pungent tang of ozone stung my sinuses as though I'd pressed my nose to the inside of a copy machine. Before I could sneeze, a riot of conflicting emotions assailed me—elation and regret; confidence and jealousy; satisfaction and frustration; joy and self-loathing and ... anger.

This was him. All him. This whole time I thought he was so self-assured, so cocky and emotionally untouchable. But he wasn't! What kind of friend was I to not notice?

I looked up from Tíereachán's hand, the taste of his blood still lingering on my tongue. As soon as my eyes locked on his, desire slammed through me, a solid, scalding surge that swooped low, catching my breath. Briefly, it overshadowed everything, until, just as I managed a single, hard-fought gasp, he withdrew his hand from mine. All at once, the stifling burden of his emotions vanished, and I wheeled backward as though he'd dropped the rope during a exuberant game of tug of war.

I tripped over my feet and might have fallen on my butt if Tíereachán hadn't darted in to catch me by my elbow. Wide eyed and breathing hard, I stared up at him.

Holy cow.

I blinked stupidly while I puzzled over what had happened.

Tíereachán was attracted to me? He wanted me? Judging by his emotions (and those were unquestionably *his* emotions I'd felt pouring through me), it sure seemed that way. Certainly, his desire had been unmistakable. The revelation was so startling I didn't know what to do with it.

This whole time, I'd dismissed his licentious flirting. We were friends. He felt indebted to me for freeing him from Azazel. But the whole flirtation thing wasn't serious. He didn't really want me.

Except ... apparently, he did.

I didn't get it. I mean, why me? It wasn't as if anyone would mistake me for a goddess. I was a freckle-nosed reluctantly-athletic redhead with a face that hadn't launched any ships that I knew of. Girl-next-door material, perhaps, but certainly not a supermodel contender. Honestly, if Tíereachán had confessed his attraction to me before I'd experienced the proof of it, I would have assumed he had some ulterior motive. It's not that I thought I was an ugly duckling. I didn't. Well, not much. Tíereachán was just *that* eye-catching. His body was exquisite to behold. Mine was ... above average. He was indisputably gorgeous. With some effort, I might qualify for pretty. He was, without question, sex on a stick. I, on the other hand, had endured more solitary Friday nights over the last ten years than a cloistered octogenarian nun.

Anyone with eyeballs could see this was a bad joke. Tíereachán was so patently out of my league it wasn't even funny.

I frowned. But ... that, right there, was hinky. Wasn't it? Because Kieran was almost as good looking as Tíereachán and yet, when Kieran made his pass at me, I hadn't discounted him as readily as Tíereachán. What's more, all along, I knew that Kieran's motives weren't entirely pure— even if I hadn't anticipated the extent of his duplicity. Yet I'd thrown myself into his arms and hardly thought twice about it. And now confronted with mounting evidence that Kieran had actively and deliberately deceived me, I *still* persisted in mistrusting Tíereachán.

Why was that?

"Because you've been transfixed," he replied.

I jumped at his unsolicited answer and then bristled. "I thought you said you couldn't read my mind."

"That was before you accepted my blood." Inside my head, he added, *Our binding is whole and you're not shielding yourself.* He smiled and, this time, it went all the way to his eyes, crinkling the delicate skin at their outer corners. *Not that I mind. Hearing your unguarded thoughts has been enlightening and ... motivating.* He grinned, raising a devilish eyebrow. *Sex on a stick, am I? Here I thought I disgusted you. Who knew your disapproving frown hid such extraordinary revelations?* His expression sobered. *Although you plainly have no idea how captivating you are. I believe I'll enjoy convincing you otherwise.*

My stomach clenched and rolled as though I'd bungee jumped off the Royal Gorge Bridge. *Crap on toast!* He'd heard every damned word? Every ridiculous stray thought since I'd licked his palm? God! No doubt he knew how much his tongue affected me, too. *Please, just kill me now.*

His chuckle reverberated inside my mind. *I'd rather not.*

I cursed my brain. *Jesus F. Christ. I have thought diarrhea.*

As Tíereachán burst out with a peal of the most deliciously musical, full-bellied laughter I'd ever heard, I uttered a strangled sound of frustration and fortified my psychic shield, which I'd inadvertently dropped during the intensity of our ritual.

Shoving my hair behind my ears, I attempted to patch up my shredded composure, a hopeless task with seconds instead of years at my disposal. And Tíereachán's continued mirth didn't help.

I squared my shoulders and reluctantly met Tíereachán's amused gaze. Finally, his earlier response penetrated my befuddled state. "Did you say I've been ... spelled?" I examined him. "You could tell?"

His smile dwindled. "Not ensorcelled. *Transfixed.* It's an encapsulated form of glamour. Not easy to detect unless you know what to look for."

Again, the impulse to run away surged through me, enough that I wavered on my feet. I squeezed my hands into fists, and the answering pain from my cut helped to ground me. "What does it do?"

He angled his head, side to side, ever so slightly. "It's similar to an attraction charm. A compulsion used to keep the quarry focused on their pursuant and to discourage them from finding others attractive or diverting." He gazed at me significantly. "It's particularly effective on a subject who already finds their stalker physically attractive and can be used to sway their actions."

Sway my actions? I grimaced at the words.

Earlier, I'd tried to imagine how I'd feel to hear that Kieran had done this, that he'd truly laid magic on me to make me do something I might not have done otherwise. I figured I'd be angry. Hurt and humiliated. Maybe it was denial, but now that I knew, all I felt was uncertain and ... detached. I realized this must be how someone might feel after being told a telepath had altered their memories. With no demonstrable proof, it was hard to believe. It didn't seem real or even possible.

"I thought— " I caught myself before saying something that implied I doubted his word. I didn't, not precisely, but I needed more. "I don't feel anything," I said. "I thought strengthening our bond would, I don't know, make it plain for me to see what Kieran did."

Fisk said something in Silven to which Tíereachán nodded without taking his eyes from mine and then replied, "The effects are subtle and you don't know what to look for. Now that we're bound, I can show you ... if you want."

"Anything I need to know about ... doing this? Are there dangers? Side effects?" I hated that I was compelled to voice the questions, but Kieran had now ruined me for assuming that people I cared about had my best interests at heart.

"If we weren't blood-bound, then, yes, there would be. Finding and countering the compulsion requires that you open yourself to me and accept my power and my presence in your mind. If we weren't bound and I was a *dishonorable cur*, it would be possible for me to do precisely what Kieran's done, or worse."

"Oh." Even though the censure wasn't undeserved, I found it difficult not to cringe at his reproach for Kieran. I wasn't sure whether this was because, in spite of everything, I still cared for Kieran, or because I felt like the biggest fool this side of the International Date Line. "Why does being bound make a difference?"

"Because I'll be just as open and vulnerable as you are," he replied. "It will be impossible for me to hide my intentions and, because you've had my blood, you'll have more power to shut me out."

When I looked at Fisk, he returned my gaze with a superior slant and folded his arms, clearly growing impatient.

I gave Tíereachán a go-ahead nod, and he drew closer to once again take my ungloved hand. He grasped it lightly to avoid aggravating my cut, which had clotted but still looked slightly wet.

"Open to me, Lire. I'll not hurt you. You have my word."

I couldn't help but think Kieran had once said the same thing, but I shoved the bitter thought from my mind and dropped my shield. All at once, Tíereachán's thoughts and emotions crowded me from all sides, and I fought to keep my own from spiraling out of control in response. It occurred to me, stupidly late, that with him inside my head like this, anything I remembered or thought would be open for his perusal. He'd see and feel everything that came to my mind!

I lost myself in a wave of panic, wheeling from one private, distressing memory to another. I was an open book, one that continually flipped to a random page, revealing a new, embarrassing secret with the speed and impetus of a stray thought. The more I fought to keep them hidden, the faster they seemed to come—my mother's horror when she discovered the proof of my clairvoyance; Daniel kissing me under the stairwell behind the school library in eighth grade; coming one shaky step from committing suicide at thirteen; Glen saying he was sick of wearing a whole body condom just to have sex with me; the wet, squishy sounds of Glen getting his throat ripped out; the sickening splat of blood hitting me as Paimon ripped strips of skin from the Circle Murderer's limp body; Maeve disappearing with Vince; Kieran, naked, pushing me onto my bed. It was enough to make me want to scream or run or both until Tíereachán took my face between his warm hands, pressed his forehead against mine, and calmly shushed me.

Easy, he thought and pushed the memory of us standing on Glacier Point into my mind, unabashedly sharing everything—his guilt over telling Fisk to put me to sleep, his fury at not noticing Kieran's deceit sooner, and his unconditional affection for me even as I scolded him and threatened to push him over the cliff's edge.

His thumbs caressed tiny circles over my cheek bones, and he stared unflinchingly into my eyes. *Listen to me. There is nothing you can think, remember, say, or do that will convince me that you are anything but the most loyal, caring, generous individual I have ever met. After living the past thousand years under Azazel's cruel thumb, do you honestly believe I'd be offended by even your worst, most uncharitable thoughts? Do you think you could drive me away? Or that anything in that beautiful head of yours will cause me to think less of you?*

He shook his head, rolling his forehead against mine. *You peered into the depths of my soul and yet you didn't run from me. You saw me for who and what I am, in spite of the horrors I've experienced and the terrors I've inflicted on others. If anyone should be afraid of being abhorred, it's me.*

I rolled my eyes. *You make me sound like some kind of saint. You were under Azazel's rule and subject to the command of whoever summoned you. You had no choice but to do their bidding. That wasn't hard to see.*

Yet no one in over a thousand years bothered to look, he thought.

I pulled away, so our foreheads were no longer touching. *It's not like I had much choice in the matter,* I told him. *I touched your essence out of desperation. You tried to drag me to Hell.*

I knew you'd escape me, but I couldn't help myself. There's something magnetic about you, Lire, which you don't seem to appreciate. Even under my demonic guise, I felt its pull. Yet now that I'm free, I wouldn't see you caged by anyone, least of all by me. Which is why, earlier, I didn't ask more of you than you were prepared to give. You can shut me out at any time. But, if you don't, you'll finally feel the truth of my words and know in your heart that I do not deceive.

There it was. The elephant that had been riding shotgun ever since Tíereachán began speaking to me in my dreams—the truth that I'd never trusted him, not fully, even after I'd freed him from Azazel's grasp.

Shame hung heavy in my chest, poisonous and thick, but before I could formulate my apology, Tíereachán pushed another memory at me. This one was of him in his demon guise, cutting my hand to bind me to a one-sided blood pact. His own guilt suffused my own and I gasped, trying to breathe past it. But instead of stifling and overwhelming me, seeing the event through his eyes and feeling his wretchedness as he brutalized me softened the edges of that horrible memory. It mitigated the terror and eased the racing of my heart that normally accompanied it.

Both of us were victims; I just hadn't known it at the time.

As I stared into those shockingly blue eyes, my pulse shot into overdrive. What was I thinking standing this close to him and holding his hand? *Bad, bad idea.* Tíereachán would read more into things than I wanted. We were friends. Nothing more. In fact, even the act of *considering* something more saddled me with that panicked, deer-in-the-headlights feeling in the pit of my stomach. Sweat sprang out on my forehead and back of my neck. I had to get away from him, post haste. What if he—

I stopped short. *Oh, God!* With him inside my head, he knew what I was thinking and feeling. I was such a dope!

I aimed to jerk away, intending to shut him out, but Tíereachán's power spiked through me, halting my spiraling thoughts and momentarily stealing my breath. Stunned, I gaped, trying to form words, but nothing came out.

Holy cow. That had felt freaking ... nice.

"Did you ..." My voice dwindled and I blinked up at him. *Share power with me?*

He tipped his head in affirmation and then squeezed my hand, which he'd managed to keep a hold of, despite my earlier efforts to yank it away. *Lire, you have nothing to fear from me. Look inside yourself, to your center. It's there. Can you not feel it?*

I stilled. For once, there was no second guessing him. No reason to doubt his words or his care for my well-being. Because of our connection, I knew precisely how he felt—outraged, angry, regretful, impatient, frustrated, and intensely protective. His emotions churned inside my mind, but as he'd promised, his feelings revealed the truth behind his words and actions. Which was why his power infusion had felt so good—it had been accompanied by his clear respect and concern for me.

After gawking at him for longer than was polite, I succumbed to his gentle urging. I pulled my focus away from his presence and turned my gaze inward, toward the wellspring of my power. In my mind's eye, it shined brilliant with a comforting warmth, as tempting as a patch of sunlight on a frigid afternoon.

Intrigued and bolstered by Tíereachán's confidence, I waded into my power's nebulous heat, allowing the familiar pulsing of my energy to surround me. It was a heady feeling, knowing that I could wield such power, one I'd not experienced when I'd simply been a clairvoyant.

As I expanded my awareness, I realized that there was no way Tíereachán could enter my mind or seek my power by stealth. Even now, I felt his presence at the fringe of my consciousness. His power, his magic, even his thoughts, vibrated in a distinct way that was very different from my own. In fact, now that I considered it, I realized his power resonated in time with his essence. Somehow, I'd missed noticing this. And, now that I was paying attention ... another discordance, deep within my core, became noticeable, one that didn't match Tíereachán's resonance, nor my own. The variance stood out, like a black ribbon in a maypole dance, but instead of driving me to pluck it away, its familiar tune drew me closer.

This was no trespasser. Its song suffused me. So dear ... so comforting. The urge to protect it overwhelmed me. It was a treasure. Helpless. I should keep it safe. Cherish it. Tuck it away and never let it go.

In fact ... what had I been thinking? Why had I opened myself to anyone else? Tíereachán was the outsider here. He was the one that didn't belong!

Push him out. Push him out before it's too late!

I gasped as Tíereachán pulsed his power into me, once again disrupting my panicked thoughts.

"Oh, God." I groaned once I'd come back to myself. "You were right. I can tell ... it's his magic." I stared at him. "This feeling ... I know it. It's been there this whole time."

I blinked, remembering, and gasped. "I wanted to stay. Before the party, I told him I didn't want to go to the Otherworld. I couldn't leave my friends and family unprotected. But Kieran ... he touched me and I ... felt this wonderful warmth radiate through me—*his* warmth. And I ... I changed my mind." I pressed my free hand to my abdomen, remembering where I'd sensed it, remembering how good it felt.

I rocked back on my heels, shaking my head. "How do I get rid of it? It's ... I can't— "

"Relax," he said, pulling my hand to keep me from spinning out of his reach. Although where I thought I'd go, I had no idea. He leaned close to peer into my eyes. "More than half the battle is seeing the transfixing for what it is. You must pierce it with your power. Take it for your own and pull it apart."

"No!" I took a breath in a useless bid to calm down. "I can't. That would be like ... like mutilating a puppy!"

"*That* is no puppy," Tíereachán countered. "It is a malevolence, planted inside of you to control your behavior."

I started to shake my head, but one look at Fisk's disapproving sneer stopped me cold. Face heating, I gritted my teeth and stood firm. *Son of a bitch.* I was acting spineless. Time to get a grip.

"Fine," I ground out. I could do this. I'd yank it out fast, like ripping off a bandage.

I closed my eyes and pushed my inner vision toward my center.

It's magic, I told myself. *Controlling magic. It's not something precious.*

But my instincts all screamed otherwise. Soft. Fragile. It should be protected, just like Kieran. He was flawed, damaged by years of being told he wasn't worthy of respect and that he'd never be anything but a deceiver. But that wasn't all there was to him! There was goodness in him. I'd seen it.

I enfolded the pulsing swirl of Kieran's magic within my power. I cradled and cuddled it, allowing its resonance to pulse through me. I smiled, my heart swelling. So beautiful, like the man. And ... *God.* It felt right having a little piece of him so close to me. It felt good. So very, very good.

I practically purred until a growing sense of unease crept through me.

This ... it was too good ... too precious.

My smile faded. *Christ.* Any minute I'd be groveling and muttering like Gollum.

I opened my eyes. Trembling, I extracted the precious bundle from the safety of my center, tugging until it manifested above my upturned palm. About the size of a marble, the near-translucent mass of energy pulsed with a sallow glow. Such a small thing and, yet ... it changed everything.

How could Kieran do this to me? I didn't understand it. Because, it wasn't as if I hadn't found him attractive from the beginning. My furtive, glassy-eyed looks and dazed stammering were too obvious to have been missed, especially by a twenty-seven-hundred-year-old experienced Lothario.

"Bastard!" I focused my fire on the sphere. For half a tick, it flared phosphorescent and then faded to leave my hand empty, which felt entirely unsatisfying. A mushroom cloud and a black, smoldering husk would have been preferable.

I cursed. The sidhe were nothing but trouble. And, now, I'd tied myself to another one. Was that a mistake too?

Brooding, I retrieved my glove and pulled it over my wounded hand. At least Tíereachán and I weren't soulbound. Our connection was more akin to what I shared with the djinn. Besides, if not for his help, I wouldn't have discovered that my will had been circumvented.

Without a word to the two men, I thrust my telekinetic fingers into the material plane and whisked us to the telepath's building, feeling the way by fingering the sidewalk ahead of us. Absurdly, I thought of Thing, the disembodied hand from *The Addams Family*.

Terrific. Now, whenever I visualized my magic crawling through the material plane while I stayed in the higher dimension, that's the ridiculous image I'd be seeing.

I whisked us around the corner and counted walkways until we reached the third one on the left. I didn't dare feel for the building to confirm our location, in case it triggered the ward and announce our arrival. Instead, I withdrew my magic—*Come here, Thing!*—and propelled us blindly through the twisted darkness, sloping upward by memory alone to account for the front steps. I knew we'd made it inside when the lighting went from Stygian to dim. Instead of blurred darkness, we were faced with a gloomy, kaleidoscopic view of the telepath's front entryway.

Yay me. We'd made it.

Sadly, my satisfaction didn't last long. The lump near my feet, which conspicuously resembled a dead body even when accounting for the distorted view, took care of that.

"Oh, shit."

Fisk echoed my opinion.

I glanced around us, scrutinizing every contorted shadow for hints of a higher body count.

Please, please. Just be someone passed out after a wild night of tequila shooters and synthetic pot.

"Veil us," I rasped. "I'll slide us back."

When the world rushed to meet us, all at once spinning closer, elongating, and snapping into focus, the first thing I noticed was the smell. Unfortunately, it was a combination I'd encountered one too many times—wet copper and excrement. With the dizzying shift, it was all I could do to keep from throwing up. Plugging my nose didn't help. I imagined the fumes sticking to my tongue and almost lost it.

Dammit to hell! Couldn't we catch a single effing break?

When I'd gained a modicum of self control, I reluctantly looked down. *Christ.* No need to check for a pulse. The man's throat was utterly ravaged. He was crumpled on his side, facing away from me, but I recognized him regardless. It was blond-Eric, one of the two Erics in the Seattle coterie, his preferred wakizashi still gripped in his right hand. I didn't know him well (I didn't know any of the coterie well, to be honest), but I remembered the distinctive sword.

Across the spacious foyer, another man sprawled near the stairs, his chestnut hair fanning out over the oak floor. I wondered if this was the other Eric.

Kim must have ordered both men to guard the telepaths in the off-chance Lorcán decided to pay them a visit, but even with their rigorous training and sidhe magic, the two of them had been no match for strigoi amped up on Lorcán's transfusions.

And that wasn't the sole disturbing thought.

There wasn't much in the way of spilled blood. Both men had been drained. Both of them, *part-bloods.*

"Crap," I muttered, but before I added to the sentiment, a shout followed by a pain-filled scream shocked me away from the forethought.

Was that Michael?

God, please, let him be alive!

I zipped out of Tíereachán's shroud, past the oblong table that decorated the center of the large entryway, to the stairs.

"Stop!" Tíereachán hissed.

I halted in flight, a few feet shy of the other dead part-blood, not because of his admonishment but because I had no intention of charging into a potentially explosive situation without discovering what we were up against. Firstly, where had the scream come from?

A man's shout drifted up from the basement, answering my question. I could make out just a few words, but the menacing tone was clear enough. "... open ... or ... another ... !"

As I cast out in the direction of the voices with my telekinetic fingers, a dark blur flew at me from somewhere to my right, crashing into my side with a flash of looming height, dark hair, and pale skin. We hit the floor in a jumble, the solid, hollow thump of our joint impact reverberating through the smooth wood surface, piercing the air around us, and announcing our presence louder than a DEFCON 1 alert in a nuclear bunker. Pain flared along my left side as the hit drove the wind clear out of me in a rough, involuntary whoosh.

The takedown happened so fast, I scarcely had time to gasp for breath, much less react. The alarming gleam of pointed canines, however, jerked me into action. With zero finesse, I lashed out at my attacker, clouting him with my TK, but to my shock, my magic slipped over him and barely nudged his head. Only then did I remember Jackie's comment about magic not working against Lorcán's vamps.

Distantly, I noted the mixed grunts, squeaking shoes, and the sonorous clashing of metal that told me both Tíereachán and Fisk were engaged.

I wasn't a sword fighter. I wasn't a fighter at all. I was a goddamned clairvoyant ... with extras. Magic was my solitary weapon.

Without that, I had nothing.

My attacker shifted hard, pinning my legs under his heavy thigh and keeping my hips twisted toward the floor so that my top leg curved to trap my bottom leg. Even though his thighs were parted and his groin open, I had no leverage to take advantage of the vulnerability. With my left arm numb and immobilized under our combined weight, I could do little more than flail and push at him with my right hand, but it was like trying to dislodge the mass of a house. Before I dug my thumb into his left eye socket, he snagged my wrist and pulled my hand down to cup it against the center of his chest. In another situation, it might have been the position of a dominant lover, but the way he looked at me was anything but loving.

The vamp grinned broadly. The sight of his inch-long fangs, glistening with saliva, jolted my heart like a starting gun in the 100-meter dash.

"He said you weren't to be killed or maimed," the vamp informed me, licking his lips. "But he didn't say anything about bleeding you."

When he snapped his mouth shut with a dramatic *clack*, I noticed his fangs angled neatly over his lower teeth in such a way that they didn't interfere with his lips or tongue. Interesting, but I could have done without the anatomy lesson.

He closed his eyes while drawing in a breath through his nose. "You smell like nothing I know."

When his eyes opened, they no longer appeared human. The white sclera had all but disappeared, pushed out by the expanded navy-blue of his irises. He devoured me with his hungry stare, his pupils so dilated and reflective they resembled two black-backed mirrors. *Cat's eyes*, I thought and shivered. Except this cat wanted to bite me and drink my blood.

My breath, coming in fast, heavy pants, buffeted the air between our bodies as I struggled against his masterful hold. It took everything in me to keep from escaping into the higher dimension. If I did, it would leave the vamp free to attack Fisk and Tíereachán. For their sake, I needed to keep this guy distracted.

"Delicious." He shuddered. "Your scent spikes when you're frightened. I wonder if you taste as good as you smell."

I snorted. "Keep wondering, blood breath. Let me go and maybe I'll let you live." By some miracle, my fear didn't reveal itself in my voice.

He quirked an eyebrow and barked out laughing. "Brave, too," he said and then lowered his head and practically purred next to my ear, "Fucking delicious."

I shivered as his breath flitted over the tender skin of my neck. Before I chickened out, I turned to press my cheek against his cool lips, making skin contact and breaking through his shroud. I felt his muscles tense, whether to bite or recoil, I didn't wait long enough to find out.

In less than a blink, I encompassed his body within my power and drew so hard and fast on my cryokinesis that my vision compressed to a sparkling pinprick. The nerve endings throughout my body flared white-hot, every synapse firing to produce a blistering pain so complete I thought I might die of it. I screamed, hoarse and ragged, but managed to discharge the stolen heat away from our bodies. As darkness pulled me under, I vaguely registered my assailant's muscles going hard as if to strike.

My senses returned sluggishly. The rapid pounding of footsteps vibrated through me, amplified by my body's contact with the wood floor. The footsteps faltered and a resounding "Fuck!" exploded above me. A decisive shove against my back, probably backed by a boot and a muscular thigh, jolted me forward, savagely driving my forehead against a cold, hard object. Even if I'd wanted to defend myself, I was semiconscious, my body leaden and feeling raw, as though my insides had gone ten rounds with a sandblaster. I didn't even have the energy to open my eyes, much less stiffen in anticipation of another kick.

A second, even raspier voice queried, "What the—?" but a loud grunt from across the room cut off the man's question. "Shit! Leave them," he said in a rush as their heavy footsteps moved away.

A fierce cry, followed by the increased number and rhythm of metal clangs, jolted me out of my stupor, reminding me where I was. With my psychic shield in tatters, Tíereachán's rage, frustration, and overwhelming fear that I'd been irrevocably harmed rolled through me. He was so focused on fighting his opponents, while haranguing himself and imagining all the horrors he wanted to inflict on the vampires, that he hadn't noticed I'd awoken. The vamps required all of his skill and they knew better than to allow him the opportunity to attain skin contact, using their inhuman speed to continually dance out of reach while keeping him and Fisk busy at the end of their swords. Fighting three such adversaries, even with Fisk's skilled help, pressed Tíereachán to the edge of his abilities.

He cursed. *If only ... we had Wade ... for her I'll fight ... until I can no longer ... lift my sword ... could always order Fisk ... to take her and run.*

Take me and run?

Not happening.

I'd perform a psychic reading of Ted Bundy's boxers before I allowed Fisk to steal me away and abandon Tíereachán and Michael.

When I opened my eyes, my bleary gaze settled on the prone strigoi embracing me. His inhuman eyes peered through me, distantly focused and unblinking. The coating of frost that covered his skin appeared almost indistinguishable from the paleness of his complexion, everywhere except his lower jaw and left cheek where my forehead had melted the surface ice and tinged his skin to a pale blush.

Well, at least now, I'd learned one thing firsthand: Like the sidhe, strigoi were immune to clairvoyance.

I wiggled out of his frozen hold, gasping at the searing pain that shot through my core with every move, and muttered between breaths, "If it's ... any ... consolation ... I think I hurt ... *myself* ... more than ... I hurt you."

I grunted as I slithered away from him and rolled into a pained crouch. "You're just lucky ... I didn't ... burn you. You'll be fine ... once you thaw out," I added, feeling the need to reassure him, even though I had no idea whether he could hear me with frozen eardrums. "But if it's all the same ... let's not do this again."

I removed my gloves, tossing them aside, while I evaluated the spectacle near the front door.

Tíereachán and Fisk stood side by side, magic blades in both hands, perfectly coordinated as they fenced three sure-footed, sword-wielding strigoi. It was a testament to the two sidhe's prowess and their four whirling swords that they'd managed to keep the vamps busy enough that the odd one could never circle behind them. Still, I could see the sweat pouring down their faces, and Fisk had been bloodied above his right pectoral muscle. The three strigoi, on the other hand, looked fully rested, as though they'd arrived for the fight after a solid twelve hours of sleep, healthy breakfast, and long leisurely shower.

I could see where this was headed.

Ignoring the non-stop burn inside me and the agony of my bruised shoulder, I wrapped my arms around my knees, aimed for one of the two vamps fighting Tíereachán, and, using my telekinesis, shot myself across the room. I flew six inches from the floor, tucking my chin and doing my hare-brained best to impersonate a bowling ball, while trying not to pass out. With pain erupting through my center whenever I drew power, the fetal position was about all I could manage.

As I'd envisioned, I slammed into the vamp's calves, whipping him clear off his feet. He hit the floor with a thunderous *boom*. And no wonder. The guy was built like a freaking bison, a lot of beef with that cake. I spun around and all but threw myself at the fallen man's feet as the clashing of swords echoed loud in my ears. Parked so close to the action, I relied on Tíereachán to keep the closest vamp from taking my head off with his ridiculous scimitar. Although, to be fair, he looked Egyptian. For all I knew, the sword was authentic.

I shoved my hand up the fallen strigoi's pant leg. If 'Brutus' here wore knee socks, I'd be screwed. He was already curling to sit up. No way I'd get above his knee before he kicked me in the face.

Or gutted me.

Memories from all the humans who'd touched the vamp's fashionably ripped jeans spiraled into my mind. As I staved them off with my mental shield, my fingertips found lukewarm skin. *Thank you, God, for bootcut jeans and drooping crew socks.* I immediately sucked the heat from his body, disbursing it into the nearest adjoining room.

Not wanting a repeat of my previous encounter, I paced myself, even though what I wanted to do was instantaneously freeze him to get away from the threatening guillotine above me. Twice already, I'd felt Tíereachán's alarm explode into my mind when he nearly missed deflecting a blow that had been aimed at me. If my insides hadn't felt as if they were being flayed with a blow torch at every pull of power, I might have risked siphoning energy at a faster clip or simultaneously levitating our bodies to the side, but the pain was already excruciating and I knew if I pushed any harder ...

Although, at this point, I didn't think it mattered. I was pretty sure I'd already damaged myself beyond recovery, but I shoved aside the frightening thought. Tíereachán and Fisk were here because of me. I'd do almost anything to keep them from harm.

Brutus, who'd risen to a sitting position, attempted to kick me loose, but his move turned into a slow motion parody. I followed his leg's trajectory, the action too slow to dislodge my fingers from his fast-freezing skin. His leg ground to a halt, raised and bent at the knee as though he was about to adjust his sock while half reclined. It was a ridiculous pose, and I felt bad about leaving him stuck that way, but I didn't dare stop. By the time ice crystals sprang out on his face, cementing his surprised expression, my vision had narrowed to a monochrome tunnel and my insides burned with the volcanic fury of a well-used furnace.

I withdrew my hand from his pants and somehow found the strength to scoot myself backward, collapsing when my back hit something solid behind me. My breath heaved in and out of my throat in jagged bursts, and everything around me took on the grainy appearance of an old, brittle, black and white photo, surreal and stark and threatening to disintegrate.

The overarching pain sucked away my will, and, although I fought it, the relief of oblivion was too much to resist.

I fell headlong into the dark and ... another life.

SEVEN

With a shout, I lunge into my swing, but my strike misses the mark when my opponent flees after Lorcán and his fellow confederates, who are fast escaping through the building's rear exit. I resist the impulse to pursue.

John dashes away, whether to give chase or observe their escape I don't know, but accompanying him isn't an option. All my focus is on Lire's limp form.

Fearing the worst, my heart thunders loud enough, no doubt, to be heard in the Otherworld. She's slumped against the wall, her body alarmingly slack, her head canted so far to the side it rests on her slender shoulder. Her hair is plastered to her cheek, russet tresses obscuring her face. She looks small and fragile, nothing like the bright, strong-willed woman I've come to admire. I gently tuck the smooth strands behind her ear and then check her pulse.

Alive, thank the Three Winds. *Frustration flares in my chest as I recall the agony of her overburn, the pain so debilitating I had to shut her out of my mind to avoid being skewered by my opponent. Locked in combat, I couldn't help her. Never have I been so desperate to vanquish my foes. And when she took down that mountainous vampire, right under my nose, I'd not experienced such relief followed by so much terror in ... possibly,* ever.

I cup my palm to her cheek. She's far too hot, burning, and alarm shoots through me once again. When I hear John return *from his walkabout, I shout at him, "Come! She mustn't wake before Wade can tend to her."*

He stops at my side, standing over us. "My lord, if you care about her, and I think you do ... you won't ask for this."

I tear my gaze away from Lire to scowl at the infuriating part-blood as he crouches next to me. "It isn't a request, it's a command," I tell him. "Overburn has broken men stronger than the two of us put together. I don't want her to wake to that kind of pain, and we need to leave. Quickly."

"She won't thank you for it." He grunts and looks away. "And it'll give her another reason to hate me."

I snort at that. "I thought you were too busy resenting her to care."

John's jaw tightens as his gaze snaps back to mine. "And what about the telepath, Michael? He's alive, but they fucked him up good, extracting what they wanted. The safe is open. He won't make it to Wade. I did what I could to stabilize him, but he needs healing. Now."

I stiffen. This is why I avoid involvement with humans. They're fragile and short lived and a majority of them don't know how to defend themselves. I didn't want to care about Michael, nor any of the other telepaths, but my rising guilt tells me it's a futile wish. Three weeks sharing quarters with them has seen to that.

Although, when it comes to Lire, I'd live with any amount of remorse to ensure her safety. I owe her my life.

"The draíoclochs?"

He shakes his head. "Gone."

I nod. "Call Kim, their emissary. She'll send someone to help him. Or summon an ambulance if you believe that to be the better choice."

I frown at John's disapproving expression. Iterating the reasoning behind every damned order has become tiresome. Whatever does Wade see in the man? It's not hard to imagine that his second-guessing has more to do with Azazel's taint than anything else.

I've come to the end of my patience, though, and I grit my teeth, fighting the urge to flay a matching wound on his alternate cheek. The Prince of Thìr na Soréidh will be obeyed!

"We cannot risk staying," I clip out, instead. *"Lorcán's presence means one thing: There's a high-level spy among the king's retinue. Once Lorcán's success in stealing the draíoclochs and his efforts to blackmail Lire are revealed, my uncle will realize a palace revolution is in the making. He'll order Lire's capture. Without any draíoclochs, my uncle's options are limited, but he is nothing if not cunning. Like Lorcán, he'll use any means to compel her obedience."*

"And if Lorcán and Maeve should succeed in their overthrow?" John asks. *"What then? Faonaín is, at least, bound to the Compact."*

He stands to his full height and folds his arms, his golden eyes bearing down on me. *"I've already relayed the situation to my mate. She's sought your mother's counsel and her orders in this are unequivocal: Endorse and defend her brother's continued rule. Wade is on his way. They've secured air travel and will arrive in a few hours. We've been ordered to contact Faonaín's emissary immediately."*

Bastard. *The man enjoys seeing me run free only to be cut short and whipped off my feet by the length of my chain. I've underestimated him. His soulmate must be one of my mother's handmaidens, or perhaps, even, her Vicegerent. This would explain Wade's faith in him despite his insolence.*

Jealousy and frustration rear up but I hammer the feckless emotions down. Thank the Oracle Lire accepted my covenant, and none too soon.

My mother hasn't survived in her position all these years by being short-sighted or imprudent. She serves her interests and those of her people with a keen mind, sharp wit, and undeniable allure that the longest serving and universally loved rulers seem to possess. The question is: Are those interests currently aligned to Lire's benefit? Even in my mother's domain, humans are granted about as many rights as our surface-dwelling animals, and, no doubt, a demon-tainted sidhe will be afforded fewer still, princely birthright or not.

Together, Lire and I will need to tread carefully, indeed.
Together …
Of course.
Mother must have ordered John to maneuver Lire into ac-
cepting my blood oath. A clever move, and not simply because
two heads are better than one. My royal connection will grant
Lire ambassadorial rights under our laws. At the same time,
our blood bond partly diminishes Azazel's hold over me. The
king, too, will be stymied by our bond. Lire will no longer be
defenseless against his magic and assassinating me will risk
the full weight of my mother's wrath. The only better deter-
rent would be if Lire and I were to bind our souls.

Maybe, in time—

I quash that line of thought.

Lire's feelings on that matter have been undeniably clear.
Besides, the Oracle is never wrong. If that doesn't put an end
to any thought of pursuit, I'll deserve every last torment that
comes with such foolish want.

The front door bursts open, prompting John and me to go
for our swords. When Kim, Jackie, and a contingent of Faonaí-
n's coterie, all of them armed and primed for battle, pour into
the room and then stop at the sight of us, I straighten and re-
call my weapon.

After assessing the room for possible threats, Kim issues a
curt nod to me. "Didn't expect to see you here, Tíereachán,
John." Her eyes widen at Lire's motionless form. "What hap-
pened?"

I notice she hasn't relaxed, nor has she issued a command
for her compatriots to stand down. "Overburn," I tell her. "We
arrived about twenty minutes ago and found your people"—
I gesture to the fallen warriors— "already dead. The vam-
pires attacked as soon as we broke shroud. Do you have a
healer with you? Lire's not in any distress at the moment, but
John tells me Michael is in a bad way, downstairs. Wade is on
his way, but it will be too late for Michael by the time he ar-
rives."

She eyes me before straightening and turning to the people
around her. "You three, secure the basement. Duran, Jackie,

as soon as they give you the all clear, go take care of Michael. Tina, take everyone else and secure the other floors. Check every square inch. All the crawl spaces. Every damn closet and bed. I don't want any surprises. And I want to know how the hell they got past the ward."

Her people stream by, expressions grim and intent, leaving Jackie and a svelte, blonde woman, who I assume is Duran, still standing near the front door.

Kim examines the coterie's two dead warriors, crouching down at each body in turn to mutter something and stroke their hair. When she finishes and stands, her expression is grieved. "I should have sent the entire Seattle contingent," she says, her voice hollow. "At least the telepaths had the sense to listen to Michael and flee."

"Too bad he didn't follow his own advice," John says.

"He stayed to make sure everyone got out—the telepaths, anyway." She walks to the vampire who looks as if he's been frozen while trying to climb a mountain from his back. She gives him a hard shove with her foot. "Lire's too softhearted by half. She should have burned them. Now we'll have to take their heads with a damned chainsaw or risk letting them thaw first."

"Be grateful. Her benevolence is what will save us," I reply. "Besides, one building set ablaze is enough for one night, don't you think?"

Her calculating blue eyes assess me. "Why are you here?"

"She wanted to see Michael before heading to her apartment."

The petite woman nods. "And, now that you've delivered her to us, what are your plans?" She folds her arms and examines me, sending the clear message that there's just one answer that will satisfy her.

John and I are on the verge of overstaying our welcome.

"Even if my mother hadn't ordered it, I'll remain at Lire's side," I reply, knowing that every word will be relayed to the king by her soulmate, Brassal. "I am sworn to protect Earth's first adept and, now, to ensure my uncle's continued rule."

145

If the twitch of her eyebrows is any indication, this surprises her. "Is that so?" She smiles, an insincere flash of teeth. "Please do thank your mother, but King Faonaín hardly needs such ... help, however capable. His rule is as assured and everlasting as the immortal amaranth."

"Yet even that enduring flower can be smothered by weeds, especially in a garden that grows unchecked," I say archly.

Her gaze sharpens, but I'm spared a response when one of her contingent returns from the basement. He murmurs a few words to Jackie, who then hurries downstairs with her companion, Duran, presumably to heal Michael.

I hope they're in time.

At least Lire's been spared the distress of waiting for word of the telepath's survival. I know she cares for the man deeply. Despite my twinge of jealousy, I hope their healer is as skilled as Wade and has the energy to save him. For a human, Michael is refreshingly honorable, and it's been clear to me, from our first meeting, that he'd do anything for Lire's benefit. Obviously the man is half in love with her.

A short but brawny part-blood tips his chin at Kim. "Emissary, a word?" he asks, flicking a suspicious glance at me and John.

Frowning, she strides to his position near the stairs. He speaks intently at her ear for a few minutes without interruption. His words are too subdued to overhear at this distance, but Kim's posture tells me she's not happy with much of what he tells her. She issues a terse reply and the warrior positions himself at the front door, sword at the ready.

Kim strides toward us, expression fierce. "You know what was inside that safe," she accuses. "You came to destroy them."

"No, not destroy," I say since there's no point being coy. I tip my head and admit, "Temporarily misplace—to allow Lire the opportunity to confront Kieran and make her own life's choices free of my uncle's coercion. I won't permit her to be unduly influenced or taken against her will."

"Right. And I suppose your motives in this are purely magnanimous," she sneers.

I take one stiff step toward her, piercing her with my narrow-eyed glare. "She freed me from torment. My motives are clear and absolute: My life, my very blood, is hers."

Her condescending glare turns to outright surprise. "You've forsworn your mother? Lire is your primary allegiance?"

I acknowledge it with my unwavering gaze and the barest nod. "Bound for all time."

Surely, her eyes couldn't get any wider. "You're mated?" Her voice is so breathless I can barely make out the question, but her stance redoubles and she exclaims, "You're tainted. You can't possibly think our people will follow you!"

"If they follow me, it will be because I remain close enough to kill her enemies." It's petty, but needling her is too satisfying to resist.

She pulls in a breath as if to explode, but John interrupts my sport, "Emissary, calm down before you pop a vein. They're merely bound by blood." He folds his arms. "But you do realize, the king has only himself to blame."

"You dare to impugn my king?" Her magic charges the air around us.

"Of course not," he replies. "I simply state facts. If the king had curbed his daughter's self-indulgent behavior years ago, the events that have led us here, today, would never have happened. My prince wouldn't have been tricked into selling his soul to save Maeve. If that hadn't happened, Tíreachán and Lire wouldn't have met. Without Maeve's influence, Kieran wouldn't be the ruin he is today."

He pulls a face. "Scratch that. He'd probably still be a prick, but he wouldn't have been asked to deceive Nuala. He would never have had a reason to lay a compulsion over Lire." He glares at Kim from beneath his brow and adds, "And then Lire *wouldn't have needed to seek a blood bond in order to shatter it."*

Kim blinks at him, now deflated and seemingly lost for words.

"Did you know Kieran had shared his power with her?" he asks.

Her wide-eyed gaze flicks down to Lire, still slumped against the wall, and then back to John. "No, I didn't, but that doesn't necessarily mean— " She stops and frowns at me. "Are you certain the compulsion is his?"

"Was his," I stress. "Yes, but more importantly, Lire is certain. She broke it with very little help from me. Just feeling my presence in her mind was enough to call attention to it. She's familiar enough with Kieran's resonance to know."

"Fuck a duck," she mutters. "What the hell was he thinking?"

"Pretty sure thinking didn't have much to do with it," John replies.

Kim scowls at him and then turns to me. "Did Lorcán get all the draíoclochs or did you manage to squirrel any away?" She sounds angry and hopeful at the same time.

"You have my word, on my mother's life, I don't have them, not one, not more than one, not in my possession nor hidden. I never made it downstairs, and John didn't make it down until after Lorcán and his cursed dhêalas *fled the building through the back door."*

She eyes John. "Do you have them, one ... or any?"

He spreads his hands wide. "No. When I got downstairs, Michael was unconscious and bleeding, and the safe had been left open. There were no draíoclochs. Don't think I didn't look."

Her shoulders slump and she runs her fingers through her short blonde hair. "Okay. Fine. Brassal will inform the king." She eyes John. "Trent told me that someone applied a tourniquet to Michael's arm. Was it you?"

John issues a brisk nod, and she manages to give him a grim smile in return. "Thank you. He'd be dead if you hadn't done that. Hopefully Duran can reattach all of his fingers."

Something inside me rears up violently, making me sick and dizzy, and I sway on my feet, too stunned to speak.

Michael! *Lire's thought rips through my mind as pain, searing and debilitating, tears through me—*

E IGHT

I woke screaming and disoriented, the pain so encompassing I could only screw my eyes shut and pray for a return to that other place, that other life, where I'd been hale and healthy, even if I hadn't been precisely happy. I had no room for any other thought. Agony ruled supreme. It roared through my body and poured from my mouth in a series of ragged shrieks. I barely registered the feel of hands pressing over me, moving my arms, supporting my head, shifting and jolting my body.

"Lire."

It took me longer than usual to relate the voice to the person. Tíereachán. It was Tíereachán. His breath buffeted my cheek and I realized I must be sitting in his lap, reclining against his chest.

The pain was ever present. It went on relentlessly, growing worse when I moved but never easing—a continuous agony that pierced every fiber in my body. Would it ever stop? I didn't know how much more I could take.

Oh, God! What if I damaged myself irreparably? What if th—

Tíereachán made soothing sounds at my ear. *Lire, stay with me. Wade is on his way. It won't be much longer. John can help your body sleep, but the ass refuses to do it unless you give him permission.*

There was no way! I could hardly muster the wherewithal to think. Speaking was beyond me.

Forget him. We can do this without his help, Tíereachán assured me. *Come to me. Join me in my dream. I'll sleep with you until Wade arrives. I won't let you go. I promise.*

I despaired and probably would have burst into tears if I'd had the energy. I wanted to escape. I wanted out of this pain, but without knowing how to go about it, I was trapped inside my ravaged body.

He shushed me again and through the torment, I dimly felt his fingers stroking my head. *Focus on my thoughts. I'm here with you, always, but you have to look past the physical, past the pain. I know it's difficult, but you can do it. Find me, Lire. I'm here. Right here.*

He continued to plead with me, encourage me, harangue me, until finally, beneath the torture that consumed my body, I caught the barest whisper of his resonance, so feather light in my mind I almost missed it.

That's it. Come to me. Come dream with me.

He didn't need to ask again. I slipped free of my body and found him waiting for me, someplace soothing and warm.

NINE

As awareness returned, I registered a brightening behind my eyelids, followed, not long after, by the feel of something firm yet yielding beneath me. I was blessedly pain free and warm, particularly along the front half of my body. I snuggled my cheek into that comforting heat, and my pillow ... shifted.

Blinking and bleary-eyed, I lifted my head, only to be stunned speechless at the blurred sight of Tíereachán, lying shirtless (and, by the feel of it, pantsless), half beneath me in my bed. When I realized my arm was splayed across his chest, my outstretched fingers covering his left nipple, I snatched it away and scrabbled back from his body as though I'd been caught groping him in his sleep. Unfortunately, the move pulled much of the covers with me and I was rewarded with the stunning view of his torso all the way down to his half-bared hip.

Good grief. If he wasn't nude, then his boxers or briefs were riding pretty damned low.

I clamped my eyes closed before my gaze could take in the baby-fine, golden hair that sparsely decorated his chest or the enticing line of it below his taut belly button. I'd seen it all, more than once. Although, not in such proximity or intimate surroundings.

To my relief, I seemed to be clothed in what felt like a t-shirt and panties, but I peeked through my slitted eyelids to be sure. Yep, my well-worn Seattle Seahawks jersey, the one I'd left under my pillow yesterday morning despite not knowing when I'd be back. I could feel that my bra was missing and wondered who had undressed me.

"Feeling better?" the prime candidate asked, his voice deep and coarse with recent sleep. I heard the rustle of sheets and felt the shifting of the mattress as he probably moved to sit up.

When I opened my eyes, the magical sight hadn't dissipated. In the dim morning light of my bedroom, he looked sleep-rumpled, warm, and completely off limits to a woman who'd been tricked and used by one too many sidhe males. The comforter had eased up his body a fraction, enough to cover his hips, which left his tight abs and everything above it open to my view.

Whoa. Easy does it, hormones.

The latest guy wasn't even out of my system yet.

And what in the hell was this anyway? Grand effing Central? Now, another one was sleeping with me?

Not okay.

On the positive side, the fact that I wasn't freaked out, running for the door, confirmed one important thing.

Kieran's compulsion was gone.

Of course, that didn't mean I wasn't perturbed ... and, okay, maybe a teensy bit unsettled. But considering the startling situation, I didn't think those feelings were out of line.

"Why are you in my bed?" I asked, doing my best to avoid screeching at him. Fortunately, my sleep-graveled voice helped. I merely sounded exasperated.

"It seemed the logical place to watch over you." His lips curved into a smirk. "Besides, last night, you refused to let go of me."

Lord. Based on the smugness of that smile, I must have done something cringeworthy. I struggled to remember anything after our fight with the strigoi, but the memories surfaced about as easily as a boot stuck fast under three feet of mud. All I got for my trouble was a headache and an elusive flashback of palm trees waving in a placid breeze, which made absolutely no sense.

Ignorant of my desire to shove my head under the closest pillow, he continued, unperturbed, "In any case, Wade's on your couch and I didn't think you'd thank me for allowing Kieran to share your bed." He gazed at me pointedly. "Or am I mistaken?"

Frowning, I grudgingly replied, "No. You're not." I glared at him. "But if you're naked, you are *so* asking for a fat lip."

He grinned, stretching and massaging his chest with his left hand in a deliberate and distractingly masculine fashion. "Purely your fault. I was unsuccessful in my bid to find men's pajamas in your wardrobe. And I'm afraid Kieran beat you to my lip."

He touched his fingertips to the right side of his mouth, which, upon closer scrutiny, appeared red and slightly swollen. He also sported a scrape along his right cheekbone that I'd chalked up to his fight with the strigoi but now speculated about.

"He missed my right eye, though, if you want to go for that instead," he offered.

I tried to reconcile elegant, well-mannered Kieran hitting his cousin and failed. "Kieran hit you?" I gaped at him. "You guys got into a … a *fistfight*?"

Sure, Kieran was a renowned warrior. I knew that. I'd seen him wielding both his magic and his sword against our enemies, looking shockingly vicious, but I'd never seen him lose control. Even in the most dire of circumstances, faced with a room full of demons, he'd been violent yet composed and self-assured. For the most part, anyway.

Tíereachán snorted at my incredulous reaction. "Indeed," he replied. "My cousin didn't enjoy hearing that he was no longer welcome to sleep in your home. It was quite a scene. You seem to bring out the worst of his base emotions." He looked thoughtful. "Of course, clinging to me and calling my name in your delirium when I handed you off to Wade didn't help matters."

I gaped at that visual and then scowled at him. "Don't look so pleased with yourself," I snapped. "It's unbecoming. Besides ... *this*"—I wagged a finger back and forth between our bodies— "is *not* happening again." I pinned him with an unflinching glare. "My bed is by invitation only. Understand?"

He arched a single lofty brow. "Of course, my love. That's precisely why I'm here."

I gritted my teeth and it took all of my willpower to avoid exploding all over him. "You know darn well, last night, I wasn't in my right mind."

"No. You weren't. You were inside mine. So deep, in fact, for some time, I hadn't realized you were there." He frowned at me, and if I hadn't known better, I might have thought he looked uneasy.

The expression stopped me short, and a fleeting image of Kim, scowling as she kicked the burly strigoi I'd frozen, flitted into my mind.

My eyes widened. *That* was not one of my memories.

I strained, desperate to remember more, but came up empty. "Kim was there ... wasn't she?"

"Yes." He narrowed his eyes, scrutinizing me. "You don't remember?"

"No, I— " I frowned and then gasped. "Michael!" I practically jumped at him in my haste to clutch at his shoulder, stopping myself at the last second when I remembered where we were and that he was probably naked underneath my disheveled covers. "What happened? Is he okay?"

His look of sympathy drove my stomach into free fall.

"He's alive," he replied softly, but his statement hung in the air, frighteningly incomplete.

"But?"

"It will be some time before he regains full use of his hand." He paused and then added an ominous, "If ever."

Horror hit me, an icy punch to the gut, as Kim's haunted expression and chilling words reared up, unbidden in my mind, like a snippet from a forgotten nightmare.

Hopefully Duran can reattach all of his fingers.

"Lorcán— " I choked out. "He cut off Michael's fingers ... he tortured him to get the safe combination. Didn't he?" I shook my head, seeing the answer in his expression but not wanting it to be true. "Somehow Lorcán found out about the draíoclochs ... knew Michael had them. That's why the vamps attacked the telepaths ... for the same reason I wanted to steal them—it's a way to get to the Otherworld, to get Maeve." I fisted my hands. "And if not for my decision to stop and deal with Kieran's fucking transfixing— "

"Then John, Michael, and I would be dead," Tíereachán said flatly. "Make no mistake. And you would now be Lorcán's chattel."

A single choked sob ripped from my throat, but I swallowed the rest and took a shuddering breath.

Why was this happening? Why?

I slammed my hands into the sheets, fighting the despair that threatened to bury me, trading it for something more productive and satisfying. Unfortunately, it often brought my pyrokinesis along for the ride.

"Lorcán's a dead man," I hissed. "He just doesn't know it yet. He and that bitch *Maeve*. Everything, all this grief—Michael, Daniel, Vince, Kieran, my friends ... *you*—every shit thing that's happened to the people I care about, it's all because of *them* ... because of their sick, filthy greed." The words poured from my snarling lips, coated in derision and hate so heavy they all but choked me. "They destroy and destroy and destroy!"

As bitter resolve settled over me, I drew in a long, raking breath and heaved it out. "I've had enough. They're going down. I'll make them pay. I swear it!"

Ignoring the spiking temperature, courtesy of my unruly magic, Tíereachán leaned forward to curl a strong hand around the back of my neck and stare into my eyes. "They will feel the brunt of our combined fury. I promise you," he said, punctuating the words with a firm pull at my neck. "But you need to leash that anger, Lire. Save it. Cultivate it, until you've received your training and come into your full power. Until then, they have the advantage. Lorcán will kill or disable you before you can touch him. His vampires underestimated you, *this time*. They've not lived in a place where a majority of the population can kill with one touch, but they'll learn from their brethren's mistake, especially with Lorcán guiding them."

I frowned. "Kieran warned me. He said Lorcán has no offensive magic, so he's spent his whole life training and perfecting his physical skills." I stiffened my jaw at the memory. "He told me to sidestep away, if I ever saw him." *Even if it meant leaving others to fight Lorcán alone.*

Tíereachán released me and barked out a scornful laugh. Once again, he reclined lazily against my tufted headboard, as if there was nothing at all unusual for him to be hanging out, naked, in my bed. The man's gall was epic.

He folded his arms across his chiseled abdomen, hiding half the cans in his sublime eight-pack, and clicked his tongue disapprovingly. "My dear cousin should have known better, considering the rather unimaginative pet name he gave you. *Bídteine*," he scoffed. "Evidently, he hadn't looked past the color of your hair to notice that your fire goes deeper than a surface trait. And there's nothing *little* about it. He'd have had more success forcing the sun to reverse course than pressing you to hide when your friends' lives are threatened." Expression darkening, he added, "Which is why he resorted to a transfixing."

I recalled Kieran's demeanor when I'd asked him what his foreign endearment meant—an endearment he'd uttered when we'd made love for the first time. 'Little fire ... if you like,' he'd said, looking almost boyish. It was a memory I'd cherished. Now, though, it would be forever tainted by the knowledge that he'd magicked me.

I looked away, angry that Tíereachán had made me remember. No lover had ever given me a pet name, until Kieran. Unimaginative or not, the diminutive had made me feel prized. Attractive. *Wanted*. Tíereachán's disdain for the moniker cut me as readily as if he'd told me I was nothing special.

Withdrawing, I whipped off the covers and threw my legs over the side of the bed to stand up.

"Lire— "

He sounded apologetic, but I didn't give him the chance to finish.

"Go downstairs, Tíereachán," I said, each word as tightly fashioned as a clenched fist. "I'm taking a shower. You and Wade can have your turns when I'm done." I walked to my bathroom, not caring if my hip-length jersey revealed more skin than I wanted to display. When I closed the door, I didn't look back.

I took a long shower. I shaved my legs. I conditioned my hair while painstakingly scrubbing every square inch of skin. Sitting on my shower's built-in bench, I combed through my hair as though the fate of humanity depended upon silky, untangled strands and then oiled my skin for good measure. After countless minutes of trying to lose myself with all the methodical, senseless preening, I stood, defeated, under the body-pounding jets. I faced the hot spray, alone in my decadent shower, until my skin was a ruddy pink and prunes had formed on top of my prunes.

Under normal circumstances, a long shower relaxed me better than anything else, but with all of my troubles, I emerged more exhausted than ever.

By the time I'd finished getting ready and trudged downstairs, my fingertips were no longer puckered. Harshly muted voices emanated from my kitchen, along with the scent of brewed coffee, even though it was nearly lunch time. I wondered whether Red had helped direct breakfast or if Tíereachán and Wade had rooted around in cabinets until finding what they were looking for.

Or, maybe, Kieran had helped them.

I hadn't seriously considered that idea until I carved a path through the family room and got a clear view of my kitchen. Kieran sat in his customary chair at my battered farmhouse table (which, my helpful voice reminded me, had been Vince's favored perch too), leaning back with his arms crossed. He scowled at Tíereachán who had planted his hip against my kitchen's center island, casually sipping from a large black mug, clad in nothing but his leather pants from last night. A pink box of what I suspected were doughnuts sat next to him on the granite counter. Wade, looking tense, observed both men from the safety of my kitchen's built-in desk while eating a glazed cruller. The atmosphere was so thick an entire tank of nitrous oxide wouldn't have lightened it.

Drawing upon a lifetime of moderating my expression, I breezed into the room and plucked my favorite pink coffee mug from its place next to the sink. "Shower's free, Tíer, if you want to go next. Morning, Wade." I glanced at my former lover and added, "Kieran."

"Good morning, Adept," Wade replied as he stood to greet me.

I'd forgotten how tall he was. The man was a shoe-in to play a Viking on that History Channel show. And who knew? He was a half-blood, mated to the amhaín—no doubt he was the genuine article.

"I hope you don't mind," he said, raising his half-eaten cruller. "We're trading you doughnuts for coffee. The proprietor at the shop a few blocks over ensured me, rather ... tersely, that everything they make is psi-free."

As I poured my coffee, I glanced at the box, spotting Donut In My Pie-Hole's signature logo. "Yeah, Bob's an interesting guy. Thanks for going to the trouble."

"No trouble at all. It's the least I could do," he said.

"Seems to me, I'm the one who should be saying that." I looked at him inquisitively. "I haven't gotten the whole story yet, but ... I think you healed me last night?"

He nodded, his gaze kind and attentive. "I stepped in to help when your friend—Duran?—could hardly stand after expending herself healing the king's telepath." He looked me up and down. "How do you feel?"

"Good. Really good." Even the wound on my hand had been healed. "Physically, anyway," I muttered, trying to ignore the feeling of Kieran's gaze on the back of my neck. I frowned down at my filled mug as I stirred sweetener into my coffee. "I wasn't sure ... I thought I might have damaged myself beyond repair." I shot him a weak smile. "So, thank you. I owe you, big time."

Wade dismissed the notion with a shake of his head. "I was happy to help." His expression clouded over. "I know the circumstances were dire, but you shouldn't have pushed yourself after overburning. Another hour without healing and I might not have been as successful in reversing the damage."

Again, he shook his head. "You owe me nothing." He arched a pale eyebrow and added, "Besides, seeing John humbled by your ability to incapacitate two empowered vampires in practically as many minutes was, in itself, a reward." He grinned. "He hasn't stopped scowling about it."

Since that was all Fisk seemed to do around me, this didn't sound like much of a transformation.

Mention of the two strigoi again triggered the memory of Kim, kicking the larger of the two. But this time, I also recalled her comment about using a chainsaw. Even though they were our enemies, I hated thinking their heads had been cut off while frozen and helpless.

I straightened. "What happened to them ... to the vamps I froze?"

As Wade's speculative gaze met mine, I pondered whether the amháin was inside his mind, watching me. How much of that perceptive gaze belonged to her?

"That wasn't left for me to decide," he replied. "But I believe the king's emissary has them in custody. Are you concerned for their well-being?"

"Of course I am," I said, gripping my mug hard. "They were helpless. And if I'd wanted them dead, I'd have burned them to ash."

"Even though they've enslaved your friends and tried their utmost to kill John and your *mionngáel*?" he asked, gesturing to Tíereachán.

The jarring *thunk* of a dropped cup made me jump.

When I turned to its source, I watched Kieran stagger back from his chair, his eyes widened by shock as his spilled coffee streamed over the edge of the table to splatter on the maple floor at his feet. But his stunned gaze wasn't directed at the mess. Instead, he stared at me, his expression a dizzying mixture of confusion, horror, and anger.

Everyone seemed to freeze until Tíereachán put down his mug and began to pull a handful of paper towels from my countertop dispenser. He glared at Wade. "That could have been handled better, my friend."

Wade sighed and then muttered, "I assumed John had already opened his big mouth about it."

"You're bound?" Kieran stood rigid, hands clenched.

It wasn't until he leveled the question with such frank disapproval, his dark-eyed gaze pinched with regret and jealousy, that I realized how angry I was. The telltale heat of it blossomed in my chest and threatened to explode from my mouth in the form of poorly chosen, incendiary words. I wanted to throttle him. Rage at him. I wanted to lash out and hurt him the way he'd hurt me. He'd betrayed my trust. He'd made me feel small and stupid and he'd keep doing the same things over and over because it seemed that's all he knew how to do!

I closed my eyes when I realized ... *that*, right there, was precisely why I couldn't do it.

Because of my gift, I'd read thousands of people's thoughts by coming into contact with the objects they'd touched. Seeing cause and effect, witnessing their thoughts followed by their actions, gave me a unique insight into the human mind. Most people drew on a sample of one—*themselves*—and based their assumptions about others on that limited viewpoint. But I had a sample of *thousands*—thousands of people's deepest thoughts and desires. I'd witnessed, from the inside, what motivated them, what drove them to do the things they did. Millionaires and peasants, bishops and thieves, actors and regular working folks, the powerfully endowed, the meek, the depraved—folks who lived in modern times and long ago—I'd encountered it all. One thing I'd learned is that people are complicated creatures whose actions are, more often than not, driven by emotion. And nearly all emotion is derived from an individual's prior history, from their past associations, from their experiences, both good and bad.

Kieran had a difficult past. He'd made a mistake that had plagued him for close to two thousand years.

Screeching hurtful things in his face and watching him wince wouldn't make me feel any better. It would be like kicking an injured animal.

And I had no desire to damage him further.

So, instead, I took a breath and did my best to let it go.

It wasn't easy, and without the anger, I simply felt sad— for him, for me, and for what could have been.

Opening my eyes, I replied, "Tíereachán and I were bound before you and I met. Something you were well aware of, since it was one of the reasons you transfixed me." I peered at him. "Wasn't it?"

He stared back, hiding behind that stony face of his, but I didn't wait for a reply.

"I think the thing that upsets me the most *isn't* that you felt the need to lay the compulsion on me. I mean, I understand why you did—in the beginning, at least. With a demon haunting my dreams, telling me secrets, and helping me break glamour, I can see why you thought I was headed to the dark side. Still not okay to spell me, though—not by a long shot—but I understand and I might have forgiven it." I shook my head. "The thing that upsets me the most, the thing that wrecks me, is that you didn't believe in yourself enough to *remove* the compulsion once you realized I wasn't tied to a demon at all ... but to your cousin."

After a moment of enduring his continued silence, I sighed and put my coffee on the counter.

I intercepted Tíereachán and took the wad of paper towels from his grasp. "Go take your shower," I said and then opened my mind to him. *Please.*

As soon as he received my thoughts, his expression went from narrow-eyed concern to thoughtful. *I'm here if you need me.* His gaze shifted to Wade and he jerked his chin toward the front door.

They both left the room without another word, leaving me alone with a stiffly silent Kieran.

After evaluating the table and floor, I snatched the entire roll of towels from the dispenser and advanced on him.

I pressed the loose wad I'd taken from Tíereachán onto the tabletop.

"Jesus, Kieran. The things you do ..." I sighed and righted his toppled mug. "You break my heart, you know that? Half of me wants to slap the living shit out of you and the other half wants to hug you hard enough that you get a god-damned *clue*." I turned to glare at him. "But I know, even if I did, it wouldn't make a damned bit of difference."

His austere expression shattered to reveal the depth of his regret, his frown so pained, it was almost a grimace. "I know it means less than nothing, coming from me, but ... I *am* sorry. I never intended to cause you pain," he said, his voice coarse and ragged, as if it hurt to speak. The muscles in his jaw jumped, and he took a half-step backward, clench-ing his fists. "I'll not ask your forgiveness. Not because I don't wish it but because ... I know I don't deserve it. I don't deserve *you*." He glanced away. "I never did."

"Only because you're still living in the past!" I huffed. "For shit sake! Two thousand years of self-loathing isn't long enough? You want to wallow there so badly that you'd repeat your past mistakes in this ... twisted *need* of yours to save me from Nuala's fate?" I frowned, searching his face. "You know that won't bring you peace, right? Deceiving and manipulating me to serve those ends? It won't bring her back. It won't change the past. All you're doing is setting yourself up to live another two thousand years in a state no better than the last."

I bent my head to catch his elusive gaze. "I'm not your ticket to redemption. Do you hear? I'm. Not. *Her*. Until you can honestly look at me without seeing her ... until you can live in the *now* and look ahead instead of behind ..." I stepped closer to peer at him, as though my pleading look might make him understand. "You'll always have my hope, Kieran. But I can't— " I shook my head and sighed.

He nodded in bleak understanding, and I watched as he rebuilt his cool façade, leaving only resignation in his eyes. "Tíereachán ... he always was honorable."

"Oh, for the love of— " I clenched my teeth together and grunted. "Yes. I know. Most of my friends *are*. Of which you are one, by the way. But I suspect you're too busy reveling in a new round of self-hatred to see that." I sighed. "Just ... do me a favor, will you? Don't go and do something stupid, like bond with this woman Jess, out of some sick desire for punishment. She doesn't deserve that. Neither do you, for that matter. But I don't expect you'll listen to me about that either, will you?"

He gave me an indulgent smile. "Little more than a single phase and you know me so well, do you?"

It was a gentle, half-hearted tease, I knew, but it pissed me off anyway. "A month is plenty of time, especially when actions speak louder than words," I snapped. After a meaningful glare, I blew out my renewed anger and then searched his face. "I want so much for you to be happy. Can you not see that much, at least?"

"I do, and more's the pity."

I opened my mouth to call him on that, to figure out what he meant, but my response was cut off by a loud knock followed by sounds of my front door opening and Kim's demand, "Kieran! You here?"

"In the kitchen with Lire," he called back.

"Kier, I'm here for you," I blurted. "You know that. Give me the word and I'll take you away. We'll figure something out. You don't have to— "

Kim strode into the kitchen, blue eyes flashing as she scanned him up and down. "Good. Brassal has some things to discuss. No more excuses."

Kieran's soft touch at my elbow drew my gaze to his face. His brown eyes were somber as they peered into mine. "I want the same for you, Lire. Truly. You made the right choice. He'll not let you down." He walked away, leaving me alone in my kitchen with a puddle of cold coffee at my feet.

I don't know how long I stood there, but after a time, Tíereachán appeared at my side, accompanied by the scent of citrus. He nudged me toward my family room. "I'll get this. Come. Sit down."

Numbly, I did what he asked, which is how I found myself on my couch a few minutes later, hot cup of coffee in my hand, Red perched in his usual spot on the back cushion, and Tíereachán watching me from the adjacent leather club chair. His blond hair, still damp from the shower and temporarily the color of wet sand, hung in perfectly combed furrows to brush the tops of his shoulders.

"What does ... myon— " Frowning, I bit my lip. "You know, whatever Wade said that upset Kieran. What does it mean?"

"*Mionngáel?*"

"Yeah, that."

He tipped his head to the side in thought. "There's no concise word for it in your language. Blood-mate, I suppose. Oath-bound or oath-kin would be other possible translations."

I nodded at my coffee, but with the way my stomach felt, I couldn't bring myself to drink any.

"You know what he's doing, now, don't you? He's off playing martyr," I scoffed, resigning my cup to the nearest coaster. "The idiot is determined to be miserable. He thinks that's all he deserves. Makes no difference what I say."

"This doesn't surprise me," Tíereachán replied. "Kieran always was stubborn to a fault."

I slumped into the plush cushion at my back. "I want him to be happy, to feel good about himself."

If he had, we might've stood some chance together.

"You can't do that for him, Lire. He has to find these things for himself."

"I know. Don't you think I know that? It just— " I closed my eyes and pressed a hand to the center of my chest. "He didn't even try. Do you know how that feels?"

Tíereachán sighed. "I do have *some* idea."

Red's paw brushed my cheek and I turned to give him a wistful smile before returning my gaze to Tíereachán.

"Speaking from experience?" I asked. "Or have I not been vigilant with my shield now that I'm home?"

"Both." The right corner of his mouth twitched upward, displaying the barest hint of amusement.

He looked comfortable sitting there, his leg cocked, right ankle resting on his left knee, in his distressed jeans, black t-shirt, and bare feet. Absently, I realized he must have snagged a change of clothes from his temporary digs at Invisius HQ. Apparently, he'd 'forgotten' to bring some pajamas when he'd packed.

Now it was my turn to sigh. "Go ahead. Say it: 'I told you so.'"

His crooked smile flattened and he narrowed his eyes. "Is that what you think? That I relish my cousin's continued downfall so much that I'd enjoy gloating at your expense? That I couldn't possibly feel a fraction of your anguish?"

Taking in his affronted expression, the pain in his voice, and what little I felt through our shielded connection, I blinked at the sudden clarity. "You care for him," I said, my eyes wide. "You love him."

"Of course I do. Growing up, he was the closest thing I had to a brother."

God, I was such a bitch. Even without Kieran's compulsion, I still persisted in selling Tíereachán short.

"Stop thinking such things. You're nothing of the sort," he admonished, which told me that my shield wasn't blocking my stronger thoughts, at least when we were in such proximity.

"You're understandably distraught," he added. "And, to your ears, I haven't been easy on my cousin."

That was true, and it made me feel a little better hearing it. I considered him. "I assumed you were older—Maeve's generation. I didn't realize you and Kieran had grown up together."

"My mother is younger than her brother by several centuries. Kieran and I are removed by one generation, but we were born a mere two seasons apart."

"And the hostage thing isn't what I thought," I observed. "You were part of the family."

His eyebrows shot up. "That would be an embellishment. I was tolerated. I was educated and trained in battle as befitted a prince. It is how things are done."

"Oh." I eyed him curiously. "And Kieran spent a lot of time with you at ... I don't even know where ... King Faonaín's castle?"

He snorted. "Putting stock in human fairytales, now?" He shook his head. "The king's royal residence is more than an insignificant castle. It's a palatial fortress. It is the seat of power in his realm, both literally and figuratively."

"And underground, like most everything else."

"Yes." He canted his head as he examined me. "Kieran told you about it?"

"No." I drew in a quick breath and clicked my tongue as I reconsidered. "Some. Not about the king's palace. He told me a little about your planet when I pestered him about it." I shrugged. "Kieran's never been one for volunteering information."

"He never was."

"Never? Not even when he was a child?"

Tíereachán paused, looking thoughtful. "Kieran was always introspective, but I suppose the tendency grew more pronounced after his disgrace."

"Why didn't he follow you to your mother's territory when you escaped? Or later? He seems so unhappy. And the things Maeve goaded him into doing ..." I frowned. "She broke him, and the king did nothing to help. And yet, Kieran stayed. Why?"

"It was expected. Until Kieran's fall into disrepute, his father was the realm's prime ætheling and King Faonaín's tánaiste, his second-in-command. When the truth about Nuala came out, his father abdicated his position in exchange for Kieran's pardon."

"What's an ... ætheling?"

"Heir apparent."

"Heir? But I thought the sidhe council, or whatever it's called, voted on the next ruler."

"The Tribunal. Yes, but the ætheling is heavily favored unless a number of the lesser houses band together to support another worthy candidate."

"So, when Kieran was disgraced, Maeve succeeded in killing two birds with one stone—both Kieran and his father out of favor in one fell swoop," I said, scowling. "And because she never gave Kieran an official order to seduce Nuala, she got away with it. What a manipulative, *effing*— " I stopped short, issuing a frustrated grunt instead of saying what I was thinking.

Tíereachán smirked.

"And then, with Kieran out of the way, she turned her attentions to you," I said.

He shrugged as if it were inconsequential. "Not immediately. But, yes."

"I don't want to break her out of jail, Tíer. I want her to suffer there for a long time, but I can't stand by and let my friends die." I gave him a pleading look. "What am I going to do?"

"Whatever you have to."

No hesitation. No admonishment to avoid foolhardy decisions. No demand that I consider my welfare to the detriment of everything and anyone else. That steadfast, four-word reply told me so many things, not the least of which was that he'd support me in anything I wanted to do, any decision I made. And not just support it—he'd back me up, put his body on the line, without question.

The realization both reassured and terrified me.

"Easy to say, but I'm pretty short on options," I groused. "Either I embark on a reckless jailbreak attempt, or I go all *Kill Bill* and try to take out Lorcán and his contingent of über-vamps at their stronghold, wherever that is. Since my magic is less than useless on anyone with a shroud and I'm not a bad-ass super ninja, I honestly don't see either scenario going well." I pressed my back into the cushion and folded my arms. "For all of my supposed power, I'm remarkably useless."

He fixed me with an unwavering stare. "Yet there is something you can do that no one—no sidhe, no human, no demon—can do. Even my mother cannot walk unhindered between worlds, Lire."

I barked out a laugh. "Neither can I!"

"Maybe not yet, but you soon will. Sidestepping to the higher dimension is merely the beginning."

"World walker," I scoffed.

So pretentious. It was right up there with being called 'the one.'

I glowered at him. "I don't understand how you can put any faith at all in Azazel's prediction."

"Because Azazel wasn't the only one to make it."

"God," I groaned, rubbing my face with both hands. "Not the oracle again."

"Even demons know to listen when she speaks."

"If she's so darn great, why didn't she warn everyone about Azazel and Maeve?"

"Who said she didn't?"

I narrowed my eyes, skewering him with a dubious look. "She warned people? She said, 'Hey everyone! Maeve's in league with an archdemon,' and no one did a thing about it?"

"I didn't say that."

"Exactly," I said, thrusting my open hand at him as though giving him an offering. "That, right there, is why prophecies are dangerous. They're so vague all they do is get people all spun up and freaked out about anything that remotely fits the prediction. Most of the time they're wrong, but, meanwhile, some poor sap has his life ruined because of it."

"The oracle has never been wrong, not once in over five thousand years."

"I didn't mean the prophecy," I exclaimed. "I meant the people thinking they know what the darn thing means!"

I.e. You! And seemingly every other sidhe I'd encountered.
He stared at me like I was an unruly teen.

I sighed. When it came down to it, at twenty-seven-hundred years old, I supposed Tíereachán was more qualified than anyone on the planet to know what he was talking about. But I sure as hell wasn't going to admit it aloud.

"Do you know her exact words?" I asked. "How long ago did she issue this divination anyway?"

"After the Battle of *Athainne* about fifteen hundred Earth years ago. And, yes, I know the prediction. Most sidhe do, especially the ones who were alive at the time."

"All right, then, let's hear it." I curled my fingers back and forth at him. *Sock it to me.*

He shot me an impatient look. "Call me a pessimist, but I don't believe you'll be impressed."

"Probably not. But tell me anyway."

He sighed. "Very well. Enter my mind. Translating will just provide another reason for you to discount it."

I rolled my eyes, but then bit my lip and admitted, "I'm not sure I know how."

Dubiousness intensified his gaze. "You don't recall the events of last night?"

"You mean after the vamps and Lorcán took off?" I frowned as I scooted backward to tuck my legs underneath me. "Not really. Snippets, maybe. I remember Kim kicking one of the frozen vamps and making some crack about having to use a chainsaw to remove their heads. And then her comment about Michael—about his fingers." I shivered. "And pain. So much pain that I thought I'd lose my mind. I couldn't think past wanting to escape from it, so anything after that ..."

I searched my memory and then caught a glimpse ... no, not a glimpse, precisely. It was more of a feeling ... the feeling of being surrounded by Tíereachán's resonance. "Wait. You helped me. You ..." I blinked and looked around the room, as though searching the carpet, coffee table, and walls might help me conjure the elusive memory. "You took me away from the pain."

As I lowered my psychic shield, opening to him, I recalled how he'd entered my mind and then lured me into *his.* He'd enticed me into his dream of a warm beach, palm trees, and an oversized hammock that we ended up sharing. Serenely swinging for hours beneath his dream-conjured trees, we'd talked about inconsequential things, personal things, like what he thought of Seattle, what my job entailed on most days, our favorite foods, whether he liked to cook, how much I missed my dad, the places we each wanted to visit someday, both of us avoiding any mention of demons, the king, Kieran's betrayal, or Tíereachán's own compromised status. It had been relaxing and peaceful, and thinking back on it made the whole thing seem almost surreal. If his own memories weren't currently mirroring my own, I might have been tempted to think it *had* just been a dream.

I remember, I told him, giving him a smile that sprang from my heart. *The pain was driving me over the bend and you saved me.* "Thank you."

He almost shrugged it off as nothing. He'd done what anyone would do when a friend was suffering.

Because our minds were open to each other, I heard his feelings on the matter. But after he realized how much his small yet significant effort meant to me, he reconsidered his dismissal and, instead, returned my smile. "Anytime."

After a moment, he cleared his throat and then leaned forward, pinning his forearms on his thighs, left hand clasped atop his right wrist. "Now then ... the prophecy." *Come.*

At his invitation, I entered his mind and parsed his thoughts, translating them aloud for Red's benefit while Tíereachán occasionally interrupted to offer a more accurate version.

Even now, settled into estrangement,
our people divided
and our strength diminished,
the seeds of our future are sown.
Planted by greed
under the guise of protection,

in our sylvan haven's fertile soil
they take hold.
So it will be
for scores of seasons hence.
We abide from afar,
while our worlds drift apart,
forced to watch
as our issue grows and stumbles.

One traitorous act
conceives demonic claim,
endowing the gifts which the One
shall wield like no other.
An adept by birth, a magus by chance,
past seed descended,
the One will straddle worlds,
walking between to redeem the lost.
Yet not magic nor power
but benevolence of heart
shall bind the One to the crown
and a mate unfettered,
the ruler who will rise from duplicity
to reunite our people,
to defend our sylvan home
at the converging, unholy dawn.
And in our time of need,
our prior glory will be restored,
rekindled by the One,
even as worlds collide.

The prophecy complete, Tíereachán leaned back and evaluated me with an inquisitive eye.

"You must admit, it fits much of what has transpired," Red observed.

It was an effort to avoid rolling my disgusted gaze to the ceiling. "Sure, I guess ... if you squint real hard."

"There has been no other adept since the prophecy was issued," Tíereachán said. "You are the first, and the timing is right. We stand at the unholy dawn, the dawn before this world and Hell converge. 'An adept by birth, a magus by chance.' Lire, you are the one—*Anóen*—our next adept, the one who will walk between worlds and rekindle our prior glory. There is little doubt."

Anóen. This wasn't the first time I'd heard that term. I shook my head. "The convergence you're talking about is a few years out, both you and Kieran have said so. The demons still can't come here unhindered. Until then, anything could happen."

I glanced at Red, who sat atop the cushion back to my left, his pudgy legs dangling over the edge. "Red and I talked about this only a month ago. Divinations are notoriously malleable. Even the smallest disruption along the timeline can alter the outcome. Just because your oracle's portent seems to fit my current circumstance, right this minute, doesn't mean anything. Someone else could come along next week. I could lose my powers … or incinerate myself or … or— " Frustrated, I threw up my hands. "Or I could end up on Mars while trying to sidestep across town!"

An infuriatingly patient smile slid over his lips.

Seeing that my argument had zero effect, I huffed, "I don't get how you can be so obstinate about it. You both know, the only reason I can do the higher dimension trick is because my building's djinn happened to take me there first. Half the stuff I do is out of sheer desperation." I lanced Tíereachán's continued amusement with a pointed glare. "How is it that you and Kieran know with one hundred percent certainty that I'm an adept? Do I smell like pancakes or something?"

He snorted. "You do smell delicious," he said with a grin, finally getting a word in edgewise, before his face fell back to seriousness. "But no. Anyone with intimate knowledge of another adept would know. Your essence, your magic, even your aura, all resonate with a tremor that is distinct. From my first breath in your presence, I suspected, but I knew you were an adept for certain when I touched you, as did Wade."

"And yet you chose to bind yourself to me," I observed. "What was it ... 'benevolence of heart will bind the One to the crown and a mate unfettered?' I notice the oracle didn't say 'soulbind,' just 'bind.'" I examined him. "I know you don't believe that you're the long awaited ruler. I've heard your thoughts on that score. So, knowing the prophecy, why'd you do it? Why tie yourself to me?"

I detected a hint of resolve, of something he expected to happen, but before I could make sense of it, his shield slammed down, shoving me from his mind and cutting off his clear thoughts.

I recoiled, shocked. "What the—? You don't think it matters ... because ..." I blinked as I replayed what he'd been thinking. Somehow, he knew, without a doubt, that our connection was moot. I knifed out of my seat and jammed my fists on my hips. "Damn it. What are you hiding from me?"

I watched him intently to little avail. His expression was as closed as his mind.

"You needn't concern yourself, my dear," he replied, plucking at an invisible speck on his sleeve and then smoothing the fabric. "Merely another prophecy that's not worth considering, right?"

I took a breath, ready to tear into him, but my phone rang, vibrating inside my back pocket and breaking my concentration with the wild notion that it was Kieran wanting immediate rescue. I peered at the screen. Not a Seattle-area number.

After spending half a tick berating myself for being a heartsick moron, I considered the long string of unfamiliar numbers. The last time I'd received an international call it was from an antiquities dealer in France. Was 354 France's country code? I couldn't remember.

Ever since the sidhe insinuated themselves into my life, I'd been neglecting my duties at Supernatural Talent and Company. Two weeks ago, I arranged for a leave of absence with my partner Jack, but eventually, I had to find a way to balance things. Jack and I had spent the last ten years building ST&C into the success it was today. No way was I giving that up. Besides, I loved what I did for a living. Appraising antiques by using my clairvoyance to uncover their varied histories was my calling, and I missed doing it.

I swiped to answer before the call went to voicemail. "Lire speaking."

After a brief hesitation, a smooth male voice, tinged by a slight Northern European accent, queried, "Ms. Devon?"

I didn't give my cell number to just anyone, so the fact that he didn't use my first name had me regretting not letting the call go to voicemail. I wasn't in the mood to deal with a telemarketer.

"Speaking. Who's this?"

"To a limited few, I am known as Roman, although, at this stage, I imagine such a fact means little to you," he replied smoothly. "Miss Devon, you have sent me a rather ... provocative collection of photographs."

I heard rustling through the earpiece, followed by muted scrunching sounds, as though he'd leaned back in his leather chair to get more comfortable. "I must admit, if you hadn't mentioned knowing Diedra in your charming correspondence, I might have dismissed it as yet another shameless attempt to draw me into some imbecilic YouTuber's five minutes of fame." In spite of sounding crisp and cultured, his menacing tone left little doubt about what might happen to someone with such aspirations.

Even if his reference to my letter hadn't clued me in to the fact that this was the vamp—excuse me, *strigoi*—domn, his mention of my friend Diedra seemed to confirm it. She and I had been friends at Coventry Academy from the time she arrived partway into my junior year (both of us being clairvoyants bonded us from the get-go) and we'd kept in touch over the years. From what she'd said in our e-mail exchanges, she was the primary administrator for a small strigoi clutch and even migrated with them—six months in Patagonia and six months in Iceland. Since strigoi didn't trigger our magic, it was a clairvoyant's ideal job, provided you could tolerate living with little sun exposure and being surrounded by creatures who viewed you as a potential food source.

However, the mention of my friend didn't guarantee that this man was the domn. He could just as easily be an underling or, even, one of Nathan or Lorcán's cronies.

My research had turned up almost nothing about the strigoi leader's identity. Even his birth name seemed to be a closely-guarded secret. All public records referred to him as 'the domn' with little other information. The Wikipedia page wasn't much better. Topped with 'This article needs additional citations for verification,' the useless entry consisted of a five-line paragraph imparting the fact that the leader's commanding title came from the Romanian word 'domn,' which was derived from the Latin 'dominus' and translates to 'lord' or 'ruler.' Go figure. An image search had turned up various stills of actors portraying vampires, random people in Halloween costumes, and dozens of blurry, clandestine snapshots, mostly of dark clothed men, but in one case, a woman. That I insisted on imagining the domn as a man offended the feminist in me, but I couldn't seem to stop myself.

The strigoi leader was utterly enigmatic—the Keyser Söze of the undead. (And even more vicious than the fictionalized crime boss, if rumor was to be believed.) The fact that my caller had given me an actual name made me highly suspicious.

I opened my mind to Tíereachán, so he could 'hear' the call.

After a disapproving sniff, the man added, "Your childhood friend has assured me, however, that you are smarter than the average human and, one would hope, in possession of an adequate sense of self-preservation. Although, she did acknowledge she hasn't seen you in over ten years."

He paused, and I could all but see him buffing his finely manicured nails against the lapel of his multi-thousand-dollar custom-tailored suit.

I refused to be intimidated by a voice on the phone. I erased the image and replaced it with a rumpled, over-weight blond, sitting on his couch, clad in ratty pajamas.

Tíereachán snickered, and the unexpectedly boyish sound almost pressed a giggle from my throat. I shot him a warning look.

"So, Miss Devon, before we proceed, I will give you this one opportunity to apologize for wasting my time, other-wise, I suggest that you be sure of your facts. If you did not take these photos, then you must be supremely confident in whoever did. It won't be their existence on the line, should I discover that these are, in fact, doctored."

Tíer's amusement vanished. I could practically feel the heat of his ire radiate through my mind at the speaker's mi-nacious warning.

"You're threatening me?" I laughed. "Isn't that a little counterproductive? Nathan and the rest of your minions al-ready have my friends enthralled and at their mercy. I'm pretty sure killing me totally defeats the purpose of last night's blackmail and hostage taking, since it'll be hard for me to do your pal Lorcán's bidding if I'm dead. Just saying."

The forbidding silence on the other end of the connec-tion didn't impress me. What was this guy's game? Every-one knew the domn's power over his subjects was nothing short of omniscient. He was their supreme ruler in all ways, connected to every single strigoi through their blood. They could do nothing without his knowledge. His absolute au-thority and unwavering enforcement of their strict laws was how the vamps had managed to stay under the radar for so many years and why, back in the day, they weren't subjected to the infamous Department of Paranormal Af-fairs ID program. Of course, the going joke was that the stri-goi PR department could have gotten Nixon reelected for a third term.

Although it was true that the strigoi enforced their laws with a severity that rivaled Singapore, everyone in the magic community knew they policed their public image with equal fervor, which meant any criminal wrongdoing was covered up with the efficiency of a well-funded, far-reaching crime syndicate. Witnesses were nonexistent—either strigoi saliva guaranteed their silence or the grave did.

"Your lack of response isn't exact— "

"You are the clairvoyant who aided my Alexei sixteen years ago, are you not?" he asked sharply.

The abrupt change of subject stopped me short. Sixteen years ... Did he mean the strigoi cursed boy I knew from Coventry Academy?

"If you mean Alex, the one everyone called Hacker— " I stopped short before I overfilled my mouth with my foot and said, "Yeah, we were at school together."

Even at a youthful and true seventeen, it had been clear to everyone that the newly-turned strigoi was a computer genius. He'd been known by a couple other nicknames, too, but 'Hackervamp' was the most flattering. Thank goodness it had been the one to slip out. I reminded myself to think before speaking.

"He told me that you were one of the few people who possessed any integrity at that school."

I blinked. "He did?" I chuffed out a breath. "I can't imagine why."

I'd been a shy, awkward, socially inept freshman with few friends. I couldn't fathom why Alex, a senior at the time and a favorite target for all the popular girls' ogling, would say such a thing.

"You came to his defense and kept him from making an egregious mistake. It is something he has not forgotten."

That's right ... I hadn't thought of it in years. I'd threatened the school bully with revealing an embarrassing secret of his if he didn't stop harassing the blond vampire.

"Skyler," I sneered. "Yeah, I remember. The guy was a jerk. He got off on giving all the vam—I mean, all the strigoi—a hard time because he knew they couldn't do anything about it."

If a strigoi so much as touched any of the students, they'd be expelled. It was too dangerous to do otherwise. Plenty of students possessed more powerful magic than those affected by the strigoi curse, but because of their powerful saliva, superhuman strength, and varied gifts, the strigoi were held to a higher standard. It wasn't fair, but it was the way things were.

"You saw Alexei in his true form," he pointed out. "Yet you stepped in before he could strike."

I remembered. At that point in my life, it had been the scariest damned thing I'd ever seen, but without thinking, I'd charged between the two older boys, putting my back to the one with scythe-like teeth, wicked claws, and eyes dark as pitch. Me, a gangly, ninety-pound fourteen-year-old with no offensive or defensive magic, but I hadn't cared. In my mind, Skyler had been the monster. Seeing him taunt Alex to the breaking point had infuriated me.

"Yes," I replied, unsure how we'd ended up on this subject or why.

"It is not possible that you would mistake us for something else," he said, sounding satisfied, and then demanded, "Explain this recent attack."

Haltingly, at first, I told him what had happened, starting with Julie's party and ending with Lorcán's theft of the draíoclochs. My caller, the purported domn, remained remarkably quiet throughout my account, murmuring occasionally, mostly, I think, to keep me from stopping every thirty seconds to ask whether he was still on the line.

After I'd finished, he said, "I haven't felt Nathan or his clutchmates for some time. There was a massacre. A fire. I had assumed, wrongly it seems, that they had all rejoined their souls. Partaking of elvish blood would explain this ... uncoupling." He paused and then barked, "What of the two frozen strigoi?"

"I'm told they're in custody, but I haven't confirmed that personally. I passed out afterward," I admitted and then kicked myself for giving that part away. Never tell a potential adversary about your weaknesses. Pretty sure that was a golden rule. "I haven't spoken to Kim, King Faonaín's emissary, yet. It's late morning here." I sighed. "But, I'm sure I don't need to tell you that this attack ... it puts you at odds with the king."

I glanced at Tíereachán, wondering where his mother would stand on these events. She'd given the order to defend the king's rule. Would she consider all the strigoi to be the enemy based solely on Nathan and his clutch's actions?

"And, yet, this *sidhe*—Lorcán—ventured uninvited into *my* territory, killed at least six of my people, and incited the defection of twice as many more. It is not *I* who must seek amends. I will, however, withhold my final judgment until after I have dealt with my disloyal subjects."

Great. Exactly what I needed. Another pissed-off warlord.

"Okay," I drawled. I mean, what could I say? 'No, please don't. We've got it covered?' Yeah, uh, *not.* "So, *Roman*, no offense, but why should I trust anything you say? I don't even know whether I'm talking to the domn or not. And even if you're legit, there's no way for me to know whether you're playing this straight. You could be working both sides, and I'd be none the wiser."

"Perhaps you will take the word of a friend? Or two?" he said. "Alexei and Diedra will arrive, momentarily. Alexei has my full confidence. When you address him, you address me. A larger party is on their way."

Before I could volunteer my opinion that injecting a bunch of angry strigoi into the mix was asking for trouble, he said, "You intrigue me, Miss Devon. After this business is settled, you and I will meet to discuss these photos," and then he promptly ended the call.

I stared at my phone's termination screen and then added the number to my contacts.

"Well, that was ... interesting," I said, returning my cell to my back pocket. "If we can take any of that conversation at face value, it seems Nathan's been a naughty boy."

Tíer snorted. Whether his derision was instigated by the 'face value' comment or comparing Nathan to a rebellious child, I didn't know. Likely both.

"If this is some kind of ruse coming from Nathan and Lorcán, what would be the point?" I asked. "They already have me over a barrel. Calling to pose as the domn doesn't make any sense. And how would either of them know about that whole incident with Alex and Skyler? Nobody else saw it. Red will tell you: News would have been all over the school in a flash if someone else had seen it."

"Agreed," Red volunteered. "Your classmates were not known for their discretion."

I flopped back on the couch and thought about Alex and Nathan. Although they were both strigoi, I couldn't have found two more polar opposites, and not just because of their contrasting hair and skin color. Although my impression of him at Julie's party had been brief, Nathan struck me as brash and thoroughly modern, bordering on flashy. Certainly, he dressed that way. Alex, on the other hand, I remembered being modest and conservative, as if he'd been from another generation even though he'd been newly turned at the time. Even on casual Fridays, when students were allowed to dispense with the school uniforms, his wardrobe had never veered from the pressed khakis, crisp oxford shirt, and brown loafers that were the norm. I wondered whether it was a look he'd outgrown.

Whenever I'd caught glimpse of him at school, Alex's subdued and controlled manner captivated me. He'd conducted himself with a grace and natural aplomb that was unusual for someone his age—confidence without the need to prove it. To a self-conscious fourteen-year-old like me, Alex's poise had been a heady thing. If not for the incident with Skyler, I'd never have dared approach him. Afterward, I couldn't say we'd gone on to become friends, but he went out of his way to greet me whenever our paths crossed, much to the shock of the other students.

"I can't see Alex colluding with someone like Nathan, but then, I didn't know him all that well. He was a senior when I was a freshman, and the strigoi didn't tend to mix with the rest of us. Alex was the exception, but he seemed to spend most of his time in the computer lab."

"Why?" Tíereachán asked.

"I don't know. I guess because he loved programming or whatever. From what I understood, he was some kind of techie wiz-kid."

He gave me a bemused look. "No, love. Why didn't the strigoi mix with the rest of you?"

"Oh," I replied sheepishly and then shrugged. "I figured that would be obvious. The strigoi took their classes at night. And they had their own dormitory. We could take the night classes if we wanted, but most of us didn't."

I frowned as I remembered the secret club some of my classmates perpetuated, The Grim Reapers. To join, you had to take at least one night class and get a strigoi to kiss you. Another stupid club, The Daredevils, required their initiates to sneak into the were's compound during the full moon.

I shivered. Those were memories best left buried.

"I guess if this is a setup, we'll find out soon enough," I mumbled.

"Indeed."

I frowned at his expression. "What?"

"The way you remember yourself." He shook his head. "I can't imagine you as a ... what was it? A gangly teen? A social misfit?" He gave me a disbelieving look as though he'd now heard everything.

I shrugged. "It's true. Ask Red."

"No, not a misfit," Red volunteered. "Guileless and ... socially awkward, perhaps. But so are many teenagers, even ones who grew up hundreds of years ago. It is astonishing how little things have changed in that regard."

"My years of ridiculous behavior have numbed you to it. That's all."

"That goes without saying," Red replied stoutly, startling a laugh out of me.

From the kitchen, my landline trilled, jolting me to my feet. The ringtone, which I'd recently programmed to sound like an old-time telephone's clanging bells, told me it was my building's front desk.

"Why do I have a bad feeling about this?" I muttered.

"I can't imagine," I heard Tíereachán say as I hurried to my kitchen desk. His response was so deadpan, my gate faltered and I looked over my shoulder at him, which, judging by his satisfied smirk, seemed to entertain him.

I jogged into the kitchen and all but dove for the handset, mostly to put a stop to the incessant racket. I was greeted with Darren's rumbly baritone.

"Good morning, uh … Ms. Devon. This is … reception. I have an … Alex Slavskaya and Diedra Yamaguchi here to see you. Shall I, uh, patch them through on the lobby phone?"

"That's okay, Darren. Tell them I'll be right down. Hey, is the conference room open?"

"Yes. You want me to reserve it for you?" He sounded surprised.

"That would be great. Thanks."

"Uh, sure."

I hung up, wondering at the man's unusually flustered demeanor, and circled back to the family room. "Come on. They're here. We'll stop by and see if Kim wants to join the fun."

Tíereachán frowned and glanced at the patio doors where the cloud-blocked, late-morning light filtered inside through the panes. "They?"

I followed his gaze and realized why Darren had seemed out of sorts. "Yeah. Okay. I guess I forgot to mention … Alex has an … unusual ability."

Besides the typical gifts that balanced their curse—increased strength, immortality, and powerful saliva—some strigoi were graced with a unique, and often unparalleled, power. Though, as far as I knew, day-walking was the most prized. It was also unaccountably rare.

His eyebrows arched. "Does he, now?"

Not the startled surprise I'd expected, but then, Tíereachán had been around a long time. Over his twenty-seven-hundred years, it stood to reason that he'd met his fair share of strigoi, even ones with extraordinary talents.

"And does he manage this with scales, hair, or projections?" he asked.

I imagined Cousin Itt from *The Addams Family* and laughed. The campy show seemed to be on my mind a lot, lately.

"Hair?" I gaped. "You've got to be kidding."

His superior look was all the response I got.

Hair. *Unbelievable.*

"Scales," I replied and then hedged, "I think. I didn't see him very often during the day and when I did, we were usually passing in the hallway or the library. I didn't stop to examine him in minute detail."

To be honest, Alex had intimidated the hell out of me—'Daytime Alex,' with his onyx-like skin, doubly so. In fact, the night of that memorable confrontation, I hadn't lingered to chat even though he'd shifted back to his pale-skinned nighttime form with remarkable swiftness. After Skyler had skulked off, my indignant anger evaporated and left me tongue-tied and embarrassed and half-convinced that Alex had been affronted by my interference. I vaguely remembered saying something inane and fleeing as fast as my feet would carry me. Even now, my stomach was tied in knots with the anticipation of speaking with him.

Good Lord. You're not a sputtering, pimply-faced, pubescent school girl anymore. Get a grip.

Tíereachán cleared his throat.

One look at his expression was enough to tell me that my shield hadn't kept him from hearing my thoughts.

Cheeks burning, I levitated Red to my shoulder and strode away.

This was, without a doubt, one reunion I could have done without.

TEN

As I rode the elevator to the lobby, I again wondered whether inviting Kim to my meeting with Diedra and Alex wouldn't turn out to be one of my more costly blunders. Given the circumstances, it had seemed smart to include King Faonaín's official representative in our discussion, but then things spiraled out of control when Kieran, Wade, and Fisk all demanded to be present for the proceedings. No doubt Jackie would have wanted to come too if she hadn't been out grocery shopping.

Arms folded, I glared at the brushed steel doors.

My decision to meet my two friends in the lobby *unaccompanied* had turned into a ridiculous argument. If not for Tíer's open disdain for Kieran's 'scaremongering' (his word) and my threats to shove the most vocal of them into the higher dimension until they calmed down, I wouldn't be alone in the elevator, right now, to fume and worry in peace.

Before I could work myself into a pronounced snit, the elevator dipped to a halt and its doors coasted open, revealing Darren at the reception desk, an armed guard to the right of the elevator, and a couple gawking tenants. Every single one of them had their wide-eyed gaze fixed on the hooded figure standing motionless in front of the lobby's tinted, bomb-resistant windows, his face hidden from my view by the thick cowl of his wool coat. Diedra, standing beside the imposing figure, looked exceptionally petite in comparison to her companion's large stature.

As I walked toward them, I examined the man while he still had his back turned.

The strigoi I'd known as Alex had been slender, almost lanky, yet he'd moved with the grace and power of a gymnast—albeit a potentially lethal one. In my teenage daydreams, I remember wondering, more than once, what he'd been like before he was turned. Had he moved with that same assured stride? Had he been his hometown high school's star basketball player? He'd plainly been fit for it. Did all the girls dream of slow dancing with him at the eighth grade Sadie Hawkins? I know I would have.

The whole vampire thing fascinated me. *He* fascinated me. I'd wanted to know why he'd given up a normal life. What had driven him to accept the strigoi curse and how had it come about? Ever since the strigoi went public as a formal organization in the 1960s, it had become common knowledge that they rigorously controlled their numbers and rarely turned anyone not borne of a few designated familial bloodlines.

At the time, though, the thing I'd pondered, most of all, was what it would be like to touch a strigoi without my gloves. Would their skin be cold? Did their hearts still beat? Were the rumors true? Could a clairvoyant touch (and—gasp!—maybe even kiss) a strigoi without the need for protection? Of course, I'd never worked up the courage to ask any of those things, because, despite his slight build, Alex had unnerved me.

Though, as I approached the hooded figure, it quickly became obvious ... this man was about as slim as a Freightliner, which put him at odds with the seventeen-year-old boy I remembered.

When Diedra spotted me, she squealed and rushed at me, smiling broadly. "Lire! Oh, wow! It's been so long. Look at you. You didn't tell me you changed your hair," she gushed, grasping and swinging our mutually gloved hands between our bodies like we'd always done in school. The clairvoyant's version of a girl hug. "It looks awesome. I never understood what possessed you to dye it in the first place. God, otherwise you've hardly changed. You look great!"

I'd changed plenty, just not where she could see it. Diedra, on the other hand, had acquired some nice curves over the last ten years. In high school, she'd been flat as a board and so diminutive that she had to order from the youth uniform catalog long after the rest of us girls had gone on to women's sizes. One boy, who I suspected had a crush on her, made the unfortunate mistake of comparing her to a tiny Asian doll. To her face. Poor guy. Pretty sure, after the resulting profanity-laden explosion, he never looked at a doll the same way again.

"Hey, Deed. Looking good yourself," I replied, practically staggering under the weight of her enthusiasm, and tried to paste a smile on my face.

I couldn't believe Diedra thought I'd mistake this person for Alex. This had to be a setup, otherwise, why the bait and switch? Had she been forced into doing this? Strigoi saliva wasn't effective on clairvoyants or telepaths, but regular strong-arm tactics worked fine, as Lorcán had amply demonstrated.

Likely sensing my unease, Diedra frowned and glanced over her shoulder at the hooded figure, who'd turned toward us when Diedra waylaid me. Releasing my hands, she stepped aside to include him in our conversation. "Lire, I think you know Alex, from high school, right?"

She sounded so genuine, but there was no way this guy was Alex. From the day they were turned, strigoi were eternal, their bodies frozen in time, a gift for which they supposedly traded their souls, among other things.

I peered into the shadow of the figure's generous hood, but with the lobby's gloomy lighting offering nothing in the way of contrast, I couldn't discern much beyond the vague contour of a dark face. The hand that extended from the man's sleeve was a lustrous black, like brushed coal, marked with a distinct pattern of tiny, rounded tiles, similar to a snake.

As a general rule, gloves or no gloves, clairvoyants didn't shake hands. No clairvoyant wanted to throw away a pair of gloves every time they greeted someone. But with their immunity, strigoi were a special case, and this guy assumed I knew it.

Under normal, friendly circumstances—with *Alex*—I might have gone along with it.

These were hardly normal circumstances. And this wasn't Alex.

I enveloped the two of them within my telekinetic grasp. Subtle? No. But I learned one important thing as I indecorously picked up and restrained them. Neither one was affected by a shroud.

Diedra's eyes went wide and she gasped at the intrusion. The cloaked figure stiffened, but without a shroud or a way to counter my magic, there wasn't much either of them could do about it.

I smoothly whisked Diedra behind me, wanting her out of the impersonator's easy reach. I was done playing into my enemy's hands.

"So ... here's the thing. I had an exceptionally shitty night, last night, no thanks to your buddies, Nathan and Eva and their newest pal, Lorcán. Call me crazy, but I get a little bit *irritated*"—I punctuated the word with a firm shake of his body— "when a herd of vampires enslave and kidnap twenty of my friends and murder a guy I used to date. So you'll have to indulge me when I say: *I'm not here to play your fucking games. Okay?*"

I speared him with a vehement glare as my fire fluttered along the surface of my skin before I could smother it. "You." I poked his steely chest with my index finger. "Are not." Poke. "Alex." Poke. "The Alex I knew intimidated the hell out of me because the guy had presence with a capital 'P,' not because he was the size of the goddamned Terminator." I folded my arms. "So, let's begin again. Shall we? Who are you and what do you want? And you better make this good. If you haven't noticed, I'm not a shy, fourteen-year-old clairvoyant anymore."

"Lire— "

"I know who *you* are, Diedra," I snapped without taking my eyes off the creature in front of me. "I wasn't talking to you."

"Lire!" she exclaimed.

"It's okay, Deidra," the man said, his voice sending tingles down my spine. "I'm not offended by the confusion. Being compared to the Terminator isn't such a bad thing, I don't think. But it's pretty ironic, since you're the one who suggested that I bulk up in the first place, Clotilde. I believe your exact words were: 'If you worked out some, put on some muscle, idiots like shit-for-brains Skyler who can't see past the end of their own noses wouldn't assume you're easy prey just because you're a computer geek.'"

He barked out a laugh. "Frankly, it's one of the most shrewd observations I've ever heard." His voice lowered to a menacing snarl. "No one mistakes me for prey."

The tingles turned into a full-on shiver as I brought a small ball of fire to the palm of my hand and cautiously raised it to illuminate the inside of his hood. A familiar yet ominous face stared back at me, his eyes black as jet. The orange and yellow of my flame glinted over his scales, making his skin appear almost opalescent.

"You can't be Alex," I said, but my voice lacked conviction. "Vampi—I mean, strigoi are eternal. They don't change."

He shook his head. "Not true. We don't age, but our hair and fingernails grow and, as you can see, we can build muscle, given the right ... circumstances."

I stared at him, sure I didn't want to know about these 'circumstances,' and wondered what the hell to do. Although I hadn't spoken to him all that often, I had to admit, this strigoi sounded a hell of a lot like Alex. He had that same Midwestern drawl.

"That night ... what did I say to Skyler to get him to back off?" I asked.

"You told him there wasn't a secret you couldn't uncover if you set your mind to it, like how he jerked off to a photo of Jennifer Randal and what her older brother might do to him if he ever found that out."

"Oh my God! You never told me that!" Diedra exclaimed, although I wasn't sure whether she'd directed the complaint to me or Alex.

"Well ... *hell*," I groused, releasing them and extinguishing my fire. "You know, they don't teach you this stuff in school, dammit. I swear, half of my idiotic blunders could be avoided if people told me important shit like this."

"Yes. Important shit," he said, voice low and severe. "Like how a clairvoyant has the power of a magus and how she plans to make amends for violating the Fourth Law."

"Uh ..." I blinked at him. "Sorry?"

"I suppose that's a start," he said dryly.

"No. I mean— " I blew out a flustered breath. "I'm sorry for, you know, the misunderstanding and manhandling you guys and stuff, but, uh ... what's this Fourth Law? Another strigoi thing that I don't know about?"

"The Fourth Law states that a magus will not use his or her power against another individual without permission or express cause," he informed me. "Violation is punishable by the Arcane Council's discretion, but can include banning, imprisonment, and/or arcane shackling."

Okay, yeah, I'd heard of the Arcane Laws, I just wasn't familiar with their finer points.

By the time he said 'shackling,' my eyes probably resembled a pair of ping-pong balls. "Oh," I replied and then added, voice rising to a near squeak, "I have doughnuts. Upstairs?"

Behind me, Diedra made a choking sound, I think to stop herself from snickering. At least, that's what I hoped. Could be she was girding herself for Alex to take my head off. Alex, for his part, simply loomed.

"Look, I'm not a magus. I have more than one psychic ability," I explained and then shrugged. "It's kind of a long story."

"That's one story I'd be interested to hear." He paused, drawing in a slow breath. "Fortunately for you, Clotilde, it seems you share the domn's favor. But don't let it go to your head. He's notoriously fickle and unpredictable." He leaned forward and, beneath the hood, I swear his eyes glowed with an unearthly black light, which dimly illuminated a pair of exceedingly long fangs. "And bear in mind, I'm no longer the seventeen-year-old computer geek you knew in high school," he said, and with his menacing voice came the unmistakable smell of death.

I staggered backward, almost clobbering Diedra, but managed to stop myself before my hindbrain had me scurrying for the nearest exit.

"I never thought you were," I croaked and then turned on my shaking legs toward the elevator.

But I wasn't stupid. I kept my telekinetic net extended and monitored every move he made while he was behind my back.

By the time the three of us shuffled into the elevator, I'd restored my composure. "We're going to my building's conference room. I assume the domn filled you in on what happened last night?" When Alex answered with an affirmative, I continued, "Good. I don't know how much you know about the sidhe, but their society is comprised of two opposing factions, one led by King Faonaín and the other by his sister, the amhaín. Kim, the king's emissary, is waiting for us, along with the amhaín's liaison and several other sidhe representatives. Are you familiar with how their emissaries and liaisons work? Each one is soulbound to a sidhe who stays in the Otherworld. Since they communicate through their bond, it provides a way for the sidhe to— "

"Speak with people here," Alex interrupted with a nod. "What's your role in all this?"

I grunted. "I guess that would depend on who you ask."

"I'm asking *you*."

"My role is … complicated. In all honesty, I'd be happier not having one at all, but the alternative is doing nothing and that's not an option. I know it sounds crazy, but demons are planning to invade Earth, and I've found that I'm in a

unique position to help stop them. They've already executed most of King Faonaín's emissaries and, a little over
three weeks ago, they murdered eighteen Invisius Verso telepaths before we were able to close their gateway. Soon,
though, they'll have the means to come here without being
summoned, and if we want to survive, we need to work together to keep them out. All of this sidhe political bullshit— " I sighed. "It comes with the territory. The sidhe have
been preparing to counter this invasion for a long time."

"The half-breeds," Alex said.

"Yes. You know about them?"

"Of course," he said gruffly. "Immortals tend to take notice of each other. Their progeny were hard to miss."

"Did you guys know why the sidhe were breeding an
army?"

"Most of the strigoi assumed they were planning an invasion of their own. What you've told me doesn't negate
that possibility, you know."

"The Compact forbids it. But if the king is usurped by his
daughter Maeve and her loyalist Lorcán ..." I shook my head.
"Then all bets are off. That's why the amhaín is supporting
her brother's continued rule, even though they don't see eye
to eye on some pretty serious issues. Unfortunately, your
strigoi *renegades* have aligned themselves with someone
who wants to overthrow the king. So, with that in mind, it
would be ... wise to tread carefully in this meeting. Right?"

The darkness of his hood stymied any sense of his reaction, but based on his stony stance and Diedra's fearful expression, I got the distinct impression that one didn't
instruct the strigoi on matters of conduct, no matter how po-
litely worded or sensible the advice.

"Your counsel has been noted, *mortal*."

He said 'mortal' the same way a medieval monarch
might say 'peasant.'

For the first time, I found myself wishing I was 'the one,'
so I could rub his condescending face in it.

Dangerous thought, I scolded myself.

In the end, who cared whether Alex acted like a douche? If we could number the domn and the strigoi among our allies, he and the rest of them could be as superior as the day was long for all I cared. It's not as though I wasn't already inured to it. Imperiousness seemed to be a sidhe national pastime.

My reasoning didn't squelch my disappointment, however. In all my childish daydreams, I'd never imagined Alex being a jerk. Scary and powerful and possibly predatory, *yes*. An arrogant jackass, *not so much*. I was beginning to think immortality was synonymous with hubris.

A dozen scathing responses flirted with the tip of my tongue, but I made a meal of them and kept my lips firmly closed. When the elevator door parted on the second floor, I strode ahead, aiming for the conference room with a mind more primed for battle than diplomacy.

Some people are jerks; get over it, I told myself.

I waited at the closed conference room door, my hand on the knob, and forced myself into calm, arching my head to each side to ease the tension in my neck. When I heard Alex and Diedra approaching, I donned a neutral expression and ushered them inside.

As I opened my mouth to make the introductions, Alex issued a guttural roar and leapt at Tíereachán with all the ferocity of a ravenous grizzly but ten times as fast. My former classmate slammed into the unprepared sidhe, knocking him six feet through the air before landing on top of him. The sickening *thwack* of Tíer's head striking the wood floor reverberated through the cavernous room, followed by Diedra's shrill scream and my shocked gasp.

I sensed the exact moment Tíer lost consciousness, not a split-second later. The steady, almost imperceptible static of his shielded thoughts, which continually rumbled just below my surface awareness, vanished so completely that I feared Alex had killed him. I hadn't realized how accustomed I'd gotten to his presence at the periphery of my mind until he was gone.

It all happened so quick; I was rendered dumbfounded, eyes cranked wide like a hapless victim in a B horror flick. For all of my power, I was pathetically inept at protecting my friends. To my right, Kim clutched at Kieran's sword arm as his weapon manifested in his grip. On my left, Fisk surged forward, his own sword already drawn. Although Fisk was closer and unencumbered, he was still too far away to do anything to prevent Tíereachán's certain death, if he hadn't been killed already.

As Alex reared back, his hood now flung wide to reveal his gaping, unhinged mouth and enormous fangs, my frozen body finally unlocked. Swift as a thought, I latched on to Tíereachán's limp body and shoved him into the higher dimension, leaving Alex to fall on hands and knees to the floor, poised to bite but now empty handed. At the same time, Kieran's shadow wholly engulfed the crazed strigoi. From experience, I knew Kieran's darkness was suffocatingly impenetrable, but given Alex's strigoi nature, I wasn't sure whether the total lack of sensory stimuli would keep him down for longer than a moment.

Clutching Tíereachán possessively within my invisible grasp, I nearly cried out when I realized his heart was still beating. He was alive! I whisked him through the higher realm until I could pull him back to the material plane, safely at my feet. I dropped to my knees beside his still form. He looked alarmingly pale.

"Wade!" I shrieked.

In an instant, the part-sidhe crouched opposite me, Tíer's prone body lying between us.

"I've got him," he said, placing his left hand atop the fallen sidhe's forehead. Warm tingles pricked my skin as his healing magic surged into Tíereachán's body.

"Tell me what to do. As his ... *mionngáel*, can I do anything to help?" My hands fluttered, practically of their own accord, hovering over Tíer's right shoulder and chest like two butterflies too timid to land on a favorite flower.

Wade peered across the room, eyes pinched with fatigue. "I have this," he forced out on a grunt. "Fisk ... could use ... your guidance ... however."

I looked up in time to see Fisk raise his gleaming sword over the opaque shadow that obscured Alex.

I surged to my feet. "Stop!"

Fisk's savage downward strike wavered before he slashed through the black cloud.

"Son of a bitch!" I bellowed at him as I pinned Alex to the far wall. I'd plucked the vamp from Kieran's darkness with not a second to spare. Thankfully, Kieran hadn't extended his magic shroud to prevent it. I shuddered at the thought.

"We are supposed to be building alliances here, goddammit!" I shouted. "Not killing each other."

As my heart pounded out a rhythm loud enough to be a distress beacon, I leveled an unwavering finger at Fisk. "You! Back off! Your prince is alive."

"I don't take orders from you," he snarled, weapon raised.

All at once, I felt the undercurrent of Tíereachán's fury burning at the outer fringes of my mind.

"You will retract your sword," Tíereachán bit out from his position at my feet. With Wade's help, he struggled to a sitting position and then directed his livid glare at Fisk. "And if you ever raise it in the adept's direction again, you stand to lose far more than a scant strip of skin."

"John, stand down," Wade seconded. "Lire has earned the amhaín's trust, and as your prince's *mionngáel*, she deserves your regard." He stood up, offering his hand to Tíereachán, and added, "Especially in areas where she isn't wrong. Killing this *dhêala* will not make things better. For any of us."

"The strigoi do not ally with demon spawn!" Alex snarled from his position against the far wall where I continued to hold him fast. "That one killed three of our people. It will die, here, now—or there will be war between us."

I flew toward the restrained vampire.

With his hood no longer covering his head, his short blond hair and thick eyebrows stood out against the burnished ebony of his skin. When I hovered, close enough to appreciate the delicate pattern of his supple scales and the frightening length of his fangs, I snapped, "He's no demon."

Alex snorted.

"The demons attacked you? When?" I demanded.

"Demon," he corrected. "Just one. *Him*." He glared over my shoulder.

"When was this?"

His alien eyes, black and fathomless, narrowed as his gaze met mine. "Many years ago. I am not as young as you naïvely believe. That one"—he jerked his chin in Tíereachán's direction— "invaded our compound in an attempt to kill the domn. The creature might have succeeded if I hadn't found its summoner and forced her to send it back to Hell."

"He's not a demon. He is a sidhe, the amhaín's son, Tíereachán, Prince of *Thìr na Soréidh*. He was tricked by Maeve, his own cousin, into enslaving himself to the archdemon Azazel and spent the last thousand years under its dominion. If he attacked your people, it's because he was compelled by Azazel and his summoner's will. He had no choice and, until recently, no memory of his prior life. Azazel took both when it enslaved him, but my blood restored Tíereachán's memories and I managed to free him. Since then, he has saved my life more than once. He's had every opportunity to deceive and manipulate me, and, yet, he hasn't. I trust him with my life."

"*Trust*," he sneered. "A human's sense of trust is meaningless. Humans are virtually blind in their powers of observation, prone to hysterics, and easily influenced. I put zero faith in your *feeling* of trust, mortal."

"Normally, I'd be inclined to agree with you." My gaze flicked to the side in search of Kieran, but I stopped myself. Squaring my chin, I met Alex's glare. "But, as it happens, Tíereachán and I are blood-bound."

His eyes narrowed to bare slits. "Prove it."

"And how am I supposed to do that?"

He lowered his voice to a menacing whisper and spoke to me as though *I* were the one currently restrained and under his power instead of the other way around. "The demon-slave knows my true name. If you are bound, as you say, you have the ability to learn it." Before I was tempted to turn, he commanded loud enough for everyone's ears, "Eyes on me. You will seek his guidance through your bond."

Uncomfortable with the thought of silently gazing into Alex's eyes, I focused on my former classmate's pointed chin and nudged Tíer's presence at the periphery of my mind. When he opened himself to me, I thought, *He's testing me. Don't speak to me out loud. He says you know his true name. Do you?*

Yes, he thought back. *He is Tsarevich Alexei Alexeyevich, second son and heir of Tsar Alexis of Russia and his consort, Maria Miloslavskaya. He is more than three hundred years old. But more importantly, Lire—he is the domn.*

At that tidbit, my eyes widened, as did Alex's when he realized what my shock might mean.

"Son of a— " Snapping my mouth shut, I glared at the ceiling. What was all of this about? Why in the hell would a three-hundred-plus-year-old Russian royal-born strigoi overlord pretend to be a teenage student at Coventry Academy? The need for it boggled my mind.

How do you know this? I asked.

Because, my mionngáel, demons may covet souls above all else, but secrets are often more prized. Secrets are how Azazel and the other high demons plot their many schemes. Secrets are the foundation upon which demon society rests. The more a demon knows, the more discord it might sow and the more souls it might reap. Why do you think Azazel wanted you under its command so badly?

I sucked in a breath. *That's why Azazel went after the Invisius elders,* I guessed. *It wasn't just because of their connection to the king. It's because of their skill for learning the secrets of everyone around them.*

Yes. Their connection to the king was a bonus.

"Jesus," I muttered.

After a moment to restore my composure, I lowered both Alex and myself to the floor. I released my hold, but loosely draped my magic around him, in case he decided to be 'fickle and unpredictable' and elect to kill me. Not that he'd get the chance, with my building's djinn protecting me, but it didn't hurt to be cautious.

I folded my arms. "You're Tsarevich Alexei Alexeyevich," I told him. And then, with a pointed look, I mouthed the words, 'the domn,' knowing, with my back to the room, no one would see.

His head jerked back with a silent snort as he studied me intently. "Indeed—a fact known by very few." Somehow he succeeded in looking both menacing and amused at the same time. "You're surprised?"

"You could say that. Why would the"—I almost stumbled into revealing his secret, but continued with barely a hitch— "one time heir to the Russian throne and three-century-old strigoi impersonate a seventeen-year-old Midwesterner and attend Coventry Academy?"

"For the same reason most students attended Coventry: To get an education."

I raised an eyebrow at his placid expression. "What? The universities in Iceland weren't good enough for you?"

"Not if you want to learn the ways of the coming generation and the technologies that will ultimately dominate them." His eyes glinted with deviousness. "My domn believes you can tell a great deal about a population by studying its youth."

This was Alex, a.k.a. *Hackervamp.*

Holy shit. A computer hacking domn.

I was speechless.

Stop thinking of him as the domn or you're going to blow it, I chastised myself.

This is Alex. Alex. Alex. Alex.

He continued, "In fact, because of our memorable ... *encounter* at school, you reminded my domn of two important lessons: The power of confidential information and the significance of image to the self-absorbed masses. Not revelations, but when you're as old as the domn, it's easy to become complacent. If it weren't for my time playing a teenager, he might not have fully appreciated a clairvoyant's usefulness."

I wondered whether this was a good thing. "And do clairvoyants find the strigoi as useful?" I asked tartly.

"I've not heard any complaints," he said, but his tone held a wicked edge that was as suggestive as it was pernicious.

Since the strigoi cursed were the only other creatures, besides the sidhe, who were immune to a clairvoyant's magic, I didn't have to wonder about the seductive implication of his reply. Heck, until a couple of months ago, I might have been intrigued by the possibility. Ten years without skin contact had a way of spurring some monumentally bad decisions. And I suspected 'bad decision' was an understatement where the domn was concerned. I held little doubt that he put the big 'D' in dominant.

Complaints? *Ha.* Who would dare?

"I imagine you wouldn't," I said, careful to keep my tone neutral. "Which brings us to our current ... dilemma. Your former brethren enthralled more than twenty of my friends and took them hostage at the bidding of a traitorous sidhe. One murdered my ex-boyfriend. All to coerce me into doing something that will probably get me killed or, at the very least, jailed by King Faonaín."

Kim gasped.

Whoops. Apparently, Kieran hadn't revealed the true purpose for Lorcán's earlier attack.

The shock of it momentarily flustered me before I added, "So ... I was hoping we could work together on this."

Alex considered me for a long moment, no doubt wondering about the level of my competence.

"There is still the matter of your mate," he said, glaring over my shoulder to survey the people behind me as he spoke. His eyebrows twitched. When his ominous gaze once again met mine, his harsh expression held a note of curiosity. "It would seem not everyone is pleased by the bond you share with this ... *prince*. Why is that, I wonder?"

I could well imagine what he'd gleaned from that glance over my shoulder.

"I guess that would depend," I mumbled, feigning indifference in spite of wanting to steal a look for myself.

"Upon whom I ask?" He smirked. "Right. Then, by all means, Clotilde, introduce me to your *allies*." His tone all but painted the final word in quotes.

"My name is Lire," I pointed out. "Nobody calls me Clotilde."

"Is that so?" he replied dismissively.

I might have taken issue with his arrogance if I hadn't turned and gotten a load of the scene behind me.

Yes, I supposed the picture it painted *was* somewhat telling.

At the far end of the conference table, Kim stood inches from a grim-faced Kieran, her right hand overtopping his left forearm in a loose hold that was obviously meant to encourage restraint. Earlier, she'd stopped him from leaping to Tíereachán's rescue, something I wouldn't forget anytime soon. Now, though, I wasn't sure what Kim hoped to prevent since I couldn't decide who Kieran wanted to throttle more, Alex or *her*. Actually, he looked predisposed to doing both.

Tíereachán, on the other hand, lounged in one of the padded guest chairs, looking elegant and relaxed, with his right ankle crossed over his left knee. Fisk, his amber eyes narrowed and guarded, watched Alex closely from his position near Tíer's left shoulder, looking every bit the FBI agent, complete with dark slacks and conservative blazer; although, his non-standard weapon, a ten-inch Bowie knife, spoiled the image. Absently, I speculated if, like his katana, the wicked looking knife materialized from nowhere or whether he'd pulled it from a sheath hidden somewhere under his jacket. Several feet away, Wade leaned against the conference room's interior wall, apparently satisfied that Fisk had Tíereachán sufficiently guarded.

Diedra, her expression pinched with worry, huddled to the left of the doorway, her gaze darting between Alex and anyone who moved. When she spied Red perched at the edge of the conference table, her face lit up in recognition and she gave him a tentative wave.

With that small gesture lightening my heart, I introduced my former classmates to everyone in the room, starting with Kim and ending with Wade.

Alex grunted as though he'd discovered an illicit secret. "Interesting. The objection to your chosen mate seems to be shared exclusively by King Faonaín's representatives."

I glared at him. Why was it that immortals seemed to delight in picking at fresh scabs? He knew darn well that Tíereachán wasn't my soulmate. We were bound by a blood covenant. The arrogant ass had countless strigoi tied to him in a similar manner, and I'd bet a year's income he didn't refer to them as his 'mates.'

He'd used the inaccurate term deliberately, hoping to provoke a response, like a kid brother taunting his older siblings.

"Does their king want you bound to one of his own, instead?" he asked.

I found it difficult, if not impossible, to avoid squirming.

His eyebrows shot up, as though I'd told him everything despite not uttering a word. "Ah. As I suspected. He covets you for himself, doesn't he?" He looked thoughtful. "A clairvoyant-turned-magus is unique, I'll give you that, but I find it hard to believe the sidhe king is so hard-up for companionship."

At the sound of a scuffle, he glanced at Kieran, whose tightly coiled body strained against Kim's hold. She hissed something at his ear that I suspected was Silven, and I wondered whether Brassal was speaking through her to issue commands.

Alex smiled, looking thoroughly satisfied. He gazed down his aquiline nose at me. "I'm referring to King Faonaín's notorious dislike of humans, of course. Anyone with eyes in their head can see you're a desirable woman."

He shook his head and tsked, casting his gaze about the room. "Nevertheless, if the sidhe king wants you, it isn't because of your obvious charms nor is it for your combination of psychic gifts—as unusual as that is. No. I think it has everything to do with this *prince* calling you 'adept' and the fact that he isn't lying dead at my feet." He fixed me with an irritated look. "Thanks to your timely intervention, I believe."

Dismissing the offense with a perfunctory wave, he sauntered to the end of the conference table, apparently unconcerned that it was the furthest point from the exit.

"Years ago, I had the pleasure of meeting a sidhe," he said conversationally, slipping off his coat to reveal attire that would give a Wall Street CEO a run for his money.

Sleek body armor, like something out of an X-Men movie, might have been more in keeping with his formidable appearance. Still, I had to admit, he wore his black trousers and crisp dress shirt well.

As he continued his commentary, he tossed his coat on the neighboring chair and took the seat at the head of the table. "His name was Caiside. During that first visit, he told the domn, and anyone who'd listen, about his home and his queen." His eyes cast upward as he appeared to search his memory. "Her inner and outer beauty were unrivaled, as was her magic, which, quite literally, supplied the lifeblood of his world. Without her, their cities would eventually fall to darkness, his society to chaos. And he'd called his queen 'their last and only adept.'"

"I know of this sidhe," Red said, astonished. "He visited my uncle at his London home when I was a young man, in 1689, or perhaps the year prior, if memory serves. My uncle told me he was an ambassador."

"Not an ambassador," Alex countered, relaxing in his chair and crossing his legs. "A *siritóir*—a tracker—one of many. I first encountered him a few years earlier than you, Master Necromancer, when I was still within my normal span, and then several more times over the intervening centuries. It was his job to find their next adept—a discovery, he assured me more than once, for which his queen would reward handsomely. Here on Earth, such a power isn't easy to detect, but he told me it might manifest as an ability to move from one location to another, instantaneously. If I ever came across a human with such a skill, he urged me to contact him." His gaze combed me from head to toe. "But it would seem the adept has already been found."

The amhaín had offered a reward for me? A goddamned finder's fee?

"That's what they keep telling me," I grumbled and scowled at the others, although I was relieved to feel the evidence of Tíer's shock as it leaked into my mind.

"All's fair in love and war," Alex told me. "Or haven't you heard?"

"Then this must be war. Very little love going around that I can see."

"Is that right?" he said, but both his amused tone and expression disagreed with my assessment.

No doubt he'd mistaken Kieran's barely leashed aggression for the behavior of a devoted lover. No way was I going to explain things.

Instead, I latched onto the headline that finally struck me. "You said Caiside urged you to contact him. How?"

The question drew an indulgent smile to his lips. "He left something with me. A beacon."

"A beacon?" I echoed, perking up. "Is that … like a draíocloch?"

When I looked at the others, I noticed they were all positively riveted to the strigoi. Wade had come away from the wall, staring hard at Alex, as though the strigoi leader had revealed a map to the holy grail.

Sparing me a distracted glance, Wade shook his head and said, "Rarer," before looking back to Alex. "Do you still have it?"

"I might."

Wade's eyes narrowed. "And *might* you be able to describe this beacon?"

If it were possible for someone to shrug using their eyebrows and a slant of their head and look refined while doing so, Alex nailed it. "An oval stone about so big," he said, pinching his thumb and index finger a couple inches apart.

"What color is the stone?" Wade asked.

"Blue."

I half expected Wade to continue with, 'What type of blue?' or 'How many facets does it have?' but instead he jerked his chin at him. "He told you how it works?"

Alex nodded, looking smug.

"You know you can't invoke it," Wade told him.

"I'm well aware of that."

"Why not?" I asked. "And what does it do?"

The firm set of Wade's shoulders eased and he moved to take a seat near Tíereachán.

Since it seemed as if Alex had decided to forgo killing anyone for the time being, I also took a seat, positioning myself adjacent to the relaxed strigoi but pulling my chair away from the table in case I needed to get up quickly.

"Come sit, Deed," I offered, gesturing to the chair at Alex's left. I shot a pointed look to Red, hoping he'd take the hint and move closer to Diedra once she sat down. I imagined she must feel uneasy at being surrounded by so many imposing people she didn't know. Although, working alongside strigoi on a daily basis probably wasn't a cakewalk either, so maybe she was used to it.

I resisted pulling out my cell to check the time. *Stupid sidhe politics.* The day wasn't ticking by any slower and every second we wasted with this bullshit, the longer my friends were forced to endure Lorcán's tender care. I battered my heel against the wood flooring, until Alex's sly look drew my attention to it. I pressed my foot flat and tried not to scowl at him.

While the others took their seats, he leaned toward me, indicating he wanted a private word.

Judging by his smug smile, I wasn't sure I wanted to hear what he had to say, but after shooting him a warning glare, I reluctantly inclined my head to meet him halfway.

"You aren't afraid of me in the slightest, are you?" he asked, his breath buffeting the skin of my neck as he spoke softly, inches from my ear. His Midwestern accent, I noticed, was absent, replaced by the cultured European one I'd heard earlier on the telephone. After learning Alex's true identity, I'd suspected he'd been the caller, but the accent had thrown me.

Jarred by the question, I jerked my head so I could see his face out of the corner of my eye. "No. Should I be?" I said and immediately wanted to smack myself.

Never ask the question if you don't want to know the answer. *Idiot.*

"Undoubtedly," he replied, sounding bored. "Most people are, particularly in this form."

He paled in comparison to the horror of Azazel, but I didn't point that out. No sense making him think it was necessary to prove himself.

He considered me for a moment before drifting dangerously close to my neck to inhale deeply. I stomped the impulse to flinch away from him. Running was something prey would do, and I sure as hell wasn't food. As I allowed him to take in my scent, a ruckus erupted at the opposite end of the table and Kim shouted something in Silven.

I didn't need to turn to know that Kieran had forced his way past Kim just to be intercepted and physically restrained by Tíereachán.

Honestly. Did Kieran think I'd be so stupid as to let down my guard? Ever since Alex's initial attack, I'd kept my TK loosely draped around everyone in the room. Although, at this point, it hardly seemed necessary. I'd decided that Alex wasn't normally the type of guy who would kill someone at the least provocation. From what I'd observed, every one of his actions had been calculated and deliberately executed, no doubt with a clear response in mind. The whole thing with Tíereachán? I was pretty sure that had been an anomaly. Alex had been caught off guard, coming face to face with his previous attacker. And having suffered my own showdown with Tíereachán's demonic alter ego, I could understand Alex's violent reaction. I didn't like it, but I understood it.

Alex's derisive snort blew the loose strands of my hair against my cheek, reminding me to stay focused on the predator next to me.

His voice rumbled into my ear, "Please tell me this boldness isn't due to human sentimentality and the mistaken belief that you and I are *friends*." He sneered the word. "Or do you think your sidhe allies are skilled enough to save you?"

In spite of my confidence, my stomach tipped at the implied threat. "We were never friends, Alex. More like acquaintances. And I'm fully capable of saving myself, thanks." I shifted in my chair so I could stare at him, our noses a scant few inches apart. "But I'm fine with not having to prove it. What about you?"

He went unnaturally still, and, at that moment, I worried that my instincts about him were wrong.

After staring into his cavernous eyes for what seemed like an interminable time, his brows pinched together. "I've disappointed you." It came out as a flat statement, but as close as we were, I could see the revelation surprised him.

In truth, I might not have stopped to dwell on my reaction if not for his comment, which was kind of sad when I considered it. Apparently, disappointment had, now, become such a common occurrence it hadn't even warranted a stray thought.

I shrugged. "Pretty sure I'll get over it."

He grunted, still eying me, but I couldn't decide whether it was an expression of amusement or dissatisfaction.

"So ... are you done pushing buttons yet?" I asked archly and then forced my stare to the other end of the room where Kieran and Tíereachán were still caught up in a heated yet muted argument.

While Alex had been in such close proximity, I hadn't dared to split my attention to dwell on Tíereachán's strenuous emotions. I knew he was angry, but when I tuned in, I was surprised to learn that his anger wasn't directed at Alex. Tíer was furious with Kieran.

Jesus. When had my life turned into a Spanish soap opera?

Chuckling, Alex shifted his coat to the second chair over and then gestured to Diedra, giving her permission to sit next to him.

Seriously? She had to wait for his approval?

When she took her appointed seat, she sat stiffly and positioned herself as close to the chair's left arm as possible, putting as much space between her and Alex as possible without being obvious. She didn't cringe, but it was a near thing. And if I noticed it, I had to believe Alex did too.

Somehow, I needed to get Diedra alone so we could talk.

Before I could analyze the gravity of my growing to-do list, Tíereachán bit out something scathing, a question, by the sound of it, ending with 'Nuala.' Kieran flinched, looking stricken as the incriminating name echoed through the room, prompting an awkward, intense silence. When Kim told Kieran to take his seat, his customary cool mien slammed into place and he did as she asked, but every one of his rigid steps advertised his displeasure.

Boy, oh boy. I sure knew how to pick the guys with the baggage, didn't I?

I wondered what Tíereachán had said but resisted the impulse to ask, even though the privacy of our bond. Now wasn't the time. Besides, I wasn't sure I wanted to know.

See? I was learning.

Floor show over, Tíer returned to his seat, appearing deceptively complaisant, with Fisk once again standing to his left, his unsheathed blade proclaiming that he was taking nothing for granted.

Alex shifted in his chair. "If I'd known things were going be this entertaining, Clotilde, I'd have visited you a long time ago," he quipped, his American accent firmly in place.

"Oh, shush," I snapped without thinking, earning Diedra's gasp, but my response had lacked heat. Alex simply chuckled.

Still grinning, he directed his attention to Wade. "*Ámsach*, please continue. Lire wishes to know what a *ríutcloch* does and why a lowly strigoi like myself is unable to invoke one."

"I'm the amhaín's liaison, not an ambassador. Wade is fine," he replied and then turned to me. "Once it's imprinted, a *ríutcloch* forges a connection between two people. Calling it a beacon isn't too off the mark, I guess."

"Okay," I drawled, frowning. *Gee, thanks, Wade. Clear as mud.* "What does imprinted mean?"

"Tied by blood. Before a *ríutcloch* can be invoked, it must, first, be bound to its owner. They're exceedingly rare. Caiside had the last few known to exist, passed down for hundreds of generations through his familial line. They were created by his ancestor Tasgall, the previous adept, thousands of years ago. When Tasgall died, his particular brand of magic passed with him. Even the amhaín can't replicate them." Eying Alex doubtfully, Wade observed, "Caiside must have trusted you greatly."

"What about the draíoclochs?" I asked. "Were those created by the previous adept too?"

"No. Those come from the amhaín," Wade replied. "A draíocloch is less sophisticated and potentially more dangerous since the temporary gateway it creates is tied to a place. It doesn't dictate or control how many individuals use it to cross between worlds. *Ríutclochs*, on the other hand, are restricted to two people. Years ago, they were how the sidhe communicated with their liaisons and emissaries, instead of resorting to a soulbond."

"So, this stone—once it's invoked—it creates a gateway between the two people?"

"Of sorts, yes. Between the *ríutcloch's* imprinted owner and its invoker."

I glanced at Alex. "And strigoi can't invoke it because ..." I frowned. "Because their blood isn't wholly their own?"

Wade cocked his head, considering it, and then shrugged. "It's as plausible as anything else I've heard."

"Most people would say it's because we're dead," Alex said flatly.

I snorted at the absurdity. "You're not dead."

They weren't. Like therianthropy, vampirism was caused by a curse. When I was in high school, I'd done a fair amount of reading on both werewolves and strigoi. I'd never admit it out loud, but it's possible I'd been a tiny bit obsessed with a certain blond strigoi. So sue me.

Alex stared at me for one stunned moment and then burst out laughing.

His mirth went on long enough that I cast my mystified gaze to the others at the table. "What the hell's so funny?" I asked, but all I got in response was a series of inscrutable smiles and a frown from Kieran.

"Oh, Clotilde," Alex said. "I can see why you have such fierce admirers. You are so deliciously naïve."

Did this mean he honestly thought he was dead? If so, how did he explain his animation? Or his hair growth, his brain activity, his muscle building, and everything about him, for goodness sakes! I gaped as a myriad of perplexing questions swarmed through my mind like thirsty mosquitoes, until all I managed to force out was a frustrated, "Whatever," which made him crack up again.

"The amhaín wishes to know *when*, exactly, you last saw Caiside."

Wade's raised voice cut short Alex's laughter. In fact, Alex's expression turned pitiless so unnaturally fast that my arms broke out with goosebumps and I wondered whether his amusement had been genuine at all.

"He last enjoyed my domn's hospitality in May of 1858," he replied. "Before that time, not more than a few years elapsed between visits."

Wade assessed Alex for a moment and then issued an ambiguous grunt. "It's been many seasons since Caiside has returned home to *Thìr na Soréidh*—at least 150 Earth years. As the eldest son of House Ruiseal, his absence has been sorely felt. My lady believes he may have fallen prey to those who wish to elicit his progeny, or died at their hands."

At Alex's stiff silence, I frowned and peered at Wade. "I'm sorry ... Those who want to do *what*?"

"Breed him," Alex clipped out. Though, with his jaw practically turned to granite, I was surprised the words came out at all.

"What do you mean 'breed?'" After receiving several raised eyebrows, I waved my hands in front of me to erase the question and sputtered, "I mean … Jeez. *Why*? Why would a woman do that?"

I heard Fisk mutter something that sounded snarky, but Wade shut him up before turning to me. "Even if you hadn't demonstrated your potential, there are those who would have taken you, regardless—for the same reason, Lire."

And then, with the horror spelled out for my stupidly naïve brain, it penetrated: Like Caiside, I was related to an adept, even if she hadn't come into her full power prior to her death.

"Are you—? You're saying … you think Caiside's been held hostage for the past century and a half—all the while, being bred like a champion racehorse?"

"Yes," Wade answered.

"It's not the first time one in Caiside's line has gone missing," Tíereachán commented.

Christ. If this was true … it made King Faonaín look positively saintly. He hoped to claim me as his soulmate, not breed me like some prized heifer. At least, that's what I'd come to believe. Although, now that I thought about it, being soulbound did seem to imply a certain level of intimacy.

"Please tell me this is a crime in your world," I said, frowning at Wade and then Kieran. "This isn't standard practice … right? I mean … this is kidnapping and rape we're talking about."

I didn't like the haunted look on Kieran's face.

"It is categorically prohibited in *Thìr na Soréidh*," Wade said, his expression hard. "Violators are severely punished in accordance to our laws, but outside of my lady's borders …" He frowned, letting the statement trail off and then admitted, "I'm afraid, where humans are concerned, there are too few protections—an oversight my lady is taking great pains to amend. Fortunately, now that you are bound to her son, even if only by blood, our current laws provide you with some guardianship in the mean time."

"But not necessarily outside of her borders," I guessed.

Wade looked at Kim and issued a precise, "No."

She straightened, her nose flaring. "My king has expressly guaranteed Lire's safety from those who wish her harm. To imply otherwise is a grave insult."

Wade tipped his head. "I wish no disrespect, Emissary, of course. But over the seasons, my lady has received every indication that the individuals responsible for kidnapping adept descendants reside *outside* of her borders. Even after her numerous entreaties, King Faonaín has yet to call for an investigation into the suspected crimes, nor has he issued an edict increasing the penalties for such despicable acts. The fact remains, without the benefit of a soulbond, as a human, Lire has zero judicial protection in the king's realm. Under his laws, livestock is afforded more security than a human, isn't that so?"

"Not unlike your lady's, if I'm not mistaken," she replied sourly. "As to these purported crimes, if my king's sister has proof, I'm assured he'll be all ears, but until that time, he won't devote precious resources to what amounts to a wild goose chase."

"No, I'd think not," Tíereachán said placidly. "Especially when most of the suspicion centers on several of the king's most powerful supporters."

"What are you implying, *briódair*? That my king lacks the means to keep his vassals in line?" Kim asked, her tone scathing, which was out of character for the woman I'd come to know and like.

If the Silven term 'briódair' was an insult, Tíer remained stoic. "Nothing of the sort. I merely agree that there's little sense disrupting a hornet's nest without good cause." He examined his nails. "However, I'll make the observation that it's equally unwise to leave a nest untended, since those stinging pests might find cause to merge with another colony. Or … take on a new queen."

Kim's eyes blazed, confirming that her mate Brassal was unquestionably in charge. "When my king requires counsel from a demon slave who hasn't set foot in the Otherworld for over a millennium, I'll let you know, until that time I suggest you— "

With a clack of teeth, Kim abruptly shut her mouth.

Blinking rapidly, she daintily shifted in her chair and pursed her lips before finishing Brassal's admonishment. "Perhaps you might consider keeping your opinion to yourself."

Somehow, I didn't think Brassal would have chosen those words, a guess confirmed by Kieran's surreptitious smirk.

"It seems to me, proof of such a crime would be of great value to most everyone here," Alex observed.

"So it would," Wade said dryly. "Is this when you tell us you have the means to attain such proof? For a price, of course."

Alex met Wade's disapproving scowl with a patronizing smile. "Of course," he said, his grin flattening to something more grim. "Unfortunately, there's just one person in this room who has the means to pay. And it's not you, Liaison."

Instead, the oppressive weight of the domn's fierce obsidian gaze landed squarely on me.

Of course it did. With the way my life was going lately, why was I even remotely surprised?

(E)LEVEN

Alex reached inside the collar of his shirt and pulled out a thick silver chain. Dangling from the lowest curve of that gleaming rope, beneath his ebony scaled fingers, was a delicately-wrought, two-inch pendant boasting an azure-blue cabochon. Its massive asterism glowed as if possessed of its own power source. I had no doubt even the famous Star of India paled in comparison to this dazzling gem.

"Whoa," I breathed.

"The domn has a proposition for you, Clotilde," Alex said, drawing my attention from the impressive jewel to his determined gaze. "Use the *ríutcloch* to reach Caiside. If he's alive, as the domn believes, bring him here to me. That's all he asks. Rescue him from his tormentors, give us proof of it, and the domn will employ his considerable power and efforts to locate and help your captured friends."

While the room erupted with the cacophony of raised voices, I reeled.

Of all the demands I'd expected to hear from the domn, rescuing Caiside hadn't been one of them. In fact, I thought use of the *ríutcloch* would be the *reward,* not the demand.

Holy crap. Could this be the answer to my prayers?

Until now, I'd begun to worry that the sole way to guarantee my friends' safety was to negotiate with King Faonaín for his help. The power of the domn, while maybe not as inescapable or relentless as the Wild Hunt, wasn't something to discount. What's more, the domn's price that I rescue

Caiside in return for my friends' safety wasn't as onerous as the demand the *king* would likely impose on me. Never mind that negotiating with the king was fraught with peril. I'd have to see him in person. And once I entered his domain, I wasn't entirely sure I'd be allowed to leave again.

Risk being bound to a megalomaniacal king for all eternity or rescue Caiside?

Quick, let me think!

I sighed. There had to be a catch. It couldn't be as easy as invoking the *ríutcloch* and waiting for Caiside to stroll through the resulting portal.

"You cannot be serious!" Kieran's rant broke into my fevered thoughts. "You honestly believe this is a good idea?"

"What I think is immaterial," Tíereachán replied. "Lire is capable of making her own decisions. She isn't an object to be possessed, *cousin*, not by you or anyone. She doesn't need, or want, your constant, suffocating protection."

At least someone *believes in me*, I grumbled to myself.

When Red moved to stand on the table in front of me, paws on his hips in a deliberate show of support, I smiled at him. *Make that two someones.*

Ignoring the scowls and charged silence down at the other end of the table, I turned back to Alex. "What's your motivation in this? Why the interest in Caiside? If you want me to rescue him just so you can punish him for something he's done to the strigoi, you can forget it. We'll find another way to do this."

"Maybe you need to rethink who've you been associating with," Alex said caustically. "Caiside is a good man, a loyal sidhe. Is it so hard to believe that I simply want to see him released?"

I studied him closely, but his alien complexion made it difficult to read anything beyond the stony set of his features. "So, you're telling me that if I pull this off, and Caiside comes through the portal, the domn will ensure his safety? He'll be free to leave with Wade, to return to the amhaín's realm, if that's what he wants?"

"Yes."

I frowned. "I don't get it. If you're so concerned about Caiside's welfare, why wait until now to use the beacon? You could have done it years ago by finding a willing human to invoke it." *Or an unwilling one, for that matter.*

"When I accepted the beacon, I swore an oath." Alex removed the necklace and held it firmly within his grasp, the pendant dangling enticingly below his fist. "I can only allow an adept to invoke it."

"Then it isn't your right to withhold it for services rendered," Kieran declared.

Alex swung his callous gaze to the opposite end of the table. "Wrong. As this *ríutcloch's* sworn custodian, I may deploy it as I see fit. In fact, my oath doesn't require me to give it to the adept at all. But as it happens, over the years, Caiside has curried the domn's favor, a consideration the domn wishes to reward."

Although Alex seemed earnest, I couldn't shake the feeling that he hadn't told me everything. Of course, the sidhe were no different. I knew for a fact that they, too, had their own secrets, yet it hadn't stopped me from trusting them. Of course, sidhe, as a rule, didn't lie.

I jerked my chin at the pendant. "Have you ever given the *ríutcloch* to someone else? Someone you thought or hoped might be an adept?" If I accepted his deal, I'd need to touch it with my bare hands. I wanted to know what I was getting into.

"No. You're the first candidate to come along in all the years I've owned it."

"So, as far as you know, no human has touched it?"

"I rarely remove it from my neck," he said with a wry smile, as though the thought of a human touching it amused him.

I sat back in my chair and studied him. "Dude, I'll be honest. You showing up, out of the blue, offering me this deal—a deal that looks too good to be true ..." I narrowed my eyes. "It makes me think it probably *is*."

"You're the one who contacted the domn with those photos. I'd hardly call his response to send us here 'out of the blue.' Although, discovering your adept abilities was unexpected, I'll give you that."

No doubt. Still ...

"Then why can't I shake the feeling that I'm missing something?"

When all I received in response was his raised eyebrows, I rolled my eyes and then turned to the others. "Anything important I should know about the *ríutcloch*? Have any of you ever used one?"

Kim and Kieran, both looking pissed off, shook their heads.

Eyes closed, Wade raised his hand in the universal 'gimme a sec' gesture that stopped the conversation. After thirty-seconds, while I tried not to fidget, he opened his eyes to consider me. "The amhaín has never used one, but several of her liaisons do. Invoking the *ríutcloch* will permanently imprint it to you. It establishes a connection, a conduit, to the *ríutcloch's* owner—whoever *originally* primed it with his or her own blood. The two of you will be able to communicate through this conduit. Unlike the bond you share with Tíereachán, the conduit is transient but more ... substantive. You can think of it as a singular gateway for lack of a better description. As long as the *ríutcloch* stays in close proximity to your body and your mind remains open to it, the connection will hold."

"What happens if it closes?" I asked. "How do I get it back again?"

His gaze briefly shifted away while he considered it. "My lady believes it takes an investment of will, similar to the way you'd open a mental connection to her son."

I frowned at a sudden, unpleasant thought. "What if Caiside is dead?"

"Nothing can forge a connection beyond the void."

Wade's response didn't precisely answer my question, but I took it to mean nothing untoward would happen.

"Any other pearls of wisdom?" I looked from Wade to the others.

"Lire ..." Kieran began, but when he took in my expression, which wasn't all that accommodating, he forced out a sigh. "Just ... consider your actions carefully. Don't take any unnecessary risks."

"I don't plan to." I think Fisk snorted, but I managed to turn back to Alex without flicking anyone on the ear.

"Okay," I said, pressing my gloved hands flat on the table as if I needed to draw strength from the wood. "I'll use the *ríutcloch* and see whether I can do something to help Caiside if he needs it—but only if you swear that the domn will spare no effort or expense to save my friends if something goes wrong. If I'm ... you know ... not here to do something about it myself." I glared at him. "Because I can't imagine this is going to be as easy as you're making it seem."

He studied me for a moment before steepling his fingers together. "Agreed."

"Oh, and I might not have mentioned ... there's a deadline. We need to neutralize Lorcán and his strigoi groupies by dawn on Wednesday or they'll start murdering my friends. Promise me, if I can't— "

"Clotilde," he said, growing impatient, "I promise you, if you're somehow prevented from coming to their aid as a result of trying to rescue Caiside, the domn will personally do everything in his power to help your friends."

"Help them *return to their former lives*," I clarified. 'Help your friends' was a little too wishy-washy for my taste. He could 'help' by whisking them off to his Iceland compound.

"Yes," he bit out.

"And if I succeed, he'll do the same," I said, "That still stands."

"Of course," he snapped, his fangs lengthening.

Hoo-boy. I'd pushed him close to his limit. But instead of alarming me, the fearsome display had me wanting to stick my tongue out at him. I was so sick of people trying to intimidate and push me around.

Fortunately, though, I showed some restraint.

I turned his promise over in my mind, searching for loopholes, until I decided it was as airtight an assurance as

I was going to get. If he went back on his word, both the am-haín and the king would know about it. With their height-ened sense of honor, I was pretty sure they wouldn't look kindly on any splitting of hairs, especially if this barely thought out, ill-considered plan got me maimed, impris-oned, or killed.

Of course, I had no intention of getting reckless. I'd in-voke the beacon, get the lay of the land, and then decide what to do next. If things looked too dicey to attempt a solo-rescue, we'd come up with another way to find and release Caiside.

And then I'll be right back to square one, won't I?

Alex frowned, his black gaze fixed on my hands as I re-moved my gloves, probably at the prominent blue tattoo just above each of my thumb knuckles, a gift from the De-partment of Paranormal Affairs and their now-defunct ID program.

"May I?" I asked, extending my open hand to him.

He pinned me with an indecipherable look but finally dropped the pendant into my waiting palm.

As soon as the talisman hit my skin, its magic jolted me ramrod straight.

Even if I hadn't known that the amulet was a summoning beacon, I would have figured it out as soon as I touched it. The tremor of magic emanating from the jewel crashed over me, drawing out my immediate shiver, as its resonance flut-tered along my skin and through my core, captivating me with its unknown yet tantalizingly familiar tune. I rolled it around in my head, savored its plagency like the taste of chocolate, until I was sure I'd recognize it, even without the pendant as a reminder.

Instinctively, I knew this was Caiside's unique reso-nance.

Too bad I didn't have the first clue about this adept stuff. Because, if I did, I could use Caiside's resonance to find and rescue him without having to use this *ríutcloch* at all. But faced with the mind-boggling expanse of this universe, not to mention parallel universes, blindly trying to find his tune would be like trying to find a needle in a ginormous—

Whoa ... wait a darn minute.

It's not as if I hadn't done something like that before. I'd faced this same circumstance when Paimon had trapped me in the Between. Except then, it was my own resonance that I'd needed to find in order to return to my Earth-bound body.

Why hadn't I thought of it sooner? The Between was my ticket. Actually, Caiside's resonance was the ticket. The Between was the train terminal—the ever-present, infinite, mother of all terminals. It was there—in that vast inter-dimensional nexus between worlds where every life force's string converged—where I would find Caiside's resonance. Once I found it, I'd follow his string, his unique essence, all the way to his physical body. And the cool thing was: If I could do it for Caiside, then I could do it for *anyone.* Well ... anyone whose resonance I bothered to memorize.

Before I got too excited, I scolded myself.

You're making a lot of assumptions, bonehead. You know what they say about assuming anything, right?

Okay, true. The theory might be complete pie in the sky. But now that I'd thought of it, I had to at least check it out.

I turned to Tíereachán. "Remember how we were talking about plagency, earlier?" When he nodded speculatively, I bit my lip and said, "I think I might have figured out how to do it with people."

"Interesting." He gave me a sly wink. "You going to give it a try?"

I smiled. He was acting so relaxed when I knew for a fact his emotions were anything but. I could feel his doubt and growing concern through our connection, even with my shield firmly in place, but he was playing it cool, supporting me when I needed it most. I could have hugged him for that.

"Maybe," I replied. "I don't plan on going anywhere yet. Lemme ... feel around, see if it's possible, first."

To be honest, I wasn't enthusiastic about participating in yet another blood ritual. If I could find and rescue Caiside without tying myself to another person, I was all for giving that a go.

I turned to Alex. "I'm going to try this real fast. If it doesn't work, then I'll use the *ríutcloch*."

He didn't say anything, just studied me with a grave expression and then nodded his assent.

I looped the necklace over my head and dropped the pendant inside the collar of my shirt. The chain was long enough that the stone hung low, between my breasts. Ready as I'd ever be, I put my hands in my lap, so I didn't have to worry about accidentally touching anything, and closed my eyes. I refused to let myself think about how I didn't have the first clue what I was doing. I thought of that singular place, the Between. I remembered how it felt, played its unique tune in my mind, and then, when I couldn't delay any longer, forced my telekinesis into that barren, resonant world beyond.

I don't know why I was so surprised when it worked. But I was, and it took me a moment of stunned inaction, astonished by the overwhelming sensation of the Between blaring at me through my magical conduit, before the true significance of the move sank in.

I'd sidestepped my magic to a destination based solely on a *feeling*. Interestingly, it wasn't all that different from how I sidestepped into the higher dimension.

This discovery was so revelatory, I had to think about it, follow the chain of reasoning a dozen times, until I was left with one amazing truth ...

If I could sidestep my magic directly to the Between, I could, without a doubt, follow with my body. And if I could do that, then I could sidestep to other locations—like my bedroom. Or the telepath's headquarters. Or my office.

Or any freaking place I'd visited and could recall its plagency.

And if I could do that, it meant—

I gasped, jolting to my feet, and staggered away from the table. My heart beat a fierce tempo in my ears, almost blocking out the collective eruption of voices around me, calling my name, asking me if I was okay. Tíereachán appeared at my elbow. His fierce blue eyes bored into my own.

"Lire, what is it? Is it Caiside?" he asked, alarm lining his face and penetrating our mostly closed connection.

"No. I haven't checked yet. I'm sorry, it's not that. Well, it is sort of that. I ..." I pressed my hand to my chest, trying to catch my breath. "You were right. I didn't want to believe you ... or Kieran ... or anyone."

I swallowed, shaking my head. "Tíer, I ... I'm what you thought. I'm ... a ... a world walker." I frowned. "I mean ... I could be. I think. I have to know the plagency of the place before I can sidestep there, so the *world* thing ... I don't know about that part, exactly, but here, on Earth, I think ... I could do it. I could take you places ... places I know ... places I've been."

I stopped shaking my head when I realized I'd been doing it the entire time I'd been babbling. Whether it was because I didn't want this to be true, couldn't believe it to be true, or didn't know it to be true, I hadn't the foggiest idea.

Tíereachán, however, didn't have any such doubts. "Show me."

"Show you? You mean ... right now?" Eyes wide, I looked past his shoulder to find everyone's focus affixed to our discussion.

"Of course," he replied blithely, as though there weren't a half-dozen other people in the room, including the domn, all of who were waiting for me to find Caiside. "It won't take long. After all, I can hardly say, 'I told you so,' until you prove it."

I gaped at him, probably doing a credible imitation of a startled walrus.

And then ... he winked at me!

It was the wink that snapped me out of it. Well, that and the pride and confidence wafting from him, effectively soothing my fears.

As he stared at me, broadcasting nothing but absolute faith in my abilities, I knew where to go. Holding the desired memory in my mind, I reached for that favored place, the one I most wanted to share with him.

"Stop pushing her," Kieran ordered. "If she doesn't— "

When the answering song resonated down my conduit, matching the one in my head, I wrapped Tíereachán and myself within my TK and sidestepped our bodies along its path.

The room disappeared before I heard Kieran finish his admonishment.

After a disconcerting blur and nauseating lurch, I stood beside a wide-eyed Tíereachán, atop the familiar mountain overlooking Yosemite Valley that I remembered so well from my childhood. The cold, pine-scented breeze was the first thing I noticed, followed by the shocked gasps and startled shrieks from several nearby hikers.

Ignoring them, along with my goosebumps, I grabbed Tíer's hand and dragged him down the dirt path to the nearest railing. Excitedly, I pointed to Half Dome and the luscious valley below, both of which were shadowed by an overcast but no less magnificent sky.

"I can do it. I can really do it!" I stared at him, seeing my own excitement mirrored back in his expression. "All these years and I didn't realize that when I visit a place, my memory of it isn't strictly what I can see, but also what I *feel*." I squeezed his hand, mainly to stop myself from jumping up and down like an ecstatic five-year-old. "Ever since you guys started telling me I was 'the one,' I resisted it because I couldn't understand how I could have this gift and not know. What I didn't realize was that all my life I've been aware of the plagency of places, I just didn't know they were significant."

"Does this mean you plan to listen to me, now?"

"I listen to you," I said. "I might not agree with you, but I always listen."

He snorted and then leaned forward to peer into my eyes. "Told you so," he said, grinning broadly. He released my hand and turned to consider the view. After a few moments of companionable silence, while I tried not to shiver at every biting gust of wind, he sighed. "Thank you for this. I never dreamed I'd stand in this valley again."

He took a deep breath, closing his eyes momentarily, and then let it out in a rush. "Perhaps— " He frowned and then shook his head as if to clear his mind. "We should get back." Gaze darting to the ground, he strode a few steps to my right and bent down to pick something up. A pine cone.

"I'll take you anywhere you want to go, Tíer. You know that. Anytime. All you have to do is ask." When he straightened and looked at me, I grinned. "And sometimes even when you don't."

Feeling lighter than I had in weeks, I swathed him in my magic and whisked us back home.

We sidestepped into the stuffy confines of the conference room, a few feet from where we'd departed. In our absence, Wade and Fisk had backed away from the table and now stood in our prior footprints. I'd adjusted our landing instinctively, eliminating another one of my unfounded worries—that I'd accidentally sidestep us into a wall or table or, God forbid, inside a person. Now that I'd done it a couple times, I could see how such a thing wasn't remotely possible, since my magic forged the conduit before I sidestepped along its path. If there was something in the way, I felt around until I found a safe spot to slide into.

We materialized behind Wade and Fisk as the two men faced off against an angry Kim, Kieran, and Alex.

Wade and Fisk whipped around to see the reason for Kim's shocked gasp.

Tíereachán didn't miss a beat. He tossed the pine cone at Kieran, who jolted in surprise but managed to catch it. Looking mystified, he turned it over in his hand and then cast his inquisitive gaze at the two of us.

"*Búancodail* sends her regards, cousin," Tíereachán said. "The valley's as breathtaking as ever." He sauntered to his chair. "Now that we've gotten that detail out of the way, shall we continue with our business? I believe *Cúairtine* was about to contact our lost tracker."

I rolled my eyes, but inside, the warmth of satisfaction blossomed and spread through me. Instead of tearing me down by pointing out how wrong I'd been, Tíereachán built me up, made me feel strong and capable. The guy was better for my ego than getting *Final Jeopardy!* right. I didn't even mind him using the nickname.

"World walker?" Wade asked. "She took you to *Búanco-dail*? Just now?" He frowned at the pine cone in Kieran's grasp before stepping around Kim, Kieran, and Alex to follow Tíereachán to his chair.

"Of course," Tíereachán replied. "Don't tell me you doubted it."

"No," he said. "Only surprised she learned to do it without training."

"Hello. I'm right here," I muttered.

"There's no doubt. She is *Anóen*. The One," Tíereachán said. "The prophecy will be fulfilled, with or without training."

"Adept, *Anóen, Cúairtine*, the one ..." I stomped to my chair, grumbling, "I swear, if anyone calls me anything else, they're in for the mother of all atomic wedgies." I leveled an accusing finger at Tíereachán. "Dude, you've been warned."

He laughed. "After two thousand years of waiting, what did you expect? Both sides have come up with several. If you don't like that one, may I suggest another?"

I growled inarticulately at him.

He grinned back, chuckling. "Lire, sit down. Caiside waits."

I landed in my chair and snatched up my abandoned gloves.

"I take it you did something significant, something you've not done before?" Alex asked once he'd retaken the seat adjacent to me.

"Not merely significant," Tíereachán replied. "It changes everything. It means she can go where she pleases. Now, no one can hold her."

"Would you stop! I'm sitting right here," I exclaimed, although the pride in Tíer's voice tempered my exasperation.

"So, it's as Caiside described. You can move instantaneously between locations. But more than that. You can take people with you." Alex frowned, his gaze briefly flicking to Tíereachán. "Or, perhaps, only him, because you're mated."

"You know damned well that we're blood-bound, not mated," I said, looking up from putting on my gloves to shoot him an irritated look. "And I can sidestep whoever I want."

"Excellent. When you go to Caiside, you'll take me with you," he announced as if it was a foregone conclusion.

"Whoa, wait a minute," I said. "I thought I was invoking the *ríutcloch*. Who said anything about going *anywhere*?"

"If he could escape, he would have done it by now," Alex replied. "Invoking the *ríutcloch* may not be enough, a fact you and everyone here already suspects."

"Right. And if any of them were asking to go, I could understand. But you?" Eying him suspiciously, I leaned in and said in a pointed undertone, "Why would you risk yourself for a sidhe you haven't seen for a hundred and fifty years?"

"Why did you choose to bind yourself to your prince?"

I blinked. "Is that supposed to answer my question?"

When he stared back silently, one superior brow raised, I rolled my eyes. What was it with immortals and their cryptic responses?

I shifted in my chair. "If you must know, his bond helped me break a transfixing that had been laid on me without my knowledge." Heat sprang to my cheeks as I pretended not to feel Kieran's stare boring into the back of my head.

"Presumably that wasn't your sole reason," Alex said.

Someone at the other end of the table coughed. It might have been Fisk.

I sat back in my seat, frowning at him. "You asked why. That's why."

"Ah." He stared at me, amused. "Breaking this spell was so dire that you simply bound yourself to the nearest sidhe. Is that it?"

"Of course not," I snapped. "Tíer's a friend and a good guy and I— "

The light turned on.

I scowled at him. "You know, you could have just told me that Caiside is your friend. Would that have been so hard?"

Instead of a reply, I got the *look*—the one that said my unique brand of naïveté charmed him to bits. Although, I couldn't fathom what I'd said that was so foolish.

"Fine," I grumbled. "I'll take your *request* under advisement."

After straightening in my seat, I mumbled something about getting started. With the Between's unique tune in my mind, I pushed my telekinesis into that remarkable, desolate place. Easy peasy.

Once again, the sheer number of resonances vibrating through the nexus left me feeling light headed. In fact, the idea of finding Caiside's resonance was so overwhelming, it was hard not to resign in defeat without even trying.

But if I'd done it once to find my own string, surely that meant I could do it for someone else's, right?

Pressing the *ríutcloch* to my chest through the fabric of my blouse, I recalled my previous visit, weeks back when I'd been trapped in the Between. Last time, I hadn't searched the strings so much as *played* them. With that in mind, I cast my magic wide, allowing it to slip over countless resonances at a time, touching upon the individual connections like chords in an otherworldly instrument. Covering territory fast as a thought, I couldn't have said how many strings my magic caressed at any given moment, but the drive to find Caiside propelled me ahead with blinding speed.

I wasn't sure how much time passed, but when I least expected it, I touched upon Caiside's intimately familiar tune, lighting me up like the Eiffel Tower on New Year's Eve.

My surprise came out in a gush. "Oh my God. I found him."

"How is he?" Alex asked. "Is— "

Eyes closed in concentration, I cut off Alex's inquiry with my outward facing palm.

I latched onto Caiside's vibrating string and then slid my TK down its nebulous length toward its source.

The moment my magic slipped to his body, the Otherworld's answering sonority reverberated through my conduit like the tolling of countless bells, all of them ringing in a resplendent, captivating symphony that was as familiar to me as a long forgotten lullaby. With a start, I realized why. I'd felt a strikingly similar tune before, whenever I'd touched the depleted *draíocloch*—the one that was sitting, even now, in my backpack upstairs.

Holy cow! I'd made it to the Otherworld and Caiside's body. Or, more precisely, my magic had made it.

I tentatively spread my invisible fingers over the sidhe, cataloging every square inch, relieved to feel his heartbeat vibrating down my conduit. From what I could tell, he was lying prone on a firm surface. As I moved my magic over him, intent on his condition, it took me a moment to notice that he'd turned to stone beneath my touch. In fact, it wasn't until his heart rate had nearly doubled and he began slapping his hands over various parts of his body that I realized my intrusion was freaking the hell out of him.

Horrified, I withdrew my magic so he could no longer feel it.

Idiot! Of course he's going to freak. What else would he do?

I was reluctant to release him completely, but I didn't want to scare him any more than I already had.

"Do you have him or not?" Alex asked tersely.

"Yes."

But I still didn't know his situation. Unceremoniously grabbing him and yanking him out of there struck me, now, as a bad idea. Besides scaring him senseless, he might not be there against his will. And wouldn't *that* be embarrassing?

"What's the problem? Get him out." I could practically feel the anxiety coming off the strigoi domn in waves.

"Lire— " Kieran began, but I overrode him. I didn't need to hear any more of his admonitions.

"Look, my magic totally freaked him out. I can't just grab him like a claw in one of those cheesy arcade prize machines. I need to talk to him, first."

Alex and someone else, Wade, I think, spoke at the same time. All I heard was: "Take me—use the—there—*ríut-cloch*," but I managed to parse out who said what.

"Alex, if I take us there, he'll probably wig out. I don't want to die doing this, okay? Unlike you, *I'm* not immortal."

"He won't hurt you," he replied forcefully. "Not if I'm there with you."

"You can't know that," I shot back, my eyes still closed as I struggled to keep my magic pinned to the Otherworld. "You haven't seen him in one hund— "

"He'll know me," he snapped. "We're bound."

Fisk erupted, "The fuck you are."

"Do you accuse me of lying, half-breed?" Alex snarled, the sound so low and guttural it made my skin crawl.

My eyes didn't need to be open to know Alex had vamped out. The caustic, putrid smell of death wafted over me, and it was all I could do to maintain my tenuous grip on Caiside.

"Stop," I wheezed as I hunched over the table, fighting the overwhelming urge to slide to the floor and crawl away.

The atmosphere cleared, and Alex's voice soothed me. "I'm sorry, Clotilde. Please, take me to him. We are bound in the same way you and your prince are bound. I assure you, he'll know me."

"If that's true, then you can speak to him through your bond," I rasped, straightening in my chair, but I didn't dare open my eyes for fear of losing my line on Caiside. "Tell him what I'm doing so he doesn't freak out."

"I can't. How is it you don't know this? He can't hear me in the Otherworld."

"It's why we bind our souls, Lire," Wade said. "Only a soulbinding can span between worlds."

That explained why I'd been cut off from my building's djinn when Paimon had pulled me into The Between. Stupid that it hadn't occurred to me sooner.

"I could grab and sidestep him here," I said. "But I don't want— "

"Do it."

Disregarding Alex's command, I released Caiside and withdrew my magic.

I opened my eyes to find the strigoi chieftain on the edge of his chair, his black gaze boring into me and his body taut enough to bounce quarters off. "Alex, calm down and listen. He's more than a little worked up. Put yourself in his shoes for a minute: Out of nowhere, an invisible entity starts groping you in your sleep. What you experienced down in the lobby was a small taste. To sidestep someone, I have to learn their body down to the last cell. Ask Fisk or most of the others here. It's intrusive and aggressive and, unless the situation is dire, I try not to do it to someone without their consent."

I pulled the pendant from under my blouse. "Fortunately, we have a way to do that. How do I use this?"

He sat back in his chair and folded his arms. "Caiside told me you invoke it the same way you'd close a circle. Blood and an investment of will."

"Terrific. Guess it's time to bleed again," I muttered.

Before I could turn to ask Fisk for his knife, Alex extended his hand, palm up. "May I?"

When I frowned down at it, he added, "Give me your hand. I won't bite ... much."

My entire focus snapped to his face, and he snorted, plainly amused. "Clotilde, trust me. After three centuries, I do have *some* self-control."

I removed my left glove and, hesitantly, placed my fingertips on the center of his palm. With a speed and efficiency that drew a small gasp from my throat, he nipped my middle finger and returned my hand, releasing it with considerable formality.

Sweet baby Dracula. I hadn't even noticed his fangs elongate, much less seen him move. Stunned, I blinked down at the drop of blood that welled from my tiny wound. Beyond a mere pricking sensation, it had hardly hurt.

Steeling myself, I pressed the crimson drop to the smooth stone at the center of Alex's former pendant, investing it with my will. Having been through a similar ritual with

Tíereachán, I wasn't surprised by the answering surge of magic that plowed through me, raising goosebumps and instantly telling me that the *ríutcloch* was now mine. Shield firmly in place, I waited for the onslaught of thoughts and emotions that would accompany the new connection.

And waited.

When nothing untoward happened for a full thirty seconds, I cautiously lowered my shield and searched my mind for a new presence. After the surge of magic, I was certain that I'd managed to invoke the *ríutcloch*, but while I could feel Tíer's ever-present rumbling at the fringes of my consciousness, I didn't feel anyone else's.

That's odd.

Maybe our connection was more like the one I, along with all the tenants in my building, shared with the djinn. The djinn were incorporeal. They didn't have blood to share. So, instead, each tenant was bound to the djinn's circle, essentially becoming one of their summoners.

Now that I thought about it, this made a lot of sense. Caiside and I weren't blood-bound to each other, per se. We were each bound, individually, to the *ríutcloch*.

With that in mind, I directed my will at the talisman, calling on Caiside in the same way I called the djinn and was instantly rewarded with the subsonic tremor of a connection.

Caiside?

The response I received was baffling and it took me several seconds to figure out why.

First of all, unlike my communication with Tíereachán, I had zero sense of the speaker's emotions. It was a bit like receiving a text message, except instead of reading the words on a bright screen, they streamed directly into my brain. Once I got past that weirdness, I realized he was speaking Silven. And by the speed of his words, he was anxious to know why I wasn't responding.

I hope you speak English, I thought to him. *Otherwise this is going to be a short conversation.*

Haltingly, the following words came to me: *You? Or is this yet ... another cruel dream? Do you ... torment me ... spirit?*

Spirit? I'm no spirit. My name is Lire and I'm with several people who are concerned about you. They think you're being held prisoner somewhere. Is that true?

Right about the time I'd decided to repeat my question, his response came to me: *Udh, tani hessio ... antìgaid nunn. But it cannot be. Nothing pierces the enebráig. You are a figment. Begone ... drogleum. Cease tormenting me.*

Caiside, in English, please. I don't understand Silven, I reminded him. *Where are you? Do you need help? Is someone holding you prisoner?*

But all I got in response was more Silven with several words repeated over and over, as if he was chanting something.

"What does *drogleum* mean?" I asked the room at large.

"Dream," Kieran offered.

"More like a bad dream," Tíereachán corrected, "Or spirit."

Kim nodded. "Agreed."

"What about *enebráig*?"

Kieran's pinched gaze flicked to Tíereachán and he uttered something in Silven.

Tíereachán frowned. And he wasn't alone in that response. Everyone who understood Silven looked either alarmed or displeased or both.

Before I could get an English explanation, Fisk volunteered something that was no doubt contentious because the room exploded in a riot of raised voices, everyone to my right talking at once, so that, even if they hadn't all been speaking in another language, it still would have been difficult to make heads or tails of the conversation.

As I slipped my glove back on, Alex leaned over to speak to me. "It doesn't matter if he thinks you're a dream. You spoke to him. Bring him here. He'll realize you're for real when you grab him. He's not stupid. He'll know you're helping him."

After turning the idea over in my mind, I couldn't argue with it. My reason for not bringing Caiside here, earlier, was because I didn't want to nab him without warning. But now that I'd spoken to him through the necklace, Alex was probably right. As soon as Caiside felt my magic, he'd realize I wasn't a dream. I was real and I intended to help him. And, if this ended up being a huge misunderstanding, if he wasn't a prisoner, I could send him back. No harm, no foul.

Given my understanding of the situation, it seemed like a reasonable conclusion at the time. So, in my defense, it's not as though I acted without thought, okay?

It was afterward, when I was dazed by nausea and the stifling atmosphere, that I realized my mistake.

Of course, by then, it was too late.

Using the *ríutcloch*, I reached through the conduit to wrap my magic around Caiside, feeling the echo of my decisive efforts reflected back through our connection as I deftly cataloged his body. I thought it was strange that I could feel my own magic traipse over my skin as I applied it to him, but dismissed it as a side effect of our mutual connection through the beacon.

Moments later, when I had his body wholly within my grasp, his resonance chiming through my mind, I yanked him toward me, intending to drop him behind Alex's chair.

Bizarrely, my world heaved and spiraled in response, constricting down to a blurred point at the center of my vision. Feeling weightless, Tíereachán's aggrieved bellow resounded in my ears and sliced through my mind before darkness consumed me, instantaneously severing our connection.

It all happened so fast, I didn't even have time to gasp.

TWELVE

I flew sideways in absolute darkness before striking a cool, hard surface. I landed skewed, my shoulder hitting first, preventing a more painful and potentially serious blow to my head. As it was, pain shot up the side of my neck and the wind whooshed out of me. Still spinning from an inexplicable force, my body whipped over to my stomach and my left arm twisted cruelly up behind my back. A monstrous weight fell on me, crushing me flat.

Blinking against the dizziness and struggling to get air, I came to my senses, prone and restrained, the cause of my confinement breathing heavily against the side of my face. He spoke sharply, his foreign words coarse yet musical, right next to my ear.

Oh my God! What the hell is happening?

I reached for my magic, desperate to get away from this surprise attack and found …

… nothing.

No power.

No magic.

No escape.

It felt distinctly as though I'd fallen backward, butt first, to find that my chair had dematerialized when I wasn't looking.

Still ranting incomprehensibly, the man on my back yanked my wrist harder, sending an agonizing jolt of pain all the way up my arm and through my shoulder.

Sobbing, I cried out, "Stop! God! Please stop!"

To my shock, my attacker did. In fact, he released me.

Woozy, I managed to roll over and come to my knees. I slumped, bracing my hands on the cool floor. Everything felt sickeningly off kilter. I tried to pop my ears, but the futile effort didn't alleviate the odd pressure inside my head. It took more than a minute of taking deliberate, steady breaths before the feeling of nausea passed. When I was pretty sure I wouldn't throw up, I eased back to sit on my heels, smoothed my disheveled hair out of my eyes, and got my first clear look around me.

The conference room was gone. In its place, I knelt in a cavernous, sparsely furnished, monochromatic room. Oddly, there were no windows and, stranger still, every-thing, including the floor, walls, ceiling, small table, single utilitarian chair, bookcase, and unadorned bed were all carved from a creamy yellow stone that reminded me of limestone. If there were doors or windows, they weren't ap-parent. The room was dimly lit, every surface seeming to ra-diate a subtle glow, giving the impression that I'd been confined to a stone bubble that floated inside a sea of light.

A male sidhe, the room's sole occupant, stood in front of the massive bed staring at me with an expression that could only be described as enraged puzzlement. As soon as I laid eyes on him, I realized what had happened.

Somehow, when I attempted to yank Caiside to Earth, I'd been pulled into his world instead.

It had to be. Like the figure I'd examined with my TK, this man was tall and thin. He was at least as tall as Fisk, but where Fisk was a solid wall of muscle, Caiside appeared al-most ethereal. Of course, it was all relative. After feeling the whole of him on top of me, I knew this guy was no feather-weight. He wore beige drawstring pants and nothing else. No shirt. No shoes. His smooth skin was paler than the stone that surrounded us, making the defined muscles of his slen-der torso appear even more chiseled than they might have otherwise. When my gaze made it to his face, his blue eyes were narrowed with suspicion as he examined me with a keenness equal to my own.

"Well, there goes my theory that sidhe are genetically incapable of having curly hair," I said, eying his long brown ringlets as I indecorously wobbled to my feet. "Although, I guess the jury's still out on copious body hair. Or anything but perfect, luminous skin."

My inane comment earned me his perplexed frown, but even scowling, the man was beautiful. Of course, that went without saying when it came to the sidhe.

Staring at him, I rubbed my wrist and rotated my neck and shoulder, relieved to discover I'd suffered nothing worse than some bruises.

"Human, you may dispense with your pathetic attempts at seduction," he said, his voice sounding rustier than a dilapidated chain-link fence. He cleared his throat and, gesturing dismissively, he croaked, "Alone one season or twenty, it matters little. Your charms do not entice. Inform Evgrenya, her newest ploy, while somewhat ... interesting, will not— " Eyes widening, his mouth snapped shut, cutting off his haughty command.

He charged toward me, faster than I'd have expected a lanky six-foot-four man to move, his expression fierce. "How did you come by this?" he demanded, his ragged voice echoing through the cavernous space, as he, none too subtly, made a grab for the pendant hanging between my breasts.

Pressing the pendant protectively to my chest, I darted to the side, barely escaping his ham fist. "Keep the hell off me. Where are your manners?" I backed away, putting more than a body length between us. "Alex gave it to me. He also said you were smart enough to figure out that I'm trying to help you." I looked him up and down. "Apparently, he was wrong. I swear to God, when I get back home, I am kicking that vampire's ass into next week."

He froze. "Alexei? He ... still lives?" His expression turned pained, and I wanted to slap myself for being so bitchy. It was starting to look as though he really was here against his will, held hostage by Evgrenya, judging by his earlier comment.

"Yes. And he's worried about you. I think he's been worried for a long time, but it took him a while to find someone he could trust to use this." I opened my palm, allowing the pendant to hang freely.

He shook his head, his eyes growing shiny with emotion. "All these years … and he is yet more honorable than any sidhe."

"Yeah, well …" I glanced around the room uncomfortably, giving him a chance to compose himself. "I'm glad to hear you say that because I'm pretty sure we're dealing with a worst case scenario here, and he swore to do something for me in case that happened."

I searched my mind for my link to Tíereachán, but not surprisingly, found nothing.

Fasten your seat belt Dorothy, 'cause Kansas just went bye-bye.

Musing on the all too appropriate *Matrix* movie quote, I spun on my heel to more thoroughly examine my surroundings. Unfortunately, the effort left me no closer to spotting a way out. "I swear, one of these days I'm going to learn my freaking lesson. No good deed goes unpunished."

"You should not have come," Caiside announced.

"Tell me something I don't know," I groused, meeting his gaze. "No offense to you or this lovely locale, but I wasn't planning to show up here at all. What I *tried* to do was use my magic to pull you through this thing's conduit"—I flicked the pendant— "but per goddamned usual, instead of a rescue, I'm dealing with yet another clusterfuck."

At his shocked expression, I added, "Pardon my French."

He blinked at me. "Mademoiselle, your manner of speech is almost as … *remarkable* as your dress." He scanned me up and down and marveled, leaving little doubt that 'remarkable' was a polite way of saying 'scandalous.' "You are no figment, my imagination could not have conjured such a thing. You are *Anóen*. It must be so for Alexei to bestow the *ríut-cloch*."

My brows went up. Had he concluded, in his raspy but no less cultured accent, that I must be real because of my coarse words and distressed skinny jeans?

"You think *I'm* bad," I muttered. "Just wait until you get a load of Fisk and his Bowie knife."

He straightened. "Lord Fisk? You speak of … Lord Jonathan Fisk?"

"Lord?" I think my jaw bounced a few times after hitting the floor. I almost laughed until the implication of our exchange penetrated my dense brain.

Caiside had been here for over a century.

Unlike Fisk and the others, he hadn't experienced the gradually changing times or seen his compatriots reinvent themselves as the years went by.

I sure had a difficult time imagining Fisk in the role of a titled lord, though.

"I think you'll find things have changed a lot while you've been here. The John Fisk I know isn't a lord. He's a— " I pressed my lips together, resisting the urge to say something unflattering and admitted, "I'm not the best person to ask, but I will say, he's a good guy to have on your side in a fight."

I cocked my head to the side, studying him. "So it's true—what the amhaín and the others suspect. You've been here for a long time … held prisoner by Evgrenya? She's been— " I snapped my teeth together as heat rushed to my cheeks. "Does King Faonaín know? Is he involved in this despicable scheme too?"

"I know nothing of the king. Evgrenya's degenerates captured me …" He seemed to think for a second and then sighed heavily. "Alas, I have no account of how many seasons ago." He eyed me. "But it would seem, by your blush, you have knowledge of Evgrenya's purpose, if not her folly."

He stepped closer, gazing at me earnestly. "Therefore, do you yet understand your plight? Once you are discovered here, she will employ all means to harness your power. And I have come to learn, there is no limit to her depravity."

His haunted expression, combined with the tone of his voice, raised the hairs on the back of my neck.

"I'll take your word for that," I told him. "Better yet, I'll take it all the way back to Earth with us. Problem is: It's hard to sidestep when I can't even pull enough magic to trip a car alarm. Is this place shackled or something? Is that how they keep you here?"

His brows furrowed. "I stay because this is *enebráig.* There is no egress."

Now, it was my turn to look confused. "Okay," I drawled. "Yeah, I can see there're no windows or doors, but presumably people do come and go? Someone has to bring you food and stuff, right? How are they getting in and out of here?"

"What you humans term 'earth magic' creates a temporary opening for one who is keyed to enter, but I've not received a visitor for many ... many a season. Evgrenya has come to believe that depriving me of attention will encourage compliance. Food and water are supplied through the conveyor."

If his hoarse voice, awkward, somewhat robotic manner, and the halting lilt in the way he spoke were any indication, I suspected Caiside hadn't simply been deprived of attention—he'd been *starved* of it, maybe for years. God knew, maybe for *scores* of years. No wonder his voice had sounded so rusty.

Jesus.

I didn't know how similar our psychological makeups were, but I had to believe Caiside would need some major therapy after all of this.

"We're getting out of here," I told him. "I promise you. If I can't figure something out, then Tíereachán and Kieran will."

His body jolted. "Tíereachán?" He stared at me, mouth agape. "The amhaín's son—he, too, survives?"

"Yes. And I can guarantee he won't give up until he finds me. Besides that, I seriously doubt the king is going to sit back and do nothing. This is one of those times when being *the one*"—I rolled my eyes and wiggled my fingers in the universal 'woo-woo' gesture— "might work in my favor."

"What do you mean by ..." He imitated my mid-air finger waggling. "Do you not believe yourself to be *Anóen*?"

"For a long while, no, I didn't. Now, though ..." I shrugged. "I guess it's more a case of not *wanting* to be 'the one.'"

He nodded gravely. "It is a heavy burden."

"Oh, I don't know. For all I know, it could be fun if I didn't have to deal with all the assholes. Seems like everyone wants a piece of me, which has me pissed about it most of the time."

He looked startled. "It has compelled you to drink?"

"Drink? What are—?" I frowned at him and then shook my head, chagrinned. "Oh, God. No. That's slang for ticked off. You know, angry. Sorry. Half the stuff I'm saying must sound nuts to you. Just ... give me a heads-up if— " I held up my hands, palms out. "Let me rephrase that. Whenever I say something you don't understand, please say so. Okay?"

"Very well."

I bit my lip. "Tell me about this place. You called it *enebráig*. What's that? A prison colony or something?"

"No. *Enebráig* is the nature of this confinement. The very rocks are imbued to disrupt spellcasting. Any spell, any enchantment, whether it be for good or ill, is reflected back to the caster."

"But why bother? There's not enough magic here to light a match."

"Not true, *Anóen*. You are merely accustomed to Earth and her vast, global reservoir. But even if that weren't so, *enebráig* also interferes with spells cast from afar where magic might be more plentiful, as you discovered when your rescue attempt resulted in— " Frowning, he blinked. "How did you so charmingly describe it? A *clusterfuck*?"

"I would never say something so unseemly," I said, pressing my hand to my chest, feigning indignation.

After a moment of wary consideration, he gave me a slow smile, but it disappeared too quickly. I could have smashed Evgrenya's face for her role in diminishing such a lovely sight.

We were *so* getting out of here, and if I ever got my chance, I'd find a way to repay his captors—in spades.

Of course, I wouldn't be doing much of *anything* if I couldn't garner enough potential to power my TK.

After another fruitless effort, I blew out a frustrated breath. "If it's not dry as a bone here, then why do I keep coming up empty?"

He paused a beat, his head tipping to the side like an inquisitive bird. "You refer, of course, not to water but to the available potential." He looked doubtful.

I scoffed. "What potential? Whenever I pull what I need for my TK, I get a big, fat nothing-burger."

Being without reliable access to magic made me distinctly uneasy. All I needed was for Evgrenya or her goons to show up. Tíer's boast, 'Now, no one can hold her,' had clearly been premature. This is what I got for getting cocky.

I paced the width of the room and raked my fingers through my hair, briskly forcing it behind my ears. "If there's potential here, I need it ASAP. I'd like to get out of here. Alex and Tíereachán are probably freaking out, along with everyone else."

I shuddered to think how Kieran might have reacted. Tíer's bellow before it all went black was bad enough. I grimaced when I considered what might have happened after my abrupt disappearance. It didn't take a psychiatrist to realize most of the people in that room were going to be pretty darn unhappy when they learned Alex had encouraged me to snag Caiside. I hoped they were smart enough to know that Alex wouldn't have encouraged me to do it if he knew I'd get sucked into the Otherworld. The idiot would have made sure I took him with me.

Caiside looked perplexed, which meant I'd been speaking gibberish again. Remembering to moderate my speech was harder than I expected it to be. Being a stress-case didn't help.

"Sorry," I said. "I need magic for my telekinesis, but every time I pull from my core, I get nothing."

"The magic here is a trickle compared to Earth's torrent, I grant you, but I would not describe it as insignificant." His brows dipped together as he considered me. "Perhaps you have little experience drawing from such a meager source. On Earth, one might cast spells with the barest of preparation since the supply fills one's center without delay. In this world, you must allow the potential to fill you beforehand. But I must dissuade you, *Anóen*. Casting in this place, while not always fatal, may cause you irreparable harm."

"Call me Lire, okay? And you don't need to worry. With what I have in mind, I won't actually be *casting* my TK on anyone."

Please, God. This had to work. If I couldn't sidestep my TK through the anti-magic barrier, like I hoped, I wouldn't be able to establish a conduit to Earth. And, without one, I didn't know how the hell I was going to get us out of here.

"As you wish, Mademoiselle Lire." He bowed from the waist. "Caiside, at your service." After straightening, he said, "I believe you might enjoy greater success if, instead of drawing upon your magic as though yanking fabric from its bolt, you pull but a single thread until you possess the necessary potential for your casting."

I'd never thought of my psychic abilities as something that required casting. They weren't spells. It was true that each boon required the raw power that all spellcasters utilized, but I didn't need a focus or a gesture or a chant to initiate them. In fact, my brand of magic had always come so naturally, with very little in the way of preparation, that until now, I'd never considered the minutia of *how* I went about it. This wasn't all that surprising, I guess. If your bathtub was always full, why learn how to use the faucet?

This time, instead of spooling the necessary magic with one greedy heave, as I'd always done, I imagined myself sucking the potential into my core through a tiny juice-box straw.

Slow and steady ...

For the first time since arriving, I felt the reassuring re-verberation of potential as it, ever so gradually, filled me. I sagged, closing my eyes in relief, and blew out the pent breath I'd been holding. It would take a while to accumulate the necessary potential to feed my TK, but at least now, I had no doubt I'd eventually get there.

"Jesus. No wonder you guys are all such skilled swords-men," I blurted. Talking while trying to keep up a consistent pull through my imagined straw was a bit like rubbing my head and patting my stomach, but I managed. "Between your shrouds and this scant dribble of magic, offensive spells must be next to useless."

He nodded gravely. "Now you may appreciate that which inspires Evgrenya and those like her to not merely find but also control an adept."

"Because an adept can access Earth's reservoir."

He tipped his head in acquiescence. "Thereby providing the lifeblood for our world. Without Earth's vast potential, we would be forced to the surface to live and die as savages. Thus, since time immemorial, whoever controls the adept, controls our very destiny."

Goosebumps broke over my arms and crawled up the back of my neck. "And what about your lady?" I asked. "Does this drive to control your world's destiny also inspire the amhaín's actions? Does she want to control an adept too?"

"My lady is not immune to the desire for power," he ad-mitted. "She has sought it, if only to protect herself and the lives of her people. But having been bent to the will of her own brother, I believe with all fervor that her ambition was tempered by that experience. While it's true that she has in-fluenced the furthering of certain ancestral lines, including her own, she has never resorted to coercion. Of this fact, I may personally attest. Nor has she, to my knowledge, kept prisoners for the sole purpose of breeding such offspring." Shifting his gaze to our surroundings, he added, "As others do."

While I was relieved to hear this, it didn't escape my notice that he hadn't answered the one question that mattered most. Would the amhaín attempt to hold and control me?

As I contemplated whether to push him for an answer, my thoughts slid to the absurd when I sensed a growing vibration beneath my feet and found myself wondering whether Caiside had a washing machine running in the next room.

It didn't take long, though, for my mind to leap to the rational and infinitely more worrisome thought: *Nuala died in an earthquake*.

"Do you feel that?" I asked. "Or is it just me?"

As I shifted my feet into a wider stance, I looked for any outward sign to explain the tremors, but there were no chandeliers with their tell-tale swing to betray the earth's movement. Nothing to see except immobile stone furnishings and the dozens of leather-bound books stacked neatly in the four-shelf bookcase.

"I feel it, too," Caiside replied calmly, but I noticed he scanned our surroundings like a cat eying a tub of flea dip, which didn't put my mind at ease.

As a long-time Seattle resident, I'd been through my share of sizable earthquakes, including the memorable South Sound quake. Anyone who lived in the area for that 7.2 temblor remembered where they'd been and what they'd been doing when it hit. I'd been in seventh grade chemistry class where a cabinet full of equipment toppled over, shattering glass beakers and injuring several students, including me. My right ankle still bore the scars.

I backed up to plant myself against the nearest wall and waited for the ground to begin gyrating under me. Strangely, although the vibrations seemed to grow to the point of near audibility, I had yet to feel the weird swaying, wave-like motions that I associated with earthquakes on Earth. Whatever this was, it seemed too restrained to be an earthquake. It felt ... more like a herd of wildebeests stampeding next door.

Caiside's eyes widened in alarm. "*Anóen*, you must leave! Leave now! The king, he— "

The ominous report of a bugle and the braying of hounds drowned out his warning, but it hardly mattered. I didn't need his explanation to know what was coming.

That type of horn call was synonymous with one thing.

A hunt.

And, with my core not even half-filled, sidestepping wasn't an option.

Son of a bitch! Brassal must have told the king that I'd been pulled into the Otherworld, stuck inside an *enebráig* prison, giving his *Wuldrífan* an ideal chance to snap me up.

Cold air washed over me before a pack of ghostly dogs bounded into the room, their lean, dappled forms materializing from nowhere, white-tipped tails trained upward and black snouts busily scenting the frigid air. Great clouds billowed past my lips, betraying my fear-quickened breaths, as I flattened myself against the wall. Ludicrously hoping for obscurity, I gawked at their gyrating, etherial bodies. Sleek and muscular, with elongated muzzles, long legs, and unusually large, erect ears, they were unlike any Earth canine breed I'd ever seen. And, when their penetrating silver eyes locked onto my position, I knew without a doubt they were also considerably smarter.

In unison, they charged, snarling and yapping and looking more than capable of drawing blood in spite of their phantom-like appearance. And, if that wasn't enough, directly on their heels, five armored huntsmen, each astride a towering, black horse, exploded into the room, their formidable beasts adding to the discord with their stomping hooves and labored breathing. The lead horseman, who rode the largest charger, taxed the room's high ceiling with his massive horned helm, both of which marked him more plainly than a blazing neon sign as the Master of the Hunt.

I might have remained frozen and agape if a dog hadn't nipped my right calf, rending a terrified shriek from my throat. If I'd been a gecko, I would have climbed the wall, but when another dog readied itself to lunge, fury roared through me.

Instead of tender flesh, the second hound got a taste of my size eight steel-capped Doc Marten. I wasn't fast enough to deliver a direct kick, but I clipped the aggressive hound hard enough under the jaw to elicit its startled yelp and send it plowing into the dog on its right, prompting a brief skirmish among its jostling pack mates.

"I'm not food, bitch!" I screamed, poising to fend off the next attack.

Presumably, King Faonaín wanted me alive, but I wasn't sure how much control he maintained over the Wild Hunt once he released it. As I watched the dogs snarl and vie for position, I decided 'wild' wasn't an exaggeration. An animal expert didn't need to tell me I was a whisker away from a savage attack, and once that happened, lug-soled boots or not, I'd be torn apart in no time.

A definitive sour note from the rear huntsman's horn, however, recalled the dogs as though they were attached to him by springs. Filling the fast emptying gap, the Master of the Hunt, sheathed in the battle accoutrements of a bygone era, surged toward me on his charger, the clamor of slithering chainmail, creaking leather, and pounding hooves providing deadly musical accompaniment.

From on high, the spectral huntsman loomed over me, his face hidden behind the macabre faceplate of his massive helm, which, by all appearances, had been molded from the skull of a monstrous Otherworld beast. The column of frozen air displaced by the horse's swift move swirled around me, and I hugged myself against the redoubled cold as my teeth chattered.

The horned specter leveled his metal encased index finger at my face and issued a lengthy command, his hard, baleful voice grating unpleasantly through the room.

I enjoyed being singled out by this creature even less than being bitten by a spectral hound, but when I realized I'd again retreated to plaster my backside to the wall, the heat of indignation blossomed in my chest.

Enough!

I was *not* prey.

Squaring my shoulders, I stepped away from the wall and snapped, "I don't speak Silven," from between my clattering teeth.

"He asks whether you will ride with him willingly or be trussed up and strapped to his saddle like game," Caiside volunteered before he uttered a pained hiss at the hands of the huntsman who'd leapt from his mount to hold a wicked dagger to the defenseless sidhe's throat.

I held up my hands in the universal gesture of appeasement. "Please, he's trying to help." I shot the lead huntsman a beseeching look. "I'll go with you. Please, don't hurt him."

Without further discourse, the horned hunter clamped his massive, gloved hands to my shoulders and plucked me from the floor as though I weighed no more than a paper cutout. I gasped as he dropped me crosswise in the saddle atop his frozen lap, my right leg skewed to the outside of the saddle's rounded pommel. With my butt penned by his right hip and my legs dangling over his left thigh, I had no choice but to grapple with his armored torso, snaking my arms around him to avoid going ass over teacup when he released me to take up the reigns of his horse. Bitter cold engulfed me, numbing my body wherever I sat in direct contact with the Master of the Hunt or his horse. The chill seeped into my bones and clouded my vision so that my surroundings took on a wavy, muted aspect, as though I viewed everything through a pane of antique glass.

The horned rider's voice rumbled harshly above my head, as harmonious as an ocean liner running aground.

Caiside grunted and then bit out, "He advises you to hold fast unless you wish to experience the void's merciless grasp."

As the charger's muscles flexed beneath me, I struggled to peer past my captor's broad shoulder to meet Caiside's tortured frown. I was relieved to see that the huntsman had released him unscathed.

I was tempted to ask them to take Caiside too, but I'd heard and read many things about the Wild Hunt, including dire warnings against crossing their path during a hunt. If they took him, there was no guarantee he'd arrive at the king's palace alive.

"Caiside, I'll come back! I swear it," I exclaimed as the horse beneath me sprang violently skyward, jostling me hard enough against my captor's metal clad chest to momentarily drive the wind from my lungs. I locked my right ankle under my left calf, pinning the minimal swell of the pommel between my thighs, and hoped like hell it would help keep me in the saddle.

"I'll get you out. I promise," I wheezed, even though I knew my voice had been swallowed by the huntsman's horn and the raucous tumult of the hunt as the riders spurred their mounts into the realm where the living surely dared not tread.

Icy-tipped agony tore through me as the world tried to shift away, the warm yellow rock twisting inward like a rubber sheet sucked down a vortex, and for a long tortuous moment, I felt every molecule in my body stretching along with it, refusing to let go, until I thought I'd be torn apart. Desperate for relief, I tore off my right glove and shoved my hand beneath the leader's massive helm, relieved when I found cold skin instead of razor sharp teeth. I pulled what little magic I had in my core and, with an aggrieved scream, severed my attachment to Caiside's prison, seeking instead to anchor myself to the resonance of the creature beneath me.

His body stiffened as the resulting snap of release catapulted the three of us—rider, horse, and captive—violently into the unknown like a death-seeking, transcendental missile.

The preternatural, bloodcurdling screech that emanated from both horse and rider accompanied us into oblivion.

THIRTEEN

Somehow, I stayed in the saddle. For countless seconds, I clamped my eyes shut, squeezing the horned rider's thick body like a lemur clutching a wind-whipped tree trunk. When his chest began shaking beneath me, out of sync with the horse's unnaturally smooth stride, I risked cracking my eyes, hugging him even tighter as I readied myself for yet another pain-filled trial. Beyond my captor's shuddering chest, a bleak, gray landscape blurred past as his powerful steed sped us toward our destination.

No threat in sight, as far as I could tell.

Above me, I registered the harsh discord of repetitive barks, which penetrated the combined din of the baying hounds, his charger's huffed breaths, and the jangling of armor. Strangely, his horse's hooves made no sound as it galloped and there was nothing in the way of wind, which made everything feel oddly surreal.

I eased my iron grip to stare up at the Master of the Hunt. "You're ... *laughing*?" I asked, too stunned to remember he didn't speak my language.

"Not without considerable challenge," he replied, his powerful, acerbic voice reverberating from beneath his hideous helm. "How is it the only quarry I cannot hold is the one who clings to me as tenaciously as death's eternal shroud?"

I gaped up at him. Tenacious or not, at that moment, he could have knocked me from the saddle with a feather boa.

"You speak English."

Apparently, such an astute observation barely merited a dismissive grunt.

"Why didn't you speak it once you knew I couldn't understand Silven?"

"Human tongues are a punishment to the ear," he rumbled.

With a voice that matched the lowest notes from a decaying pipe organ, I didn't think it was the particular language at fault. Still, I had to admit, even his guttural delivery had a certain musical quality that seemed to go part and parcel with the sidhe.

He whooped something at the other riders, a bellow that jolted me against his icy body. His horse's furious pace slackened as a plaintive call on the horn echoed around us.

My stomach clenched. "Have we arrived?" I gripped his left arm. "Please, I can't manage another transition like that. Not this soon."

I'd depleted most of the potential in my core with our escape, and, although the flow of magic seemed to increase the closer we drew to King Faonaín's territory, I wouldn't be anywhere near full for several minutes yet.

He tilted his head downward, and I could practically feel his black, disapproving gaze on my hand as he replied curtly, "It will be some moments yet before we reach the king's fortress."

I withdrew my hand. "Will you warn me when we get close?"

"If it will avoid a repeat of the discomfort of our departure, then, yes," he grumbled. "Had I known what you are, I would have done things differently."

I wondered what this 'difference' would have entailed. Nothing good, by the sound of it.

"What did you mean when you said I'm the one quarry you can't hold?"

He snorted, whether in disbelief or disdain, I couldn't venture to guess without seeing his face. "You are a *cú-airtine*," he ground out. "You may cross worlds at will, yet you cling to me as if falling from my horse will commit you to oblivion."

"But that's what you said!" I blurted, bristling at his derision. "What the hell did you expect? Besides, I said I'd go with you. I've no desire to be lashed to your horse, thanks."

This, to my astonishment, garnered another round of gruff laughter.

I scowled. "I'm so glad I could be the object of your amusement."

"Yet, is that not the appropriate response to a *cúairtine* who pretends she hasn't the power to condemn the Hunt to eternal chase?"

Huh?

I thought back to what Tíereachán had told me about the Wild Hunt, about their singular, relentless pursuit. "If I sidestep to Earth, you can't easily follow me. Can you? You'd be forced to ride until ..." I blinked and then sucked in a breath. "Since the king doesn't have a gateway, you'd be forced to ride until I happened to come back to the Otherworld. That's what you meant about eternal chase." I frowned. "So, I guess that means the king can't recall you."

At his responding wall of silence, I muttered, "Jeez. That's a hell of a downside."

I looked up at him, although I don't know why I bothered. It wasn't like I could get any sort of read from him by gazing into the black holes of his terrifying helm. Curiosity finally won over intimidation, though, and I asked him why he was obligated to King Faonaín. "Did you commit your soul to a binding when you died?"

"Of a sort," he admitted. "For another king."

"You and the rest of your hunting party are bound to an object. Aren't you? One that's passed down to the reigning king or queen."

"The *Bráigda*, the perennial collar. Yes."

I thought of Red. Over three hundred years ago, moments before his execution during the Salem witch trials, he'd allowed his soul to be captured by a coven of local witches. Since that time, he'd been bound to many vessels and had coped with four previous masters. I was just the latest. I often wondered whether that impulsive decision, long ago, was one he'd come to regret.

"If you could do it over again, would you?" It was a question Red would never be able to answer, as much as I wished knowing.

"There is no greater pleasure than a righteous hunt for a benevolent king."

That didn't exactly answer my question, which made me wonder whether he was under a geas similar to Red's that limited what he could divulge about his binding.

"A righteous hunt for a benevolent king, huh? So ... this"—I swept my hand to indicate the hunters around us— "is a righteous hunt?"

"It does not displease."

"And if you'd been told to kill me instead of capture me? What then?"

"Then I imagine we would not be having this conversation."

Despite my unease at his dry response, I snorted. "No. I imagine not. Would that be righteous? Would that please the *Wuldrífan*—hunting me to my death and thereby avoiding this delightful exchange of ours?" I couldn't help adding my own hint of sarcasm.

The sounds of his shifting armor and the occasional yipping hound filled the intervening the silence. I didn't expect an answer to such a charged question, so when he replied, I jerked in the saddle at his deep voice.

"No, *Cúairtine*," he clipped out. "It would not please."

Interesting. It seemed the Master of the Hunt wasn't the robotic, unfeeling land-shark that my research had led me to believe. That wasn't too surprising given the lack of credible information about the sidhe. Most people still operated under the delusion that all elves were magnanimous and had pointed ears, too, no thanks to Professor Tolkien.

"Well, that's something, I suppose." I shifted in the saddle, trying to find a happy balance where I wasn't so dependent on clinging to him to stay upright. "By the way, my name is Lire. Will you … tell me yours? Master of the Hunt is a mouthful."

"Drustan," he replied after some hesitation.

"So, Drustan, what about Faonaín? Is he as benevolent as your king of long ago?"

When his body went solid beneath me, I didn't need to pursue the ensuing silence for an answer.

"That's what I thought," I mumbled, turning my gaze to the scenery around us. Or, rather, the lack of scenery.

The horses had slowed to a speed more akin to an easy canter, which had rendered the panorama clear to my view but no less bleak. All around us, the brownish-gray surface appeared parched and, as far as my unaided sight could discern, devoid of life and contour. Flat and barren, even its resonance felt as hollow and inert as the unremarkable landscape. The sky, which appeared gray and dead, possessed a uniform dullness that hardly distinguished it from the color of the landscape. Here, there was no sun, no moon, no stars, nothing to mark the passage of time, nor, even, of distance.

To our left, a river of quicksilver paralleled our level path, flowing from horizon to horizon, providing the sole source of relief to the unrelenting desolation in every direction. With nothing nearby to offer any sense of scale, it was difficult to get a sense of its width or how far away it was.

"What is this place?" I asked. "It feels empty and … wrong somehow."

Strangely, though, I no longer felt cold. I speculated that it had something to do with being fully immersed in this plane's resonance, as opposed to sitting at the doorway and feeling its draft. Now that I considered it, both Drustan and the rest of his contingent seemed to appear more solid here, too—less ghostly.

"*Nàsaig*," he replied and then added, "The shore where alone the forsaken linger."

I shivered and pointed to our left. "And what's that?"

His head swiveled to regard the undulating swath of silver. "The river *Crònathir*. I believe humans call it Styx, the unending boundary between the land of the living and death's domain. To enter without sufferance is to be drowned by its waters for all eternity. Be warned, *Cúairtine*, none have the power to escape its grasp, not even one such as you."

With a shudder, I considered the stripe. "Not much to look at, is it? Nothing like it's portrayed in stories ... or the movies. According to myth, there's supposed to be a ferryman, Charon. He carries souls across for a toll—a gold coin, usually."

He snorted, still looking toward the river. "If there is a ferryman, I have yet to see him."

Something told me he'd endured countless opportunities to see everything there was to be seen in this place.

"Is this where you go when you and your men aren't off hunting for the king?"

He nodded, a stiff up and down jerk of his helm.

"And ... I guess you've been bound to this collar thing for a long time, then?"

He didn't deign that with an answer, but I knew he'd been bound for a minimum of three thousand years, because I remembered Kieran saying that's about how long King Faonaín had reigned. Of course, Drustan didn't mention which prior king he'd committed himself to. For all I knew, he'd been stuck as Master of the Hunt for tens of thousands of years.

A sobering thought.

With my core finally filled to the brim, a crazy impulse went through my mind, one that would provide Drustan with a long overdue change of scenery and also give King Faonaín the middle finger.

"So ... I know I told you that I'd come with you and everything," I began. "But if I were to, let's say, sidestep to Earth and maybe accidentally take you along for the ride ... what would happen?"

His whole body stiffened as he jerked his head to stare down at me. "I am compelled to bring you to the king."

"Uh-huh. So, on Earth, you won't die or dissolve into mist or turn into goo or something like that, right?"

He shook his head, I suspected, more in bewilderment than anything else.

"What about your men?" I asked. "What will happen to them if I take you to Earth for a little R & R?"

"The hunt cannot be thwarted," he replied. "We hunt until our quarry is captured or killed, as charged by our master."

"And your horse? Nothing bad will happen if you're parted from each other, right?"

When he stared down at me, in what I guessed was confusion, I blew out a breath. "Look, I don't know the constraints of your binding. Can you dismount from your horse without anything bad happening, or not?"

"Of course I can dismount," he replied as though I'd asked him if he knew the horse's withers from its tail.

"Fine. Hang on. We're gonna take ourselves a little detour."

Before he could argue, I enfolded him within my telekinetic grasp (which, incidentally, drew an entertaining grunt of surprise from beneath his helm), thought of my destination, and sidestepped my magic through the nether.

As soon as my tendril pierced the veil between our worlds, slipping into my building's conference room, the exuberant torrent of Earth's magic, combined with the reassuring tether of Tíereachán's bond, filled me with such utter relief I might have stumbled without the support of my telekinesis.

If someone had told me a bomb had detonated in the conference room while I was away, I wouldn't have questioned it. The conference table laid in two jagged pieces, overturned chairs were scattered everywhere, and I had a heck of a time finding a clear spot to slide us into. With the exception of Red and Diedra, my building's djinn had restrained everyone inside individual, nearly transparent bubbles.

I gaped at the spectacle. Besides the wrecked furniture, Kim looked as though she'd been through a wind tunnel; Wade's clothing was somewhat charred but he appeared otherwise okay; Fisk had a seeping gash on his forehead, bloody scratches down his neck, and his suit jacket was tattered; Tíereachán's left eye had swollen shut, his arms bore slash wounds as though he'd been raked by a clawed animal and his clothes were blackened in spots; Kieran's shoulder was covered in a mass of bloody, clotted punctures; and, lastly, there was Alex, curled into the fetal position, unconscious, his clothing covered in soot, blood clotting at his ears, mouth, nose, and staining the tips of every finger.

The smell of ozone, blood, and burnt fabric assailed my nose, but what caught me flatfooted was the intensity of Tíer's astonishment at my appearance and the overwhelming surge of relief that followed. For a moment, my own surprise mingled with his before his injuries (which were painful but not life threatening) sparked my anger.

"Jesus H. Christ," I shouted, glaring at the lot of them. "I leave for half a goddamned hour and you guys destroy the conference room trying to kill each other? Are you all insane?"

More than one of them gasped at my abrupt return. Or it might have had to do with the enormous armored warrior standing next to me.

Fisk blurted, "What the ...?" His eyes nearly bugged out as he stared at my horn-helmed companion. "You brought us the Master of the fucking Hunt? What the hell happened to Caiside?"

"A certain someone decided to send the Hunt to collect me before I got the chance to sidestep the both of us out of Evgrenya's prison." I lowered my voice. "I don't take kindly to being abducted."

Kim drew herself up straight, nose held high, and it wasn't hard to imagine Brassal doing the same thing in the Otherworld while he used her as his conduit. "Ungrateful human, the king was rescuing you!"

Their lack of reaction to my 'Evgrenya' bombshell told me it was something Kim, Brassal, and Kieran already knew about or, at the very least, suspected.

"I'm a world walker," I snapped. "I don't need rescuing. Caiside—he needs rescuing. My friends—they're the ones who need rescuing."

I took a cleansing breath and fought for a more conversational tone. "You know, I'd be a little more understanding had the king instructed the Hunt to rescue Caiside too. But His Royal Highness didn't bother. The Hunt took only me, and I had to watch Caiside's face when they carried me off, leaving him to rot where he's already spent the past century and a half. Can you even begin to imagine how devastating that must be for him—to have freedom so close at hand just to see it plucked away at the last second?"

Clenching my hands into useless fists, I added, "So don't you dare characterize that as a heroic move. Sending the Hunt for me when the king knew I couldn't get away was anything but heroic. It was a power grab, and you know it."

Turning my back on them, I strode to Alex's unmoving body. I knelt next to him, outside the strange bubble's shimmering shell. Curious, I hesitantly extended my naked hand, now remembering that I'd lost my right glove. When I received no warning from Maya and Tanu, I skimmed my fingers over the surface of their handiwork. Although the bubble's tactile feedback told my brain that I touched something smooth and unyielding, the resonance vibrating beneath my fingertips said something quite ... *other*.

This was not a construct of Earth.

I marveled at it until curiosity got the better of me and I plucked at the bubble with my telekinesis. As the resulting tremor rippled through the shell, I understood what the djinn had done. They'd forged a magic circle around Alex, but instead of utilizing Earth's resonance in its construction, it rang of their own world's.

It hadn't occurred to me that when a spellcaster on Earth crafted a circle, they naturally drew in Earth's resonance when sealing it with their own blood. It made sense. It was all they knew. But the djinn weren't creatures of Earth and, as far as I knew, they didn't have blood. Yet, somehow, they'd forged a circle utilizing their home world's resonance and their own will, which had the effect of creating an unbreakable barrier, a ward of sorts, through which nothing of this physical plane could pass.

Ingenious.

"Is he okay?" I asked the two djinn, who hovered nearby, their gray misty forms swirling like two miniature tornadoes.

"The cursed human is healing his wounds," one of them replied. With both of their incorporeal bodies churning so close to each other, it was impossible to tell which had spoken.

"The djinn interfered before unalterable damage occurred," the other added.

Not sure the conference table would agree, I thought to myself as I surveyed the room. It was pretty clear that the djinn had waited until the last second to intervene. I puzzled over whether they'd done this on purpose. Had watching the fight entertained them?

I gasped as something cold clamped my upper arm and hauled me to my feet.

Drustan, in full master-mode, yanked me toward him. "*Cúairtine* or not, you cannot escape the Hunt. I will bring you to my king, regardless," he boomed, towering over me, once again appearing ghostly.

I cast a withering glance at his grip and stifled an involuntary shiver at the drop in temperature. "Would you lighten up? I already told you, I'm not trying to escape. I'm still your captured quarry, all right? This is just a detour so I can finish what I was doing before I was so rudely interrupted." I shot Kim a pointed glare.

Looking back to my helmed specter, I added, "There's no gateway that you can drag me through, so you may as well relax and enjoy the change of scenery. Don't worry, we'll see the king soon enough."

And when we did, he was going to wish he'd never messed with me. I was done being threatened and intimidated.

I yanked my arm out of Drustan's slackening grip. "By the way, you're on Earth now. No offense, but the helm is a little overkill for a business meeting, even if it does look like the aftermath of a drunken brawl in here."

What was I saying? The armor and helm were overkill period, here or elsewhere. He couldn't be killed. He was already dead! Though, now that I considered it, despite his spectral appearance, he possessed a corporeal form. Was it possible he could be injured? Was that why he wore all that armor?

As I gazed at him, wondering about all this, his helm dissolved to reveal a thick-necked sidhe with smooth plaits of shoulder-length black hair, henna-brown skin, narrowed eyes, and a mouth pinched in displeasure. He also possessed one of the most expertly groomed beards I'd ever seen, which enhanced his high cheekbones and intensely blue eyes.

Wow.

Apparently, the sidhe weren't as homogenous as I'd come to believe.

He was so striking, with his tawny skin and bright eyes, it was hard not to stare, but I managed to stop goggling and looked for a chair that was still intact. "Here," I said, pulling one upright, which was somewhat awkward since I was forced to use my left hand. "Have a seat. This won't take long."

His expression turned caustic. "I have no need to sit."

"Fine. Loom all you want. Just stay out of my way or you'll find yourself in another dimension faster than you can say 'Doctor Who.'" I briefly tightened my TK around his body for emphasis. "Understand?"

He glared down at me and folded his arms, his expression telling me he wasn't impressed but planned to behave—for the moment, anyway.

"Lire, tell your heavy-handed djinn to release us," Kim demanded.

"I have an idea. How about I grab Caiside and let him decide whether they were heavy-handed or not?" I snapped.

"Lire," Tíereachán said, turning my name into a mild reprimand.

"Fine," I groused and shot a look at the two djinn. "Maya, Tanu, please release— "

"Not the vampire," Wade said. "Not until he regains his senses."

As I reexamined Alex, it dawned on me that it probably took a lot of effort to overcome a strigoi as powerful as the domn—hence, the destroyed room. And, I didn't have to be an experienced blood patron to know that an injured strigoi might not wake up well.

"Okay, release everyone except Alex," I clarified.

"As the Lire wishes," the entities replied in unison, prompting the disappearance of their force fields.

I cast a scathing glare at Kim and Kieran. "You know, it's a good thing I figured out a few things while I was over there, otherwise I'd be pretty pissed off at you guys right about now."

I sat down in the chair I'd initially pulled upright for Drustan, careful to avoid touching it with my right hand. I speculated whether my glove had floated to the floor of Caiside's prison or if it was trapped in *Nàsaig*, somewhere along that forsaken shore.

I grumbled at them, "Think you guys can avoid wrecking anything else for the next two minutes while I get Caiside?"

"That's what started this mess in the first place!" Kim exploded.

Right. It was all my fault.

"What was I thinking?" I said with mock gravity before glowering. "The world might explode or something if anyone other than Tíer and Red actually had faith in me."

I had to remind myself that I liked Kim. She was an intriguing combination of sweet and irreverent that I found endlessly entertaining. I loved hanging out with both her and her partner Jackie. Their camaraderie and mutual affection was adorable, plus they were a hell of a lot of fun to be around. Whenever the whole demon-invasion-you're-the-one thing was getting me down, the two of them never failed to cheer me up.

Today, though, there'd been no trace of fun-loving Kim. I'd mainly seen dour-and-moody Kim, thanks to Brassal's influence. Granted, she had a job to do as King Faonaín's emissary, and, as far as I knew, they hadn't added any new ones to replace the part-bloods who'd been murdered. Kim and Brassal were it—the king's sole means of communication. Heck, Brassal was no doubt standing—or kneeling—in the Lord on High's presence, right now, which put both Kim and Brassal in a difficult spot. I kept reminding myself of these things, but when she came across like such a jerk, it was hard to not take it personally.

Nothing was ever easy with these people.

Ignoring her pinched expression, I closed my eyes. This time, I eschewed the beacon still around my neck, in favor of my sidestepping ability, and reached into the Between in search of Caiside's essence.

I'd realized something profoundly important when I matched Drustan's resonance in order to escape Caiside's prison—I could sidestep through a ward, even one as powerful as the *enebráig*.

But that wasn't all.

I could sidestep my telekinesis through a sidhe's shroud too. And once I knew an individual's resonance, I could go through the Between to do it from afar.

Even from a trashed conference room on Earth.

Levering my heels up and down with excitement, I sought Caiside's resonance within the Between's infinite nexus and, upon finding it, followed the tremulous string to his body. As I sidestepped my TK to envelop him within my grasp, he jolted, his body tensing, but he didn't swat at my ministrations. And, unlike the time I'd used the necklace, there was no tell-tale reflection of my magic, which told me definitively that I'd bypassed the prison's ward. If I'd done it this way in the first place, instead of going through the necklace, the whole fiasco with being sucked into his prison wouldn't have happened. Of course, I wouldn't have learned some important lessons either.

Before I sidestepped him to stand in front of me, I stroked his cheek with my magic.

A split-second later, he materialized three feet away, blinking back the bright lights and breathing hard.

Yes!

"Am I cooking with gas or what?" I exclaimed, jumping to my feet.

After a moment of awed fascination, Caiside's expression turned to alarm and his focus snapped to Alex, who was struggling to a sitting position within the confines of the djinn's last remaining bubble.

"Alexei," Caiside rasped, settling to his knees near the injured strigoi.

He pressed the flat of his hand to the shimmering prison and then considered me, his eyes turning angry. "He needs blood to fully heal. Release him."

I stepped closer. "Is he in control?"

The more I looked at Alex, the less I liked the idea of setting him loose. He was breathing erratically with extended fangs and hooded eyes, and I could hear him growling.

"Release him. I will care for his needs," Caiside replied.

"Fuck that. Give him the Deceiver," Fisk sneered. "He's the asshole who started this shit storm."

"Sidhe blood will empower him," Kim said, striding closer, her lips curled in disgust. "It's forbidden!"

As I considered them, with their ruined clothes the sole evidence of their dust-up, I realized Wade must have been busy healing everyone while I'd been distracted with rescuing Caiside. Now, Alex was the only one left with injuries.

"I won't let him suffer," I said curtly. "And if he ends up empowered, all the better for when he helps me save my friends." I nodded at the djinn. "Release— "

"Lire, no. With a shroud, he'll be invulnerable," Kim said, dismayed. "It was already hard enough to keep him from killing Kieran. Your friend is more powerful than you can imagine. Why do you think your djinn had to interfere? Even my lightning was hard pressed to subdue him."

"It won't get that far now that I'm here," I said. "Caiside, you ready?"

"Yes," he replied.

Kim huffed, but she didn't interfere when I nodded at the djinn. "Okay, release Alex, please. If things spiral out of control, you'll restrain him. I don't want anyone getting hurt."

"As the Lire wishes," they answered.

In case things took a turn for the worse, I surrounded Alex with my TK and watched, stomach clenched, as he hungrily launched himself at Caiside. Although he may have looked the weaker of the two, Caiside enfolded Alex within the circle of his arms and fed him his wrist before the hungry strigoi could think about going for his neck. Eyes intent and gripping Caiside's arm like it might escape at any moment, Alex sank his teeth into flesh, driving a pained grunt from the sidhe. Caiside's expression, though, was far from injured. He lovingly held Alex's body, pulling the strigoi leader into his lap and rotating so that his broad back shielded Alex's feeding from our curious gazes.

Caiside's voice rumbled, rife with emotion, words too subdued from my distance to understand. Alex's labored breathing and wet suckling echoed through the room, but after ten seconds or so, the sounds diminished to a less frenzied level. I hoped this was an indication that Alex had gained control of himself and Caiside wasn't about to be sucked dry. Because it wasn't hard to see—Caiside wouldn't hesitate to give his life for his mate.

"Maya," I murmured, motioning the djinn toward me. "Don't allow Alex to take too much from Caiside, okay?"

"The djinn will not allow the sidhe Caiside to suffer unalterable damage," it assured me.

As Maya drifted toward Caiside's hunched form, I caught Diedra's suspiciously narrowed gaze as she observed the two men from the other side of the broken conference table. "Deed, you okay?"

She jerked at my question, her expression clearing, and then nodded a little too rapidly. After a beat, though, she seemed to think better of it, shrugging and giving me a small smile that said, 'Not really, but I'll survive.'

I could sympathize. But before I could return her smile, Kim issued a hair-raising shriek and crumpled to her knees as if she'd been summarily kicked in the kidneys.

Gasping and distressed, she raised her head and choked out something in Silven. I distinctly heard 'Brassal.'

All the sidhe stared wide-eyed at Kim, their bodies rigid, and then the room exploded with a riot of agitated Silven, all of them speaking at once. Nonplussed, I glanced in Diedra's direction—knowing, like me, she wouldn't understand what the heck was going on. Interestingly, though, instead of confused, she looked almost victorious.

Whoa. She detested Kim that much?

I stared at Diedra, puzzled, until I realized she'd been helpless to do anything but watch when Kim attacked Alex with her lightning until he lost consciousness. No wonder Diedra disliked her.

My friend continued to observe the sidhe's animated discussion, her gaze bouncing avidly from one speaker to the next, looking as though she couldn't get enough of the conversation, until she caught me watching her. Her slender eyes rounded at my curious gaze and then a dizzying array of emotions flashed over her features—fear, anger, guilt— so quickly that I could hardly keep up. Finally, she frowned, looking bewildered, but even that expression didn't seem to sit comfortably on her face. It left me with the odd sensation that her confusion was feigned—which made no sense because it wasn't as though she understood Silven.

Proving my point, she jerked a thumb toward the agitated discussion and mouthed, "What's going on?"

They were no longer all speaking at once. Kieran knelt next to Kim and the others had moved closer as they all listened to her anxious, halting words. My stomach tried to dive into my shoes when I noticed Kim had tears in her eyes.

I shook my head at Diedra and mouthed back, "I don't know."

Plainly, though, something bad had happened. I got that in all caps from Tíereachán's emotions, which were strong enough to overpower his shield. His distress, mixing with the general feeling of turmoil in the room, formed a toxic cocktail that left me tense and jittery and somewhat queasy.

Just when I thought I'd gotten my stomach under control, Kim said something in a highly anxious tone that prompted everyone to stare at me.

Uh oh.

Kieran stood, looking about as conflicted as a person could look without imploding, and he might have started toward me if Tíereachán hadn't beaten him to it.

"Brassal's been gravely injured," Tíereachán said, moving close enough to touch my arm. "Kim isn't sure what happened, but she thinks he was attacked, and she can no longer communicate with him. There's reason to believe this is the work of an assassin. Kim thinks he'll die unless we can get to him in the next few minutes."

"Okay," I said, wondering what they expected me to do. "I'll help in any way I can, you know that, but I've never met Brassal. Without knowing his resonance, I can't bring him here like I did with Caiside. And I can't take us to him without knowing the plagency of where he was last standing."

At this news, Kim issued a strangled sob.

"My lady's nearest gateway is three hours away," Wade said. "But it is open for the emissary's use, should she wish it."

"He'll be dead in minutes, if he's not already," Kim cried through her tears. "Why didn't I tell Michael to bring me the draíoclochs? If I had— " She broke down, unable to finish.

I snapped my gaze to Tíereachán.

The draíocloch!

He frowned in confusion.

"Lire— " Red started, but I already knew what he was about to say.

"I know!" I shook my hands excitedly, looking to him for guidance. "My backpack ... Red, where'd I leave it?"

"In your bedroom, I believe," he replied, standing on his chair, a few feet to the left of Diedra.

"What do you have in mind, *mionngáel*?" Tíereachán asked discretely. He glanced at Kim, who had stopped sobbing and stared at me with hopeful, red-rimmed eyes.

"I'm trying to figure something out. Give me a second," I said, looking down at the floor to better concentrate.

With my bedroom's resonance in my mind, I pushed my TK directly there and searched for my backpack. On my slipper chair, in the corner, I found it half covered by my bathrobe. I didn't stop to marvel at my new skills. I grabbed the bag and then sidestepped it through my conduit, depositing it on the floor at my feet.

I dropped to my knees, ripped open the drawstring top, and dug around inside until I found what I wanted—the depleted *draíocloch*.

"Yes," I hissed before transferring it to the palm of my gloveless right hand.

On contact, the familiar resonance coursed through me, reminding me of that fateful day, last month, when Maeve and Kieran first showed up to screw up my life. Although the magic had been drained, the captured essence of the Otherworld remained. As its wondrous tune flowed over my skin and permeated my senses, I opened myself to it. And this time, I memorized its unique symphony, so nothing could ever keep me from traveling to its source—*draíocloch*, in hand, or not.

As I ran my fingers over the egg-like object's delicately carved surface, I recalled Red's prophetic words, uttered after Vince had been abducted, back when I foolishly thought things were at their darkest.

True, the magic has been consumed, but I sense something more. It may yet have a role to play.

"Red, you were right. It did still have a role to play." I grinned at him as he regarded me from the other side of the broken conference table. "You're one smart cookie, you know that?"

Kim stood up with Kieran's help and shot a watery glare at Tíereachán and Fisk. "You told me you didn't have any of the *draíoclochs*!"

"They don't," I said, lurching to my feet. "This is the one Daniel invoked to call Maeve and Kieran, last month. The magic is depleted, but it's still attuned to the Otherworld." I turned it over in my hand and then looked at Kieran. "If I follow the resonance, where will it take us?"

"The Great Hall, inside the king's palace," he replied, watching me with growing alarm. "But you can't risk traveling there yourself. Send Kim and me, but you have to stay here."

Before I could get up a head of steam over being told what I could or couldn't do, Kim barked at him, "She has to come! What if Brassal needs to get to a healer? What the fuck is wrong with you? He's your best friend."

"You don't understand!" Kieran erupted, startling the hell out of me. Kim, too, jumped at the unexpected outburst. Staring at her, he shook his head violently, his face twisted into a mask of horror mixed with an undeniable dose of fury. "He'll take her! Don't you see? He is without compunction. He'll use her as he did Nuala. He'll rape her until she's with child and even then, he'll not let her go. He'll break her!"

"Oh, Kier." I pressed the flat of my hand to my chest.

Now, it all became clear. This is what drove his overarching obsession with my plight. King Faonaín had raped Nuala. He'd done to Kieran's mate what Evgrenya had done to Caiside (and who knew how many others), possibly for as long as Kieran and Nuala were bonded, until her death in that earthquake. And, by the sound of it, she'd had at a child in the process.

No wonder Kieran was so screwed up.

I looked at Tíereachán, but the shock coming through our connection already told me this had caught him flat-footed too. His expression only mirrored it.

"Fucking hell," Fisk muttered.

Diedra, oblivious to the gravity of Kieran's disclosure, echoed her earlier protestation, "Lire, if you go, you'll be taken to the king." Bizarrely, she looked almost as anxious as Kieran. She jerked her chin at Drustan. "You heard what he said earlier. You can't escape the Hunt."

"I'm not worried about the king. He and I are going to come to an understanding, one that won't entail my subjugation." I looked at Kieran, willing him to understand. "I'm sorry, Kier. This must seem like history repeating itself, but you haven't been paying attention. I'm not Nuala. I have skills she couldn't have dreamed of—not to mention the support of some powerful and steadfast friends." I glanced at Tíereachán and the others and then returned the *draío-cloch* to my bag.

I donned an extra right-hand glove and picked up my backpack. "I need to know who's coming," I said as I levitated Red to my shoulder.

"At least, leave the Master of the Hunt here," Diedra persisted, sounding more than a little distraught. "It would be bad, otherwise."

"That won't make any difference. The rest of the Hunt is still seeking me in the Otherworld." I frowned at her. "Besides, I gave him my word."

What was up with her?

Wringing her hands, Diedra shifted on her feet and, if not for the damaged conference table between us, I think she would have tried to grab my arm. "Please, Lire, don't go. You can't go. You have to stay here ... please."

I opened my mouth to ask her what this was all about, but Alex interrupted me.

"Diedra." The domn's commanding voice thundered through the room as he stood with his arms folded, observing us from his position ten feet away, totally healed. Caiside stood at his side, looking pale but otherwise unaffected by Alex's recent meal.

"Brassal's dying," Kim exclaimed. "We don't have time for this!"

She was right. Another person's life was more important than taking the time to ease an overanxious friend's jitters.

"Caiside, Alex, and Diedra are staying here," I announced. "Everyone else is going unless you tell me—right now—that you're not." I looked at each of them in turn. "Don't shield against my TK. It'll just make my job more difficult."

I easily wrapped up Kim, Kieran, Fisk, Tíereachán, and Drustan since I'd already learned their resonances. Wade, though, required some effort. But before I could get started, Tíer's overarching alarm spiked through my mind as a heavy body crashed into me, knocking me to the floor, making new bruises, and driving the wind out of me. At the same time, an explosive report tore through the room, constricting my eardrums and adding yet another painful sensation to my growing list of ills.

As I struggled to breathe, I found myself looking into Fisk's contorted face while all two-hundred-plus pounds of him kept me pinned to the cool floor. If I hadn't been out of sorts, I might have kicked the jerk in the nuts or at the very least used my TK to do something—anything!—other than lay beneath him like a gasping lumpfish.

Where was Red? He'd been on my shoulder. Why didn't he zap Fisk senseless?

"Breathe," Fisk ordered. At least, I think that's what he said. My ears were ringing and my lungs had seized up somewhere beneath my body and the hard floor.

After he glanced away to consider our surroundings, he temporarily shifted his body to look me over. "You're okay," he reassured me, looking rattled. "You're fine. Your djinn were in time. Fuck. Just breathe, okay?"

After several excruciatingly long seconds of all-consuming distress while my vision darkened and I fought to draw breath, I finally, *finally* sucked in a mouthful of life-affirming, delicious air. It was then, when I could breathe, that I registered the fact that Fisk cradled my head, which seemed to be resting in his palm. He must have wrapped his hand around the back of my skull to protect me from our fall. He'd also positioned himself on top of me so that his weight didn't impede my breathing, leaning on his left forearm as he loomed over me.

I blinked at him in confusion as he stared into my eyes, his amber gaze intensely focused. Outside my line of sight, I vaguely registered shouts from several of the others, a woman crying, and the djinn's calm responses.

"You okay now?" Fisk asked.

This has to be my most surreal experience, to date, I thought inanely. *And I have cotton in my ears.*

"What happened?" I rasped. My lungs still ached with that dreadful hollow feeling, my upper-back and left elbow throbbed painfully, and, although Fisk did his best to lean to the side, he was still a big guy who needed to get off me.

As though reading my mind, he pushed to his knees and then helped me to a sitting position.

Red toddled up from behind my back where he must have gone flying when Fisk turned me into his football tackle dummy.

"Diedra pulled a gun," Red informed me. "She tried to shoot you."

My brain function promptly seized. I rubbed my sore elbow absently while the image of Diedra with a gun—never mind trying to kill me—took shape in my mind. I shook my head. It didn't compute.

"That ... can't be," I stammered. Maybe I'd misheard him.

"She did," Fisk said. "If your djinn hadn't interfered, my prince would be dead. He put himself in the line of fire, trying to take her down."

Fisk didn't spell it out. He didn't have to. Tíereachán had charged a gun to save me and, if the djinn hadn't been on their game, he would have taken the bullet. Even with a healer in the room, there was no coming back from a gunshot to the head or heart. This knowledge thundered through me, shaking my breath and making the world look as grainy as an old-time movie. Tíereachán might have died for me. If it were possible to be both astonished and unsurprised at the same time, I managed. It was one thing to hear the oath and know intellectually what it meant; quite another to see the results play out in real life. It didn't matter that if our roles had been reversed, I would have likely done the same thing.

I couldn't let this happen again.

If Tíer died because of me …

I shuddered. The thought was too horrible to consider.

"You didn't exactly sit on your hands either," I said, giving his arm a squeeze. "Thank you."

His body jolted, his eyes rounding with surprise.

What the—?

He thought I was so ungrateful that I wouldn't even appreciate or acknowledge what he'd done?

Now that I was sitting, the top arch of the djinn's silvery forcefield was visible above the broken conference table. Inside the bubble, I spied the crown of Diedra's quaking head as she sobbed. Alex towered over her, his black eyes reduced to murderous slits, a small handgun held loosely in his grip. Tíereachán stood opposite, speaking to the fuming strigoi leader as Caiside placed a comforting hand on his shoulder. To the far right of the table, Kim paced anxiously while Kieran stared at me, hands clenched to fists at his sides.

Brassal.

Forgetting my indignation, I leapt to my feet and soared over the conference table to stand between Tíereachán and Alex.

We'd have to deal with Diedra later. It was well past time to go.

My friend raised her tear-filled gaze to meet mine. "Please," she blubbered. "He'll kill them. He'll kill them and share it. He told me! He'll kill them … and he'll make me watch. Inside my head I can't … close … my eyes! I can't not see it!" She issued a wailing sob and pulled savagely at her hair. "Just kill me and get it over with. He already knows! Please. I can't live this way!"

Holy crap. Had Lorcán and his cronies kidnapped Diedra's loved ones? Her family maybe?

I looked at Tíereachán, my eyes probably as large as two scrying orbs.

Caiside knelt next to the shimmering force field. "I need to touch her. Now."

Instantly suspicious, I examined him. "Why?"

"He's an animtùr," Wade said and then clarified, "An aura reader."

"If your friend is under an enchantment or a geas, it would be best to learn it now," Caiside reasoned.

Diedra had attempted to kill me, which was so totally out of character it wasn't even funny. An enchantment would certainly fit.

After considering him, I nodded. "Okay. I'm gonna trust you on this. But if you harm her ... I'm here to tell you, you *will* regret it."

Keeping a watchful eye on Caiside, I gave the djinn the go-ahead.

The force field didn't disappear, but Caiside was able to reach into the bubble. Diedra didn't fight him when he pushed up her sleeve to touch her skin.

"As I thought," he said after their brief contact. "She is mated to a sidhe. Soulbound."

Whoa. I hadn't necessarily expected *that.* I seemed to be a magnet for unpleasant surprises, lately.

"Right." I considered the others. "Any bets on whether Lorcán's her mate?"

Weeks ago, Kieran had mentioned that Lorcán's previous mate had committed suicide, so presumably he was unbound.

Until now, perhaps.

"The perfect spy," Alex hissed.

"He has my parents and my little sister." She stared up at me. "Lire, he has Megan! He ... he ..." She shook her head vehemently.

I could imagine all too readily what Lorcán had done to her family in order to elicit her cooperation. Spying on the domn wasn't a smart choice unless you had a death wish. Anyone with half a brain knew that much.

I'd met Diedra's sister a few times over the course of our time at Coventry Academy. She was five years younger than Diedra and me, and, even as a kid, it'd been easy to see Megan would grow up to be a smart woman, just as beautiful and outgoing as her big sister.

Diedra's face hardened and she glared through her tears at Alex. "This is all the domn's fault! If he'd allowed Nathan to expand his business interests, instead of being an asshole, Nathan never would have done this!"

If it were possible for Alex to look any more deadly, he managed. His fangs dripped with venom and his body coiled as though ready to strike. Without the djinn's protective bubble, no doubt Diedra would currently be in a world of hurt.

Not good, but I didn't have time to deal with it.

"Goddammit." My stomach in knots, I ran my fingers through my hair. "I have to help Brassal," I said, and then lowered my voice to a determined growl, "but right after, I'm coming back to deal with that bastard Lorcán. He has people I care about, too. We'll get them out and he'll pay for what he's done. I promise you, we'll do everything in our power to help your family."

I turned to the djinn. "Take her to Jerome and Peter's apartment. Don't let her leave and keep an eye on her to make sure she doesn't harm herself. Tell Jackie what's going on, okay?"

"As the Lire wishes," they replied. The three of them disappeared in a blink.

"Who are Jerome and Peter?" Alex's angry voice boomed through the room.

"My neighbors," I replied, ignoring his furious stance. "Kim and Jackie are house sitting for them. She'll be safe there. More importantly, it gets Lorcán out of the equation so he doesn't learn our every move." I turned to include the others in our conversation. "Do you think he's the one behind Brassal's attack? Because if you think he is, then we need to consider the possibility that rescuing him is a trap."

Poor Kim looked ready to detonate. She paced at the far side of the broken table, raking her fingers through her hair and muttering under her breath.

"I believe it would be wise to examine Diedra's conduct," Red suggested from his position on the floor, still standing a few feet from Fisk. "She resorted to extreme measures in order to prevent Lire from going to the Otherworld. If Lorcán is indeed behind Diedra's actions, you must ask yourselves why he would not want Lire to travel to the Otherworld at this time."

I frowned. "It makes no sense. It's what he wanted me to do in the first place. He took my friends hostage to coerce me into breaking Maeve out of prison. Being in the Otherworld puts me one step closer to that goal. So why would that suddenly change?"

"That's easy," Fisk said. "You're here with the Master of the Hunt. As long as he's trapped here, the *Wuldrífan* is tied up. It puts the king at a significant disadvantage."

Wade folded his arms. "I believe Lorcán's use of the strigoi rebels was calculated. Lorcán must have learned of Alex's connection to Caiside. He knew using them to attack Lire would draw out the domn and provide a means to insert Alex and his spy into our midst. And once Alex learned of Lire's abilities, Lorcán knew Lire would use Alex's ríutcloch to rescue Caiside."

"And with Lire so close at hand, the king, predictably, fell to temptation," Tíereachán said.

"That's all fine, but what are we going to do about Brassal?" Kim exclaimed, still pacing.

"Where was Brassal the last time you were connected to him?" I asked.

She stopped and turned to me, hugging herself. "The king's antechamber."

I nodded. "How far from there to the Great Hall?"

"It depends on the route," Kieran said. "The most direct is by way of a guarded passage between the king's private box and his anteroom."

I plunked down into the nearest upright chair, the one Red had been standing on earlier. "Okay. Let me feel around a bit."

When I closed my eyes and sidestepped my TK to the Great Hall, the Otherworld's plagency instantly thrummed through me, like the completion of an electric circuit.

Wow.

"I'm there," I said, casting my net wide.

In my mind's eye, I 'saw' a cavernous space supported by colossal pillars, which stretched three stories up to the coffered ceiling above. "It seems to be a large space—holy cow—with giant carved columns, right? Jeez, this place is frickin' huge. Is there anywhere we can slip in undetected?"

Alert for signs of unrest, I poked further into the large space, feeling for the edges of the room and the entrance to the antechamber that Kieran had described.

"In the gallery, above," Kieran said, his voice taut with surprise. Apparently, the extent of my new-found powers was sinking in.

"The royal box would be the best," Kim added. "And then we can decide how to get to his antechamber."

As my magic flowed along the smooth floor, which I guessed was stone, my mental map grew to include at least one massive archway leading into a tunnel that felt big enough to fit a semi-trailer truck.

"I found an archway, but it's gigantic," I announced.

"Two public avenues intersect the Great Hall," Kieran said. "I concur with Kim, the royal box is a good idea. It has access to the king's private passage."

I slipped my magic upward, looking for the gallery Kieran had mentioned and the king's box. As I searched, my expectations conjured a gilded, royal balcony in a grand European theater circa 1850, which probably bore no resemblance to reality.

"Seems like everything's sculpted in this place," I mumbled as I snaked my way up the wall's contoured decorations and found a recessed area, about fifteen feet above ground level, which was fronted by a carved balustrade. "I found the gallery, I think, on the next level up. Stone benches down the center? It's an area where people can view the Great Hall's floor, right?"

"Yes," Kieran replied.

"Does the gallery run all the way around, you know, like private balconies at an opera house?"

"Yes. Although the king's box doesn't connect to it," he explained. "Imagine your opera house, except put the stage at its center and the gallery spanning three sides. The fourth side is reserved for the royal box." He paused. "Do you understand?"

"I think so." Similar to a stadium but without any seats at ground level.

Keeping the solid interior wall at my left, I traced my way through the gallery until I hit a corner. Since the space continued to the right, I guessed I hadn't hit the king's box yet.

I thought it odd that I hadn't encountered any signs of life. This being King Faonaín's fortress and all, I'd have expected a guard or two, especially in the gallery, since it offered such a good vantage point.

"I'm surprised you guys don't have guards up ..." I faltered, and the word 'here' leaked from my throat like the air from a punctured tire.

I'd stumbled upon two headless bodies splayed prone on the floor, and it took most of my willpower to keep from recoiling all the way back to Earth. Their severed heads had ended up some distance apart, in different directions as though someone had kicked them away haphazardly, no more important than discarded soccer balls.

"What is it?" Tíereachán asked. I heard his movement and felt the heat of him near my right thigh, so I wasn't surprised when his body nudged the outside of my knee.

Eyes squeezed shut and stomach reeling, I grasped at whatever part had brushed up against me and held on tight. It turned out to be his shoulder, and I realized he'd knelt next to me. "I found ... two bodies," I croaked and then added in a low tone, "They've been decapitated."

To my left, Kim gasped. "No. It's not Brassal," she said, her voice thready and uncertain. "It can't be. He was in the king's rooms, not the gallery." She said 'rooms' as though the word should be capitalized. "What are they wearing?" she demanded.

Still gripping Tíer's arm like a drowning victim, I 'looked' closer. "Chain armor, by the feel of it. Smooth pants, probably leather. Boots. Something long and cylindrical on their backs." I frowned. "A rocket launcher, maybe?"

Fisk snorted. "Hardly. Wielding material explosives in a magic dominated world would be suicidal. Why do you think we arm ourselves with swords? They're wearing quivers. Given the location, I'd say those are two of the king's archers."

That explained the strange shape on the ground next to one of the men—a bow.

"Agreed," Kieran said. "There are normally two, sometimes three, in each span."

"*Mionngáel*, keep going," Tíereachán said, unhooking my hand from his sleeve and squeezing it between his palms. "I'm right here."

I nodded, a reluctant bob of my chin as though my head was attached by a rusty hinge, and continued to push my magic fingers through the gallery. When I found additional bodies sprawled at the next corner, the shock wasn't as jarring. "Another two bodies."

These guys still had their heads at least. Although, I wouldn't have called it an improvement per se, since they both appeared to have been savaged by a vampire.

"It's weird," I said weakly. "Their throats have been ripped out, yet the ones who were decapitated ... Why is it their deaths seem so much worse?" My voice came out as a bare whisper, and I took a breath to steady myself. "It makes no sense."

Strong hands grasped my shoulders. "Steady, love," Tíereachán said as he gently forced me upright.

At some point, I'd listed to port.

Find your backbone, I scolded myself. *Brassal needs your help.*

Squaring my shoulders, I plunged my tendrils ahead, thoroughly checking the rest of the gallery. Unfortunately, I found eleven more bodies along the way, two in the next span, four in the main stairwell that fed the public gallery, three in the royal box, and two at the bottom of the stairs that led down to the king's private passage. Most of them had been killed by strigoi, but four had been slain by an edged weapon of some kind.

I told the others what I'd found. "As far as I can tell, except for the dead guards, the royal box is empty. The stairs are unobstructed, but there are two more dead guards at the bottom. I haven't looked far beyond that."

The king's box was a shorter duplicate of the main gallery—a rectangular room with benches running down the center like the dotted line on a two lane road. Smack dab in the center was a raised platform, a dais, containing a single grand high-backed chair, clearly meant for King Faonaín's royal tush.

"When the king released the Hunt, Lorcán and his conspirators must have decided it was time to make their move," Wade announced. "My lady has received word that Evgrenya's forces and those aligned with her—Houses Ilíandaeon, Faisleanne, and Maleos—are marching under a combined banner and have breached the outer walls of the city."

Kieran and Fisk both issued a fervent curse, Kieran's in Silven and Fisk's in English.

"The rats have come to nest, traitors all," Tíereachán scoffed.

"Anóen, with your aid we can be in a position to help the king until my lady's forces arrive," Wade said. "She'll not stand by while her brother is usurped by those who associate with demons and endorse the torture and rape of her people." He paused and I heard him step closer to me. "Will you help us?"

I opened my eyes, squinting back the brightness of the overhead lights, and found him standing on the other side of the broken table. When I stood up, Tíer followed suit, steadying me with a hand at my right elbow.

"I really shouldn't involve myself in your politics, but judging by what Maeve and Lorcán have done and seeing how Evgrenya treated Caiside, it's pretty clear having them in charge would be a bad thing all the way around." I nodded toward Kim. "I've promised to find Brassal. After that, I'll do what I can to help you."

"No. King Faonaín must come first," Kim said, her voice coarse with unshed tears. "Drop us in his box and then go with the Master of the Hunt. Brassal wasn't far from the king when he was attacked."

I frowned. "Okay ... that makes sense." With all this, I'd forgotten about the whole thing with the Hunt. I gave Drustan a sheepish shrug. "Right, let's— "

"You will take Caiside and me with you," Alex ordered.

I opened my mouth to argue, but he cut me off. "If my people are there, they will answer to me for their treachery."

I looked at Wade for guidance. When I received a subtle nod from him, I turned back to Alex. "Fine, but you'll stick with Wade and the others. Follow their lead when it comes to dealing with the sidhe. Agreed?"

"Very well."

"Caiside? You on board with this?" I asked as I whisked Red to the safety of my backpack's outer pocket. I learned Wade's resonance before Caiside had a chance to answer.

I was definitely getting the hang of this adept stuff.

"I am," he replied, although he sounded somewhat uncertain. I wondered whether this was due to my choice of words or the task at hand.

I shot him a crooked smile. "Okay then ... buckle up, people," I quipped, and promptly sidestepped us along the path of my magic, making sure to leave the tether of my magic in place after landing.

Never again would I make the mistake of showing up without access to Earth's potential.

Now I just needed to prevent King Faonaín from getting his greedy hands on it.

Or, rather—on *me*.

(F)OURTEEN

We slid into the king's box, easy as can be. Caiside didn't even have time to tense up.

When the blurred walls swirled into focus, I had about one-point-two seconds to gather my footing before Drustan blew a series of plaintive notes on his horn, grabbed me about my hips, and hefted me over his shoulder like a trussed, one-hundred-twenty-pound bipedal deer. The air in my lungs woofed out of me in a surprised gush when my abdomen impacted and then folded over his massive ice-cold shoulder, effectively depriving me of the ability to issue any parting comments to the others, much less take in the conditions of our surroundings.

My inverted view (which afforded me little more than dizzying flashes of creamy-yellow stone between his booted feet) and painful bouncing against the meat of Drustan's unyielding body made for an uncomfortable ride as he strode to the box's turned balustrade. I managed an alarmed squeak from between my chattering teeth as he vaulted over the thick railing toward the floor, an unsettling fifteen feet below. I braced myself, readying my magic to prevent a jarring landing and possible broken spine. Astonishingly, Drustan's enormous black charger appeared beneath us and we alighted onto his back, sliding smoothly into the saddle as if my sidhe abductor had wings.

Evidently, the Master of the Hunt packed some serious mojo in the magic department.

So do you, I reminded myself. And I refused to be served up to King Faonaín like a side of venison.

Tíer's concern nudged his way into my thoughts. *You okay?*

Yeah, I thought back. *The bastard caught me by surprise. I hadn't expected him to be quite so gung-ho.*

Using a combination of levitation and gravity, I slid my body down the front of Drustan's armored torso, twisting my butt to the outside, to land sideways in his lap, exactly how I'd ridden when he'd plucked me out of Caiside's prison. This time, though, I maneuvered my right leg over the horse's broad neck to sit in the saddle like a normal person, albeit without the benefit of stirrups. On top of all my other bumps and bruises, my butt and thighs were definitely going to be feeling it in the morning.

I leaned forward in the saddle to keep from squishing Red, who'd kept his footing inside my backpack's outer pocket.

Since Drustan continued to sit tall in the saddle and wasn't currently laid out on the ground, I figured Red's close proximity deterrent spells didn't work on the dead. The thought prompted me to wonder whether strigoi had the same resistance, and I had the ridiculous notion of asking Alex to be a test subject in order to know for sure. Neither Drustan nor strigoi reacted to my clairvoyance, so if they ever did touch him, I breathed easier knowing Red would remain psi-free.

After I called Red up to my shoulder and could lean back comfortably, I had my first look around.

A breathy, "Wow," along with a vaporous cloud of my warm breath, was about all I could manage.

'Great Hall,' indeed. At a near gallop, it took almost thirty seconds to make a full circuit of the immense chamber. I'd say the space was one hundred fifty feet on a side, but that alone wasn't what made the Great Hall 'great.' This wasn't just a hall. The four supporting columns and, even, the very walls, had been expertly carved to mimic a sea of massive sequoias. Overhead, a dense canopy of intricately chiseled leaves loomed at least forty feet above us. The entire arena had been etched into bedrock to resemble an old growth forest, replete with elaborate trompe-l'œil painting over every square inch, tricking the eye to a masterful degree. It was, hands down, the most convincing deception I'd ever laid eyes on, not to mention the most exquisite interior space I'd ever seen. Even the lighting seemed to filter down through the canopy and from between the sculpted tree trunks, as though the trees provided us respite from the noonday sun.

"Beautiful," Red murmured.

"And then some."

Jeez. You guys weren't kidding with the name, I thought at Tíereachán. *It's enormous. But 'Great Hall' doesn't do it justice. It's breathtaking.*

Merely a humble place name, he explained. *Its true name is Sylvan Hallâ—Hall of Trees.*

I relayed what Tíer had said, for Red's benefit, and then added, "No wonder they built a gallery. I could sit here for hours and gape at it."

"The king I served in life saw to its creation," Drustan informed me. "He would be pleased to know *Anóen* and her servant approve."

"Servant?" I blurted, almost barking out a laugh. "Red isn't my servant. He's my best friend. I'm sorry for not introducing you earlier. John Redborn, former necromancer, meet Drustan, Master of the Hunt."

"An honor," Red said as he managed to turn and bow while still holding onto my hair.

"I do not understand," Drustan said. "Are you not bound to this form and sworn to obedience until your mistress' death?"

"Indeed, I am," Red replied.

I frowned, tensing up. "Maybe technically, but that's not how I think of you. I've never thought of you that way. Not ever."

Red gave my hair a gentle tug. "I know. In all eternity, I could not have found a kinder, more caring owner."

At his final word, I sagged and murmured, "I'd release you in a heartbeat if you could tell me it's what you wanted." I meant this wholeheartedly, but the nature of our binding prevented Red from seeking the release of his soul, so there was no way for me to know whether it was something he desired. "I'd miss you terribly, but I'd do it—*for you*. You know that. You're not my slave."

He shushed me. "My dearest Lire, rest easy. Had I the chance, I would not wish for things to be any different, binding or not." He caressed my cheek, the softness of his paw drawing out an involuntary shiver. "Truly."

I nodded, taking his heartfelt words at face value, allowing them to soothe the ache I always felt whenever I allowed myself to consider the moral ambiguity of our relationship. As a bound servant himself, I wondered what Drustan was thinking. He remained curiously quiet behind me.

As Drustan and his charger completed our initial circuit about the perimeter, I noted the colossal archways framing each opening to the public avenues, carved to resemble a tangle of buttressed tree roots and thickly twining vines. Sadly, my delighted ogling was cut short by the bodies of half a dozen soldiers sprawled on the ground at the nearest archway where they'd obviously been cut down in battle.

When Drustan drew his steed close enough to distinguish their causes of death, I spied the notched ends of several arrows sticking from at least four soldiers. The rest had either died from sword wounds or, possibly, offensive magic. All of their throats were intact. Blood pooled on the stone surrounding the soldiers' prone forms, looking more brown than red in the filtered light. The bodies that sprouted arrows, I noticed, wore burgundy and silvery-blue color-blocked tunics with an embroidered coat of arms featuring a creature that resembled a hydra.

"The red and blue livery must belong to the rival faction," Red observed.

When Drustan paused his horse beneath the towering archway, nothing stirred nearby except the jingling of his chainmail and creaking of leather. A strange lifelessness permeated the air, but somewhere in the distance, I could hear the unmistakable sounds of armed conflict.

We're heading down the king's private passage, Tíereachán told me.

Be careful, I beamed at him. My already clenched stomach swooped at the thought of something bad happening to him or any of the others. *I can hear people fighting somewhere ahead of us and there are at least six dead soldiers at this entrance. None of them were killed by strigoi, so ... God. It's a good bet Nathan and his followers took the king's passage.*

We're all seasoned champions, he returned briskly. *You needn't distract yourself with worries for us. Keep your wits about you. As long as you are in the master's grasp, you share his spectral protection, but once he relinquishes you to the king, you will stand alone. Be yourself, mionngáel. Listen to your heart, don't shy from your power, and you will prevail.*

Once again, I was struck speechless by the twist of fate that had brought this man into my life. How crazy was it that the one creature who I'd initially distrusted above all others would end up being the only other individual in my life, besides Red, to express so unequivocally his belief in my abilities? Every day since our disastrous first meeting, he'd showed me this faith with his words as well as his actions. That I hadn't seen this, until recently, turned my stomach, even though we both knew it was Kieran's enthralling glamour that had influenced my dismissal.

I will. Thank you, Tíer. Your support ... I can't tell you how much it means to me. I invested the thought with all the warmth that radiated through me whenever I considered our growing friendship.

You make it easy. Now pay attention, he admonished and then shielded his thoughts from me, managing to get in the last word.

It seemed horrible to smile, even briefly, given what lay on the ground a few feet away from me, but I couldn't help it.

I tried to peer over my shoulder at my captor, catching the edge of his horned helm in my peripheral vision. "They've decided to take the king's private passage," I relayed, pitching my voice low in case the tunnel carried our voices further than I wanted.

At my back, Drustan had gone ominously still, and his horse, perhaps made uneasy by the proximity of the dead soldiers, edged sideways and threw its head impatiently. After our expeditious departure from the royal box, I'd expected us to beeline straight to the king.

"What's wrong?" I asked, inwardly cringing at the ludicrousness of asking that question when there were dead bodies practically under our noses.

"I cannot gain bearing on my master."

"What does that mean? Is the king … dead?" I again struggled to peer over my shoulder. Sitting this way might have been more comfortable, but the point of view made it impossible to converse normally.

"No," he replied. "If the wearer dies prior to bequeathing the collar, my servitude ends and I, too, pass on. I sense no new owner. He is alive."

"So, maybe unconscious?" I posed, but then had a more disturbing thought. "Or in another realm."

"Perhaps."

"I take it this has never happened before."

"No."

He sounded almost lost, a state which was so contrary to his prior steadfast confidence that I felt the absurd need to reassure him.

"Brassal and the king were together in the king's antechamber," I said. "It's starting to sound like both of them were subdued at the same time. It would be great if we could sneak in there and see what's going on without being seen. Can you do that?"

In lieu of an answer, he shifted in the saddle. Instantly, our surroundings took on an unnatural, muted aspect as his horse sprang ahead, slamming my already bruised spine into Drustan's mail-clad torso and catapulting us through the scenery at a speed that left blurred streaks in my peripheral vision. I snatched Red from my shoulder and hugged him to my chest, something I typically refrained from doing—he was a grown man, not a stuffed toy—but the thought of losing him over the side scared the bejeezus out of me. I wasn't sure whether we were in the physical realm anymore.

Directly ahead, something that reminded me of a sci-fi movie wormhole filled my vision, all the more terrifying because this wasn't make believe. My stomach seemed to take refuge in the vicinity of my throat, and I might have barfed all over the saddle if our journey hadn't screeched to a halt just as precipitously as we'd departed. Drustan's arm snaked around my waist to pin me to his icy body, sparing me the indignity of becoming a projectile at our deceleration. If I'd sailed over his horse's ears, beyond his camouflaging veil, our arrival would no longer be a secret.

This would have been a big problem, since we'd come to rest at the far end of a spacious, sumptuously appointed chamber that had clearly been ground zero of a ferocious battle.

More than a dozen dead soldiers, along with at least three shriveled husks that were probably deceased strigoi, littered the floor, most of them concentrated near each of the two magically sealed archways that led into the luxurious apartment. But what drew my eye were the three people standing near the room's center, surrounding a pale blond, amply-built sidhe who'd been strapped to one of the room's gilded chairs, his head flaccidly canted to the side. Blood, wet, glistening, and alarming in its quantity, coated his mouth, jaw, neck, and torso, saturating the supple leather of his formerly tan-colored tunic. Tarnished metal chains, which wrapped securely around his chest and waist, fixed him to the opulently decorated chair, while black leather ties at each knee, ankle, wrist, and elbow secured his limbs to its adorned wood frame. His hands, also covered in blood, splayed limply atop the chair's wide arms. And no wonder. He was missing at least three fingers from his left hand and two from his right. On the floor, blood and gobbets of flesh peppered the carpet, obscuring a portion of the rug's elaborate design.

It didn't surprise me to find that Maeve, Lorcán, and Nathan were the torturers. For a strigoi surrounded by fresh blood, though, Nathan appeared decidedly unhappy and somewhat green around the edges, a tough feat, considering his dark skin.

I could see why. Not since witnessing the Circle Murderer's demise at Paimon's hands had I seen anything so horrifying. A groan eked past my lips, and I promptly slapped my free hand across my mouth to stop any further outbursts, verbal or otherwise. That's all we needed—to be noticed by these three. The mere thought of it drove away my nausea with a hefty dose of good old fashioned fear.

It soon became clear I needn't have worried. With the way Maeve was shouting and carrying on, I didn't think they'd hear anything shy of a foghorn. Even within the muted surroundings of Drustan's veil, her angry, musical voice came through clear enough. She gesticulated wildly, her wavy blonde hair sliding across her back as she ranted in her native Silven, occasionally punctuating her tirade by roughly shoving at the unconscious man's head or shoulder.

Please don't be Brassal, I thought fervently. On the other hand, if this wasn't Brassal, then he might be one of the dead, which wasn't any better.

"We are not fully within in their realm," Drustan said. "They cannot detect our presence."

I released Red with a murmured apology and allowed him to scramble back atop my shoulder.

"Is that—?" I started to ask, but stopped when Maeve cruelly yanked the unconscious man's long platinum-blond hair, which jerked his head backward to expose his neck and the thick gold torc that adorned it.

A collar.

I jolted against Drustan's one-armed embrace, sitting bolt upright. "Oh, God. That's ... is that the king?"

In all my imaginings, I'd pictured him wearing elaborately tailored, flowing robes and a silvery circlet that arched delicately across his forehead, not unlike Elrond in *The Lord of the Rings* movies. But this man was dressed as an ordinary sidhe in his fitted leather tunic and matching leggings. Even his boots, where not covered in blood, were scuffed and plain. Unbelievably, Maeve's formal-length dress swished about her long, slender legs like a sleek emerald waterfall. She'd donned a gem-studded frigging gown for a torture session. The mind positively boggled.

"Yes," Drustan confirmed.

"And his own daughter is torturing him!"

Jesus. This woman knew no bounds.

Granted, by all accounts, King Faonaín was hardly a saint, and I could imagine he hadn't been the best father, but that didn't excuse ... this. It was one thing to kill a bunch of soldiers in a coup d'état, which was bad enough, quite another to strap someone down and start cutting bits off, piece by piece. This was the act of a depraved, thoroughly evil individual. Make that *individuals*. As Lorcán sauntered to a nearby couch, he paused to wipe his bloody dagger clean on a tufted pillow before sprawling languorously at the opposite end.

At my back, I heard Drustan take a breath as if to respond, but he ultimately held his tongue. I suppose because there wasn't much to say in response to my declaration. It's not as though he could argue. The proof of it was right there in front of us.

"Aren't you supposed to protect him?" I as much as screeched.

"I am the king's huntsman, his bound servant. I follow his express command to pursue, capture or kill, and return his marked quarry. I am constrained by my binding to do no less. Once the game is delivered, he may command my obedience again."

I guessed this meant 'no,' although his precise wording puzzled me. He could do 'no less' than return his quarry. Did that mean he could do more, whether or not he'd been asked? My gaze went back to the king, unconscious, re-strained, and without the Hunt.

Bloody frigging hell.

I couldn't sit back while a man was slowly tortured. There'd be no living with myself. Besides, if King Faonaín died, who'd take his place as ruler? Maeve? Evgrenya? Some other bigoted, sadistic jerk nominated by the Tribunal, someone more like Lorcán?

Better the devil we know than the one we don't.

Besides, there was the whole issue with the Compact not being binding if the king was usurped. That alone was rea-son enough to ensure he stayed in power since it's what pre-vented the king and his people from exterminating humans whenever the impulse arose.

My thoughts stilled as I plotted my course of action. First, rescue the king. Second, find Brassal. Third, get them both to Wade for healing. After that, Kieran and the others could decide how to proceed.

I reached out with my telekinesis and immediately ran up against a ward that encompassed the king and the sur-rounding eight feet on all sides of his chair. Since King Faonaín was no doubt a badass in the magic department, this wasn't much of a surprise. I suspected he'd turn Maeve into a smoking pile of ash, given half a chance. As I side-stepped my TK, weaving past the ward to encompass the king, it struck me that I had no idea what type of magic he commanded. Somehow, in all of my discussions with Kieran and Tíereachán about the threat the king posed, I'd never bothered to ask.

"What's she going on about?" I asked, jerking a thumb at Maeve as I became acquainted with the king's resonance.

"She is furious at my master for refusing to relinquish the *Bráigda*—the binding collar. She says it is her birthright and will see him whittled down to a stump if that's what it takes to get it. She has ordered the *dhêala* to stop the bleed-ing but take no further blood. As soon as my master wakes, she wants her fair-haired co-conspirator wielding the mis-ericorde to remove his ears, strip by strip."

Drustan paused while listening to Lorcán and then continued, "But he counsels her against further attempts at persuasion. Even though they have taken the precaution of cutting out my master's tongue, he says keeping the king alive is a risk."

"Jesus Christ! They cut out his tongue? What the hell kind of precaution is that?"

As I asked the question, Maeve shook her head at Lorcán, clipped out a heated sentence, and then turned to deliver a brutal slap across the king's left cheek that echoed throughout the room, making me cringe.

"It prevents— " Drustan began and then stiffened, his arm once again pulling me hard to his body.

The king's head lolled a few times, but he eventually straightened and opened his eyes. Even bloody and ravaged, he regarded Maeve with a look of fury that would have stopped me in my tracks if I'd been on the receiving end of it.

Before I could think to protest, Drustan slid from the saddle, yanking me and Red along for the ride as he deftly dropped to the ground. If not for his unyielding two-handed grip on my shoulders, I might have fallen to my knees. My irritation promptly evaporated, though, when I considered the four shocked gazes that locked onto our location when Drustan's veil vanished.

"My lord," he called out. "Your quarry as commanded. I await your next call when you *charge me by name*."

He turned to me, bowed deferentially, and then, just like that, the master was gone—*poof*—horse and all.

But with his final words, Drustan found a way to answer my question. To invoke the Hunt, King Faonaín had to call the master by name, which was impossible now that his tongue was missing.

Lorcán, still relaxing on the couch, looked me up and down as a condescending smirk spread over his cruel lips. "My, my. Look at what the huntsman dragged in. But where is your attack dog, I wonder? Left behind, foaming at the mouth, I don't doubt." He chuckled. "Poor Kieran. He never was particularly good at keeping up with the play. Always a day late and a dollar short, isn't that the saying?" He grinned, pleased with himself.

My lips curled into an involuntary grimace. "Jesus. How can you even stand yourself?" Shaking my head, I looked at Maeve. "And you. He's your father! No wonder you've taken up with demons. You guys are birds of a feather. While we're on the subject of human sayings, here's another one to consider: *You reap what you sow.*"

Pretty sure the king was finding that one particularly insightful, right about now.

Maeve laughed and placed her hand lovingly on the king's shoulder. "How quaint—*father*. Do you see this? The adept is honestly upset for you. *You*—the one who encouraged his marischal to dabble with plagues and cause untold human misery and death. The same sidhe who methodically impregnates any and every female descended from adept blood lines, whether they're bonded or not. The king who would risk everything to possess his prophesied *Anóen*, body and soul, by any means necessary."

Folding her arms, she stared at me pitilessly. "Go home, Adept. I am rescuing you from a lifetime of torment. Save your sympathy for someone who deserves it."

Her gruff yet earnest declaration caught me flatfooted and, for a moment, I didn't know what to say. Talk about a surreal moment. I'd come face to face with one of those mind-bending philosophical questions: If you could kill Adolf Hitler, would you do it? And not merely that, how about making him suffer a little too, for good measure?

Except, in my case, the question seemed to be: Would you go out of your way to save his life and alleviate his suffering?

My head swam.

Maeve had given me a choice—walk away or risk my life for a man who probably made Josef Stalin look like a petty thug, although, perhaps that was an unfair comparison. None of my sidhe compatriots had ever taken the time to recount all of the king's supposed crimes. Maeve mentioned plagues. Could the king's ordered 'dabbling' be responsible for the pandemics that wiped out millions back in the fourteenth century or something less deadly, like the common cold?

Even if it was the former, did it make a bit of difference what he'd done or how many he'd killed? Was prolonged systematic torture *ever* an acceptable punishment?

I wasn't proud of myself. The question was more difficult to answer than I'd like to admit, especially when I considered the evils perpetuated by some of the more depraved serial killers in human history. Deep down, though, when I honestly considered it, I knew, even if King Faonaín had killed millions, even if he'd been as villainous as Ted Bundy in his efforts, if I walked away and allowed these three to continue their torture, I'd be condoning their crime. I'd be an accessory to the king's dismemberment, suffering, and eventual murder and it would make me no better than them. No better than Azazel.

There was no choice. Not for me.

And so, for better or worse, I seized the king and sidestepped him out of his chair as though he were a thread that I pulled through the fabric of the universe. Thankfully, I'd gotten a head start learning his resonance while hiding behind Drustan's veil, otherwise, taking his clothes along for the ride at a moment's notice might have been a problem. Keeping his limbs steady was more of a challenge since I had to account for standing him upright as I sidestepped him to my side. When he arrived, pain lanced his expression, but he stood with squared shoulders, taking his full weight without needing the support of my telekinesis. With the amount of blood he'd lost, he had to be running on fumes, so I kept my webbing draped around him, in case.

I tried not to grimace at the combined smell of his blood and sweat or the closeup view of his gore coated jaw and neck. As I considered him, my thoughts went to Michael's suffering down in Invisius' basement at Lorcán's hands while I dawdled in the higher realm dealing with Kieran's unwanted magic.

Indignant, righteous fury bloomed in my chest and radiated through me, a welcome heat, searing in its intensity but delicious as hell. It narrowed my vision and heated the air around us as efficiently as a radiator on a gray Seattle morning. Before I panicked about how to safely release the excess potential, King Faonaín cupped his ruined right hand to my neck and turned to regard his three torturers.

I don't know what in the Sam Hill I'd been thinking when I grabbed the king. I should have whisked us back to his royal box, or sought Tíer's resonance or, even, taken him to the higher realm, away from Maeve and Lorcán and Nathan, for a cooling off period. But no. Instead, I'd removed him from his shackles and expected him to act like an honorable, scrupulous ruler by affording his usurpers due process of law. At most, I figured this would entail throwing the three of them in jail to await the Tribunal. Why I thought this would follow, after Maeve and her cohorts had essentially riled up the bull by cutting off his horns, I can't imagine.

So I had to wonder whether a not-so-small part of me knew what would happen, even if I couldn't have foreseen precisely how things would unfold or the dangers involved.

At the king's touch, an odd tremor pulsed through me. If the sensation possessed a voice, it would have said, 'Please, come to me,' but the request hadn't been directed at me, not exactly. It was an ardent, desperate plea, a broad, sensual stroke that delved straight to my core and teased my potential. The caress of this connection felt so incredibly right, so pleasurable, that nothing short of forced separation would have prevented my wholehearted compliance. By the time Tíereachán's alarm slammed through me and I realized what was happening, it was too late.

Unchecked power, supreme in its brilliance, roared through me, completing our circuit and conveying so much of Earth's potential that I lost all sense of my physical body as it rushed through me to satisfy the king's urgent need. And even though his evocation blinded me and overloaded my nerve endings, I reveled in each glorious, scorching second until the pleasure turned to pain and self-preservation reared up to slap the hell out of me. At the cusp of overburn, I tore away from his enticing grasp, stumbled backward, and witnessed King Faonaín's wrath when fueled by a briefly besotted idiot of an adept.

With an inarticulate roar, the king unleashed his magic in a single, thunderous salvo that tore open solid rock, forming a rift that fanned outward from his feet like a zipper bursting apart at its seam. The air reverberated with a deafening peal as the accompanying shockwave shook the ground so violently that even the king would have fallen to his knees if not for my telekinesis, which I'd instinctively wrapped around us.

Lorcán, who'd been caught mid-stride as he attempted to reach safety, slipped from my view as the bottomless fissure gaped under his feet, unceremoniously swallowing him whole, right along with the sumptuously upholstered couch, matching velvet settee, carved coffee table, and several chairs, not to mention much of the room's stone floor. Half of the brightly-colored rug hung over the crevasse's lip, forming an unintentional, below-ground tapestry, its trailing edge pinned topside by the magic circle, which had protected Maeve and a shell-shocked Nathan from the king's vengeance.

Maeve, now confined to a sixteen-foot diameter pillar of rock, rushed to her circle's perimeter to peer down into the depths of the sheer abyss, screaming Lorcán's name. When she turned her aggrieved gaze to her father, her blue eyes hardened and her mouth drew down to form a malevolent line. She shrieked something indecipherable at him, which may have echoed my own immediate sentiment.

"Son of a bitch! I didn't rescue you so you could summarily execute everyone! Don't you people have laws here? A little something called the Tribunal?" I shot eye-daggers at him. "And if you touch me again, so help me, I'll freeze your balls solid and then kick them hard enough to knock your goddamned teeth out."

In spite of his dire injuries, the bastard had the nerve to raise a superior eyebrow. His eyes, which were a stunning robin's egg blue, all but twinkled, which made me wonder whether he was still riding high on the pleasure of our joining or if his delight was solely due to eliminating one of his tormentors in such a dramatic way.

I wasn't sorry Lorcán was gone. He'd ordered Glen's murder and the abduction of my friends and done horrible things to the king, but knowing that I'd been at least partly responsible for his death filled me with a snarl of intensely bleak emotions that tangled in my thoughts, weighing me down. As I fought to compartmentalize my feelings, Tíer's concern, which I realized had been pulsing through me ever since the king siphoned my power, finally caught my attention, but I didn't have the bandwidth, nor the heart, to explain, so I opened my mind to him instead.

"Stupid human! Of course we have laws," Maeve sneered. "The king doesn't believe they apply to him. Why in the oracle's name do you think we've done all this? Centuries of planning, countless lives lost, all rendered meaningless no thanks to a brainless, insignificant human with more power than intellect!"

"Maybe if you hadn't been an immoral, scheming bitch who enjoys torture and consorts with demons, an insignificant human like me wouldn't have taken you for the greater of two evils." I speared her with a narrow-eyed glare. "But your undoing was messing with people I care about. Nobody screws with my friends. Daddy Dearest here might not be a prize, but at least he hasn't tortured my loved ones to force me into doing his bidding."

She regarded me, stunned for half a second, and then burst out with a round of musical laughter. "Oh. Oh, my." Barely recovered from her hilarity, she pressed her dainty fingertips to the base of her throat. "Yes, of course—your friends. You should ask the *worthy* sidhe you rescued about one friend who has spent quite some time in his company. You, my callow, unsuspecting adept, are in for a cruel enlightenment." She sighed. "I almost wish I could leave things as they are, just to see him break you. But, alas, it is not to be." Brandishing a knife, she deftly cut the tip of her middle finger and bent down to press it to the edge of her circle.

As she began to chant something under her breath, King Faonaín's grunt drew my attention to his pointed glare.

When he attempted to step close enough to touch me, I secured my telekinetic hold on him. "I'm not your personal battery pack." Frowning, I shook my head in some vain hope that Maeve had manipulated the truth. "The only friend of mine you had access to is Vince. Where is he? What have you done?"

He glared back, square jaw dead set, and jerked the bloody stump of his right index finger at Maeve.

Seeing that fiercely pointing finger and his indignant expression, knowing that he might have tortured Vince ... something inside of me snapped. I knew it was reckless to ignore Maeve, but her words had destroyed any charity or kindness I had so naïvely felt for the king's plight. I practically felt my heels dig into the stone floor. I'd resign myself to Hell before I took orders from the likes of him.

"I don't give a crap what your shit daughter is doing!" I bellowed at him, every muscle primed for a showdown. "Look at me! Yes or no. Did you hurt Vince?"

He shook his head, his blue eyes blazing at me from beneath his fiercely set brows.

I almost breathed a sigh of relief until I considered his injuries and *who* had delivered them. I fixed him with a scrutinizing glare. "Did you order or allow someone else to hurt Vince?"

His expression drew down hard, and he stared at me with a look of such righteous fury that it took all of my willpower to refrain from kicking his sorry ass right over the lip of the yawning pit.

Maeve was right. I was an idiot. I'd saved a mass murdering, sadistic monster from his just desserts. What had I been thinking?

You are not like them, love, Tíereachán thought at me. *You follow your heart. It isn't in you to do anything less than save, even, the lowest, most undeserving miscreant from torture. A quality for which I am eternally thankful, I might add. Now, bring the king and come to me. Brassal is here. We arrived in time. The king's chambers are sealed to us, but I'm told my mother's forces have engaged the king's enemies, cutting them off from the palace. It is a matter of time before Evgrenya and the rest of Maeve's co-conspirators are routed. Soon my wretched cousin will have few resources and no safe harbor.*

He didn't have to ask me twice. Hanging out with Maeve was about as pleasant as sharing a bath with a box jellyfish.

"Lire— " Red began, sounding worried.

"I know. The others found Brassal, so we're out of here."

With King Faonaín under my control, I sought Tíer's resonance, but the king's shroud slammed down, cutting off my telekinesis as efficiently as snipping a telephone line. I might have reeled back, spewing potential, but Fisk had made me an expert in dealing with that particular rebuff.

I glared at the king. "What—?"

The remaining words dried up in my throat along with all of my spit and half my breath when Azazel's malevolent voice grated through the room: "So soon, Princess? I don't relish being disturbed. I've just settled in with my newest pet." The mountainous demon picked at its curved black claws as it considered her. "Of course, I might be inclined to overlook this disruption if you have another mutually beneficial arrangement to propose."

While I'd been distracted by confronting the king, Maeve had summoned the creature that factored into my worst nightmares. Between my own caterwauling fear and Tíereachán's crushing alarm, I could do little more than stare, momentarily frozen in my size eights.

Azazel stood at the edge of Maeve's circle, displaying every inch of its nude body to frightful effect—eight feet of thick-skinned, monstrously-proportioned, slab-muscled demon. Even though it manifested in a male, roughly humanoid form, I knew better than to assign a gender to the creature. It could as easily appear as a gorgeous female sidhe if that's what it wanted. Interestingly, though, it seemed Azazel preferred this masculine, supremely powerful shape over other possibilities, since this is how it had appeared in our previous encounter. Who knew? Maybe demons *did* have identifiable genders. What I knew about their kind couldn't fill a Post-It note. *Know thy enemy.* Wasn't that a well-known saying? I seriously needed to sit down with Tíer and pick his brain about the time he spent as Azazel's servant.

Forget the king, Tíereachán cut in. *Come to me now! As long as you're safe, I'll tell you all you want to know and more.*

As I reeled from the force of his fervent demand, the repulsive creature eyed Nathan and its voice fell to even more menacing depths. "If this is your offering, my dear, I'll be greatly disappointed. The soulless do not interest me, no matter how pretty or how deliciously hard they like to bite."

Crap. I'd forgotten about Nathan. Seeing his terrified expression snapped me out of my fear-induced stupor. I couldn't leave him behind to Maeve and Azazel's tender care. The whole time I'd been here, he'd possessed the distinct look of someone who'd been thrown into the deep end of the pool and had no idea how to get out. And, now that Lorcán was gone, Nathan's life preserver had vanished, such as it was. But this wasn't just my compassion talking. If his accompanying vamps had died fighting the king's guards, Nathan was the only one here who knew where my friends were being held.

Tíereachán's concern spiked, but even though I could feel his reluctance, he didn't try to dissuade me. *Follow your heart, but be quick about it. Azazel would not risk answering an Otherworld summons without reason.*

I didn't think twice. With Nathan in my sights, I sidestepped my TK into the higher dimension, shot my invisible fingers to where I thought I'd find him, and poked my magical hand into the physical realm, piercing Maeve's circle. On my first attempt, I grabbed air, so I withdrew, but the second time, I hit my target. While I ran my magic over his body, learning his resonance, Nathan's complexion turned positively ashy, and I realized he probably thought the invasive going-over was Azazel's doing. Crazy as it was, I almost felt sorry for him.

I sidestepped the rigid strigoi to my side without a hitch. His face went from dire to astonished in lightning speed and, I swear, when he realized what had happened, he looked poised to hug me. Quite a transformation from the self-assured vamp I'd met at Julie and Steven's party.

While Azazel chuckled at Maeve's hissy fit over losing yet another pawn, I gave Nathan a pointed look. "You're going to return my friends to their former lives. If you do that and stop causing trouble, I'll protect you, even from the domn."

Before Nathan could reply, Azazel turned its unblinking eyes to our little group. It grinned widely, exhibiting a mouthful of multi-rowed serrated teeth, stained with things I didn't want to consider. Blunt-faced with flat, black eyes that were too large for its unnaturally broad face, the creature took 'uncanny valley' to a whole new level. Its appearance stirred things deep within me, an unfathomable dread that I'd only ever felt upon waking from an inconsolable nightmare.

"Ah, the adept," the demon crooned. Its guttural drawl vibrated up my spine, tightening my bowels. "How delightful. And— " It feigned a gasp. "My dear Princess, what's this? She's also stolen the prize I helped you win?"

The creature turned back to consider Maeve. "The adept seems to have a talent for taking things that don't belong to her, doesn't she?" It clucked its thick tongue with mock disappointment. "What a pity. Our mutual friend will be so disappointed. I think he deserves to know about this misstep, don't you?"

Maeve, who'd been looking like she just French kissed a banana slug, brightened with gleeful menace. "Why, yes," she drew out. "By all means."

It occurred to me that I might not enjoy knowing about this 'mutual friend,' but like a witness to a high-speed train wreck, I couldn't look away. And when Vince stepped into view, summoned by Azazel's command, I realized I'd effectively stepped into the demon's baited trap.

FIFTEEN

To Azazel's intense delight, I gasped.

Unfortunately, my agitation wasn't simply due to the fact that my former love interest had answered the archdemon's call, which all on its own would have been bad enough. No. What had shocked me most, at least initially, was Vince's lack of clothing.

Cheeks blazing hotter than my five-alarm chili, I came dangerously close to slapping both hands over my eyes at the sight of him. If he'd been a stranger—if we hadn't, not that long ago, shared a romantic interest in each other and a few stellar make-out sessions—I might not have been quite so flustered. But, although we'd been close (and, once, even slept together in the same bed), I'd never had the pleasure of seeing him full-on naked, which made this encounter all the more distressing.

Worse, I couldn't think of a single scenario in which Vince would choose to walk around in public this way. Knowing Azazel had forced him into such a vulnerable position troubled me deeply and I couldn't stop wondering what else the demon had done to him.

Heat roared through me, drawn by my unchecked anger, as I sidestepped my TK, practically whipping it in Vince's direction through the higher realm. Tíereachán's frantic warning blasted through my mind, but it came too late. I'd punched through to the physical plane, opening my senses to the most foul, unctuously repugnant object I'd ever encountered. I thought I'd miscalculated and accidentally grasped Azazel, but beneath the loathsome, slippery taint that seized upon my magical tether, I detected Vince's unmistakable resonance.

I fell to my knees, gagging. Instinctively, I drew upon my fire, which already simmered under the surface, and slung a mad flare down the length of my magical webbing, incinerating the corruption that raced along its invisible length to invade my mind.

Azazel chuckled. "My dear Adept, unlike my traitorous servant, who was weakened by your blood, *this one*"—it stroked the curved side of one wicked claw down Vince's arm— "is mine and mine alone."

I peered through my disheveled hair at Vince, now coming face to face with the ghastly truth.

Dear God. Why hadn't I seen this sooner? I might have gone to him, saved him!

It is ridiculous to blame yourself, Tíereachán thought. *This is the path he, alone, chose. Please, mionngáel, come to me. The longer you remain in my master's presence, the more likely you'll become tangled within its web.*

As I scrambled to my feet, anger heated me. *Stop calling it that! It's no longer your master. I saw to that.*

Our bond has weakened Azazel's hold on me, it's true, but don't let that sway you into thinking you can free your former love. Hear me on this, Lire. This is precisely what Azazel wants you to believe. I think this was its plan all along. It allowed me to escape, intending us to unite, for no other reason than to lead you down the golden path, to make you think you are capable of attaining something that is outside of your reach, and taking that one perilous step too far. Tíereachán paused, his emotions painting a desperate plea in my mind. *Please, love, do not take that step. If not for me, then for your friends who need you and the thousands of humans who will benefit from your power to fight the coming scourge.*

I hear you, Tíer. I do. I know the value of my soul and it isn't up for barter. I won't fall. I promise.

I felt him sag, not quite in defeat, but in grim acceptance. For a second, I saw through his eyes as he flattened his hands against the sealed door that separated us, as though he sought to touch me through the barrier. *Remember, Anóen, you are the linchpin, the one being who has the power to foil the demonic invasion. Azazel knows this. It will use any means necessary to corrupt or destroy you. If it can achieve this by turning love to hate, hope to despair, trust to suspicion—all the better.*

I examined Vince. What in God's name had driven him to tie himself to the demon?

Considering the fact that he'd been under Azazel's thumb, subjected to God knew what horrors, Vince appeared remarkably hale and at ease. In fact, he looked altogether gorgeous—better than ever. His dark glossy hair settled around his face in the most delicious tangle, his espresso-brown eyes were wide and bright, and his body ... let's just say, his toned physique exceeded every one of my pre-Tíereachán fantasies by a mile.

Unfazed by my attempt to rescue him, nor even my studious eye, Vince surveyed his surroundings as he blinked back the disorientation that came with being summoned. He stood tall and confident, as though paying a house call with an archdemon, while naked, was something he did every day.

When his eyes met mine, he looked pleasantly surprised, but at sight of King Faonaín his expression clouded over, going from sunny to F5 territory in an instant.

"What is he doing free?" he demanded, his murderous glare aimed squarely at Maeve.

She folded her arms, fashioning a taut frame for her perfect breasts, and gave him a haughty raised eyebrow.

When he whipped his glare in my direction several beats later, I realized she'd replied to him through their shared connection.

"Why?" he growled, his voice a choleric, accusing indictment. "Why the fuck did you free him?"

I jerked at his scathing censure. "Why? You can't be serious." I glanced at the wounded sidhe next to me. "Look at him. Your precious mate and her attack dog were torturing him."

His brows twitched in surprise before they knitted downward and stayed there. "Do you have any idea what he's done?"

"What difference does that make? You're a police detective, for God's sake. Since when is slow dismemberment an acceptable punishment? Never mind the fact that he hasn't even had a trial." Eyes wide, I huffed. "I can't believe we're even having this discussion. What the hell's the matter with you?"

"What's the matter?" he roared, his face a savage caricature of the caring man I once knew. "That miscreant is what's the matter!"

He strode to the leading edge of Maeve's summoning circle. "Trial," he spat. "I don't need a fucking trial. How's *this* for firsthand knowledge?"

In an instant, instead of a handsome, virile man, I gazed upon something out of a nightmare, his skin a bloody, horrifying canvas. Someone, some depraved, monstrous individual, had carved words—Silven script of varying size—into his flesh, some of it scabbed and inflamed, some of it crimson and still weeping, and since he was naked, I could see in frightening detail that almost no part of his body had been left unmarked. The effect was so singular, so ghastly, I couldn't immediately process it. And when he held out the blood-stained, fingerless stumps of his two hands for my inspection, I turned my watery, horrified gaze to the king.

"Why?" I managed to choke out, too shattered to remember that he couldn't answer me even if he'd wanted to.

"Because I refused to tell him what he most wanted to know," Vince said. "Your one weakness. The one person or object his precious adept covets above all else. The one thing he could steal and use against you, to force your compliance in every way." He shook his head, his mouth locked into a grimace. "At one time, I hoped that might have been me. But you and I both know that wasn't going to happen. There's one person at your side who comes first and always will."

I gasped and almost reached for Red's leg as he stood on my shoulder, but I resisted the protective impulse.

He barked out a humorless laugh. "All this." He jerked his fingerless hands at his ruined body. "I endured for you and your dearest love. And look!" He thrust his stump of a right hand toward the king. "The asshole still doesn't have a fucking clue!"

When my back crashed against a solid expanse and cool hands gripped my upper arms, I started, and it took me a moment of blurry-eyed confusion to realize I'd stumbled backward into Nathan.

"Steady, love," his cultured voice soothed as he whispered at my ear, his chin resting lightly on my left shoulder, the one opposite Red. "Just realized you're surrounded by monsters, have you? Here's a bit of advice: Stay true to your beliefs. Don't allow fear or guilt to sway you. It's what we seek, particularly when it comes to someone as virtuous as you."

He chuffed softly, his nose brushing the tender skin at my neck. "Listen to the monster at your back who owes you a turn. If you have the power to leave, take me with you and I'll owe you another."

"Lire ... please. You loved me once," Vince said, his body again restored to the pinnacle of health. "If you care about me at all, give back the king. You've seen what he's capable of. He despises humans. If it were up to him, we'd all be exterminated. If you think he'll treat you differently because of your gifts, you couldn't be more wrong. He plans to use you. You know this. Please, just ... go. Leave him here and go."

I stared at him, the final pieces slamming into place as my tears dried on my cheeks. "That's why you did it, isn't it? Azazel promised to ease your suffering, to make you whole again."

"Yes. The demon was the only one who had balls enough to help me. Everyone else was either too chickenshit to step up or too busy enjoying the show." He narrowed his eyes and snarled, "I'll *never* be that powerless again. Never. And I'll be damned if that motherfucker doesn't endure more than half of what he did to me!"

Blinking, I tried to swallow the wet knot in my throat. "Oh, babe. Don't you see? You already got that wish—both counts. But the real tragedy is that you've only succeeded in punishing yourself."

"What the fuck do you know?" he roared. "You haven't been maimed! You're not permanently disfigured!"

I flinched at the animosity in his words and, with a heaviness I'd not felt since my father's death, looked away from his contorted face, realizing now that Tíer had been right. There was nothing I could do to save him. Vince was as lost to me as he was to himself, and I had to live the rest of my life knowing that I'd failed him.

Biting my trembling lip, I removed and pocketed my gloves, grasped Nathan's right hand with my left, and then extended my free hand to the king. I could have sidestepped my TK past his shroud, but I didn't like the idea of grabbing him without permission.

Above Maeve's frantic ranting and Vince's furious expletives, I cleared my throat and then, with as much dignity as I could contrive, said, "We're leaving. Take my hand if you want to come with us."

As Azazel said something to Maeve about speaking thrice, Red tugged at my hair. "Hurry. Maeve is offering it her blood."

King Faonaín glanced down at my outstretched fingers as though he expected them to be festering with some communicable disease. When his narrow-eyed gaze snapped to mine, he studied me intensely before his hard expression yielded to one of frank astonishment. In a blink, the naked emotion vanished, replaced by his austere mien, but he stepped closer, reaching for my hand.

It's possible, if I'd lunged for him, I might have been fast enough to reestablish my telekinetic hold on his body and sidestep the three of us away, but Nathan's shout jerked my attention from the king in time to see Azazel's massive bulk clearing the abyss. With a ton of jagged-toothed razor-clawed monster about to crash down on us, I did the one thing I could think of that wouldn't be thwarted if Azazel had a shroud. I sidestepped my TK and pulled as much of the higher realm into the material plane as I could, forming an impenetrable bubble around us—similar, I hoped, to what the djinn had done in the conference room.

In my ridiculous millisecond-long fantasy, I visualized foiling Azazel's attack with my shimmering bubble and then waving a cheeky goodbye as I whisked the three of us to Tíereachán's side for my hero's welcome.

When Azazel's incomparable weight crashed down atop my meager shell, I hadn't figured on the pain.

The force of the demon's impact knocked the wind out of me, driving me to the floor as a thousand invisible daggers punched through to my core. If not for Tíer's impassioned shout in my mind along with Red's at my ear, I might have passed out. In spite of redoubling my telekinesis, my bubble shrank by a third. Unfortunately, Azazel's unrelenting hammering with its sledgehammer-sized fists didn't allow for recovery, much less rational thought.

I cried out, curled on the stone floor, clenched in agony, while Azazel turned my barrier into a punching bag. I struggled to remain conscious, investing all of my will in maintaining the integrity of my thin, shimmering shell. Blood from my nose, and possibly my ears, coated the stone beneath my cheek, mixing with my sweat to form a warm, sticky mess.

"It's killing her!" I heard Red cry out, although what he thought Nathan or the king could do about it, I had no idea.

Tíereachán shouted at me to hold on, they were trying break through the magically sealed door, but between the strength of that barricade and lack of available potential, it was proving to be slow going, even for their combined power. If I had the bandwidth to share Earth's stream with them without compromising our safety, I would have, but I scarcely possessed the wherewithal to parse his thoughts, much less risk siphoning off power from my core.

I lost all sense of time. There was me, the integrity of my circle, and the all encompassing pain brought with each of Azazel's unflagging concussive strikes. Through my sweat-blurred view, even I could see how this would end. As Azazel dealt yet another ferocious series of blows upon my gradually shrinking bubble, a victorious grin split its hideous lips. It wouldn't be long until my barrier became too small to contain the three of us. Already, Nathan and the king knelt on either side of my body, their heads bowed to avoid hitting the top of the bubble. Blood trickling from my nose, leaked into my mouth. I hung on to my composure with every shred of willpower I could rally, but a sob eked past my sticky lips.

As my gaze found Red, who knelt near my face, stroking my cheek, my unshed tears and sweat blurred my view of his fuzzy form. I knew, and I suspected he did too, that I hovered near my limit. The final salvo was coming, the one that would shatter my defenses, render me senseless, and leave the rest of them at Azazel's mercy.

I trembled at the memory of what those claws were capable of doing.

"Dearest Lire, let go," Red murmured, his voice as kind and soft as the paw he smoothed across my brow. "You have suffered enough for us. Faith will see us through. Our souls are not your burden to carry."

When Azazel's twin fists wound up for probably the last time, I heard Maeve's anguished cry as the king pushed Red aside, roughly lifted my head, and shoved something cool around my neck. Using the hair at the back of my head as a handle, he raised my face level with his, shook me like a naughty cat, and then swiped his fingers beneath my bloody nose before touching them to the object that weighed heavily against my collarbone.

The welcomed explosion of magic that roared through me, combined with the pain of Azazel's descending blows, shattered my barrier and tore the frantic scream from my throat: "Drustan, come!"

Maeve shrieked, "Don't kill her! Azazel, she has the collar!"

As Azazel's colossal fist streaked toward me, too late to avoid, I realized the inevitable. The king hadn't just bequeathed me the collar; he'd also given me a chance to share his grisly fate. If I couldn't speak my command, calling the Hunt was useless. Rendering me unconscious was a first step in that direction.

Out of the corner of my eye, something streaked across my vision, colliding with Azazel and diverting his strike. In a move too fast to appreciate, blood splattered my face as Azazel tossed Nathan's limp form to fall somewhere behind me with a dire thud. But the distraction provided me enough recovery time to reestablish my bubble, thicker and stronger this time, as Drustan's towering appearance next to me provided a much needed confidence boost.

Instead of hammering against my renewed circle, Azazel stepped back to sneer at the king, "Nicely played, Faonaín." It turned to me, grinning wide. "What will you do now, Adept? Order the Hunt to kill me?" The demon chortled, watching blithely as Drustan offered me his hand to help me stand, which I accepted after I'd rescued Red from the floor.

"Mistress, what command do you give the Hunt?" Drustan asked me, his rumbling voice once again coming to me from beneath his massive horned helm.

I frowned. "Don't call me that. You know how I feel about it. My name is Lire."

"As you wish," he replied. "Mistress *Lire*, what command do you give the Hunt?"

I scowled, all set to issue a rebuke, but decided I had more important things to sort out than our social footing.

"Go ahead," Azazel goaded. "Use them as your executioner. Order them to take my head and serve it upon one of the king's many gilded platters."

I took a breath, intending to do just that (minus the head-on-a-platter thing), but stopped shy of opening my mouth.

I could order the Hunt to kill or, even, to capture Azazel—but to what end? And what of the risks?

Capturing the demon would result in the Master of the Hunt dumping Azazel at my feet, like he'd done earlier when he'd delivered me to the king. And ordering the Hunt to kill Azazel wasn't much better. True, it would get the demon out of our hair, but temporarily since demons couldn't be killed. Their physical forms were conjured from the blood and magic of their summoners. If Drustan managed to destroy Azazel's current form, Maeve could resummon the demon anytime she wanted.

Then, there was the whole matter of potentially sentencing the Hunt to an eternal chase. If Azazel escaped through its portal, the Hunt would be forced to pursue the archdemon until it returned to this realm. And as long as Maeve didn't own the collar, it was to her advantage to keep the Hunt eternally occupied. No doubt she'd choose to skinny dip in the River Styx before summoning the demon to this realm again.

The bitter thought froze me in my lug-soled boots while Azazel stood little more than a yard away and taunted me. "So, little girl, nothing to say? No orders to give?" It laughed and beamed at the king. "How sad. Perhaps your ploy wasn't so shrewd after all, Faonaín. Humans really are best left as fodder."

As the demon wound up to strike yet another monumental blow against my barrier, I turned to the master and blurted, "Drustan, if you can, would you please take this demon, Azazel, and throw it into the River Styx?"

Instead of an order, I'd issued a request. And a wishy-washy one at that.

Drustan's body started, and when he looked down at me, canting his helm-clad head to the side in confusion, despair rose up to grip me by the throat.

Clearly, I'd misinterpreted his earlier comment about 'doing no less.'

Brilliant move, moron.

I'd been given *one* chance to catch Azazel by surprise and what did I do? I totally blew it by trying to eliminate Drustan's risk of an eternal hunt.

Next to me, the king uttered a furious grunt. Judging by his twisted expression and the set of his shoulders, he was about to bitch slap me into next week. Maeve, of course, burst out laughing and scoffed something about brainless humans and their belief in fairytales. But it was Azazel's shocked expression and the halt of its impending swing that truly broadcasted my failure.

Unlike Maeve, Azazel knew the Styx wasn't a myth. I could see it in the demon's abysmal eyes as its surprise turned to determination and it tensed its muscles for escape. It was about to disappear down its bolthole, taking Vince with it. At this point, even if I reissued my failed request and made it an order, it was too late. Azazel was already poised to flee. If I gave the command now, I'd sentence the Hunt to eternal pursuit for sure.

If I hadn't listened to my heart and wasted my one precious chance trying to be Miss Clever Pants, I could have delivered a major blow to the demon invasion, never mind save the three of us from a painful death. But *no*. I had to go all soft and give Drustan a way out, instead of just giving the freaking order, consequences be damned.

As Azazel turned to leap over the chasm, Drustan's shrill whistle blasted my ears, making every one of my abdominal muscles jolt in surprise.

Out of nowhere, a throng of gyrating hounds and half-a-dozen huntsman surrounded Azazel, each hunter spinning hundreds of whisper thin, spectral filaments that whipped from their fingers to stick to the demon's face, feet, and arms. With a roar that shook the ground, Azazel swatted at the nebulous fibers, swinging its hands through the air as though the strands were a swarm of killer bees, each one of them issuing a painful, debilitating sting.

In mere seconds, the blizzard of silky threads had coated the demon and pinned its arms to its sides. Blinded, it managed two stumbling steps before the substance tripped up its feet. The cocooned eight-foot behemoth fell to the ground, issuing a teeth-rattling tremor that had me flailing my arms for balance.

Drustan vanished from my side and reappeared a tick later astride his warhorse, a few feet from his circled huntsmen. Alongside his black spectral steed stood a sleek, riderless mare with a mercurial coat that made a Lipizzaner look like a flea-bitten carthorse.

With a unified, orchestrated movement, the standing huntsmen swooped their arms into the air, using their attached filaments to catapult Azazel's silk-wrapped body onto the silvery gray's saddled back. Although the burden looked capable of crushing the lean animal, she hardly shifted her elegant, long-legged stance under the demon's considerable weight. Before I had time to marvel at this, or at the efficiency of their capture, Drustan angled his horse in my direction.

"Mistress Lire, your request pleases the Hunt. It will be done." He bowed. "Until you next call me by name, we bid you a fond farewell."

He blew a series of enthusiastic notes on his hunting horn, prompting his huntsmen to reappear athwart their own imposing stallions. In near perfect accord, the horses leapt into the air, disappearing in a flash, accompanied by their baying hounds and the huntsman's rallying cries.

The entire capture and subsequent departure took less than fifteen seconds. The four of us were still gaping at the Hunt's decisive decampment when the entrance to my right exploded into the room with a deafening shower of rocks, followed closely by a torrent of at least a dozen battle primed soldiers, all of them armored to the gills with gleaming chainmail and wielding weapons alight with glowing runes. If I hadn't felt Tíer's profound relief after the explosion and then spotted Kim, striding in behind the first few warriors, I might have worried about the allegiance of these formidable soldiers.

I turned to the king, who regarded me with such blatant intensity, I ended up shifting on my feet and babbling, "It's, uh, safe to lower my barrier ... don't you think?"

He blinked, as if coming back to his senses, and then flicked his hand magnanimously at the bubble as if to say, 'Yes, humble servant. You've done well having this meager thought.'

Somehow, I avoided pulling a face. I dropped my barrier and then, ignoring King Faonaín and the irate screams coming from Maeve, I rushed to Nathan's crumpled form, several feet behind me.

The strigoi labored to push himself up, despite the grievous wound that split his abdomen. Lumps and bumps that I couldn't bear dwelling on distended the fabric of his slashed and blood-saturated shirt. My insides quavered at the gruesome sight.

"Oh, Nathan," I whispered thickly, trying not to breathe through my nose as I knelt next to him. The smell brought back the unwanted memory of my friend Daniel's death, and I hovered at the edge of tears. "God. Oh, God. What can I do?" I waved my hands helplessly between us.

He chuckled. The man actually chuckled—with half of his insides pooling in his shirt! I stared at him, flabbergasted and appalled in equal measure.

"Steady, love. You've had a busy day," he said and then collapsed to his side with a pained grunt.

"Me? I don't believe you. You're ... you're ..." I shook my head, unsure where I was going.

"Dead?" he choked out. "It will be of little consequence when my master arrives. He's here, isn't he? You smell of him."

I peered over my shoulder, searching for Alex's dark form, but the dozen or so soldiers, who'd formed a protective circle around the king, blocked my view.

"I won't let him hurt you," I said, looking back down at him. "You definitely backed the wrong horse, but you helped me when I needed it. Thank you for that." Truthfully, he'd saved my life and the king's too, but I couldn't find it in myself to point that out after what he and his minions had done to my friends.

He scoffed. "Don't sound so impressed. I did it purely for selfish reasons. *You*, my clever girl, are my ticket home." He sighed. "Alas, a world without daylight was an intriguing thought," he said wistfully. "However, I'm afraid the inhabitants weren't nearly as charming as advertised."

I could imagine what Lorcán had promised him. I frowned. "Diedra worked for you, didn't she? That's what got her tangled up with Lorcán."

His expression darkened. "Yes. I didn't realize what that bastard had done to her and her family until it was too late."

"Are they still alive?"

"Yes. I made sure they were safe." He frowned. "It was the least I could do."

"And my friends?"

He managed a stiff nod. "We took over a B & B, near your city's zoo, a charming establishment called Woodland Manor. They're fine—having a little unscheduled vacation."

I sagged in relief before glaring down at him. "Some of them have children, you know that? People who depend on them. Pets. Jobs. God knows what other damage you've done to their lives, you big jerk! I'd give you a beating to remember if you weren't already such a goddamned mess."

"He will not go unpunished," Alex growled, appearing at my left, his fangs extended, blood coating his chin, neck, and shirt.

Caiside, whose bare torso was also a crimson splattered mess, stood at the domn's back, eying the room for trouble. Apparently, they'd seen some action in the king's passage.

I sidestepped a barrier around Nathan, an act made considerably easier now that I was outside the king's shroud. I glared up at Alex. "No. I promised him my protection. I'd be in a world of hurt right now if he hadn't helped me, even if he *did* do it for selfish reasons."

Alex turned his threatening, blackened gaze upon me. "He is *mine*."

I squared my chin, gritting my teeth against the impulse to cower at his feet. "Maybe so, but I made him a promise. I won't— "

"No." Nathan's resonance rang through me as he pressed his bloody hand to the interior of my bubble. "That is one promise I cannot abide, although I appreciate the sentiment. I live at my master's sufferance." He allowed his arm to drop to the floor, plainly weakened by his efforts. "Please ... *Adept*, he can speed the healing."

Frowning, I fixed Alex with a resolute gaze. "There's no doubt in my mind—he saved me from a slow, painful death. I know you and I aren't exactly friends, but if you share even a fraction of the goodwill I feel for you, you'll spare his life."

"You ridiculous girl," Alex chided. "He shares my blood. I would no sooner kill him than run a stake through my own heart. Stand aside so I can end his suffering."

"End his suffering?" I squeaked and then glared accusingly. "You know, that's not the best choice of words unless you're planning to euthanize him. Just saying."

"Clotilde, there are limits to this mutual *goodwill* of ours," he growled. "Boundaries, I might add, that you have an unhealthy and most irritating habit of testing! I share his pain. Allow me to heal him."

When I looked to Caiside and got a nod, confirming his blood-mate's earnest mindset, I lowered my barrier.

Fortunately, Alex's actions seemed to confirm what he'd said. His hands were gentle when he helped Nathan to roll to his back, and he spoke soothingly while pulling aside Nathan's shirt to examine his dreadful wound.

At the first sight of viscera, I averted my gaze and scrabbled backward until I ran up against a firm set of legs. I didn't need to look up. The feel of Tíer's resonance, the strength of his presence pulsing so close to me, drew a sigh from my throat. He pulled me to my feet, took one look at me, and folded me into his arms, prompting Red to slide off my shoulder into the safety of my backpack. As the comfort and security of his embrace warmed me, the pent up stress and terror I'd set aside while trying to stay strong in the face of death finally broke free, and I splintered.

It was over.

Azazel was vanquished. I'd foiled Maeve's plot to overthrow the king. Soon, Alex, Nathan, and I would get my friends and, with the help of Michael and the Invisius telepaths, ensure that they all returned to their lives, unaffected by their terrifying ordeal. And I'd be damned if I didn't see Nathan personally rebuild Peabody's Beans, nail by freaking nail. Okay, that wouldn't happen, but somehow I'd ensure Nathan made good. I might not be able to get everything back to the way it was—certainly, Glen's death and Vince's torture had left indelible marks on my soul—but darn it if I wouldn't fix the things I could.

As I fell apart and then slowly reformed myself, I clung to Tíereachán, my friend, my *mionngáel*, finding refuge in the heat of his body, his scent, and the solace of our connection. And when he placed a tender kiss at my temple while wiping away my tears and soothing my post-traumatic trembling, the intimacy didn't even freak me out. Honestly, it felt … rather nice. Sweet and uncomplicated. A novel feeling, really.

If only that relative peace could have lasted.

SIXTEEN

The growing murmur of uneasy voices penetrated my temporary haven. After the initial rush of soldiers, a growing number of unarmed sidhe had trickled into the wrecked room, fanning out from the entrance along the back wall and keeping a respectful distance from King Faonaín and his soldiers. Most of them wore clothing that I'd qualify as regal—not as stunning as Maeve's ridiculous gown, but not something I'd describe as plain either. I imagined they were members of the king's staff and retinue. Possibly Maeve's too, although I'd assumed her support had waned after she'd been found guilty of conspiring with a demon and thrown in prison.

I fought the urge to hide my bloody, sweat-stained face behind Tíereachán. It was common knowledge that the sidhe were, as a rule, exceptionally beautiful. The few I'd met pretty much proved this assumption. But seeing the truth of it, in such a certifiable way ... well, it was jaw-dropping, to say the least. I couldn't avoid feeling like a pimply-faced teen who'd crashed a supermodels-only convention.

I ground my teeth.

You know what? Screw that.

No one could make you feel inferior without your consent and I sure as hell wasn't giving myself permission. So what if I looked a bloody mess? I'd just outsmarted an archdemon from Hell and saved the sidhe king from a horrifying death—not to mention depriving demon-kind of one of their most powerful leaders and setting back their invasion by several decades if not indefinitely.

Hello! I didn't need to wear a gem-studded haute couture gown to feel good about myself.

At the thought, Tíer's approval and open admiration surged through our connection, catapulting my ego into rock star territory. When I moved out of his embrace, his hand found mine and he gave it a squeeze before releasing me. It would be a lie to say I hadn't enjoyed the closeness, and if Tíereachán's reluctance to move away was any indication, he felt the same way.

Our shoulders still touching, curiosity turned my attention back to the crowd that had now swelled to number at least thirty.

As I surveyed the room, I realized some familiar faces were missing. *Where are Kieran, Wade, and Fisk?*

He gave my fingers another brief tweak. *Relax. They're fine. They're responding to a summons from my mother.*

Even Kieran?

He smiled. *Yes.*

As I mused on this, I turned my curiosity back to the crowd.

Interestingly, long straight hair seemed to be the norm, but several sidhe sported waves or curls, like Caiside. Complexions ranged from the exceedingly pale to deep-brown, although the majority seemed to fall to the fairer end of the spectrum. Ditto with hair color, and—confirming what Kieran had once mentioned—there wasn't a redhead in the bunch. What struck me, though, was that their bone structure and facial features didn't seem to differ as widely as those attributes did among humans. Aside from their varied skin, eye, and hair color, there didn't seem to be marked ethnicities, at least not in this particular subset of individuals. And, as far as I could tell, not one of them had the tapered ear genetic trait, like that brother and sister Tolkien had interviewed all those years ago.

As I evaluated the throng, it didn't take long for it to become obvious that almost every gaze I met was laced with intense shock if not grief, and, in more than a few cases, outright disgust.

I frowned, turning to Tíereachán. *Why are they looking at me like that? What are they saying?*

Instead of responding in kind, he said, loud enough for the room at large to hear, "They don't understand why their king would give a mere human the *Bráigda*. Some think you magicked him somehow, while others scorn the idea of a human possessing so much power." He scoffed, "They cannot see the truth, even when it's laid out before their own eyes—that *Anóen* came to their king's aid when his own daughter turned against him and tried to usurp the crown."

Maeve ranted in Silven, teary-eyed and holding onto Vince, who was once again a bloody mess. She was trying to sway the crowd, no doubt telling them about how the king had tortured her mate. By some of their troubled expressions, she seemed to be succeeding. Several sidhe yelled in response, whether in solidarity or disagreement, I couldn't tell.

Tíer's stance turned stony. He rejoined in Silven, speaking loud enough to make me jump. With his right hand at the small of my back, he gesticulated with the other, his motions indicating the king, Maeve, and me, all while lecturing the crowd. He said the word 'Anóen' more than once, along with a scathing 'Maeve' and 'Azazel.'

I'm not sure how things would have gone if not for the arrival of three imposing sidhe men garbed in elegant full-length robes that somehow managed to be flowing yet masculine at the same time. Their train of armed guards parted the crowd, which had gone reverentially silent at their arrival, allowing these men audience with the king.

Their verbally crippled ruler sat in one of the few remaining gilt chairs, flanked by his own guards and tolerating the ministrations of two female attendants, who I assumed were his healers given their jaundiced pallor and the fresh pink skin at the tips of each of his fingerless stumps.

Wow. The fact that the king was still awake following such a healing ... this was *not* a guy you messed with.

In fact, with his access to magic potential, skilled healers, and donors willing to endure the pain and disfigurement of tissue loss, I could easily imagine that regrowth of his missing parts wasn't outside the realm of possibility. Though, nothing about the process was easy. From what I understood, magically induced regeneration (or MIR, as it was popularly called at home) was exceedingly painful, physically exhausting, and required dozens if not hundreds of sessions. For a mortal human, it took years and many tens of thousands of dollars to regenerate *one* less-than-functional digit. Judging by what Tíereachán had said about Kieran's burns, sidhe healers were only moderately more capable.

For human or sidhe, magically inclined or not, arcane regeneration came with a near insurmountable price, even for a magnificent, all-powerful king.

And this king was most assuredly magnificent.

Now that we were out of immediate danger, I could appreciate the full impact of King Faonaín's presence. Even clad in a thoroughly stained tunic with traces of blood remaining on his squared, dimpled chin, he exuded a formidable aura of power. Everything in his bearing, from the confident set of his broad shoulders to the hard gleam in his blue eyes, screamed 'badass.' It wasn't difficult to see why he'd been crowned king.

As if to illustrate my thought, he casually flicked his hand. A monstrous *crack* jolted the room as a rectangular chunk of the stone floor, centering on his chair, popped upward ten inches from the surrounding rock, forming an expansive platform large enough for the king and his retinue. Intricate carvings of vines and flowers flowed across the newly exposed surface, matching the elaborate designs that adorned the room's columns, archways, and domed ceiling.

When the three incoming sidhe drew close to the makeshift dais, King Faonaín impatiently waved his healers away, even though they hadn't finished cleaning his face and hands free of blood. Kim and a man who I assumed to be Brassal stood regally on either side of the king's chair, facing the crowd and the three imperious newcomers. Across the chasm, behind all of us, Maeve had gone quiet but tearful, doing a masterful job of appearing meek and persecuted while she sat, confined to the stone pillar, cradling Vince's head atop her elegantly folded knees.

Who are they? I asked as the three men came to a stop, not five yards from where we both stood.

Members of the Tribunal, Tíer replied, looking grim. *The top six dominant houses qualify for a seat. These are the leaders of the three houses that remained loyal to the king. The other three joined with Maeve and Evgrenya.*

His thoughts stilled as the shortest of the three newcomers began speaking.

Even before the dark-haired sidhe opened his mouth, my eyes had been drawn to his noble bearing and the ominous, swirling shadows that surrounded him, beclouding all but his most prominent features. I didn't know what type of magic he possessed and absolutely wanted to keep it that way. The shadows, which undulated in a way that seemed sentient, gave me the creeps.

"He is a necromancer of considerable power," Red whispered from his perch in the topmost pocket of my backpack, his head peeking up enough to see over my shoulder.

It astounded me that Red had anything in common with Shadow Guy, which made me wonder (although certainly not for the first time) what Red had been like, back in the late 1600s, when he'd been a human necromancer. Surely, given the anti-witchcraft sentiment of the time, his appearance would have been more circumspect.

"Whatever you do, do not allow him or his umbrae to touch you," Red added, ratcheting up my unease.

Instead of answering, I gave his paw an inconspicuous pat.

As for the other two Tribunal leaders ... they were hardly wallflowers, that's for sure. The one furthest from Tíereachán and me, who stood at Shadow Guy's right, was covered head to toe in brilliant tattoos. The intricate patterns snared my appreciative gaze, opalescent and captivating as a butterfly's markings, each swirling line begging to be traced with the tip of my finger. So strong was the desire that Tíereachán had to shake me to my senses after I dazedly took a step in the sidhe's direction.

Don't look at the designs, he hissed in my mind as he grasped my hand and tugged me back to his side.

Honestly, I didn't know how *not* goggling at Tattooed Man was possible with so much of his glorious skin on display. He wasn't wearing robes, as I'd originally thought. His tattoos radiated color and light in such a tangible way that, unless you were paying attention, he appeared fully clothed. With Tíer's sustaining presence in my mind, though, I tore my gaze away from the dazzling sight to focus on the third leader.

This one was unusual in that there was nothing outwardly remarkable about him at all. Brown hair. Average height and build—at least for a male sidhe. But when he turned his clear gray-eyed gaze upon me, I soon realized he was the most dangerous one in the bunch, perhaps in the entire freaking room. Whereas the other sidhe had looked at me with shock and sometimes disgust, this creature regarded me with such pitiless rapacity that I knew he didn't view me as anything more than an animal, something to be watered, fed, and milked while shackled down in his basement.

I shivered. His was the implacable gaze of a sociopath. Even the king hadn't looked at me this way.

I might have taken an involuntary step backward, but a cool body at my back stopped me short. When I peered over my right shoulder, the sight of Alex baring the full length of his deadly fangs almost had me reversing course until I saw that his feral gaze was aimed squarely at Mr. Sociopath. I tried not to look astonished when the strigoi domn issued a guttural snarl and placed his clawed hand atop my left shoulder. There was nothing possessive or disempowering about the gesture. He didn't pull me against him and shield me as though I was his crystalline flower in need of protection. Alex merely stood at my back with his hand respectfully atop my shoulder, sending the message: 'You mess with her, you'll be messing with us *both*.'

With Tíereachán on my left and Alex at my back, I felt pretty un-freaking-beatable.

When Caiside and a deathly-pale-but-healed Nathan joined Alex in a unified front, folding their arms and looking more menacing than a platoon of commandos, my heart did a little dance. The fact that I'd earned their alliance and respect by just being me and following my heart made their show of support all the sweeter.

Even the frigidity of Mr. Sociopath's smile couldn't temper the warmth flooding through me.

The boom of a male voice from the king's makeshift dais jerked my attention away from our little show of strength, although I kept half an eye on Mr. Sociopath.

Is that Brassal? I asked when I discovered the voice's source was the slim, sandy-haired sidhe at King Faonaín's left who I'd noted earlier. Strangely, he appeared to be reading from a—

No way. I blinked, not trusting my eyes. *Is that ... a stone tablet?*

Yes. The king is a geomancer of unequaled power and skill.

I marveled at this. *So he's carving his commands on the stone tablet for Brassal to read?*

If the atmosphere in the room hadn't been so charged, I might have snickered at the biblical parallels.

Yes. Tíereachán squeezed my hand in warning, although, his growing disquiet, which pulsed through our connection like the timer on a doomsday device, had already squashed any remaining levity I might have felt.

He relaxed his grip and explained, *High Steward Gilios has informed the king that the rebel forces have been crushed by the Tribunal's three loyal families, with the aid of my mother's royal guard. In accordance to Tribunal bylaws, the rebel houses have been censured, their standings degraded, and*

Tribunal appointments revoked. The next three highest ranked houses have received and accepted their nominations.

Okay. I looked around. *Why is everyone so tense? Seems to me, defeating a coup would be cause for celebration.*

The Tribunal is required to include my mother's people in the rankings, which means that the three appointments were issued to, and accepted by, houses that are loyal to her.

So, you're saying the king no longer has a guaranteed majority? I studied his profile. *That's what has everyone's panties in a twist?*

I got a flash of blue as he slid his eyes to the side, giving me an amused glance, before he returned his grim gaze to the ongoing exchange between the sidhe leaders.

Yes, he replied. *In case of a tie, the king has the deciding vote, but in light of allegations of wrongdoing against the crown, the Tribunal has imposed what you would call Martial Law. Until the Tribunal's convocation, next phase, the high steward has assumed governorship of the crown with the backing of the other Tribunal leaders and their unified forces.*

Brassal, sternly reading from the tablet, pointed an accusing finger at Maeve, his lips curled in disgust. While Tíereachán had been filling me in, the crowd had grown restless, murmuring to one another, their expressions mirroring Brassal's. Several bystanders issued hoots of agreement.

Brassal demands to know why the king is being disempowered and investigated when it is clear that his daughter spearheaded the plot to overthrow the crown.

High Steward Gilios spared a scathing glance for the crowd, folding his arms in displeasure. He addressed the king and, after a stern diatribe, pointed to Maeve. He'd not spoken a dozen more Silven words when Maeve jolted, her face turning ashen. The crowd stilled. Even Tíer's thoughts seemed to freeze.

Whoa. What'd he say?

Maeve will face the capital charge of treason at the con-vocation. Due to her previous conviction and escape from official custody, if she's found guilty, she will either submit to scaradrai or be executed.

It seemed to me that she should have faced treason charges back when her demon cavorting ways had come to light, but what did I know?

What's scaradrai? I asked.

Magic—he paused to consider and then settled on—*sterilization.*

You mean shackling?

Tíer shook his head. *Shackling is temporary. Scaradrai is a permanent cauterization of one's ability to use magic. It is the worst of our punishments—most would say, worse than death.*

Living like a normal human is worse than death? I snorted. *Clearly some of your people need to try living as an Earthbound clairvoyant. There've been times when I would have jumped at the chance to undergo such a thing.*

This seemed to take him aback, and he frowned at me. *Unlike humans, all sidhe are born with some degree of magic. Even those without discretionary skill possess autonomous abilities.* He tipped his head, studying me. *To be without magic would be like carving out the core of your being, emptying yourself of the very thing that connects us to the beyond. Would you honestly wish such a thing?*

Not anymore, no. But there were times—hello, most of my adolescence—when I would have considered it. I didn't have the greatest childhood, remember? And until recently, I had virtually no love life. I shrugged. *Being normal isn't worse than death. Billions of humans live happy productive lives without magic. That's all I'm saying.*

"See all you have wrought, Adept?" Maeve snarled, jerking me away from our private conversation. She stood, safe inside her circle with Vince, who was once again restored to health, her face contorted into a beautiful, vicious mask. "You have doomed my people to untold years of strife. If you hadn't interfered, we would've had a peaceful transition

327

with minimal lives lost and a ruler predisposed to restoring relations with the amhaín." She spared a pejorative glare for the king. "Do you think *he* will be so agreeable?"

She laughed bitterly. "And now they are forced to contend with a human who wears the *Bráigda*. You may command the Hunt, my dear adept, but make no mistake, it is you who will be hunted. Soon, you'll find there is no one you can trust, not even your doomed *mionngáel*. When that day comes, when you realize the mistake you've made, you know where I'll be."

With a twirl of her stunning gown, she turned to embrace Vince. In a blink, they blipped from view, their disappearance heralded by the telltale, subsonic *pop* of a broken summoning circle.

The high steward turned his furious gaze on me and roared, "What have you done? Where did you send her?"

"Me?" Heat flooded through me. "If you think I'd lift one finger to help her escape punishment, then you seriously need to bone up on past events." I rolled my eyes and then snapped, "She was standing in her summoning circle. Evidently, she decided Hell was a better choice over what you guys had planned for her."

Tíereachán squeezed my hand in warning, but I was too worked up to heed it and added, "Next time, I suggest taking your criminals into custody *before* threatening them with dire punishments. I'm no warlord and even *I* know that much."

With the fleet of shadows gyrating about his face, the high steward's expression was unreadable, but the agitated movements of his umbrae told me I hadn't made a friend.

King Faonaín, on the other hand, who'd been almost wholly silent since I'd arrived, burst out with an unbridled, bewitching peal of laughter. I basked in the sheer delight of it, pleased that I might have been the cause for such a marvelous, captivating response, until I reminded myself *who* was doing the laughing.

The king's mirth had hardly dwindled to a chuckle when Brassal announced, "High Steward Gilios, Stewards Sùdrach and Urchardan, may I present, *Anóen*, Earth's first adept, most honored friend and favored adjutant of King Faonaín and his people. Let it be known, from this day forward, those who threaten *Anóen* also threaten the crown."

I bristled at the implication that I somehow served the king, but Tíer's fierce squeeze of my hand and Mr. Sociopath's sinister stare wisely instigated my silence.

Terrific. I had no idea what 'adjutant' would entail, but I was willing to bet I wasn't going to be happy about it. On the plus side, the king had acknowledged my status as Earth's adept, so theoretically he didn't plan to keep me chained in some adept-proof oubliette like Mr. Sociopath surely did. Of course, I didn't for one minute think the king wouldn't try to bend me to his will. I'd have to be on my guard where he was concerned, especially if he ever regrew his tongue. I had a feeling it was pure silver.

As the king came to his feet, Brassal lowered his tablet and addressed the Tribunal leaders, "King Faonaín bids the Tribunal welcome. After these trying few turns, I'm sure you understand that his focus must be devoted to his people as they grieve for their lost loved ones. In the mean time, I will show you to your quarters. If additional billeting is required for your soldiers, the king will create the necessary accommodations."

Brassal stepped from the raised platform as the room exploded into a hive of conversation and activity. All at once, everyone had a job to do and little or no time to do it.

Before Mr. Sociopath turned to follow Brassal and the rest of his associates, he gave me one final penetrating stare, tipping his head ever so slightly in my direction as the hint of a callous smile tainted his thin lips.

I suppressed a shiver.

"There is one who will strip the skin from his live prey and not bat an eye," Alex whispered at my ear. "In case you missed it, take this warning from a predator who knows: He has just marked his next quarry. Even if the chase takes a millennia, he will not rest until he has captured and tamed you."

When I gazed at Tíereachán, I didn't like the flatness of his expression as he watched the otherwise nondescript sidhe walk away. There was a distance, a fateful set to his eyes that said he'd glimpsed his future and knew it wouldn't be ending well.

His reaction had 'prophecy' written all over it, which immediately raised my hackles. I swear, if I ever came face to face with that bat of an oracle, I'd seal her effing lips shut with super glue. The woman was a menace.

I stepped in front of him and got all up in his face, and then, for good measure, I poked his firm chest with my index finger. Hard. "Let me remind you, in case you've forgotten. That oath of ours goes both ways. Make sure you think about that, long and hard, before you go deciding how your future is going to end. Because, for better or worse, we are now in it together. And I can promise you this, right now: Mr. Sociopath over there will not be the cause of *our* demise." I scowled and poked him again. "You got that?"

As I wound up to poke him a third time, he grabbed my hand, squeezing it tenderly, and then held it to his chest. His gaze was patient but resigned. "The oracle has never been wrong, Lire. Not once, in over five thousand years."

"And yet, I still manage to surprise you, don't I?" I raised my eyebrows and then leveled him with a steady glare. "She can't account for everything. Don't be so quick to consign your fate on the say-so of an old woman who's never met me or witnessed the chaos field that surrounds me." I squared my chin and narrowed my eyes at him in challenge. "Embrace the chaos, *mionngáel*. I dare you."

After a beat of silence, Nathan piped up, "Bloody hell. If he doesn't take you up on it, I know I will."

"Good to hear," Alex said dryly, "since, following your punishment, it is *you* who will be answering to *Anóen* for the foreseeable future as proof of strigoi goodwill and the domn's trust."

Nathan blinked, astonished, but swiftly regained his composure. He went down to one knee and kissed the back of Alex's hand. "Master, it's an honor I don't deserve. I will not fail you. I swear it."

"See that you don't," the domn replied, his voice turning to granite as he waved the man to his feet. "My tolerance goes only so far."

When I gazed back at Tíereachán, noting his raised eyebrow, I tipped my head at Alex and murmured, "Chaos field. I'm telling you—it's real."

He pressed my captured hand to his lips and then replied solemnly, "Of that, I've no doubt."

As I stared at him, my heart pounding at this blatant display of affection, his eyes flicked over my shoulder. Languidly, he relinquished my hand. "I believe someone wants a word."

I turned to find a beautiful sidhe woman approaching me from the dais. When she stopped a polite distance away, she bowed her head regally. "*Anóen*, my lord King Faonaín wishes for a moment of your time if it pleases you."

Do you think he actually said those words, 'if it pleases?' I almost snorted.

Somehow, Tíereachán conveyed his admonishment to 'behave' without issuing a single word through our connection. Pretty sure my grudging 'fine' was received in much the same manner.

In spite of my nervous stomach, I mustered a friendly smile for the king's gopher. "Sure."

But if I see any hint of an oubliette, we are gone like yesterday's chocolates, I promised.

His means of control will be more subtle. Listen to your instincts and follow your heart, mionngáel. This has served you well.

"Tuck down, Red," I whispered as I followed the woman toward the king, who stood at the edge of the abyss with his back to us.

As we approached, King Faonaín flicked his hand, causing the rock from below to well upward, restoring the floor to its formerly smooth, pristine expanse as though it were made of putty. But it was the nonexistent tremor and whispered rumbling, bearing testament to the true depth of his power, that had my neck and arms breaking into gooseflesh.

Holy dump trucks, Batman. To manipulate that much rock with nary a jolt, especially after what he'd been through ... even the most skilled geomancer on Earth couldn't accomplish such a feat.

When the damaged, indefatigable king turned to watch our advance, he studied me so intently I had the strongest urge to cover up, despite his neutral expression.

"My lord," the woman said as she performed an elegant curtsey and then gestured at me. "*Anóen.*"

Crap. Was I supposed to curtsey too? That was *so* not happening.

He didn't even deign to look at his servant as he waved her away, his eyes focused solely on my own. Before the silence could stretch into awkwardness, he tipped his head in amiable greeting and then gestured me toward an intimate cluster of chairs at the far side of the room. As we walked across the renewed floor, I couldn't help thinking about Lorcán's remains, or what might be left of them, crushed into oblivion by the mountain of rock that had filled the crevasse. Certainly, the area rug would never be the same. It had been neatly severed along the abyss's former edge. I couldn't suppress a shudder at the line of thought, and it was all I could do not to levitate myself over the immaculate surface, for fear of the ground swallowing me whole.

When I glanced in his direction, the king looked distinctly amused and I had little doubt he knew what I'd been thinking.

Gritting my teeth, I sat in the velvet chair he indicated. He took the one adjacent, sitting with his legs extended in a relaxed sprawl, which left our knees separated by scarcely an inch. At this proximity, I could fully appreciate King Faonaín's able-bodied form. The supple leather of his bloodstained pants hugged his thick, muscular thighs, and I just managed to pull my gaze before noticing what else the soft material might, or might not, be hugging.

Once again, his crooked, superior smile told me he'd gleaned my thoughts. At this rate, my molars were sure to fuse together under the pressure of all my grinding.

I think to avoid startling me, the king swept his hand lazily toward the floor and on the upsweep, presented me with a thin slab of stone, similar to the one Brassal had been reading from earlier. It was lighter and thinner than I'd imagined, hardly heavier than my iPad, yet it was twice its screen size. Almost faster than I could fathom, an intricate border of vines and flowers wove their way around the margins of the tablet, drawing an involuntary gasp from my throat. This wasn't some crude, rudimentary means of communication. It was truly artful.

As I looked down in wonder, feathery script letters rose at the center of its flat, lustrous surface, effectively stunning me for a good five seconds before I had the sense to read and consider the words the king had embossed.

'Thank you.'

I snapped my gaze to his and stared at him, those two little words rendering me speechless. I expected a lot of things from King Faonaín, but a thank you hadn't been one of them.

When he cleared his throat and cast a meaningful glance at the stone in my hands, I jerked and stared down at the tablet.

'I may be many things, but an ungrateful cur is not one of them. You saved my life at grave risk to your own, an act very few, if any, would have undertaken, especially with escape so easily within reach.'

At the scrape of nearby footsteps, the king frowned, his gaze diverting past my right shoulder, and then nodded at a towheaded boy, the first youngster I'd seen. Having received King Faonaín's approval, the boy approached me, carrying a stoneware tray that held two steaming white rolls. The child looked not more than eight years old, prompting me to wonder if the sidhe matured in the same time frame as humans did, even though age didn't wither them.

It took me a moment of frank bewilderment to realize the objects on his plate were hot towels. "For your ... comfort, my lady, a small ... charity free of ... obligation," he said in the sweetest, most delightfully halting English I'd ever heard from a sidhe.

Was he nervous or simply unaccustomed to speaking English? I looked into his perfectly formed brown eyes and decided he was both. When I didn't receive any warning from Tíereachán, I rested the stone tablet flat on my thighs and reached for one of the hot towels.

"Thank you," I said as I unrolled it, alert for any unusual smells or tingling in my fingertips.

I shivered at its warmth. When the boy didn't move away, I realized he planned to wait until I was finished so he could take my dirty towels back for laundering. He might have been cute and sweet, but there was no way in hell I was presenting anyone here with a gift of my blood.

"Please, leave the plate there," I pointed to the floor at the foot of my chair.

"I am ... instructed to ... wait, my lady."

"All right." While I toweled my face and neck clean, I speculated whether this was King Faonaín's idea or someone else's, possibly an underling hoping to score the king's favor with the means to control me. Or, worse, someone in league with Mr. Sociopath. Even with Maeve and Lorcán and Azazel out of the picture, it seemed there was no shortage of predators drawn to the scent of my blood.

Finished, I folded the now filthy towel, intending to incinerate it to ash, but the king kicked my foot, startling me. He glared at the tablet. When I looked down, the previous words had disappeared, replaced by new ones.

'Do not give him the cloth. I wish to know who instructed the boy to offer them to you. Ask him.'

I looked up. "The king wishes to know who gave you the towels and asked you to bring them to me."

He blinked and then turned to the king. Timidly, he uttered a short reply in Silven. If there was a name in there, I wasn't able to pick it out.

I glanced down at the tablet. This time, the text wasn't addressed to me. I frowned and looked at King Faonaín who impatiently waved his hand, telling me to get on with it.

Nonplussed, I turned to the boy. "The words I'm going to read are from your king, okay?" I wondered if this was as weird for him as it was for me.

When the boy nodded, I began reading, "You will confine your replies to English. When you were told to bring the towels, did you understand the reason you were instructed to wait and not relinquish the plate."

"Y-yes ... my lord." The poor kid had started trembling.

"Were you promised something in return?"

His head hung so low, his quavering chin practically touched his chest. "Y-yes, my l-l-lord."

"Members of my household do not act as tools for others and their loyalty is not for trade or purchase," I read, marveling at the speed at which the king was able to emboss the words across the stone. "Knowing Màili's intent, what should you have done instead?"

The boy switched to Silven blurting a hasty series of words as if he were trying to get as many out before being told to return to English. I heard the word 'Brassal,' at least once.

After the boy had run out of things to say, King Faonaín blew out an annoyed breath, but he didn't order the boy to repeat it in English.

"Report to Brassal, immediately," I read to him. "You are hereby ordered to divulge nothing of what we have discussed to anyone, including Màili. Do you understand?" When the youngster nodded, I continued reading, "For the entirety of the next four seasons, you are Brassal's to command for every menial task he can divine. Leave the tray and go. Brassal is expecting you."

The boy didn't need to be told twice. He placed the platter at his feet, bowed, turned in military fashion, and scurried away.

I tossed my cold, dirty towel onto the plate and focused my pyrokinesis on it, burning it to ash.

When I looked at the king, he'd raised an eyebrow.

"You thought I didn't know?" I scoffed and shook my head. "*Please*. I'm not a complete moron."

I glanced in the direction of the retreating boy. "What about this ... Màili? Will he or she be punished too?"

The previous words disappeared from the tablet and renewed script flowed across the stone, replacing it. 'His cousin. Yes. She will be questioned. Brassal will decide her fate. Why? Do you wish to be consulted?'

When I glanced up at him, his arch look told me that last bit wasn't exactly a sincere offer.

I snorted. "Right."

'Is the idea so absurd?'

I frowned at him, studying his cool expression. "What idea? That I might have an opinion regarding the girl's punishment? Or the idea that my opinion might be taken into account?"

'Both.'

I stared at him. "You're serious."

He raised his eyebrows, giving me an impatient look.

"The idea is absurd because you think humans are vermin. And in case you haven't noticed—*I'm human*."

He smiled wryly, tilting his head toward the tablet where he'd written: 'This, I have noticed. Do you believe yourself a mind reader too?'

Huh?

"I'm a clairvoyant, not a telepath."

'Yet, with considerable arrogance, you profess to know what I am thinking,' he wrote. 'I do not think humans are vermin. Vermin are small furry mammals, are they not? Humans are larger, bipedal, and lack fur. They are also more intelligent, resourceful, destructive, and greedy.'

I gave him a disparaging look. "The statement wasn't meant to be taken literally. You put humans on the same level as rats or cockroaches. We should all be exterminated. Isn't that your party line?"

'I would cull the numbers of *any* species that voraciously devours and pollutes Thìr na Étail, our treasured sylvan haven, especially a species unchecked by a rampant birthrate. For a race that prides itself on its intelligence and superiority above all other species on *their* Earth, humans are remarkably short-sighted and witless. Except, perhaps, for some of your native peoples who revered Thìr na Étail and respected its natural resources. Do you have any idea how many species have gone extinct due to humankind's unchecked expansion and insatiable pursuit of wealth? When I was a boy, the land you humans call England was covered by vast forests, so too was Western Europe and great swaths of the Americas. And, now, with the sidhe's culling curtailed by the Compact, the deforestation and destruction of species continues unabated. Or do you dare to dispute this?'

For long seconds, I stared at him while trying to formulate some sort of intelligent rebuttal that didn't come down to: *Killing humans is wrong because I'm human and we're not all greedy assholes, and, by the way, you're a murdering bastard.*

I blew out an exasperated breath. "Okay, yes, as a species we're not without our faults, but not all of us are insatiable, selfish jerks with zero scruples. Most of us cherish our environment and other living things. We care about sustainability and do what we can not to pollute. Some more than others. But like all living things, we consume to survive. Just like you guys. Hello! That's what living organisms do. We all strive for survival."

I glared at him, gripping the tablet hard enough to hurt my fingers. "What gives you the right to kill us indiscriminately for doing what any successful species does? I mean—*Jesus!*—look at *you*, Mr. High and Mighty, King of the Sidhe. You kill and torture and kidnap to stay in power. It's not like you're in much of a position to criticize." I stopped short of calling him an asshole, but it was a near thing.

Hoo-boy. If a steely-eyed stare could kill, I'd have been one big char mark at the bottom of a smoldering crater.

My tablet split in two with a resounding *thwack*, startling the hell out of me, but before I could lose my grip, stone flowed across the gap, restoring the pristine tile.

'I see your insolence is not solely reserved for the high steward.' If King Faonaín's death-ray glare and the broken tablet weren't enough of a tell, his excessively raised, embossed script sealed the deal. The words almost leapt off the stone to slap me in the face.

"I speak my mind. If you're looking for an adept who just says the things you want to hear, then keep looking."

When his ruthless frown deepened and the ground rocked beneath my feet, I hesitated but then thought, *Screw it*, heedless to the yellow flag of caution Tíereachán launched into my thoughts.

"You know what? Since you're probably already thinking of ways to torture me until I fall down and kiss your feet, I'm gonna go for broke. I mean, I've got nothing to lose at this point, right?"

Ignoring anything he might have embossed on the tablet, I leaned closer, resting my forearms on my knees, and gave him a direct glare. "Eliminating dissent and surrounding yourself with people who are afraid to tell you when you're being an asshole isn't going to create a healthy, lasting society. It *is* a great recipe for a dictatorship, though. People will follow you, not because they respect you but because they're too afraid to do anything else."

Shrugging, I leaned back. "I don't know. Could be I've misread the situation. Maybe, in spite of directing the systematic torture of my friend and murdering God knows how many humans, you're actually a great guy who instills loyalty and honor among his people. Although, I have to say, if that's the case, your own daughter sure missed the memo on that."

As the ground trembled and stone flowed around me, plunging me into darkness, Tíereachán's alarm reached a fever pitch. But he needn't have worried. I had King Faonaín's number. While I'd been giving him a piece of my mind, I'd scoured the Between and found his resonant string. I stood up, seized the king's body, sidestepped him to stand in front of me, and then enclosed us within my protective barrier, all within a matter of a second.

I shouted at him in the stifling darkness, our bodies, now, a scant three inches apart, "You know, my life would be a lot less complicated if you weren't such a dick!"

The walls that had flowed to encase us cracked and groaned, but with the king standing so close, he'd be forced to partake in whatever he dished out.

I hadn't restrained him though. With an inarticulate growl, he grabbed my shoulders and shoved me until I ran up against the wall of my bubble. Shaking my shoulders roughly, he repeated the same growl, and I realized he was trying to speak. Lorcán must have left some of his tongue behind, enough for me to eventually parse out his demand, which he repeated over and over with each subsequent shake of my shoulders.

"Why?" I uttered, finally understanding the word, my breath coming short as my heart pounded a frantic rhythm in my ears. I strained to see him through the impenetrable blackness. "Why what?"

After more inarticulate grunts that I failed to understand, he pressed his forehead to mine and exhaled a frustrated breath that heated my neck and chest, eliciting my shiver.

Relaxing his grip, so it wasn't quite so painful, he tried again.

He repeated the first word: "Why."

It took two tries, but I got the next one.

When I echoed, "Did," he rubbed his sweaty forehead against mine and grunted his ascent.

Again for the next. "You."

"Save."

"Me."

He sighed and rubbed his hands over my upper arms where he'd held me. In spite of his missing fingers, I'd probably have bruises springing up by morning.

"Why did I save you?" I sucked in a steady breath before releasing it into the darkness. "Because no matter what you'd done to deserve it, torture is just plain *wrong*. It's depraved and evil and everything I am *not*. And if I turned my back and left you there to suffer for who knows how long, I'd have been as evil as them, as evil as Azazel." I was surprised as tears jumped to my throat, watering down my voice, but I continued anyway. "I don't understand it. How can you be the way you are? How can you torture someone and still live with yourself? Vince sold his soul to a demon because of you!" In lieu of strangling him, I squeezed the stone tablet, which I only then realized I hadn't dropped. "I just. Don't. *Get it*. What is wrong with you people?"

Our dark enclosure wasn't so dark anymore. The rock beneath our feet and that of my tablet, the remaining stone inside my barrier that the king could command, radiated a subtle glow, brightening the inside of our tomb just enough to see each other. The king stepped back. Reaching out with his remaining index finger, he tipped the stone tablet away from my body so I could squint at his embossed words.

'I do whatever I have to do, for the sake of my people— for their continued survival. I am the only power that stands between them and a life of undue hardship. We are, all of us, but one faltering step away from a forced decampment to our world's inhospitable surface. Our portals are fading. Our access to magic is a whisper of what it once was.

'Your unfortunate friend provided a means for us to learn about Maeve's planned insurgency. Information regarding your loved ones was needed in order to foil the enemy's plans to use them to force your compliance. He withheld this information, not solely for your benefit, as he professed, but for Maeve's.

'I am not proud of the necessity of what was done to him, yet I will not apologize for it. I do not revel in torture, as you have come to believe. I do not rule by fiat. I do not surround myself with individuals who cannot speak their minds, although I understand how you arrived at these conclusions. I am not kind. I am ruthless. Perhaps that makes me evil by your reckoning, but you will soon learn there are others who are far more *fiendish* in their pursuits than I.'

I shivered at the words. "Yeah. Steward Sociopath delivered that message loud and clear, and he didn't even have to open his darn mouth."

'And he is not alone. My traitorous daughter was right about one thing: From this day hence, you will be relentlessly pursued. I made it clear that you have my protection, but you will find no respite from those who seek to possess you, unless you strengthen the crown by binding your soul to mine.'

I jerked my startled and no doubt horrified gaze upward to find him peering at me, a look of sympathy playing over his grimly set features. He grunted something under his breath, his own eyes rounding with surprise, before his expression turned almost wistful. He shook his head, looking amused if not sheepish, and then poked the tablet.

'If I needed yet another reminder that you are not part of our world, your genuine, unscripted reaction to my proposal would serve. I cannot recall the last time a woman has looked at me in such a manner at the mere suggestion of intimacy.'

Tíereachán broke into my thoughts, *Do not dismiss him out of hand, mionngáel. Now that you possess the collar, he has even more reason to protect you. And he isn't wrong. Binding yourself to him, you would gain more power and stature than you can imagine. His people would prosper and rally behind you. With you as his mate, tempering his stance on humans, the both of you could reunite our people. You would be revered for all time. The remaining naysayers would not have the power to stand against you, especially with my mother's endorsement.*

What the—? I'd gotten the impression that Tíereachán was attracted to me, at least a little. But maybe 'a little' was the key phrase.

Are you insane? I gasped at the notion. *No. I can't. I won't. I don't—* I shook my head. *It's ridiculous.*

We are a dying race, Lire. You could change that.

I closed my eyes, desperately fending off the words in my head. I pressed the stone tablet to my forehead. "Tíer, no. Just stop!"

Keep an open mind, he said. *That's all I'm asking.*

After a minute of me trying to fuse my head with the tablet, King Faonaín cleared his throat and then tapped on the opposite side of the tile.

When I lowered it, he looked at me with some amusement as he, once again, pulled the stone away from my body with his finger so I could read it.

'What does my nephew tell you that is so provoking? Does he tell you to kill me? You could, you know. Put the kingdom in the hands of his mother. This would surely lead to another bloody civil war. Without me, the conservative houses will not fall in line. Our already declining population would diminish further.'

"No! Just— " I uttered an indelicate grunt of frustration. "Shit. Just stop, okay? He's not telling me to kill you. Christ. He's your nephew, for God's sake. He doesn't want you dead. He cares about you." I pressed my lips together and then grumbled, "Although, I can't imagine why."

I had to get away from here, go back home, get my head screwed on straight. These people were making me crazy.

It fits the prophecy, Tíereachán pointed out.

I sent him the visual of me pinching his ear. *I can't believe you're encouraging me to bond with him. A virtual stranger. A mass murderer. A guy I don't love, much less respect!*

'Yet not magic nor power but benevolence of heart shall bind the One to the crown and a mate unfettered, the ruler who will rise from duplicity to reunite our people.' Lire, it makes perfect sense. You are Anóen. You are meant to be our queen. The timing is right. With you mated to our king, our people will reunite under your joint rule.

"That's enough!" I growled.

I slapped a hand over my face and muttered, "Nice. Now, I'm yelling at no one." I glared at the ceiling. "Keep this up and everyone's going to think I'm a lunatic. Yeah, the perfect queen. I should start screaming, 'Off with his head!' too, for good measure," I exclaimed.

I guess the king had gotten his fill of crazy talk. He huffed and shoved the tablet under my nose.

'Is this true? Tíereachán endorses me?'

"Argh!" I growled, then huffed, "You see what this has driven me to? I sound like a freaking pirate. That's it. I'm out. You can get yourself back up top on your own, right?"

I dropped my barrier but before I could sidestep away, he caught my wrist. "Aaa," he ground out and then grimaced, issuing an aggravated grunt.

Frowning, I looked down at the tablet where he'd written: 'Stay. Even if we aren't bound, you can do much to help us, to help my people.'

The ground shuddered and the walls came down. Or maybe we rose up; I wasn't sure which. Either way, we emerged right back where we'd been sitting, our chairs in the exact same position, both of us now standing in the open.

As I blinked back the renewed brightness of the room, King Faonaín's grip on my wrist tightened and his breath caught. I followed his startled gaze to one of the most beautiful women I'd ever seen, one who didn't need a gem-studded gown to appear regal. With her luxuriantly long golden-honey hair, blue eyes like her son's, and the stature of a Viking goddess, I harbored little doubt that this was the amhaín, despite her understated, pearlescent gown. Standing to her right, Wade cut an imposing figure in his formal yet simple robes with his broad shoulders and chiseled Nordic features. He tipped his head in greeting, whether directed at me or the king, I wasn't sure. Fisk stood next to Wade, looking a tad out of place in his worse-for-wear suit. His expression was as inscrutable as ever.

At the sidhe queen's left, to my surprise, stood Kieran, a smoldering contrast to her seraphic glow.

But then, I blinked because, apparently, I was seeing double. The real Kieran, the right half of his face twisted and scarred, stood further off to my right, near Tíereachán. Puzzled, my gaze bounced back and forth between the two men who, aside from Kieran's revealed disfigurement, looked so alike.

Scanlon is Kieran's father, Tíereachán explained as he eyed me from his position near Nathan and Alex. *And, yes, the woman is my mother.*

As my mind reeled at the whole idea of parents looking young enough to be their own children's siblings, the king released my wrist and extended his right elbow for me to take.

I shuddered at the thought of touching him, but I didn't want to insult the guy in front of the people I imagined he wanted to impress.

Truth be told, a tiny part of me couldn't help feeling sorry for King Faonaín with his missing tongue and fingers—which was asinine, I knew. The guy was a torturing, murdering fiend that most people would say had gotten his overdue comeuppance. Supposedly he'd done it for his people's benefit, but jeez, that was a slippery slope if I ever heard one. Is torturing someone a justified act if it means saving a million people from a life of egregious hardship? What about a thousand people? A hundred? A dozen? Where did you draw the line? Even the notion of drawing a line *at all* troubled me profoundly. And I couldn't forget the fact that he considered himself the game warden in charge of population control for all of Earth's species, including humans. The guy made my skin crawl. Maybe not as much as Mr. Sociopath, whose sinister stare ascribed to a life of merciless barbarity, but it was close.

After shooting King Faonaín a wary glare, I placed my left hand in the crook of his bent elbow, thankful for his long sleeves, and accompanied him across the grand (if not furniture-lacking) chamber to his sister. For the first time, I forgot to feel like the ugly duckling. Of course, that probably had more do to with the fact that I'd committed most of my attention to not tripping over my own feet or dropping the stone tablet.

Positioned behind the amhaín and her companions, a dozen or so soldiers stood at attention. Although these warriors wore less armor, they seemed vastly more dangerous than the Tribunal's guards, more like well-seasoned assassins as opposed to common soldiers. Not to be outdone, the king's equally intimidating bodyguards moved within deflection range, several of them positioning themselves diagonally behind the king and me.

Standing a polite distance to the side, Brassal and Kim fell in line with the king as he drew us to a stop six feet from the amhaín.

Before I could take back my hand, King Faonaín overtopped it, forcing me to keep my hand where it was on his arm. His skin warmed my fingers, sending a shiver down my spine. Tíereachán, who stood to Kieran's left, looked almost as grouchy as his cousin at seeing the king pinning my hand in place. Was that resentment I sensed seeping through our connection?

A tiny spark that I recognized as hope zinged through me. Perhaps Tíereachán wasn't quite as gung-ho to see me mated to the king as he'd led me to believe.

"Brother," the amhaín said, her voice a delicate tune that furled around us. "After such an unpleasant ordeal, I am pleased to find that your vigor remains absolute. Rest assured, Evgrenya and her fellow traitors were captured and are now confined to your *enebráig* cells, under heavy guard. Indeed, the rooms are precisely how I remembered them and will no doubt serve well."

The king stiffened. Based on his reaction and what little I knew about their past history, I suspected her offhanded remark about remembering the cells held notable significance.

Brassal's voice rang out from the king's left, making me jump. "Lady Geiléis, my lord King Faonaín welcomes you to his fortress. He's sure you'll notice a great many things have changed, although many of the infrequently used areas, like his detention block, have remained the same. It would be my honor to provide you with a tour, should you desire it.

You and your entourage are welcome to stay, along with the other Tribunal leaders, of course."

"Thank you, *Sénéchal* Brassal. It's a pleasure to see you again, even if it is under such trying circumstances. Rooms will not be necessary, but I thank my brother for his hospitality. The other Tribunal leaders have the means to contact me if the need arises." She considered me and smiled. "So, too, will *Anóen*, soon enough, I imagine."

"My lady, my lords, I beg your forgiveness," Brassal said. "Please allow me to introduce *Anóen,* Miss Lire Devon, Earth's adept, my king's favored adjutant, and current caretaker of the *Bráigda*."

Brassal regarded me, stepping out of line to see past the king. "*Anóen*, may I present Lady Geiléis, the amhaín, and Lord Scanlon who we congratulate on his recent appointment as Steward representing House Fòlais in the Tribunal."

I smiled tentatively, trying not to stare like a country bumpkin at either of them, but before I could say anything, the amhaín extended her hand. "My dear girl, we finally meet. I have taken great pleasure in watching you grow into your abilities."

At her entreaty, King Faonaín released me. Reassured by Tíer's attentive expression and the overwhelming sense of contentment that surged through our connection, I stepped closer to take her hand, transferring the tablet to my left hand to do so.

I ducked my head deferentially. "It's an honor to meet you, my lady."

She grasped my hand warmly, cupping it between both of hers. "You are truly a breath of fresh air. I see why my son has sworn himself to you." She smiled broadly. "Don't be shy, *Anóen.* Learn my resonance, so that you may find me if you ever are in the need of my advice or wish to visit my domain, where you are always welcome."

"Oh, uh … that comes with just a touch," I admitted.

"Indulge me with your full ministration, my dear. Liaison Fisk, Steward Ruiseal, and my consort have all described the sensation, but I wish to experience it for myself."

I frowned. "Steward Ruiseal?"

"You know him as Caiside, of course."

Caiside was a Steward now?

I glanced past Scanlon, my attention drawn to the sidhe I hadn't initially identified now that he wore an elaborate full-length robe. Smiling, Caiside canted his head at me in renewed greeting.

A little nonplussed, I turned back to her. "So you, uh, want me to grab you ... like I'm going to sidestep us somewhere?"

Ugh. I needed some decent terminology, stat. 'Want me to grab you?' was hardly awe inspiring.

Nevertheless, she smiled. "Precisely."

When I slid my half-wary gaze to Tíer, she chuckled.

She won't harm you, mionngáel, he replied. *Even if that's her intent, I won't allow it. My oath holds true, even in response to my own mother.*

Her request, though, left me feeling a little like a mage being asked to do a parlor trick. *Let's all watch while the cute human does something magical!*

However, the bitter thought evaporated when I took in the amhaín's earnest expression.

Squaring my shoulders, I did as she asked. I wrapped her within my telekinetic web and then efficiently learned her body, all the way down to her toenails, as if I intended to sidestep the both of us back to Earth.

"Should I release you, or is there somewhere you want me to take you, first?"

"Remarkable," she murmured, now beaming. "Thank you, no. However, someday soon, I should very much like to meet your djinn."

As I freed her from my telekinetic grasp, she peered down the line to her left, still holding my hand. "Steward Ruiseal, you were right, of course. Her magic feels like your ancestor Tasgall's. It's been a long time since I've felt such power."

She touched her dainty fingertips to the underside of my jaw. "My son will have his work cut out for him when word of this gets out," she observed, and then, with a shooing gesture and a kind nudge, she encouraged me to go stand with Tíereachán at the fringe of the group, relieving me of my obligation to return to the king.

"Indeed, my lady," Caiside replied. "But I think you will find that your son is not without help in that area."

At reaching Tíer's side, with Alex and Nathan once again standing at my back, Caiside bowed toward me, adding, "And I believe *Anóen*, too, has proven herself to be quite capable of fending off and protecting those around her from an unsolicited attack."

"Which brings us to the issue at hand," Scanlon announced, sounding impatient and, to my surprise, not at all like his son. His voice wasn't as deep or as consonant. "My lord, we bring tidings of a *confidential* nature."

After he and King Faonáin exchanged pointed stares, the king turned and jerked his chin at the closest of his guards. As they filed toward the door, Scanlon issued a similar gesture at the soldiers behind him.

When the last guard had exited the room, the king flicked his hand at the archway. Stone flowed across the large opening, sealing the rest of us inside.

Apparently satisfied, Scanlon continued, "My lord, we have been told, in light of your grievous injuries and the loss of the *Bráigda*, Stewards Gilios, Sùdrach, and Urchardan will pursue a vote of no confidence at the upcoming convocation. If one of us here votes in support of this, you will not possess the majority needed to overturn such a ruling. We *three*," he said, placing emphasis on the number and then clarifying, "myself, Steward Ruiseal, and your sister— *Mormaer* of House Loudain and duly appointed Steward of the Tribunal—offer you our support at the convocation ... provided you grant us one concession."

The king, who now looked angry enough to tackle a Lernaean hydra without a firebrand, glared at Scanlon and then at his sister. Brassal spoke his words, "Geiléis is a Bànach by birth, *not* a Loudain."

"I've not been a Bànach for a very, very long time, *Faonaín*," the amhaín corrected, stressing his name, I think to call attention to the reciprocal lack of honorific. "After I escaped from your tender care and found refuge with my mate, I renounced my birth name. On that very day, Cormac's family adopted me, and I swore my allegiance to House Loudain. Even after Cormac's essence crossed the void and the eastern houses crowned me Queen of *Thìr na Soréidh*, House Loudain named me their own and I theirs."

"With Geiléis at their head, House Loudain supplants House Gilios in the Continuum," Scanlon said.

"She will be high steward," Kieran blurted, clearly awed by this news.

I didn't register any shock or surprise from Tíereachán, so I guessed that he'd learned this tidbit earlier from Wade or Fisk.

Raising a superior eyebrow, Scanlon glanced at his son. "Indeed. A fact the remaining three Tribunal leaders remain unaware of. Right now, they are no doubt entertaining favors from the various contenders vying for kingship."

King Faonaín possessed a look of fury that was only surpassed by the glare he'd given his daughter when she'd roused him with her brutal slap.

"And what is this concession?" Brassal bit out.

"Irrevocably proclaim Tíereachán, your nephew and heir to House Loudain, as your crown prince and heir apparent," Scanlon replied. "If you do this, prior to the coming convocation, we three will vote to endorse your continued rule. As high steward, your sister will possess the vote necessary to break the tie and decide in your favor."

The resounding jolt that plowed through our bond, followed closely by utter dismay, told me Tíer hadn't seen this one coming. If not for the benefit of our connection, I'd never have guessed such strenuous emotions simmered under the surface of his steady, neutral expression.

"Such a concession does not displease," the king replied after a thoughtful pause. "It is no secret that I raised my nephew as I might have raised my own son." He glanced over at Tíereachán archly. "And apparently we share the distinction of being deceived by the same traitorous family member, who we shall no longer name." Turning back to Scanlon and his sister, he said, "It shall be done."

"I am pleased to hear it, brother, because in light of this I have one last requirement, which you shall surely embrace as it will please your soon to be crown prince and will, no doubt, allay our population's inevitable mistrust."

To my dismay, she switched to Silven, but even so, there was no mistaking her underlying tone. This was the make or break demand. If the king refused, she would hold true to her word. She would not endorse his continued rule, even if it meant throwing the realm into another bloody civil war.

What would happen if King Faonaín refused to accede to this demand? Would he attempt to bury everyone in the room beneath a ton of rock? Or open up the floor before I had the chance to prevent it?

Frustrated by their impenetrable language, I found myself squeezing Tíer's hand anxiously, which came as something of a surprise because I didn't recall reaching for it in the first place. So, when the amhaín uttered something rather pointed in the midst of her demand, I might have discounted it, except, with our fingers intertwined, I felt him stiffen.

Uh oh.

In spite of her assurance that the 'soon to be crown prince' would be pleased by her demand, I sure as hell didn't feel anything remotely warm and fuzzy through our bond. In fact, whatever she'd demanded of the king, it had Tíereachán shuttering our connection faster than a dragon protecting its treasure, but not before I caught the stray thought that I absolutely wouldn't like what his mother had in mind.

No wonder she'd stopped speaking English.

When everyone turned to look at me, I assumed the worst. She'd told the king he had no choice but to bond with me. It had to be. What else would cause Tíer to clam up? It was the one demand I'd made abundantly clear I wouldn't go for. Even Kieran was looking at me strangely, as though he couldn't decide whether to protect me or resign himself to the inevitable.

No, no, no.

I would not bind my soul to a megalomaniacal mass murderer—even if doing so meant preventing a bloody civil war. If that made me a selfish bitch, I didn't care. I didn't!

Not happening.

I gritted my teeth, preparing for the onslaught. They could beg and plead and I would *not* cave, no matter what they said. My soul was my own. It wasn't up for negotiation, not for Azazel and not for the sidhe. When I bonded my soul with someone, it would be for love and wanting to spend the rest of my life with that person. Maybe this made me a hopeless romantic, but too effing bad. It was my damned life.

At this point, I'd squeezed Tíer's hand so strenuously, it was a miracle he hadn't screamed 'uncle.'

King Faonaín affixed Tíereachán with his piercing glare, his gaze flicking briefly to our joined hands.

Brassal said, "My king wishes to hear it from the crown prince's own lips. Is his mother correct in her assumptions? Would this please you?"

Tíereachán frowned, turning to examine me.

Even though he'd closed himself off, I raged at him, *How could you even consider such a thing? He's not even a* fraction *of the man you are, and yet you'd tell me to bond with him?* I glared at him, stiffening my jaw as I now tried to yank my hand out of his grasp. *I don't care what you say. I won't do it. I won't bond with him. I'll die first.*

The bastard refused to release me. He replied, "It does, my lord."

The king regarded him skeptically, no doubt noting my furious expression, and then gave him a terse nod. As the king turned back to his sister, Brassal announced, "Very well. We are in accord. My Chancellor will draw up the writ. Scanlon, will make the official announcement. The crown prince and his intended will be introduced at the convocation. Does that suffice?"

The crown prince and his *intended*?

I stopped trying to yank my hand away.

"Indeed it does, sire," the amhaín replied, a sentiment which was promptly seconded by Caiside and Scanlon.

"My lord, we will discuss the finer points of living arrangements and duties after the convocation," Scanlon declared.

My mind reeled, and I was sure to need eye drops soon, my lids pinned as wide as they were.

Tíer had a fiancée? And soon they'd be discussing … living arrangements? Did that mean he'd be returning to live in the Otherworld?

A peculiar burn kindled in my chest and it took me more than a moment to realize it was the acute flare of jealousy.

What the—?

Before it could get away from me, I clamped down hard.

Stop being ridiculous, I scolded myself. *It's not as if you were in the running.*

"Thank you, my lord. As this concludes our business, I shall bid you farewell," the amhaín said, executing an elegant bow toward her brother. "Until the convocation."

Beside her, Wade also bowed, along with Fisk, Scanlon, and Caiside.

At the superior tip of his chin, signaling his dismissal, she pinched the fabric of her gown, gracefully holding the hem aloft to avoid tripping over it, and drifted to where Tíereachán and I stood. Wade, Fisk, and Caiside followed a short distance behind.

"My son," she said, reaching out to caress his cheek. "Perhaps we will have more time together at your next visit. With the destruction of Evgrenya's gateway, Earth is the safest place for you both for the time being. Go now. If I'm not mistaken, *Anóen* has loved ones to attend to." She beamed at me. "Dear girl, you are everything I could have hoped for."

She moved away, taking Wade's arm, but turned to add, "I will see you at the convocation. Wade will send for you two when the time comes." With that parting comment, she tossed something that resembled a glimmering lasso into the air. When the lariat fell to ensnare her, Wade, and Caiside, the three of them vanished.

Great. The convocation. Just what I wanted to do with my free time: Receive hundreds of scathing looks from all the townsfolk while watching the new crown prince and his disgustingly gorgeous fiancée announce their betrothal. My insides almost reignited at the thought. *Gee, I can hardly wait.*

It won't be that bad, Tíereachán assured me.

I shot him a dirty look. *Oh, so you're talking to me again, huh? Thanks a lot for making me a nervous wreck. Jerk!*

I succeeded in wresting my hand away from him and folded my arms around the stone tablet, pressing it to my chest. *You could have told me your mother was playing matchmaker for* you *and not me. But no. Instead, you let me think I was about to be promised to the king like you wanted! I can't believe you did that to me. I was freaking out.*

I came close to asking him why the hell he'd done it.

And then I remembered ...

He'd retreated because he knew I wouldn't like what his mother was about to announce. I'd heard that thought clearly just before he closed himself off from me. Somehow, he knew I'd be jealous and possibly hurt and he wanted to give me privacy.

I wanted to hide in a closet and die of embarrassment. For the first time since binding myself to him, I regretted doing it.

I threw up my shield and forced him from my mind, shutting him out, exactly as he'd done to me.

"Lire— "

Overriding him, I squared my shoulders and announced, "It's time to go home. I need to get my friends. Kieran, are you staying or going?"

He frowned, the action twisting the scars on his face in a startling fashion, but I kept my eyes pinned to his, not wanting to offend him. "For the time being, I must stay. But ..." He peered at me. "If you ever have need of me, I'm here for you. Any time, without question."

In my desperation to bury my lingering embarrassment, I nearly steamrollered ahead without so much as a reply, but I stopped myself because Kieran deserved more than an inconsiderate brush off. "Thanks. I like knowing that. Truly. Take care of yourself, Kieran."

With a doleful smile, he nodded and walked away, heading to join his father, who stood in quiet discussion with Brassal and Kim. The king, I noticed, had disappeared, and I couldn't suppress my sigh of relief.

I caught Kim's eye and mouthed, "We're leaving," and made my fingers walk. I pointed at her. "You coming?"

She nodded and then excused herself from their group, first bowing to Scanlon and then smiling demurely at Brassal. But when she rounded behind her mate on her way toward us, her grin turned impish and she surreptitiously groped his ass, knowing her movement was outside of Scanlon's view.

I stifled my laugh. Now, *that* was the Kim I knew and liked.

She stopped in front of me. "Okay, *Anóen*. Let's blow this popsicle stand. Jackie's probably worn a path through the floor by now with all of her pacing."

I'd forgotten about her and Diedra. I hoped they hadn't been too worried.

"Clotilde, for Nathan's sake, please bear in mind that it isn't yet night," Alex said. "A room with curtained windows is necessary."

"Right. My bedroom, then. Pretty sure I left the shutters closed in there this morning." And, since they were all safe from my clairvoyance, the psi-free environment of my home wasn't at risk.

With the plagency of my bedroom firmly in my mind, I scooped up our traveling band and sidestepped us home.

But not before I wondered whether I'd remembered to pick up my dirty underwear.

SEVENTEEN

At our arrival, Alex whisked Nathan off his feet before the comatose strigoi could hit the carpet.

I'd never thought of my bedroom as small, but filling it with six adults, four of who were tall and broad-shouldered, left us little room to rumba.

I tossed the stone tablet on my slipper chair and pointed at my bed. "Put him there."

Although my whitewashed shutters were snugly closed and the lights were off, it wasn't so dark that we couldn't see each other. Thankfully, I'd taken the time to pull up my bed's covers and plump up my decorative pillows earlier in the morning. And no discarded panties in sight.

After getting him settled, Alex removed Nathan's shoes, I think more as a concession to my lovely duvet cover than the unconscious strigoi's comfort, because when I covered Nathan with my faux cashmere blanket, snuggling it under his chin and patting it smooth, Alex shot me a sardonic look, shaking his head at the gesture.

Fisk snorted, but it was Tíer's dark expression and folded arms that gave me pause.

I shot the three of them a scowl, turned on my heel, and strode out the door to the top of the stairs. Kim had practically flown from my bedroom at our arrival, and I caught a glimpse of her pink cardigan as she raced out my front door.

I arrived across the hall a minute later, still yanking on my gloves, to find Jackie fiercely hugging Kim while Diedra looked on, an expression of profound relief on all of their faces.

When Jackie's gaze found mine, she reluctantly released Kim and pointed at Diedra. "Your friend's a fucking saint. Poor woman. I must have grilled her a dozen times about your guys' meeting. Somehow she managed to keep me from tearing up the walls and the goddamned furniture. And when she saw you show up and save the king— " Jackie huffed. "There was a part of me that wished the king hadn't killed that sorry sonnuva bitch, just so we could know what was going on."

I pressed my hand to my chest. At the time, it hadn't occurred to me that, until Lorcán's death, Diedra might have been watching the events in the king's chamber through her mate's eyes. For a time, she'd possessed a uniquely horrifying window into the Otherworld.

"Thank you. If you hadn't gone there— " Diedra shook her head. "I'm sorry I tried to stop you," she cried, bursting into tears. Trembling, she hugged herself, her sleek black hair sliding over her shoulders to obscure her face. "I'm so sorry, Lire. I knew the shot ... wouldn't hit you. I knew your djinn ... would stop it. I ... I had to make it look good or he ... he ..."

"I know, hon," I said, drawing close but helpless to do much more than rub her back. "He's dead now. And Nathan told me he made sure your family was safe. He had no idea what Lorcán had done to you or your sister until it was too late. I think— " I sighed. "I should let him tell you, but I think ... he didn't anticipate where it would all lead. And once he started down that road, he got in over his head. Big time. The Otherworld's a pretty compelling place. For the strigoi, there's no daytime. And, did you know everything there is psi-free?—the sidhe, their animals, everything. I'm not excusing him. I'm not. But ... I guess I kinda get how Lorcán was able to sway him."

She sniffled and looked up at me with red-rimmed eyes. "Jackie's wrong. You're the one who's the saint, not me, not even close. After what he's done, after what he helped do to your friends, you're still able to see his side of it. I'm not like you, Lire. I'm not sure I'll *ever* be able to do that," she spat before covering her face.

"He will be punished," Alex reaffirmed, his voice cutting through the apartment. "And he will make restitution. You and your family will want for nothing. Nathan's clutch is no more, but you have a job with me as my clucer if you wish it, Diedra."

Lowering her hands, she stared at him, shock rendering her features slack. "Clucer?" The word came out in a gush. "You would trust me with such a position?" She regarded him with rounded eyes. "Why?"

"Because you now understand the lengths the domn would go to defend what is his. And, perhaps, because a certain someone demonstrated to me the value of friendship."

At my surprised gaze, he glared at me. "But this should not go to your head."

I smiled and scoffed, "Yeah, yeah. Strigoi are fickle and unpredictable. Yadda, yadda, yadda." I rolled my eyes. "Can we go get my friends now?"

Between my sidestepping ability and Michael's Subaru, we made it to the small hotel Nathan had mentioned, less than thirty minutes later. As the strigoi had professed, my friends were enjoying the facilities as though it was a continuation of Julie and Steven's party. They were blind to the fact that they'd been there for nearly twenty-four hours with no luggage, no clean clothes, and no memory of any real world responsibilities. I was greeted with enthusiasm and a call to join in the festivities, which, at the moment, seemed to include billiards, reading in the library, or hanging near the backyard hot tub, fully clothed, favored drink in hand. The hotel staff, too, seemed oblivious to all of it, not even raising an eyebrow about their odd guests who hadn't brought their swimsuits, nor even a toothbrush between them.

Alex released them from their compulsion. I don't know if he had this ability because he was the domn, or Nathan's maker, or both. With Michael and the telepaths in tow, they helped reinsert each of the party-goers back into their lives, managing their family members, friends, or coworkers when necessary, as though their ordeal never happened.

Julie and Steven were a different story. Their coffee shop was a burned out shell, but Michael had worked his magic so that in less than a day, the fire inspector had issued his report declaring the fire the result of faulty electrical wiring and Glen, an unlucky good Samaritan who'd died trying to put out the fire. The insurance adjustors had also come and gone, leaving a letter for Julie and Steven, informing them that the full replacement cost of rebuilding would be covered with no deductible and no change in their yearly rates. In the meantime, while the rebuilding took place, Julie and Steven were booked for a two week cruise of the Caribbean and a month long stay in the Caymans, paid for by the phony electrical company whose faulty wiring was supposedly at fault.

Magic, indeed.

By the time we'd finished getting everyone's car out of the city's impound lot and returned, it was close to dinnertime, and since lunch had come and gone without so much as a cracker, I was starved. All I wanted to do was go home, make a grilled cheese sandwich, eat it in bed, and then sleep for a week. When Michael volunteered to drop Alex and Diedra off at their hotel, I begged off joining them for dinner, even though I was mildly curious whether Alex would eat something or merely sit and watch.

Since Fisk's car was still parked in my apartment building's lot, I sidestepped him and Tíer back home with me.

In my building's lobby, I bid them adieu. "Guys, thanks for the memories. I guess I'll hear from you when it's time for the convocation thing. You'll have to let me know what I'm supposed to wear, and if you can give me more than an hour's notice, that would be spectacular. If you tell me the night before, I'll bake you cookies."

As I turned toward the elevators, Tíereachán growled, "Aren't you forgetting something?"

I turned, eyebrows raised.

He glowered at me. "The vampire in your bed."

Nathan. I'd forgotten about him.

"Oh, right." I shrugged. "I'll call a taxi and send him over to Alex's hotel." When he continued to stare at me, I frowned. "Is there something else?"

"Yes. There's the little matter of our protection."

"Our protection?"

"Earth may be safer than staying in the Otherworld, but it's not devoid of those who would risk much to capture you. And with all that hangs in the balance, you are especially at risk," he paused and then acknowledged, "As am I."

"What are you saying?" I blinked at him. "Are you suggesting that ... you stay *here* ... with *me*?" If my voice rose any higher, I'd sound like a pixie.

"Our mutual oaths are ineffective if I am across town."

His tone was reasonable enough that I couldn't decide whether he was being facetious or not. I might have been able to read him, if our connection had been open, but I'd kept my psychic shield firmly in place ever since Brassal's announcement for fear of him hearing some of my more irrational thoughts.

Fisk, ignoring the fact that neither of them had been invited upstairs, hit the elevator button.

"Isn't your *intended* going to be a little upset about you living with another woman?" 'Intended' came out a little more snarky than I'd expected, and I wished I hadn't bothered to open my mouth. I seriously needed to get a grip.

He smirked, clearly enjoying the thought. "I'm thinking she might, at that."

I scowled at him. "Great. That's all I need. An elf princess with an axe to grind. As if I haven't had enough of those already."

Never mind the fact that, in spite of myself, I hated her guts with all the fervor of an angsty teen and about as much common sense. Although, when it came to the power of attraction, I didn't think common sense entered into the equation, nor did previous disastrous relationships that were a mere twenty-four hours dead. Otherwise, I would have talked my way out of my illogical jealousy hours ago, instead of wheeling from yet another tiring round of mental tug of war.

But the truth of it was I'd been attracted to Tíereachán from the first, no matter how hard I worked to deny it. And it had me wondering what might have happened if I hadn't been ensnared by Kieran's doleful eyes and ruinous magic.

Of course, ultimately, it didn't matter. Tíer was promised to someone else.

Maybe I could catch food poisoning just in time for the convocation.

When the elevator doors opened, both men wandered inside while I continued to frown. "Don't you care at all what she thinks? She won't necessarily know you're on the couch."

He leaned against the back wall of the elevator, looking more satisfied than a bobcat locked inside a tropical aviary. He folded his arms and grinned at me. "Jealousy has its uses."

Excuse me?

What happened to the man who'd been so supportive? The friend who, when I'd needed it, held me like he cared about me? Now, less than eight hours later, I was a handy tool he could use to make his 'intended' jealous?

I stomped into the elevator. "So glad I could be of service," I said caustically and stabbed the button for my floor. "By all means, move in with me. It's not like I have any reputation to uphold, right? One sidhe moves out and the next moves in. Boy, I guess I better get busy lining up the next one, huh? Or maybe you plan on picking your successor once you and your *intended* tie the knot and move back home."

Ooooh. Now *that* elicited a response.

He came away from the wall, his expression stormy, jaw stiff. "Not bloody likely."

"Oh really? Not bloody likely, is it?" I folded my arms, glaring at him. "Now you're in charge of my life? I can't wait to see what your future bride has to say about that one."

Before Tíereachán could come up with a reply, Fisk turned on him, his amber eyes narrowed in frank disapproval, and uttered something in Silven.

Tíer's belligerent-sounding response was concise. Something along the lines of *shut the fuck up* was my guess, because Fisk's jaw clamped shut, his lips forming a thin, angry line, and he turned back toward the elevator doors, folding his arms.

When I looked back to Tíereachán, his angry expression had yielded to one of intense annoyance, but it wasn't necessarily directed at Fisk, nor at me. And when he raked his hand through his hair, muttering in Silven, Fisk rolled his eyes, unimpressed.

Whatever.

The elevator doors couldn't open fast enough, and when they did, I strode through them like a woman on a mission. With my TK, I no longer needed a key to my front door. I flipped the dead bolt, but before I could head inside, Fisk called out from Jackie and Kim's doorway, "If you want me on your couch instead, let Jackie know." With a scathing eye over my shoulder at you-know-who, he added, "My mate and I don't need to play games. She knows well where my loyalties lie." He gave me a sympathetic smile and then added, "Ask the ass the name of his intended. You deserve to know."

With that parting remark, he strode into Jackie and Kim's apartment as if he owned the place, shutting the door crisply behind him.

I walked into my apartment, frowning as something like alarm rocketed through me, jolting me alert and driving away my hunger. Fisk thought the name of Tíer's intended would mean something to me. Since I knew very few female sidhe by name, and all of those were unquestionably non-mate-material, a potent combination of fear and excitement churned inside of me. Biting my lip hard enough to leave temporary marks, I drifted to my family room couch, dropping my backpack in its usual spot so Red could climb out, and continued into the kitchen, all while I ignored the man whose presence behind me had expanded to elephantine proportions. In fact, his closeness seemed to pervade the room so entirely that I could scarcely draw breath or even *think*.

"Is my company so distasteful that now you can't even stomach to look at me, nor even speak to me?" he asked.

I stopped at my kitchen table, grasping the back of a chair. "I don't think it's me that needs to do the talking." I turned to look at him, taking in his forbidding scowl. "Apparently, there's something I deserve to know."

"Yes, and so you *would* if you hadn't cut our connection."

"Ah. I see. So it's my fault." Matching his irksome expression, I folded my arms. "Well then, I guess you'll have to use actual words," I said, steeling myself, in case my suspicion was wrong. Or right. Either way, I'd be upset, for opposing reasons, and the stress of it had me feeling brittle, which I instinctively covered with a shield of bravado.

"Out with it," I ordered, twirling my hand impatiently. "Chop, chop."

After brief consideration, his narrowed-eyed gaze softened.

"You're afraid of hearing a name other than your own," he said, sounding just as astonished as he looked, and then a smile, the likes of which I hadn't seen since he'd invaded my dreams weeks ago, crept across his mouth. "Aren't you?" he asked, his voice pitching to seductive depths, matching the intensity of his gaze.

My scowl magnified. Somebody needed to get over himself. "Don't be ridiculous," I sputtered.

"Ridiculous, am I?" His grin flattened to something more serious but didn't wholly disappear. "Then you'll have no issue with taking my hand and telling me *with your actual words* that you feel nothing beyond a … a charitable regard for me."

He stalked closer, crossing into the kitchen and extending his hand as though he wished to partake in a friendly shake, but the fervor of his gaze and the challenge in his voice spoke of something far more profound. "Open our bond and show me that you feel absolutely no spark, no thrill—that I am *alone* in feeling the breathless zing of attraction and the flush of desire whenever we touch. That the mere thought of another woman sharing my affections doesn't spur a surge of jealousy in precisely the same way the thought of that vampire, sleeping in your bed, stirs in me *right now.*"

With my thighs backed up to my kitchen table and twenty-four inches of stifling, electrically charged air between us, he pierced me with a smoldering, breath-catching stare that had my heart beating triple-time and my body riveted in place. Leaning close, he said softly but no less passionately, "Take my hand and tell me you don't want it to be *your* name that my mother proclaimed as the only woman I've ever desired to have as my mate."

As I stared at him, doe-eyed and mute, reading fervency in his pale-blue eyes and the fierce set of his brows, I could hardly breathe, much less speak, but it was just as well, because if I admitted to any of those things, I'd be lying and there was no way he wouldn't know it.

"No?" he asked, brows lifting in sanguine query as he straightened. "Very well. Then this is what we're going to do. We're going to give each other the benefit of three months. Call it ... a trial period, in which you allow me the privilege of courting you. You'll go with me to the convocation as my intended, *but*—if after our three months is up, you decide that I'm a conceited blowhard who cares little for anything but himself and kisses you like a dead fish, then we'll call off the engagement and go our separate ways. However, if after three months, you still want me as much as I want you"—he looked at me meaningfully— "then perhaps we might renegotiate our sleeping arrangements."

Finding my breath, I croaked, "Are you saying you want ... to date me?"

He gave me a lopsided, decidedly wicked grin. "I think I've tacitly established that I want to do a great deal more than date you, but in a word: Yes."

Blinking, I shook my head, trying to get this newest development straight in my mind. "You're going to date me while living with me and sleeping on my couch."

"Yes."

The proposition was bonkers and, yet, so totally in keeping with my absurdly complicated life.

He smirked at me. "Come on, *mionngáel*. Embrace the chaos. I double dog dare you."

I burst out laughing. I couldn't help it. Hearing him turn my own words against me and then topping it off with something so utterly human, it tickled the mirth right out of me.

Blowing out a breath, I relaxed against the table behind me and folded my arms. After a moment of consideration, I tipped my chin at him in acquiescence. "Three months. But we're keeping things platonic until I say otherwise." I narrowed my eyes. "And you're not sleeping here. You can take the couch across the way." This probably meant Fisk would be sleeping on my couch instead, but I didn't care.

He frowned, likely realizing the same thing.

"As you wish," he finally replied, his voice as calm as you please, but his heated gaze told me he was contemplating ways to tempt me into saying 'otherwise' sooner rather than later.

To my chagrin, my stomach tilted and and I flushed, no doubt an embarrassing shade of pink, from that *one* pointed look.

I was so out of my depth with this guy.

Smirking, he announced, "Now, I believe a grilled cheese sandwich and sleeping for a week are called for." He pressed his lips together and, eyes darting to his left, snarled, "But first, I need to have a word with a *certain eavesdropping vampire*."

"Don't get your knickers in a twist, you jealous bastard. I'm gone." Nathan peeked over Tíer's shoulder to give me a devious wink. "Thanks again, love. I'll say *adieu* since I believe we'll be seeing each other again." He grinned, his straight white teeth a dazzling contrast to the tawny brown of his full lips. "The blanket was a nice touch. Smells nice too. I dare say, the fragrance alone will sustain me throughout the duration of my punishment."

The door clicked shut just as Tíereachán turned his threatening glare over his shoulder.

Wow. That strigoi could *move.* And a good thing too.

Chuckling, I went up on the balls of my feet and gave Tíer an impulsive peck on the cheek. I strolled away before he'd recovered from his astonishment.

Sure, my life might be bizarre, but at least I finally felt in control of it, eager to chart my own course.

I turned to give him an appreciative stare. "I'll tell you one thing, you sure do great things for my ego." Grinning, I tipped my head toward the kitchen. "Come on, Mr. Ninety Day Trial. Let me introduce you to the merits of grilled cheese. I'll tell you about everyone at my office and your new job. Sleeping for a week is optional."

"My new job?"

"Yep. For the past month and a half, Jack's been making noises about hiring a daytime guard. I think you'll fit the bill nicely. Don't you?"

His smug grin and raised eyebrow told me all I needed to know.

Hired.

Oh, yeah. Definitely.

AUTHOR'S NOTE

If you're anything like me, you're a rabid Scrooge when it comes to your free time. You carefully ration it and begrudge the need to spend it on ridiculous distractions like eating, sleeping, and shaving your legs. Okay, that could just be me. Even so, the fact that you spent your valuable time, reading something I created for enjoyment, means a great deal to me.

But if I don't hear from you, cherished reader, I'll have no clue whether I succeeded or failed (or maybe just left you saying 'meh') in my attempt to entertain you.

I hope you'll consider posting a review of *Reluctant Adept* on the site where you purchased it. Reviews not only help other readers decide if my novels are something they might enjoy, but they also let me know where I need to improve as a storyteller. I appreciate all reviews, whether positive or negative. Let me know what worked for you and what didn't. You're also welcome to visit and correspond with me on my website at www.katherinebayless.com. I'd love to hear from you.

You've just read the third novel in the *A Clairvoyant's Complicated Life* series. If you'd like to read an excerpt from the fourth, *Song of the Lost*, please turn the page.

AN EXCERPT FROM SONG OF THE LOST

If not for my dour bodyguard, who loomed outside my closed office door, I could almost pretend that my life had gone back to normal.

Normal? I rolled my eyes. Life as a clairvoyant ruled that out by the age of three.

At least Fisk, bodyguard extraordinaire and former FBI-agent impersonator, wasn't sleeping on my couch anymore. That was something.

My desk phone trilled, yanking my attention from my computer screen and the appraisal I'd been distractedly writing.

"Hey, Monica." I wedged the receiver beneath my chin and continued working, importing the first photo of the late sixteenth-century Nuremberg egg I'd read for a local antique dealer earlier in the week.

"Hi, Lire. Sorry to interrupt, but there's a gentleman here asking to speak with you, a Mr. Patrick Jacoby." She clipped out his name with testy precision. "I know you're done with clients for the day, but he said that you'd want to see him."

This 'Mr. Jacoby' must have been rudely insistent. Monica didn't usually get ruffled without reason.

"I'm sorry, Monica. I'm super swamped, right now. Can you ask him what this is about?"

"I did. He didn't elaborate. He said his name would mean something to you and that you'd want to see him."

Patrick Jacoby. The name rang darkly.

"Fine. Tell him I'll be there in a minute. Thanks, Monica."

After quickly importing the remaining three photos, I saved my progress and pushed away from my desk.

Red, my magical familiar, regarded me from his perch on the padded bench beneath my office window. Clutched in his teddy bear paws was his iPhone—perfectly sized to feed his voracious reading habit.

"I've got to deal with a drop-in." I stopped with my fingertips on the door handle. "Does the name 'Patrick Jacoby' mean anything to you? It sounds familiar, but I can't place it."

"Indeed." Red lowered his reading. "You will no doubt remember him from your time at Coventry Academy, your junior year, if memory serves. He was the Arcane Council's vice president and the godfather to one of your less amiable classmates."

Groaning, I slumped against the door. *Vice President Jacoby.* "That's right. Amanda's godfather. He was super creepy. And a complete jerk. Not a surprise, considering how awful Amanda was." Those were memories I was much happier not recalling. "I hope he's not here to cancel the council meeting."

Next week, several of us were scheduled to meet with Arcane Council President Kessburg to discuss the impending demon invasion.

I opened the door and found Fisk standing at the ready. The half-blood sidhe took his bodyguard job seriously. Confronted by his steady amber eyes, I tried to recall whether I'd ever heard him issue a genuine laugh in all the time that I'd known him. Certainly, his smiles were few and far between. Even Monica, who never missed an opportunity to flirt, had mostly given up on Fisk, which was saying something. It had sure been fun watching her try, though.

"I've got a drop-in," I said. "Do you know Patrick Jacoby? Not sure if he still is, but he used to be the Arcane Council's veep."

"By reputation only." Fisk's customary scowl deepened. "He's a powerful *animtùr.*"

"Aura reader," I said with a derisive snort. "It makes him sound so passive. I had a run-in with him in high school. The rumor was that he could strip a person's aura without skin contact ... among other things." I glanced toward the lobby. "Lucky me. He's waiting up front."

I didn't bother inviting Fisk to come along. He'd accompany me, regardless. While Tíereachán visited his mother in the Otherworld, Fisk had been tasked with protecting me.

Fighting it was a waste of energy. Besides, I couldn't argue that there weren't more than a few individuals who might want to kidnap, torture, or murder me. After all, I'd been publicly declared to be 'the One,' the sidhe's long-awaited adept who'd supposedly help reunite their populace and re-kindle their prior glory. (Gee, no pressure there.) On top of that, I possessed the sidhe's coveted *Bráigda,* the collar that controlled the Master of the Hunt; I was slated to be Crown Prince Tíereachán's consort; and King Faonaín had claimed me as his 'favored adjutant,' whatever *that* was.

All of it was enough to bring on a panic attack, so I made regular practice of not thinking about it.

As we ventured down the hall, Fisk lengthened his stride to keep half a step ahead of me, his eyes roving as he scanned our surroundings. "Is your TK up?"

"Yes. You don't need to keep asking, okay? I have it ready all the time." I ruffled his hair with my telekinetic fingers, which I kept draped over anything and anyone nearby. It was my freakish version of radar, one that I'd learned to keep active.

He jerked his head aside, grumbling, and smoothed a hand over his short thick hair.

I extended my TK forward, pushing my invisible net into the lobby to get a mental lay of the land. "Monica's at her desk and there's a tall, slim individual standing by the wait-ing area's coffee table. Nothing seems amiss."

Fisk grunted.

As we emerged from the rear hallway, I caught sight of Jacoby seconds before he noticed me. Memories, most of them bleak, flooded into my mind, and I had to force my ex-pression into one of cordiality.

The master ethermancer hadn't changed. He hadn't even aged. He looked exactly how I remembered him, right down to the impeccable single-breasted bespoke suit, expertly knotted tie, and slicked-back ebony hair.

Jacoby faced me, his lips curving into a self-satisfied smile. "Ah, Miss Devon. So gracious of you to receive my un-expected visit, given your weighty workload. I'm honored."

His superior tone told me what he thought about my weighty workload.

Fisk halted at the edge of the waiting area, allowing me to continue forward to greet the man whose sudden appearance had rekindled so many unpleasant details from my junior year in high school.

I remembered him being taller. No less creepy, though. "Hello, Mr. Jacoby. What can I do for you?"

"Ah, straight to the point. Good. I wish for thirty minutes of your time, nothing more. I possess information that I believe is in your best interest to learn." His eyes shifted toward Fisk before he refocused on my face. "How we proceed from there will be up to you."

"Are you here representing the Arcane Council?"

He canted his head slightly. "Yes and no. My interests lie with the Council, but I am here of my own accord."

"Okay." Steeling myself for what was sure to be another complication in my life, I sighed inwardly and turned toward Monica, who watched us with avid curiosity. "Is anyone using the conference room?"

"I don't think so, but let me check." Her glossy blonde hair slid across her shoulders as she reached for the sign-up clipboard. "No one has it scheduled, but you know how that goes."

"Yep. Would you mind penciling us in for thirty minutes? Come on back, Mr. Jacoby. We'll see if the room's open."

I led the way, waving at my business partner, Jack, through his open doorway, as Jacoby and I strode past his office. Fisk followed close in our wake. I aimed for the next door down, which, to my relief, stood ajar.

"Can I get you something to drink?" I asked once we'd crossed the conference room's threshold. "We have coffee, tea, soda, water ..."

"Thank you. No."

Nodding, I gestured at Fisk, who now loomed inside the doorway. "Mr. Jacoby, this is Mr. Johnathan Fisk, liaison to the sidhe's *amhaín*. For reasons we won't discuss, he's acting as my bodyguard."

Jacoby bypassed the head-of-the-table nearest us and, instead, took the seat at its left. "If you wish his queen to learn what I'm about to impart, I certainly have no objection. Whether you find it to be in your best interest ..." He let the cagey remark trail off with a languid shrug.

Grinding my teeth against a frustrated retort, I turned my back on Jacoby to face a stern-jawed Fisk.

Why does my life have to be so complicated?

"Mr. Jacoby isn't going to harm me," I said in a hushed tone. "I need you to wait outside."

"No," Fisk said, his eyes remaining fixed on our guest. "I am fulfilling my prince's command, not yours."

I wanted to strangle him. Why did Jacoby have to show up when Tíereachán was out of town?

To be fair, the situation was hardly Fisk's doing. At least he was being polite. Just two months ago, Fisk would have issued a flat 'no' in his best fuck-you voice. Still, I couldn't help bristling at being treated like a helpless damsel who needed protection at all costs. While I appreciated the backup, I could darn well take care of myself.

"Fine. Then I see only one alternative," I said. "Swear to me, on your honor as a sidhe, that you won't divulge or act upon any information you hear in this meeting, unless you get my express permission. This includes your mate." His soulmate, I knew, was one of the *amhaín's* handmaidens.

Jacoby hadn't been wrong. Soulmated sidhe had the ability to communicate telepathically, a bond that spanned worlds. They could see and hear everything their partner experienced—and even use them as their mouthpiece—if their mate allowed it. So, unless Fisk took steps to prevent it, whatever he learned would go right into the *amhaín's* ear by means of his soulmate.

Jaw muscles flexing, Fisk narrowed his eyes to murderous slits, still focused on Jacoby.

"Please." I tentatively stepped closer to him. "This way, we both get what we need."

"Agreed," he finally ground out. "Sit across the table from him. Do not allow him to touch you. If you venture outside my veil, I will end this."

Like many part-bloods, Fisk had the ability to shield himself and others from magical attack, but the power of that veil degraded with distance.

"Understood. Thank you."

Jacoby looked distinctly amused when I took the seat opposite him. Fisk positioned himself three feet behind my chair.

With his manicured fingers pressed together on the tabletop, the master ethermancer raised a single perfectly groomed brow. "I see you continue to inspire near fanatical protection from those who seek your subservience."

I glared at him. "You know nothing about me. I've been through more in the last three months, dealt with more monsters and more death than you can imagine. Unless you want this conversation over, *tout de suite*, you'll keep your ignorance to yourself."

He tipped his head in acquiescence. "*Touché.* The finer details of your life are, indeed, a mystery to me. However, my observation was not based on ignorance, rather, it illustrates *your own*." He sniffed. "I am privy to a detail that has been concealed from you for many years, one which I am now content to reveal."

"I'm listening."

His reptilian gaze sized me up, and I had little doubt that he found me lacking. "For the past fourteen years, you have been a vampire's thrall."

The statement was so absurd, I burst out laughing.

"That's impossible," I finally forced out. "Clairvoyants—all mind psychics—are immune to vampire saliva."

"Not when the recipient is willing." He watched me with a condescending expression that said, *You witless child. You're lucky I'm here to set you straight.*

"You're saying I willingly allowed a vampire to bite and enthrall me?"

"Yes."

"You're serious? When I was—" I did the mental math. "Sixteen?" I hesitated, frowning. "That's around the time you showed up at Coventry Academy." I scowled at him.

"That's the year you inserted yourself into that bullshit situation with Amanda, when she accused me of being a blackmailer."

"Yes."

I tried to recall the details, but my mind turned as smoothly as a rusted cog.

The situation had been ugly and terrifying, I remembered that much. I'd felt powerless, frustrated by the injustice of being accused of blackmailing a bully named Skyler when I'd done it to protect Alex—

Oh, shit …

Alex.

Alex hadn't been some run-of-the-mill student. He was a vampire—a strigoi. And not just *any* strigoi. He was their domn, their supreme leader, a fact known by few outsiders. Of course, this wasn't something I had any clue about at the time.

"The light is beginning to dawn, I see," Jacoby said, his voice a smug purr that I imagined choking off with two well-placed hands and a solid throttling.

"Enough drama and innuendo," I said curtly. "Who do you claim bit me?"

"None other than the domn's most trusted mouthpiece, Alexei, by order of his master."

"Alex wouldn't do that. And even if he had, I've been around him. Last month, in fact. I never felt any difference. I didn't fawn all over him or jump to do his bidding. People would have noticed." I glanced behind me. "Ask Fisk. He'll tell you."

"So he didn't compel you," Jacoby said, waving it away with a flick of his long slender fingers. "That neither proves nor disproves your enslavement."

"I'm nobody's slave," I shot back.

He simply stared at me, a supercilious smile on his lips.

"At sixteen, I was naïve, not stupid," I said. "I wouldn't have allowed Alex to bite me, no matter how cute I thought he was."

"Maybe so. Unfortunately, there were extenuating circumstances. Do you recall a man by the name of Sindre Treblow?"

A strange feeling, one I couldn't define, thrummed through me.

"Yes," I said, the answer sounding more like a question than a statement. "I think he was one of Coventry Academy's founders." I blinked, searching my mind. "Yes. Sorcerer Treblow. His property was next door to the school's. And ... there was something ..."

The detail flitted at the edge of my mind, just beyond reach, like a forgotten dream. It didn't leave me with the warm fuzzies. "I vaguely remember something happening with him, some scandal, maybe, but I can't remember what."

"He was murdered. In fact, you might have been murdered, too, along with a friend of yours." He gazed down his nose at me. "At one time, you knew these things, but for your protection and because his domn had plans for you, Alexei concealed them."

"For my protection." I ground my teeth together. "If I had a nickel for every time someone's said that to me ..." I glared at the ceiling before blowing out an angry breath. "Okay. Say I believe you ... Why did Alex think these memories were so dangerous? Was I traumatized or something?" I folded my arms. "And how do you even know about it?"

"Because, Miss Devon, I was there. In the thick of it, as the expression goes. Like you, I was subdued by Sindre's killer. Instead of breaking free, I played victim to rescue you and your friend."

"You rescued us?"

He pursed his lips. "I will overlook your astonishment."

I squashed the urge to roll my eyes. "So, this murderer subdued me and a friend? What friend? Was she bitten and mind wiped too?"

"Him. And, no, he wasn't."

"Why not?"

"Because he didn't commune with the spirit of Sindre Treblow and learn the *ubhnati's* deepest secrets."

Despite the blanket of unease that had engulfed me, I bit out a laugh. "And *I* did? I'm a clairvoyant, not a soulseeker."

"I'm well aware of that." He speared me with a scathing look. "You touched his blood. And before you arrogantly remind me that you were sixteen, not stupid—I suggest thinking hard on your recent activities. Touching Sindre's blood is not as implausible as you try to pretend."

I bit back my incendiary reply because he wasn't wrong about my past. Nearly four months ago, I had, indeed, touched human remains to solve the murder of a dear friend. And the consequences of my rash behavior were still bearing their bitter fruit.

Jacoby rested his left forearm on the table, appearing content to speak at leisure. "I'm sure I don't need to tell you that such endeavors always come with a price."

"And now you're seeking payment. Is that it?"

"I suppose that's one way to look at it." He shrugged. "Myself ... I like to view it as a mutually beneficial arrangement. I have provided you with information that is vital to your survival. In return, I would ask that you grant me a small favor."

"God forbid anyone would do something just because it's the right thing to do," I retorted. "What's this small favor?"

"Before he was murdered, Sindre hid the entire contents of his library in a higher dimension. As he was a member of the Arcane Council, his life's work belongs to us. I want you to relocate his belongings to the safety of our central vault once your memories are restored."

"No," Fisk's booming voice echoed through the conference room. "*Anóen*, it's unwise to oblige yourself to such a man and twice as reckless to do it without first learning all the facts."

"Yes. The facts." Jacoby peered over my head at Fisk. "I have to wonder, have you or your illustrious queen been as forthcoming? And what of the sidhe king? For example, have any of you told Miss Devon that her entire life is based on a lie?"

"What are you talking about?" I twisted in my seat to peer at Fisk. "What does he mean? What lie?"

Fisk's face was stony. Worse, he remained silent.

"Not so eager to offer your two cents, now, are you? I am undoubtedly self-serving, but at least I'm honest about it." Jacoby clicked his tongue disapprovingly. "My dear Miss Devon, you are being manipulated by the very people whose secret machinations elicited your birth. Your father, Lucien, was a sidhe. Make no mistake, you are not Earth's adept but theirs."

I shook my head, struggling to make sense of his words, all of it made worse by the absence of Fisk's vehement denial. Which meant one thing … Jacoby was telling the truth. The realization landed on me like a truckload of wet cement.

"How do you know this?" I asked.

"I'm an exceedingly skilled ethermancer, Miss Devon, one who is familiar with the sidhe and the obscure hallmarks of even the most ingenious and expertly crafted enchantments." Jacoby stood and looked down at me. "Your aura is one of the most complex I've ever encountered, but it shines with a brilliance that is unique to their kind, as did Lucien's—despite the powerful magic he employed to conceal it. Ask the king about your father. I believe there is much you don't know."

With that final bombshell, Jacoby placed his card on the table and slid it in my direction. Two golden rings glinted up at me. The one on his middle finger resembled an elaborate braid. On his ring finger, he wore a nondescript gold band. Did that mean Jacoby was married? I wondered what kind of person would be drawn to such an odious man before realizing that he'd proffered his card with his right hand, not his left. So, maybe not married. Not that I cared.

"Should you ever require my service …" He turned on his heel and strode from the room, leaving behind the scent of sandalwood and something indefinably cloying.

Papa … a sidhe?

How could this be? Sidhe didn't whither from age, and they were well-nigh immune to disease. If Jacoby was telling the truth and Papa had been a sidhe, then why had he deteriorated? Why had he gotten cancer?

My thoughts darted back to that horrible time. Papa's body had already been sent downstairs by the time I arrived at the hospital that morning. I'd decided on a closed casket funeral. I hadn't wanted my last memory of him to be of his lifeless face. Had that been my thought or one suggested by the funeral director? I couldn't recall.

No. There lay grievous wounds. I refused to reopen them.

My entire life ... based on a lie.

Fisk continued his silence. He hadn't disputed any of it, and he wasn't the type to allow lies to go unchallenged.

I'm not human. The thought reverberated through me as Jacoby's revelations weighed on my every breath. And *I'm enthralled to Alex. Are the two things linked? Can anything I remember be trusted? And what about Giselle? Is my sister a part-blood, too?*

All at once, my chair jolted, spinning, until all I saw was Fisk's face and his fiercely set amber eyes.

"Listen to me," he said, clamping a hand on my shoulder and delivering a firm shake. "You are still *you*. It is the strength of your character and your actions that define you, not the blood of your parents." He crouched on one knee to deliver his resolute stare. "This changes nothing."

"You knew I wasn't human? You knew about my father? And you didn't tell me? And Tíer—"

"No," he interrupted. "My prince was unaware. All of us were. My mate learned of your heritage a few weeks ago, after Caiside mentioned it to my queen in passing. He'd assumed that she already knew."

I couldn't fault Caiside for that. Over a month ago, I'd rescued him from one of Evgrenya's *enebráig* prison cells, where he'd been held prisoner for over a century and a half. If he'd realized my heritage wasn't common knowledge, he would have kept the information to himself. He was that kind of guy.

Fisk shook his head. "Whatever magic your father used, it's highly effective. Even after healing you, Wade had no idea that you were part sidhe."

"But my father got old and sick. How could he be sidhe?" I gasped. "Oh, God. Did Alex alter my memories? Is that how—"

"Questioning every detail of your life is a waste of time," he said. "When my prince returns, we will pool our information. We'll confront Alex and force him to restore your memories and release you from his grasp. Afterward, we'll learn what we can about your father."

We? This was the first time I could remember him speaking to me in terms of being an equal partner.

"Why are you being so nice to me all of a sudden?"

He jolted and then glowered at me. "Temporary insanity." Stepping backward, he folded his arms.

"Maybe." I considered him. "Or maybe you're not as much of a hard-ass as you want people to think."

His frown deepened.

"*Now* who's temporarily insane?" I got up, snatched Jacoby's card from the table, and stalked past him. "Come on. Time to put Alex on notice."

"No. My prince will want to accompany us."

"I wish you'd stop calling him that," I said over my shoulder. "You know how much he hates it."

"Like it or not, that's his sovereign role," he said imperiously.

Once we got into the hallway, he kept pace alongside me, but it made it harder for me to kick him. The desire to do violence came up a lot whenever Fisk and I spent more than thirty seconds together.

This wasn't a new revelation.

"He needs friendship more than he needs pompous titles," I retorted. "I'm his intended, but I don't hear you calling me 'my princess.' Why can't you do the same for him?"

"That's different."

I scoffed. "Right. Because I'm—" I stopped myself before I uttered the word.

Human.

I faltered and nearly tripped. Guess I couldn't say that anymore if—

No. Not *if*. Fisk had confirmed it. Even the *amhaín* knew the truth. I was half-human, a part-blood.

Fisk followed me into my office. "It's different because, human or no, you're a scrap of a girl, thirty years old to my two-hundred-twenty-two. My prince is near three thousand. And you weren't born into the role of princess. You stumbled into it by virtue of your magic."

He took in my affronted expression and then snapped, "Forget it." He strode out, grousing something about 'bothering to be nice,' and closed the door behind him.

I turned to Red. "He should have quit while he was ahead."

"What did the master ethermancer want?" he asked, wisely skirting the subject of Fisk's patronizing comments.

Red! Of course!

If anyone could confirm or deny that Alex had enthralled me and fill in any gaps in my memory, it was Red, the one person who'd been my constant companion for nearly my entire life.

I examined Jacoby's calling card, making a face before I tossed it into the open top of my purse. "He told me that I'm Alex's thrall. That I allowed Alex to bite me when I was sixteen, so that he could hide the memories I'd gleaned from reading a powerful *ubhnati's* blood. *For my protection*, of course," I air-quoted the offending words.

"To label you Alex's thrall is a gross misstatement of fact." Red set aside his iPhone, placing it on the window seat's cushion next to him, and stood. "You and Alex are bound by blood, this is true, but it is a narrowly constrained pact."

For a moment, I could only open and close my mouth. "You knew and didn't tell me?"

"At your behest, yes."

I staggered to my chair and sat down hard.

I dropped my head into my hands. "He also said my life is based on a lie, that Papa was a sidhe and that he used magic on the both of us to hide it." I looked at him. "He said that I wasn't Earth's adept. I was bred to be the sidhe's. He meant the king's, I'm pretty sure, because he said that I should ask the king about Papa."

"Interesting." Red paced in front of my closed blinds. "I do not doubt that Master Jacoby is capable of detecting such heritage. He is unquestionably a talented ethermancer. He is also shrewd enough to realize that his pronouncement is easily verified. All you need do is ask another experienced aura reader, like Caiside."

"According to Fisk, Caiside is the one who told the queen, unintentionally. Caiside assumed she already knew." I frowned. "But how do you explain Michael being able to enter my mind? Granted, it's not easy for him, especially if I'm on the defensive, but the fact that his telepathy works at all doesn't seem to fit with being a part-blood."

"That we know of." Red stopped pacing and considered me, clasping his paws over his round tummy. "All I can say with certainty is that sidhe gifts appear to be quite variable. Or, perhaps it has something to do with the magic your father worked to conceal your heritage."

"But he aged! Sidhe don't age, remember? And he got sick. He was in the hospital. Sidhe are supposedly immune to human diseases."

"That is true enough, in their world." He cocked his head inquisitively. "Do you know what *Tír na hÓige* means? It means land of youth. Earth may be their land of treasure, but our vast profusion of magic diminishes them."

I stared at him as the import of his words settled over me.

"Tíer," I whispered. "He'll die if he stays here."

"Yes, my dearest. Eventually, you both will."

"So stupid," I murmured, shaking my head. "I knew that. I mean ... that's why the king is breeding his half-blood army and why the emissaries live the way they do, right? One in the Otherworld and one here? But when it came to Tíereachán ... somehow I'd forgotten that."

I sighed wistfully. "This past month has been really nice, too—the both of us pretending to be normal—just two people dating and getting to know each other. I wish—" I issued a gruff laugh. "Well, that's my mistake, right there. No good ever came from just wishing. Isn't that what Papa used to say?"

Papa!

With a shuddering breath, I pressed my palms against my eyes. I sat like that for several long moments until the threat of tears had passed.

Finally, I straightened and let out a deep breath. "Tell me about this narrowly constrained pact with Alex. Can he compel me or not?"

"Not in all things, no."

I raised my eyebrows, waiting for more. "That's it? Can you be more specific? This is a little important, don't you think?"

"I do. Profoundly important, in fact."

"But you're not going to elaborate?" I frowned. "You agree there's a blood pact between Alex and me, right?"

"Yes."

"Because you were there at the time? You witnessed it?"

"Yes."

"But you won't tell me about it? Like, what the heck made me do it?" I peered at him. "Can you at least confirm whether it had to do with Sindre Treblow's murder like Jacoby said?"

Again, he regarded me in silence.

"Crap. I compelled you to secrecy, didn't I?" I straightened in my chair. "Which means I can undo it. Red, I recant any order of secrecy I gave you. Tell me everything about my pact with Alex."

"You accepted a blood pact with Alexei Slavskaya on the fourteenth of September of your sixteenth year. You exchanged blood after reciting an oath. He bit your neck. You took his blood by sucking on a wound that he opened on his wrist. The pact, itself, is limited in scope. I cannot expound any further."

"But I revoked your order of silence."

"When it comes to a command of secrecy issued by a master to his or her bound servant, if the breach of such a directive contravenes the master pact, it becomes a geas that cannot be revoked."

"Of course it would." I pinched the bridge of my nose. "So, you're saying that I can't take back my order of silence because, if you go against it and speak about what happened, it would breach our master pact, the one that binds you as my familiar." I lowered my arm, allowing my hand to fall into my lap. "Did I get that right?"

"Indeed."

"Presumably because it would violate the part of our pact that compels you to protect me from harm."

"That is correct."

"Okay." I pondered him. "Can you answer me this—besides you, did anyone else witness the actual ritual?"

"No."

"No?" I straightened. "Jacoby wasn't there?"

"Not for the ritual, no."

"But he knows about it. Was he there beforehand or something?"

"Correct."

I slumped in my chair, not sure how this information helped me. "Did I consult you before I agreed to the pact? Did you give me your consent?"

"Yes. And ... somewhat."

"Somewhat?" I looked at him agog. "Seriously, Red? This is getting ridiculous."

"I believe I said that you could do worse than place your trust in Alexei."

"Well ... at least he can't order me around like his personal automaton." I jerked my gaze to Red. "He can't do that, right?"

"Correct. He cannot."

I relaxed. "That's something, I guess."

Although, the fact that Red couldn't talk about my lost memories, even after all these years, said they still posed a clear and present danger to me.

Now, the question was: Would it be smarter to let sleeping dogs lie?

You have been reading an excerpt from

SONG OF THE LOST

by Katherine Bayless

NOW AVAILABLE at

Amazon, B&N, Kobo, and iBooks

GLOSSARY

1995 Paranormal Rights Act

The landmark civil rights legislation in the United States that outlaws major forms of discrimination against magically inclined or cursed individuals.

Adept

A sidhe who has the ability to create and manage portals between worlds.

Ætheling

Silven (also Anglo-Saxon) term for a prince or heir apparent.

Ámsach

Silven term for an ambassador.

Animtùr

Silven term for an individual capable of reading auras; an aura reader.

Anóen

Silven sobriquet for the prophesied world-straddling adept who will be mated to the ruler responsible for unifying the sidhe's fractured populace. Translated, it means 'the one.'

Arcane Council

Ruling body for all magic users (both witchcraft and sorcery) in the United States.

The Between

The vast inter-dimensional nexus where the essence of every unique life force, from any one of an infinite number of worlds, intersects. Also known as Purgatory.

Bídteine
Sobriquet that means 'little fire' in Silven.

Bráigda
The object which binds, and therefore controls, the soul of each member of the Wuldrífan. In Silven, it means 'perennial collar.'

Brownie
In English vernacular, refers to a diminutive, roughly humanoid race from the Otherworld. Often mistaken for a hobgoblin, they are smaller, less hairy, and do not typically indulge in practical jokes. They have been known to inhabit human homes and perform household tasks in exchange for small gifts of food. Bread (especially brioche) and honey are said to be particular favorites. They work only at night and do not like to be seen. Of all the fae, brownies have been the most eager to reside permanently on Earth.

Búancodail
Silven name for Yosemite National Park in California's Sierra Nevada mountains.

Circle of power
A ritually defined space, usually sealed with blood, used in spellcasting to control the flow of magic (and/or physical access) within its boundaries. See summoner, ward.

Clairvoyant
A mind psychic who can read the memories associated with an object (or person) through direct physical contact.

Clean room
An enclosed space that is completely psi-free, often within the confines of a psychiatric hospital.

The Compact
The ancient peace accord between King Faonaín, the amhaín, and the telepaths of Invisius Verso, which brought an

end to the sidhe's civil war. The covenant curtails King Faonaín's efforts to exterminate the human race.

Coterie

An exclusive group of individuals with shared interests or tastes. A witchcraft coven is a type of coterie. The king's part-blood subjects on Earth are organized into coteries, typically one or two for every major urban center throughout his territories.

Coventry Academy

The private elementary, middle, and high school, located in Coventry, WA, dedicated to the education of children capable of spellcasting, possessing a psychic ability, or cursed by magic, including those affected by the strigoi curse (vampirism) and therianthropy.

Coventry Hospital

The hospital, located in Coventry, WA, that specializes in the care of those gifted with psychic or magic powers or individuals suffering from magic related injuries or curses.

Crònathir

Silven name for the River Styx. See Nàsaig.

Cryokinetic

An individual who is capable of siphoning ambient heat from the atmosphere or other physical objects. Also known as an icemaker.

Cúairtine

Silven term for an individual capable of sidestepping between worlds. Translated, it means 'world walker.'

Curse

An enchantment that, by its very nature, imparts both positive and negative affects on an individual, location, or object. When applied to an individual, a curse is often (but not always) hereditary or transmittable via body fluids. Of all curses, therianthropy and the strigoi curse are perhaps the most well-known.

Daoine Sídhe
See sidhe.

Dark Arts
A field of magic dealing with death and darkness. Spell-casters capable of such magic are often mistakenly labeled as evil or in league with the devil.

Department of Paranormal Affairs
United States governmental agency created to oversee all citizens possessing magical abilities. Until it was declared unconstitutional twenty-five years ago, their ID program required the registration, tattooing, and tracking of all psychics, magic users, and cursed individuals from their birth (or manifestation date). The Magic User Registration Bill, if passed, threatens to restore some of these practices.

Dhêala
Silven term for a human possessing the strigoi curse; a vampire.

Divinor
An individual with the gift of precognition, the ability to foresee the future. Also known as oracle, seer, or prophesier.

Djinn
A spirit-like entity that inhabits a world beyond the dimensions of Earth. Also known as jinn, genie, or jinnī. They can be physical or incorporeal in nature and are known shape-shifters. In their dealings with humankind, they are most often neutral, neither good nor bad, typically practicing noninterference in human matters unless bound by blood compact. Other than their ability to transform and hold any physical shape, it is said they have the ability to

move between dimensions and travel great distances at extreme speeds. The full extent of their power is unknown.

Domn

Title given to the ruler of the United Convocation of Strigoi (vampires).

Draíocloch

A sidhe magic item that, when used, forges a temporary gateway to the Otherworld.

Elder race

A class of humanoid beings that existed before modern humans.

Elf

In English vernacular, a term that refers to a sidhe, popularized by J. R. R. Tolkien in his high-fantasy books. Because 'elf' has, in the distant past, been used to describe invisible demonic beings and other unsavory (and often fictional) creatures, it isn't a term the sidhe favor.

Emissary

English vernacular title given to King Faonaín's representatives who provide a means of communication between the sidhe ruler and his Earth-bound subjects. An emissary is typically a part-blood (or less commonly a human) who is soulbound to a sidhe within the king's retinue. The emissary and his/her mate communicate telepathically through their joined souls. One remains in the Otherworld and the other on Earth. See liaison.

Enebráig

A sidhe confinement or prison in which the cell or extended area is imbued to disrupt all spellcasting.

Essence

An individual's life-force, their soul.

Fae

In English vernacular, a term that refers to the many unique beings and creatures that inhabit the Otherworld.

Faery

In English vernacular, a term for the Otherworld.

Fairy

In English vernacular, an alternate term for fae that has come to be associated with the fictionalized versions of Otherworld creatures found in European folklore.

Fairyland

In English vernacular, often used as a derogatory term for the Otherworld.

Firestarter

See pyrokinetic.

Flaith

Silven (also Irish) term for a prince.

Flight 208

The plane crash that was caused by a terrorist wielding an object enchanted with an inferno spell.

Gateway

A magical conduit, or portal, large enough to provide physical transport from one place to another, often between dimensions or worlds.

Geas

A magically enforced prohibition (similar to a curse but without the required positive/negative interdependency), which imposes a certain behavior upon its subject. A geas is either compulsory or voluntary. If compulsory, the subject is physically incapable of violating the geas. If the geas is voluntary, violation of the designated stricture may result in dishonor, physical or mental duress, or, in extreme cases, death.

Glamours

In English vernacular, a term that refers to a class of spells innate among the sidhe, which can be used to deceive, lure, or otherwise charm humans and other creatures.

Glindarian

A member of the Glindarian witchcraft sect.

Golem

A magical being created from inanimate matter that possesses limited intelligence and typically requires the continued direction of its creator in order to function.

Hobgoblin

In English vernacular, a term that refers to a diminutive, roughly humanoid race from the Otherworld who are known to be friendly but, more often than not, troublesome. They are prone to practical jokes and fond of living in human homes, helping with small household tasks in return for food. Unlike their smaller cousin, the brownie, hobgoblins are shape-shifters and quick to take offense at any perceived slight.

Icemaker

See cryokinetic.

Isangrim

Title given to the ruler of the North American Rout (werewolves).

Invisius Verso

A secret organization of telepaths and divinors. Its name means 'unseen influence' in Latin.

Leprechaun

In English vernacular, a term that refers to a diminutive, humanoid race from the Otherworld who are known for their skill in shoemaking and leatherworking. They are unrivaled in their ability to evade and escape capture, often by shape-shifting, but in the event they are apprehended, will grant a favor in exchange for release. Like brownies, they are content to reside permanently on Earth.

Levitation

The act of moving objects without interacting with them physically. See telekinesis.

Liaison

English vernacular title given to the amhaín's representatives who provide a means of communication between the sidhe ruler and her Earth-bound subjects. A liaison is typically a part-blood (or less commonly a human) who is soulbound to a sidhe within the queen's retinue. The liaison and his/her mate communicate telepathically through their joined souls. See emissary.

Lycanthropy

A term used to describe the human to wolf transformation curse. See therianthropy.

Mage, Magic User, Magus

Terms used to describe an individual with the ability to cast spells. (Generally not used to describe an individual possessing a psychic power.)

Magi-phobe

A term (often derogatory) that refers to an individual who fears, distrusts, or condemns magic and those who are capable of magic.

Magically Induced Regeneration

Magical healing process in which tissue from a live donor is used to replenish missing tissue in a victim's injury or missing limb. Also known as MIR.

Magic Reservations

Government owned compounds dedicated to the care and rearing of state adopted youngsters who are spellcasters, gifted with a psychic ability, or cursed.

Magic User Registration Bill

A United States bill, which, if passed into law, would require all magic users, psychics, and cursed individuals to register with the government.

Magician

Someone who does parlor tricks. Not a true magic user.

Master of the Hunt

Leader of the Wuldrífan.

Mionngáel

Silven term for someone who is bound to another individual by means of a mutual blood covenant.

MIR

See Magically Induced Regeneration.

Nàsaig

Silven term for the border of land between the living and the dead, the forsaken shore along the river Crònathir (the River Styx).

Necromancer

A sorcerer with power over the dead.

Níláitidir

Silven term for the Between.

Normal
An individual who possesses no magical ability.

North American Rout
The official organization of werewolves in the United States and Canada.

Oracle
See divinor.

Otherworld
The world where the fae reside. Also known as Faerie.

Overburn
The physiological damage caused by burning through more magic than a person's body can tolerate.

Overspooling
The act of readying more potential in one's core than necessary prior to casting a spell. Similar to topping off (overfilling) a car's gas tank.

Paranormal Help Network
A non-profit organization devoted to providing support services to families of the magically gifted.

Paranormal Regulatory Commission
An international organization of psychics that governs the conduct of the psychic community.

Part-blood
A human with sidhe ancestry, usually having one sidhe parent.

Peabody's Beans
Coffee shop owned by Julie and Steven Peabody specializing in psi-free coffee, beverages, pastries, etc.

Pixie

In English vernacular, refers to a diminutive, humanoid race from the Otherworld who are endearingly childlike and benign in character. They live in large clans, are tremendously fond of music and dancing, and often partake in mischievous but harmless pranks.

Portal

A magical conduit, most often forged during a summoning, that connects two different locations, providing access to another dimension or world. A portal may or may not be large enough for physical transport. See gateway.

Prophecy

A prediction of the future.

Prophesier

See divinor.

Psi-free

Term used to describe something that is free of life-essence contamination, untouched by humans or animals.

Psi-ward

An area within a hospital that specializes in the care of those gifted with psychic or magic powers or individuals suffering from magic related injuries or curses.

Psychic Shield

The mental shield fortified by magic that all clairvoyants and telepaths use to control the inflow of thoughts and memories into their own minds.

Psychic

An individual gifted with a mind power, either telekinesis, pyrokinesis, cryokinesis, divination, truthsaying, or clairvoyance. Sensitives are also sometimes psychic.

Puget Pacific Towers
Office building in downtown Seattle where Sotheby's is located. Across the street and a block away from Peabody's Beans.

Purgatory
See the Between.

Pyrokinetic
An individual who is capable of generating ambient heat. Also known as a firestarter.

Ríutcloch
A sidhe magic item that, when used, forges a temporary portal between two individuals.

Rowan
A member of the Rowan witchcraft sect.

Runestone
A stone marked with a runic inscription, often used in witchcraft to focus and enhance the magus' spellcasting.

SAM
Seattle Art Museum.

Scolaca
Silven term for 'servant.'

SCU
Supernatural Crime Unit.

Seer
See divinor.

Sensitive
An individual who can detect (and often identify) specific types of magic and/or individual spells.

Shape-shifter

A being that can change its shape and hold its new form, either by virtue of magic or a curse. A werewolf is a type of shape-shifter.

Sidestep

The act of moving a person or object to another dimension.

Sidhe

An elder race that is arguably the most humanoid of all the magical beings that inhabit the Otherworld. The sidhe are known by other sobriquets—aos sí, aes sídhe, daoine sídhe, daoine síth, and (perhaps least liked by the creatures themselves) fairy and elf. Humans who are reluctant to name them directly often refer to them as 'the good neighbors,' 'the fair folk,' or 'people of the mounds.' Their Earthbound gateways are typically encapsulated by a mound of earth or encircled by stones or mushrooms.

Silven

The language of the sidhe.

Siritóir

Silven title for an individual who is responsible for tracking down or monitoring a particular person or group of individuals; a tracker.

Skin-suit

A thin bodysuit crafted from psi-free, moisture-repelling fabric, used to prevent contact between a clairvoyant and other individuals or objects.

Sorcerer/Sorceress

A magus who uses gestures for casting spells, they are typically restricted to a certain field of magic.

Sorcery

Spellcasting performed by a sorcerer or sorceress.

Stake-burner

A derogatory term often applied to magi-phobic individuals, especially those in judicial or law enforcement positions.

Strigoi

An individual affected by the strigoi curse; a vampire.

Strigoi Curse

The curse that causes vampirism. An individual afflicted by this curse is granted immortality, superior strength, and, in a limited fashion, the ability to shape-shift. Countering each of these boons is an equally powerful weakness. (This duality is the hallmark of all curses.) In the case of vampirism, the cursed individual's existence is restricted to the night—during daylight hours they are helpless and virtually comatose. To satisfy their thirst for sustenance, they must drink human blood. Precious metals cause great pain and weakness. The most powerful strigoi are almost always blessed with one additional gift that may or may not be offset by an additional weakness.

Styx

The river and adjoining shore that forms the boundary between the land of the living and the dead. According to legend, any being who enters the river's treacherous waters without sufferance is doomed to drown for all eternity. See Crònathir and Nàsaig.

Summoner

A magic user capable of summoning a spirit being, usually from another dimension or universe, to a designated location, typically a circle of power.

Supernatural Talent and Company (ST&C)

Paranormal talent agency located in Seattle, owned by Jack Beaumont and Lire Devon.

Sylvan Haven

Term used by the sidhe to describe Earth. Translated it means 'treed haven.'

Tánaiste

Silven term for 'second-in-command.'

Telekinetic

A psychic capable of levitating an object. A type one telekinetic can move only inanimate objects, a type two can move only animate objects, a type three can move both animate and inanimate objects. See levitation.

Telepath

A psychic capable of reading human thoughts without skin contact. Some (but not all) are capable of inserting memories into a human subject's mind. Fewer still are able to assume enough control to direct their human subject's actions.

Therianthropy

Term used to describe the curse of human to animal transformation. An individual afflicted with this curse is granted the ability to transform into a particular animal. Only rigorous training and self-discipline allows the cursed individual to retain their human consciousness during transformation. Depending upon their skill, this transformation can take place at will, however, during nights of the full moon, the transformation is compulsory. See werewolf.

Thìr na Étail

Silven name for the Earth. Translated it means 'Land of Treasure.'

Thìr na Soréidh

The amhaín's sealed enclave within the Otherworld. Translated it means 'Land of Farewell.'

Threefold Principal

The belief that the energy a magic user (or psychic) dispenses, whether it be positive or negative, will be returned threefold. You reap what you sow.

TK

A slang term for telekinesis. See levitation.

Tonngéar

A surface-dwelling Otherworld beast.

Touchy

A derogatory term for a clairvoyant.

True Name

A being's intrinsic name, one which is bound so closely that it's tied to their essence. When pronounced with intimate familiarity, it can be used in a ritual to summon the being between worlds.

Truthsayer

A psychic who is capable of detecting whether a person is lying.

United Convocation of Strigoi

The international society of individuals affected by the strigoi curse.

Ùruisg

A diminutive, roughly humanoid race from the Otherworld. Like the brownie, they are one of the few fae that thrive living on Earth, however, they are considerably less social and rarely provide their human neighbors with domestic help. On Earth, they live outdoors near streams and waterfalls.

Vampire

An alternate term for 'strigoi,' one that is viewed as somewhat coarse by those affected by the strigoi curse.

Ward

A type of ensorcellment that regulates or prohibits magic or physical interactions that take place within its area of effect. Such spells are often (but not exclusively) used in conjunction with a magic circle or within the natural boundary provided by a dwelling's foundation.

Warlock/Witch

A magus who can only employ spoken or chanted magic, they use runestones and/or other objects (such as wands) to power or strengthen their spells.

Were

Someone who is cursed with therianthropy.

Which Witch

The paranormal talent agency owned by Judith Kitchell.

The Wild Hunt

See Wuldrífan.

Will-o'-the-Wisp

In English vernacular, refers to a diminutive spirit-like being from the Otherworld, often seen glowing like a lantern at night, that are known to lead travelers astray.

Witchcraft

Spoken or chanted magic.

The Wuldrífan

The sidhe's phantasmal, spectral hunting party, complete with horses and hounds, outfitted with the regalia of the chase and led by the Master of the Hunt. According to legend, the Wuldrífan is comprised of fallen sidhe who died fearlessly in battle. Their leader, the Master of the Hunt, heeds only the sidhe king or queen's command and is often depicted wearing a great horned helm. Also known as the Wild Hunt.

Zombie

A human or animal corpse that has been raised from dead and animated by magical means.

LIRE AND THE PEOPLE SHE KNOWS

Amhaín

Geiléis, primarily known as the amhaín, is the sidhe's sole portal adept. (The sidhe, also known as 'elves' thanks to Tolkien, are a humanoid immortal race who live in a parallel universe we call the Otherworld.) She alone possesses the ability to create, maintain, or close the sidhe's conduits to Earth. Currently, she and her brother Faonaín are the two estranged siblings who rule over the sidhe in the Otherworld. Three thousand years ago, following the death of their father, Faonaín forced his sister to abdicate in favor of serving as his adept, by holding her son Tíereachán hostage. Faonaín's brutal stance regarding the treatment of humans and the amhaín's escape from his tender care eventually led to the sidhe's Rift War. After many battles and countless lives lost, the amhaín forced her brother's hand by closing nearly all of his gateways and threatening to do the same to his remaining conduits. Since the conduits provide the magic potential necessary for his people's survival, the move brought about the Compact and the tenuous peace that now exists between the estranged siblings and their kingdoms. The amhaín is Queen of *Thìr na Soréidh*, the territory she sealed off from the rest of the Otherworld about twelve hundred years ago.

Azazel

I first came face-to-face with the archdemon Azazel in Invisius Verso's basement when a group of us discovered the demonic gateway the corrupt telepathic elders had summoned. The demon's preferred form seems to be that of an eight-foot leviathan with thick, leathery brown skin that covers its entire body, including its genitals. More disturbing, though, are the six-inch-long black talons it brandishes instead of fingers and its exceedingly creepy, pitch black eyes. Although humanoid in its appearance, with a sure-footed stance on two massive legs, its muscular arms are long enough to run on all fours. Over a thousand years ago, Tíereachán traded Azazel his soul to free Princess Maeve from its grasp, only afterward learning it had been a ploy. Maeve had been in cahoots with the demon the whole time.

Brassal

Brassal is a sidhe of some stature in King Faonaín's retinue. Through his soulbond with Kim Pratchett, he provides an invaluable means of communication to the king's subjects on Earth. I've only spoken to Brassal through Kim, but I'm curious to meet him in person. Brassal and Kieran are best friends and share a residence in the Otherworld.

Brian Stalzing, the Circle Murderer

Brian was a telepath, member of Invisius Verso, and a power-hungry, serial-killing psycho. In his mad attempt to wrest control away from Invisius' elders, Brian murdered four psychics (including my college sweetheart) by using a summoned demon to steal their powers for himself. The arrogant ass then kidnapped me, along with my business partner Jack, and might have succeeded in murdering both of us if he hadn't lost control of his summoned demon Paimon. Instead, the demon turned on Brian, killing him.

The Circle Murderer's Victims: Nick Coulter, Jason Warner, Trinity Wilson, Patty Schaeffer

All four of the Circle Murderer's victims had been psychics, but Nick Coulter was the only one who I'd known personally. Nick had been my college sweetheart, a fellow clairvoyant, and the first man I'd been able to touch without the protection of a skin-suit. We broke up, after just a year, but remained close friends until his death. His murder drove me to aid the police by performing a psychic reading on the three other victims' remains. Not something I'd normally do—nor would any clairvoyant in their right frigging mind!—but Nick's murder had left me angry and feeling more than a little reckless. What I didn't know at the time, what none of us knew, was the murderer had been working with a demon to siphon each of his victim's psychic powers using an ancient spell. When I touched their remains, the residual magic from that spell reacted with my clairvoyance and transferred their talents to me. From Jason Warner, I received telekinesis; from Trinity Wilson, cryokinesis; and from Patty Schaeffer, pyrokinesis. Out of the three gifts, I struggled with Patty's fire the most. Patty had been an evil individual in life and I found it difficult, if not impossible, to separate her vile memories from the magic that bubbled to the surface all too readily when I was angry.

Claude Lefevre

I met Claude at our apartment building's first community mixer, six years ago. With his shoulder-length blond hair, GQ-good looks, and swoon-inducing French accent, the Rowan warlock has no shortage of admiring women vying for his attention. So it surprised me when he spent a majority of the party focused solely on me, especially since my clairvoyance prohibits anything more serious than egregious flirting. Since then, I've discovered that there's so much more to Claude than irresistible rake with commitment issues. He's intelligent, perceptive, and a steadfast friend. Even though we're both around thirty, he seems to possess a soul as old as mine. I acquired my own abiding insight after years of ingesting the memories of countless individuals through my psychic readings. How he came by his sagacity is a story I've yet to hear, but I suspect it has something to do with his childhood and family he almost never talks about.

Clotilde 'Lire' Marie Devon (me!)

I adopted the name 'Lire' when I was twelve and it's stuck with me ever since. Pronounced 'lear,' it means read in French. The nickname seemed appropriate since my father was French and, as a clairvoyant, that's what I do, I read things. Besides, by the time I'd reached seventh grade, I'd heard 'Clit-tilde' one too many times. (I discovered early that teenage boys are genetically programmed to be a pain in the ass.) I'm thirty years old, five-foot-seven-inches tall, and reluctantly athletic. I inherited my dark-red hair from Grandpa Giordano, jade-green eyes from Dad, and smattering of freckles from God knows where. Except for my years at Coventry Academy and then NYU, I've lived in Seattle, with my familiar Red, for most of my life. I discovered I was a clairvoyant when I was three and a half. My life has always been somewhat complicated, but about a month ago, I managed to acquire three additional 'gifts'—telekinesis, pyrokinesis, and cryokinesis. Making matters worse, every sidhe I meet thinks I'm an adept—someone capable of opening and closing portals between worlds. Me? I'm not sure what to think, but with the way my life's been going lately, it's probably true. It might not be so bad if every Tom, Dick, and Psycho didn't want to get their hands on my particular brand of power. Thankfully, I have Kieran at my side to keep the monsters at bay. Meeting him is the one good thing that's happened after all of my recent troubles.

Daniel Stockard

Daniel was my first love. We met in first grade at Coventry Academy and fast became friends. He was the one person at school who never shied away from me and my gloves, probably because he was another mind psychic, a telepath. Our 'psi battles' are why my shielding ability is as strong as it is today. We shared our first kiss under the library stairwell when we were thirteen, just before Invisius Verso stole him away to attend their secret school. Two months ago, after not seeing him for seventeen years, Daniel strode back into my life when the Invisius Verso elders used him as their messenger, hoping to force me into removing myself as a police consultant on the Circle Murder investigation. Daniel risked his life to help me, telling me about a divination that predicted I would reorder Invisius, something the elders sought to counter by any means necessary. Using his influence, Daniel steered Invisius away from voting to mind wipe me. Just a few weeks later, he died at the claws of the archdemon Azazel when a group of us stormed the Invisius headquarters to finally deal with the organization's corrupt elders. If I'd known how to close a demonic gateway sooner,

I might have saved him. It's a frequent recrimination that will no doubt haunt me for the rest of my life.

Diedra Yamaguchi

Fellow clairvoyant and high school alumni, Diedra and I became BFFs from her first day at Coventry Academy, partway into our junior year. She turned what had mostly been a trying school experience into something easier to bear. Anyone who takes stock of Diedra's petite frame, fine features, and porcelain skin and jumps to the conclusion that she's a soft-spoken, demure, Japanese-princess type is in for a big surprise. Next to Julie, Diedra tips the charts at being the most outgoing, fun-loving person I've ever met. She also isn't shy about expressing her opinions, and if you piss her off ... look out. She works for a strigoi clutch as their primary administrator and even migrates with them—six months in Patagonia and six months in Iceland.

The Domn

The leader of the United Convocation of Strigoi (vampires) is a figure veiled by mystery, wrapped in a thick layer of urban legend, whose identity is zealously guarded by the far-reaching influence of the strigoi PR machine. Even the Domn's gender is unknown. It is widely believed that the Domn's power over each strigoi is nothing short of omniscient, as each strigoi is bound by blood to their supreme ruler. The Domn's absolute authority and unwavering enforcement of their strict laws enabled the strigoi to remain hidden for many centuries until their recognition as a minority group in the mid-1960s. As magically cursed individuals, they are protected by the 1995 Paranormal Rights Act, along with psychics and magic users, due in no small part to the Domn's considerable influence.

Duran

Duran is everything you'd expect in a Glindarian witch if all you had for reference was the good witch from *The Wizard of Oz*. She's a dark blonde beauty with flawless skin, blue eyes, and a trim figure, but that's where the similarities end. She likes to socialize, questions everything, and is so direct, if not for her humor and tenderheartedness, she'd border on bossy. She's a powerful healer and has come to my rescue more than once. She also makes a mean chocolatini.

Evgrenya

I don't know much about this female sidhe. According to Kieran, she controls the only Earthbound gateway that lies outside of the amhaín's domain. The gateway's access point on Earth is somewhere in Ireland. A few weeks ago, Maeve negotiated a treaty with Evgrenya, which allowed Lorcán, Maeve's second in command, to travel to Earth for the purpose of claiming me.

Faonaín, King of the Sidhe

I've never met King Faonaín, ruler of the sidhe, and never will if I have anything to do with it. From what I've heard, he has zero regard for humankind and would be tickled pink if our species went extinct. From what I've been told, only the Compact—the agreement between the king, the amhaín, and the Invisius telepaths—keeps the king from resuming his extermination efforts. Ever since his sister, the amhaín, slipped through his fingers almost two thousand years ago, he's been obsessed with finding his own adept to keep his kingdom flush with potential from Earth.

Giselle Devon Stafford

Giselle is my only sibling, older by four years. She lives in the Bay Area with her husband and two kids. We were estranged for most of our lives, but we reconciled just before our mother's death.

Glen Porter

I met Glen, last year, at one of Julie and Steven's parties and we hit it off. We dated for almost seven months until one night he dropped the bombshell that he was sick of wearing "a full body condom" every time he wanted to have sex with me and had no desire to commit to a lifetime of such a nuisance. We broke up that night. Not twenty-four hours later, Julie saw him having dinner with a pretty blonde. (Actually, Julie didn't say pretty. She said something far more unflattering, but it's not the blonde's fault that Glen is a tactless jerk.)

The Insangrim

By all accounts, the Chief of the North American Rout (werewolves) is a hard-working, all-around nice guy who hails from the wilds of Montana. I don't necessarily buy into the every-man's-man-helluva-guy narrative, though. I've spent time with werewolves. Is he a good guy? Maybe. But I'd bet my left big toe that anyone who rises to a level of power in their ranks must be one tough hombre and clever as hell to boot.

Jack Beaumont

I've known Jack since my freshman year at NYU when we lived in the same dorm. Even though he doesn't have a scrap of magic in his five-foot-six-inch Bowflex body, he convinced me to partner with him in opening Supernatural Talent and Company, a paranormal consulting agency, not long after college graduation. The saying 'opposites attract' must apply to friendship too because, between his outgoing, near-manic personality and my organized, button-down nature, we've stuck together to build our business into the success it is today.

Jackie

Jackie is a Rowan witch, in her early thirties if I had to guess. She's brash, confident, doesn't pull any punches, and would do anything for her partners Kim and Brassal. She has chin-length brown hair, brown eyes, and a demeanor as no-nonsense as her wardrobe of jeans and button down shirts. With Jackie, what you see is what you get. She's high on my list of favorite people. The sidhe only allow two individuals to bind their souls, but if I ever get into a position of influence (however unlikely that might be), you can bet that's the first stupid rule I'd change. The fact that Jackie ages—while Kim and Brassal stay youthful by virtue of their bond—is a tragedy in the making.

John Fisk

Fisk was first introduced to me as Agent Fisk—as in *FBI* Agent Fisk. I've since learned that he's also one of the am-haín's part-blood (part human, part sidhe) liaisons. About a month ago, I had my first run-in with *Agent* Fisk when he asked for my expertise to read a necklace that belonged to a murder suspect. After I refused, he found a way to sneak the necklace into a group of items I was slated to read for a cable television show. The necklace turned out to be tainted by the demon Azazel and if not for Kieran's help in breaking its spell, I might have succumbed to the demon's nefarious magic. Fisk's trickery, combined with his caustic personal-ity, has landed him squarely on my personal shit list. As a result, our relationship is what you might call 'cantanker-ous.' I'll admit, like all the part-bloods I've encountered thus far, Fisk is off-the-charts in the looks department with his squared jaw, clear amber gaze, and muscular physique. For all that, though, the guy's personality leaves a lot to be de-sired.

John 'Red' Redborn

Red is my best friend, my constant companion. Techni-cally, he's my familiar, bound to me by magic just as his soul is bound to his current form—a stuffed, nine-inch black teddy bear. But Red is no animated toy. He's human—or *was*. In the late 1600s, Red was a necromancer who had the misfortune of coming to the attention of the Court of Oyer and Terminer during the Salem Witch Trials. When he was executed, a local witch coven cast a spell of soulbinding, which he accepted. Red's had several owners during the last three centuries before my father acquired him for me. Dad knew that, as a clairvoyant, I'd be unable to endure skin con-tact and worried my life would be devoid of human compan-ionship. I was five years old and thrilled beyond measure at his huggable gift. In spite of my early manhandling and countless teddy bear tea parties, Red's blessed me with a lifelong friendship that's helped mold me into the woman I am today. I owe him more than I could ever hope to repay and love him to the depth of my soul. There's almost nothing I wouldn't do for him.

Jason Warner

See The Circle Murderer's Victims.

Julie Peabody

Julie is my best friend. We met through my espresso addiction. She's my primary caffeine supplier and has been for the past seven years. She and her husband Steven own Peabody's Beans, the best coffee shop in Seattle and one of the first businesses to go entirely psi-free—selling goods that haven't been touched by human hands so misfits like me can enjoy them. Julie's a normal, but her brother Tom is a pyrokinetic. Julie has long, straight chestnut hair, big brown eyes, a contagious laugh, and a five-foot-five inch bod that says she works out but not obsessively. She dresses with an eclectic flair that I envy and is always up for trying new things. She's a hell of a lot of fun to be around and I love her to pieces.

Kieran

Kieran is a twenty-seven-hundred-year-old sidhe who doesn't look older than my thirty. I met Kieran when my childhood friend Daniel set up a meet-and-greet between the sidhe and my almost-boyfriend-at-the-time Vince. To say things didn't go well would be a massive understatement. During that meeting, Kieran attempted to kidnap me. At the same time, his cousin, Princess Maeve, succeeded in abducting Vince and once she had him in the Otherworld, seduced him into becoming her soulmate. You'd think that would have put the kibosh on any possible relationship between Kieran and me, but after I spent time with him, fighting possessed telepaths and a demon incursion, I realized that Kieran's an amazing guy. And because the sidhe are immune to my clairvoyance, I can touch him without any protection. He is the epitome of tall, dark, and devastating— six feet four, angular features, keenly tapered brows, and long black hair. Of course, since my life is nothing if not complicated, this gorgeous sidhe doesn't come without baggage.

Almost two thousand years ago, Kieran made a big mistake (see: Nuala) and now he's known as 'the Deceiver.' The sidhe border on zealotry when it comes to their honor, but I've made it my mission to convince him that he's so much more than a fallen sidhe.

Kim Pratchet

Kim is currently King Faonaín's last remaining emissary. I met Kim when Kieran and I helped her and her partner Jackie fend off a demon attack at their home on Bainbridge Island. She's a twenty-something part-blood who looks more like a preschool teacher than a skilled magus—petite, pixie-short blonde hair, and a preference for cardigans and ballet flats. Through her soulmate connection with Brassal, she provides King Faonaín with his sole means of communication to his subjects on Earth. Kim and Jackie are house sitting across the hall from me while their house, which burned down following the demon attack, is being rebuilt. Kim might look unassuming, but she is a powerful magic user who can control lightning.

Lorcán

Princess Maeve's second in command, Lorcán, is another sidhe who I hope I never meet. Apparently, the guy is beauty incarnate and has a reputation for going to extremes in doing his part to help breed the king's part-blood army. (Impregnating as many human women as possible in order to create a magically inclined force to fight the demon invasion is the sidhe's brilliant plan to save Earth. Gee, thanks guys.) According to Kieran, unicorns weep and sirens sing odes for Lorcán's exquisite good looks … or something. As far as I'm concerned, nothing can mask a cruel heart, and from what I've heard, Lorcán is a bastard of the first order. He's so awful, his mate killed herself. And years ago, when Kieran was away on an errand for the king, Lorcán attempted to seduce Kieran's mate Nuala. If not for Brassal's timely interference, Lorcán might have raped her. The guy is a waste of air. If we ever meet, you can bet I won't be afraid to inflict some serious damage, especially since Maeve's last order was for

Lorcán to glamour and claim me. Gives me the creeps just thinking about it.

Nick Coulter

See The Circle Murderer's Victims.

Maeve

King Faonaín's daughter, Maeve, is a scheming, manipulative sidhe with the face and body of a goddess. I have fantasies about getting her alone in a dark alley and beating the tar out of her. And not just because she abducted and seduced Vince, my almost-boyfriend, into becoming her soulmate. She's done real damage to people I care about. In her selfish pursuit of the crown, Maeve is responsible for ruining both of her younger cousins' lives. Thanks to her machinations, Kieran is known as 'the Deceiver' and Tíereachán spent the last millennium enslaved to the archdemon Azazel. Can you honestly blame me for wanting to scrape her face across a gravel road a few dozen times?

Maya and Tanu

Maya and Tanu are Talisman Towers' house djinn. As a loft owner, I'm bound by blood covenant to these two alien, otherworldly entities, serving as their master. They use their unfathomable magic to protect our building and its occupants from harm, answering our call whenever needed. Their true form is that of a tumultuous grey mist with mercurial, swirling eyes, but as far as I know, they can appear in any form of their choosing and are often seen in their human guise, roaming the building as middle-aged male security guards.

Michael Thompson

Just after we'd been introduced, Michael, who's a powerful telepath, made the mistake of probing my mind in a secret attempt to test my psychic shield abilities. When I felt his unwanted intrusion, I pinned him and Daniel to the wall of my building's conference room and nearly lost control of my pyrokinesis. In spite of his misstep and my overreaction, we patched things up and have become good friends. Following an impulsive meeting of minds without the interference of our shields, I learned that he'd read my thoughts over a period of years, starting when I'd attended NYU, and, in the process, he'd fallen for me. Not that he was whiling away his days, forlorn with angst or anything. He'd gotten over it and learned an important lesson about keeping himself out of other people's heads over a long-term basis, taking special care around women who intrigue him. Michael is one of my most trusted friends, and I'm pretty sure he feels the same way about me. After the deaths of Daniel and the Invisius Verso elders, Michael took the reigns of the secret organization of telepaths. Along with the sidhe, we're working together to prepare for the coming demon invasion.

Monica

Monica is our administrative assistant at Supernatural Talent and Company. She greets our clients, schedules our appointments, and generally keeps things running smoothly.

Nuala

Nuala was the amhaín's adept-in-training who, almost two thousand years ago, Kieran seduced into becoming his soulmate by pretending to be one of the amhaín's subjects. When Nuala discovered Kieran's deception (whose actions had been subtly instigated by Princess Maeve), Nuala withdrew from him. And even though Kieran had fallen in love with her, she never forgave him, never opened herself up to him, not in the near century they were mated, ending when she died in an earthquake. His mistake continues to haunt him, even after all this time, and it's why Kieran is known as 'the Deceiver.'

The Oracle

For more than five thousand years, the Oracle has been the sidhe's most revered prophesier. Supposedly, not a single one of her divinations has been wrong. I've never met her, but there are times when I wish I could give her a hard pinch on the ear.

Paimon

I first encountered the demon Paimon when the Circle Murderer, Brian Stalzing, summoned it to do his bidding. However, instead of killing me, the demon turned on Brian, killing him and saving me from becoming the serial killer's fifth victim. Afterward, Paimon forced me into a one-sided blood pact and attempted to drag my soul to Hell. What I didn't know at the time was that Paimon wasn't a really demon but an enslaved sidhe prince. See *Tíereachán*.

Patty Schaeffer

See The Circle Murderer's Victims.

Red

See John 'Red' Redborn.

Tíereachán

When I first met Tíereachán, he'd been in his unknowing guise as the demon Paimon. A thousand years ago, Tíereachán traded his soul to rescue his cousin Maeve from Azazel's clutches, only to learn that she and the archdemon were in cahoots together. A few weeks ago, I managed to steal Tíereachán away from Azazel by sidestepping the sidhe prince into a higher dimension before closing the demon's gateway. Although I go out of my way to avoid noticing, Tíereachán is the embodiment of a sidhe prince—defined physique, golden-blond hair, and graceful yet supremely masculine features. Truth be told, he checks every box on my Dream Guy Wish List, a fact I keep firmly under wraps. If he knew, I'd never hear the end of it. Because Tíereachán tasted my blood while he was in his former demonic guise, we share a connection that I try hard not to dwell on. See *Paimon*.

Trinity Wilson

See The Circle Murderer's Victims.

Detective Vince Vanelli

Vince was one of the two primary Chiliquitham police detectives assigned to the Circle Murder investigation. When I showed up as a consultant, Vince told me in no uncertain terms that they didn't need any 'magic mumbo jumbo' to help them solve the case. After just three minutes in his presence, I concluded he was a psi-phobic jackass. So, given my complicated life, is it really any wonder that he turned out to be the first normal I'd ever encountered who I could touch without the protection of a skin-suit? Later, after I figured out that Vince wasn't such a bad guy after all, we both learned that he's far from normal. The reason my clairvoyance doesn't work on him is because Vince is a part-blood sidhe. Despite the fact that we hadn't gone on an official date, I thought Vince had come to love me. At least, he said he did … once. But then, last month, during what was supposed to be a meet-and-greet with the sidhe, Princess Maeve glamoured Vince and took him back to the Otherworld, closing her temporary gateway before I could do anything about it. Next thing I knew, Vince and Maeve had become soulmates. And everyone knows, when it comes to matters of the soul, an individual can't be forced. Bottom line: Vince chose Maeve over me. The news stung at first, but I've moved on.

Wade

Wade is the amhaín's part-blood mate. We met in Invisius Verso's basement, the day Kieran, Jackie, Michael, Daniel, and I stormed the telepath's base of operations in our attempt to bring the wayward organization back under the king's control. Ever since that first meeting, I've wanted to ask Wade whether he's a Viking—like an honest-to-goodness raiding warrior from the ninth century. He sure looks the part. And since he's mated to a full-blooded sidhe, he doesn't age, so I suppose it's possible. One of these days, I'm going to work up the nerve to ask. Wade is a skilled healer, accomplished warrior, and a genuinely nice guy. He also shuts Fisk up whenever the guy starts acting like a douchebag, which always brightens my day.

ABOUT THE AUTHOR

Daydreamer and committed late-sleeper, Katherine Bayless writes paranormal fantasy and romance for fun and occasional profit. When she isn't adventuring vicariously through her stories, Katherine enjoys a variety of arts and crafts, lays waste to enemies in *Diablo III* and *Path of Exile*, and indulges her addictions to cooking shows, science documentaries, and digital photography.

Katherine's writing career began when she wondered what a clairvoyant's life would be like, an idea that sparked her imagination and added 'creative writing' to her brimming list of hobbies. In her pre-author life, Katherine worked as a software engineer in the game industry, where she not only met her awesome husband but also discovered her passion for fantasy stories and role-playing games.

Over the past thirty years, she has moved eleven times, calling California, Oregon, Washington, and Illinois home states at one time or another. She currently lives happily in view of Central Oregon's ancient volcanoes with her husband, kids, two sweet and shamelessly spoiled corgis named Sunny and Luna, and Zeke, a cabinet-opening, treat-stealing commando that doesn't know his own name because everyone just calls him Cat.

Although Katherine freely admits she'd rather live inside her head and write stories instead of blog posts, she always makes the time to respond to emails and blog comments.

You can find her website at www.katherinebayless.com.

Made in the USA
Columbia, SC
26 June 2021

41035346R00237